PRAISE FOR CAROLYN MILLER

"I LOVE THIS BOOK!! I love the uniqueness of the characters - we don't see too many hockey player heroes which is a true shame because THOSE KISSES!!"~ *CARRIE BOOTH SCHMIDT, Reading is my Superpower blog*

"I loved the dialogue and the hero and heroine, the very authentic and real challenges they faced and the unique setting and hockey slant." ~ *RACHEL MCMILLAN, bestselling author*

"This novel is perfect for readers who love hockey without being so technical to overwhelm readers who don't...grab a fan for some swoon-worthy kisses!" ~ *KARI TRUMBO, bestselling author*

"I loved reading this story and cannot wait for book #2. Carolyn Miller has crafted an incredible story with fabulous characters, great settings and wonderful swoon worthy romance. I highly recommend *The Breakup Project.*" ~ *BECKY'S BOOKSHELVES*

"Sporty? Tick. Faith-filled? Double tick. Romantic? Triple Tick. Take it from me - *The Breakup Project* has all the feels and then some!" ~ *ANDREA GRIGG, author of All Is Bright*

"*The Breakup Project* is a fun, charming, and faith-filled contemporary romance with adorable characters set in the competitive North American ice hockey world. Highly recommended." ~ *NARELLE ATKINS, Author of Solo Tu & Her Tycoon Hero*

"This new contemporary Christian novel by Carolyn Miller is so much more than the usual 'ho-hum' Christian romance. You will be challenged and inspired." ~ *MEREDITH RESCE, author of the Luella Linley - Licence to Meddle series*

"Carolyn Miller delivers a winsome exploration of life, love, and faith." ~ *PUBLISHERS WEEKLY*

"Displaying a flair for comedy and witty dialog, Miller is clearly an author to watch…with clever, snappy repartee, creating an exciting and fast-paced read." ~ *LIBRARY JOURNAL*

THE BREAKUP PROJECT

CAROLYN MILLER

Visit Carolyn Miller at www.carolynmillerauthor.com

Cover design by Marion Uekermann / The Collaborative Press

Edited by Katie Donovan

Bible references are from the New International Version.

CHAPTER 1

Detroit, Michigan
December 31

"*B*ecause it is a truth, that *should* be universally acknowledged, that the sister of a hockey player will forever have hockey in her future." Breanna Karlsson leaned forward, drawing on the purple eyeliner with a steady hand. Too much and she'd look like a clown, but just the right amount and *hello, world*. "And that's especially the case for the twin sister of someone regarded as one of the NHL's top forwards."

Laughter flowed from the phone propped up against the mirror and switched on speaker. "You poor thing. Really feeling for you here," Holly Travers said, her Australian accent holding friendly sarcasm.

Bree grinned and carefully swiped on mascara. "And so you should. I can't believe that all the guys I know either play hockey or want to talk about hockey as soon as they know I'm the sister of *the* Brent Karlsson." She wrinkled her nose.

"So what are you going to do?"

"I don't know. I think this coming year I should swear off dating hockey players. I can never tell if the guys I date are interested in me or interested in getting to know him. Mind you, the way he's been acting lately…"

"What's happened?"

"Oh, Holl, I wish you were here. You'd pull him down a peg or three. He's gotten so arrogant, like the air we plebs breathe down here isn't good enough for him. Remember I told you about his girlfriend? Apparently she's going to be at the party tonight. I can't wait."

"Yeah, it sounds like it," Holly said, her irony-detector working well.

"I cannot believe my brother would fall for someone like her. Did you see those pictures I sent of her that she'd posted online?"

"Yep."

"Don't you think she looks like a—"

"Yep."

"I can't get over how he's so shallow as to go for a girl like that. She's so fake." Fake hair, fake tan, fake b—

"I'll be praying for him."

Bree exhaled. "Thanks, Holl. That means a lot." And was probably something she should do more of, too. "I really feel he needs a God-intervention and to have the right woman come along soon. Hey, I'd better go. Mike's coming to collect me, and I don't want to be late."

"Mike?"

"Mike Vaughan. Remember him? Another of Brent's friends, plays for Boston, and here for New Year's. I'm pretty sure you met him when you stayed with us all those years ago. We've known him forever."

"Another hockey player, huh?"

"Don't tease. No, he's just a friend. One of the good ones, but he's not my type."

"No tingles and toe curls?"

"Alas, no."

"Alas? Does that mean you'd like there to be?"

"Stop making mischief. No, Mike is not my type. Never has been, never will be, so put that out of your head. Things have gotten so sad I think I'll have to find someone like one of your young men."

"Well, if you teach Sunday school, maybe you will. At least four-year-old boys have no problem sharing their emotions."

A knock came at the hotel door.

"Ooh, I should go. I'll snap a pic and send it to you so you can tell me if I look okay."

"Bree, you always look beautiful."

"And comments like that are why you're my best friend."

Holly chuckled. "Go, have fun. And happy New Year! I'm praying it's the best one yet, and that you'll meet the man of your dreams."

"Thanks, Holls. I'll be praying for your man to make an appearance too. Happy New Year to you."

"Yeah, it's January already here in Australia."

The knock came again.

"Oops! Gotta go. Bye!"

Bree ended the call, checked her appearance in the mirror one more time, and made a face at her reflection. Blessed with Karlsson genetics, she'd never owned Holly's petite frame, except maybe when she was ten. At least this dress didn't accentuate the curves newly acquired since Christmas. She twisted. Well, maybe she should keep her coat on, and buttoned across the waist...

A third knock.

"Oh! I'm coming!" She rushed to the door and opened it to see Mike, his hand raised as if to knock once more. "Oh, hi. I'm so sorry. I was chatting with Holly—remember her? She's the Australian girl who stayed with us on exchange years ago and is now training as a short track skater. Did you know she wants to represent her country at the Games in a couple of years? I think she's so impressive, and probably will make it because she's so dedicated and trains *so* hard, and—"

"Breathe, Bree."

She laughed and obeyed. "Hi, Mike."

"Hi, Bree." He smiled.

Well, she might not get tingles and toe curls, but she couldn't deny the handsomeness of the man. Fair hair, blue eyes, even features, and a smile that conveyed sincerity and laid-back good humor. Not to mention a physique that demonstrated his commitment to his sport.

She gestured to his evening attire, the navy suit stretching across broad shoulders, his straw-blond hair carefully styled for once. "You look nice."

"I aim to please." His lips pulled wider, and the light in his eyes seemed to confirm the truth of his words, causing an interesting twinge in her upper torso.

Which was *ridiculous*. Mike had been a family friend forever. She certainly wasn't interested in someone like him. All that talk of boyfriends before had made her a little loopy. Obviously her body just needed time to get the memo: no dating hockey players this year.

"Just give me a second more."

She grabbed her bag, touched both earrings to ensure they were still there, and wrapped a scarf around her neck. Perhaps that should be her New Year's resolution…

A nod. That would be her resolution. One she *would* keep. Unlike last year's to avoid chocolate and do thirty minutes' exercise every day. She sucked her tummy in. Turned back to Mike and smiled. "So, how do I look?"

"You look…" He gave her the once-over and swallowed. "You look great."

"Oh good. For a minute there I thought you didn't know what to say and were just trying to be polite, and I've tried to make an effort tonight, because it's not every day a girl gets to go to an NHL team's New Year's Eve party. Hey, do you mind taking a quick photo?"

"Uh, sure."

She handed him her phone and posed in front of the door: tummy in, chin up, face angled. He took a couple of pictures.

"Does one of them look okay?" She shifted close and peered at his handiwork.

"They all look great, Bree."

"Hey, we should get one of us together. I'm sending a pic to Holly."

"I'll take it with my phone." He stretched out his arm, she leaned close to his face, smiled, and he snapped a photo.

"Let me see." She looked at the image and nodded. "Hey, we look good."

"Yeah."

"Can you text it to me? Then I'll send it to Holly."

"Sure."

They spent the next minute sending photos, then she finally closed the door. "I'm still surprised you came tonight."

"Brent asked, and for once I can come. I hope you're not disappointed."

"No, not at all. I was just saying to Holly how good it is to have someone involved in the hockey world who is a friend, who I don't have to worry about."

His brow wrinkled. "Worry about? Has someone been bothering you?"

"Oh, no. Not really." At his frown, she hastened to reassure. "No, not at all. No, it's just something I've decided that I should do differently this coming year."

"And what's that?"

But the way he looked at her, all sincerity and care, made her strangely reluctant to share. Mike was a nice guy. It didn't seem right to lump him in with the others, but he played hockey, so must be included. But it still didn't mean she wanted to admit her New Year's resolution to him.

His lips twitched.

"What?"

"Nothing."

"It's not nothing. Go on, tell."

"Is this another resolution?"

He knew her too well. "Maybe."

"Like the year you decided not to eat bread anymore?" He chuckled softly. "How long did that last?"

Three days. But seriously, how did—"You remember that?"

"I pay attention, Bree."

Huh. They moved to the elevators, her heels clicking along the tiles. "Well, anyway, I'm so glad you're here."

He glanced at her as he pressed the down button, his features pulling into a smile. "And why is that?"

She stepped in next to him and nearly toppled, so clutched his arm. "Well, I want your opinion on something. You know Brent better than anyone, except his family."

"Brent?"

"Yeah, you know that twin of mine? Your best friend since grade school? *Hockey World*'s hottest upcoming forwards edition?"

"Oh, *that* Brent." His mouth twitched. "Yeah, I've heard of him."

She swatted his arm. "I want your advice. And tonight should be the perfect opportunity. You know he's going out with this Chloe girl?"

His lips thinned. "Yeah."

"Well, I really think he's getting a little carried away with his own publicity, chasing a girl like that."

"To be fair, I don't think he's the one doing all the chasing."

"Well, he's not exactly discouraging her, is he? And he should. She's bad news. He needs a good girlfriend—someone who's a Christian. Not someone like a Chloe."

"He is an adult, Bree."

"An adult making dumb choices. Come on. Would you want to see Chloe end up marrying him?"

Mike chuckled. "I don't think he's thinking marriage just yet."

"He better not be. He's barely known the girl two minutes."

"Which is why I don't think you should be worrying."

"Yeah, but you should've heard him at Christmas. He was all 'I want you to meet Chloe,' 'We should've invited Chloe.' He's never acted like that before."

"Have you met her?" he asked.

"No. That's what I'm doing tonight. And that's why I'm glad you're here, to back me up."

He released a low whistle. "You want me to meet someone for the first time and agree with your prejudice?"

Ouch. "Come on, Mike, it's not prejudice to make assumptions about someone when they post pictures of themselves in swimsuits that barely cover important parts."

"Isn't it? I must've misunderstood what prejudice is."

She frowned and pulled her arm away. "I didn't think you were like all the rest."

"All the rest?"

"Guys. Happy to absolve a woman just because she's beautiful."

"You think she's pretty?"

"Well, yes." Pretty plastic, too, but she sensed saying that would not go down well with Brent's best friend. How had she misread him?

"Bree, I've never met Chloe, so I'd like to reserve judgment until then."

"But haven't you seen the pictures on the internet?"

His lips tweaked to one side. "I don't go looking through the internet for pictures of other guy's girlfriends." He glanced at her. "I didn't think you would, either."

Luckily the elevator stopped, the doors finally swooshed open, and the sounds of the party overrode everything, removing the need for her to reply. Not that she'd known exactly what to say. This man kept confounding her. She'd known him nearly all her life. How could he not see things as she did?

A tall figure near the doors to the function room straightened. Brent. Bree pasted on a smile, even as she checked out the woman standing next to him in a white dress so tight you could watch her digestive system ripple. So this was Chloe. A swift glance up and down… Yep. Exactly as she'd imagined. Too low, too high, too—

"Finally," Brent said. "You sure took your time."

"Why do you always assume it's me who takes a long time to get ready?" Bree pushed her dark hair over her shoulder. "Why couldn't it be Mike who was primping for ages?"

"Because I know you both too well."

"Hmph. Well, perfection takes a while. Anyway, hello, Brent. Good game tonight." She reached up to give him a hug. Six inches taller, made less so by these heels. These heels that meant she towered over his girlfriend.

She supposed she should act like a Christian. "Hello." Fake smile. "You must be Chloe."

"Hi."

The woman's heavily-mascaraed and silver-shadowed brown eyes did their own quick scan. Bree sucked in her stomach a little more. It wasn't fair that some girls got looks in both the face *and* figure departments. And what was with the basic "Hi"? Surely as Brent's sister, Brent's *twin* sister, any girlfriend of his should try a little harder to be friendly.

Brent did the introductions, and Chloe's eyes lingered on Mike, her smile curving into something that seemed edged with interest. Indignation rose in Bree's chest. Seriously? Eyeing off another man right in front of her own boyfriend?

"So what do you do, Chloe?" Mike asked, ever the gentleman.

"Oh, I'm a model."

Of course she was. Bree caught Mike's glance and rolled her eyes. "And what exactly do you model?" she asked sweetly.

"Breanna." Brent frowned at her. "She's just getting started."

"That must be why I've seen so many pictures of you on the internet," Bree said, fake-smiling some more. Look, she was being interested, asking questions. Which was way more effort than Chloe was making.

"I'm not sure what photos you've seen," Chloe said with a coy look up at Brent under false lashes. Yep. Fake blonde hair, fake tan, fake lashes, and judging from the skinniness of everywhere else, fake curves on top.

"So, did you two meet at church?"

Brent hooked an eyebrow at Bree. "Seriously?"

She narrowed her gaze at him. What had happened to the boy who had made a Jesus commitment in his mid-teens? "Seriously. How *is* church these days, Brent?"

"I didn't know you went to church," Chloe cooed up at him, fake nails—talons, really—digging into his upper arm. "That's so sweet."

"Maybe you should ask him to take you," Bree said, her fingers—talon-free—clenching.

She grew vaguely aware of Mike moving closer, touching her arm. She sucked in a breath, released it slowly.

"So." Chloe uncoiled herself from Brent's side, eyes shifting back to Bree. "What do you do?"

"I work in a preschool." Wholesome, family-focused. Why did that seem so boring now?

"She's the assistant director of one of Toronto's leading childcare centers," Mike added.

Bree glanced up at him, surprised. His gaze warmed, tiny gold flecks dancing in the depths of his blue eyes.

"Told you I paid attention."

She echoed his smile with one of her own.

"So how long have you two been a couple for?"

"What?" Bree shifted her attention back to Chloe. "Do you mean Mike and me? We're not together. Mike's been a family friend for as long as I can remember. We're just friends."

"Yeah. Just friends," Mike echoed, shifting away.

Brent glanced at his watch, then placed a hand on Chloe's lower back. "Shall we go in, babe? I'm getting hungry."

"When are you not?" Bree muttered, noting Brent's watch seemed brand new. How much had that cost—or was it a perk from one of his many endorsements? She glanced at his product-enhanced upswept hair. Wait—did he have highlights now? Where had her down-to-earth, fun-loving brother gone? Even his tease held an edge these days.

She couldn't help but observe Chloe slink her way into Brent's side again. Ugh.

At least she didn't have to pretend politeness inside the function room, the noise and music providing a million distractions. Shoulders slumping, she trailed behind as Brent led the way to a buffet table filled with mouthwatering deliciousness. But the knowledge she must appear a size fourteen to Chloe's size four made her hesitate.

"Are you hungry?" Mike asked.

She was *starving*. But also self-conscious. And didn't want to start stuffing her face if Chloe wasn't eating. Maybe that's what she needed to do to lose weight. Just not eat.

"Bree?"

"Oh, I might get something later."

"You sure?"

She eyed the platter of savories wistfully. Perhaps if she danced later, she could earn some calories now. Or—Chloe edged into view; Bree bet no-one had ever called *her* thunder thighs—maybe not.

"I might just have water."

And maybe some lettuce. Weren't lettuce and celery supposed to have negative calories?

"I'll be back in a moment."

She watched Mike disappear into the feeding frenzy, then stepped back, glancing around her. She recognized most of the guys here, either from visits to games or from the roster, and so smiled and nodded and managed some small talk, but the music made it hard to hear. Brent seemed to have disappeared with Chloe—she didn't want to think where—and Mike was chatting to someone by the table, probably fending off questions about why a Boston player was welcoming in the new year here in Detroit.

Bree knew a sudden pang of loneliness and felt a ridiculous urge to leave, to find a space where she could cry and sift through this tumult of emotions. Because this hustling, burly, super-fit, model-on-arm scene wasn't her, wasn't where she wanted to be. She'd once loved glamming up for nights like this, but now it seemed she didn't belong. Everything felt topsy-turvy, too awkward and artificial. Truth be told, she'd rather be at home watching a chick flick, eating ice-cream, and wearing fluffy slippers instead of these ridiculous heels. Was she getting old or something?

"Hey, it's Bree, isn't it?"

She turned, caught the hockey player's eyes sliding from her chest to her face. Ugh. This was why she didn't want to date athletes. Even if they professed to be Christians or attended church, too many seemed too focused on bodies, often appearing to want only one thing, more like a player than a gentleman. Not that she needed a Mr. Darcy type—she'd always thought him a little too aloof to ever really be the kind of guy she'd want to marry—but it wouldn't hurt for guys to be a little courteous at least. "And you are?" Apart from sleazy.

"Alex Turner. I play with Brent."

She nodded. Fought the desire to cover her neckline with a dozen paper napkins. Not that she was showing too much skin —or much at all, really, compared to some girls here tonight— but apparently some guys weren't like Mike and didn't know how to treat a woman respectfully. Mike's eyes had never strayed below her chin.

"Are you having fun?" he asked—or maybe more like yelled.

"Not really," she replied. "I find some people here a little sleazy, to be honest. I don't like being looked at like I'm a piece of meat."

He choked, muttered something she didn't hear, and quickly slunk away.

Good riddance. Honestly, why did women put up with guys looking at them like that? Or maybe they liked the feeling of power that came with attractiveness.

That so wasn't her. She sighed, her gaze sliding past guys she didn't recognize to the one she did. God bless Mike. Faithful, easygoing Mike. An ever-present haven from her brother's tease. If he wasn't Brent's best friend, and if she hadn't vowed never to date hockey players, he might even be worth consideration as boyfriend material. He caught her gaze, and her discomfort eased as she returned his smile.

MIKE'S HEART SKIDDED. If asked to describe his ideal woman, Breanna Karlsson would tick every box. She always had, ever since he'd first known the Karlsson family through school and church and hockey all those years ago. Her eyes met his and drew him once more into her beauty. The violet-gray eyes, the perfect skin, the dark, glossy hair he yearned to touch.

But despite years of admiration, he'd never allowed his feelings to kindle into anything warmer. What was the point when Brent had pretty much warned every guy to stay away? Mike had seen the way Brent had snapped at other guys and taken the "out-of-bounds" caution to heart. But now, with Brent distracted, maybe he could see if there might ever be a chance.

Thumping music, more house techno than Keith Urban, thudded through his ears. He winced, moving between chattering groups, and found Bree in a slightly quieter section, now pensively staring out the window.

"Here you go."

She turned, nearly toppled. Mike held out an arm to catch her. "Whoa."

"Sorry!" Her jolt of movement jogged his elbow. Sauce now dripped down his shirt sleeve. "Oh no! Let me fix that."

"It doesn't matter."

But apparently it did. She tugged free one of the paper napkins he held and dabbed at the stain. "I'm so sorry, Mike. I'm getting everything wrong tonight."

"Hey, it's okay. It's all okay. Even the whole Brent and Chloe thing will be okay."

She blinked rapidly, as if fighting tears. "How do you know?"

"I have a feeling."

"What, like a feeling they'll grow old together and live happily ever after?"

"Yeah, not that."

"Thank goodness." She exhaled. "Wait, are these feelings of yours trustworthy?"

"Some can be." And others probably should be locked in a box and thrown—with key—into Boston Harbor.

She finished her ministrations and drew him closer to the

window overlooking the Detroit River. "Okay, so do you agree?"

"About Brent?"

"Yeah, him and Chloe. Don't you think they're just so wrong for each other?"

Yes. But... "I still think the man can make his own choices."

"It's like he's been blinded by her gorgeousness."

Did she say that because she didn't see herself as pretty? Why did so many women seem to judge their worth on their looks—and assume all men judged the same way—when it was their heart and character that proved the real deal in lasting attraction?

Still, he had to stand up for his man. "Do you really think Brent so shallow?"

"I don't know what to think anymore." She bit her lip. Eyed him in a way that made him long to amend his earlier comment that she looked great to something more appropriate, like "*I think you're the most beautiful woman here tonight.*"

But he sensed this fractured relationship with her brother needed something deeper than his own admission of attraction.

"Bree, I agree Brent isn't the same guy who started in the NHL six years ago. He's playing really well, and I guess it's natural he's a little caught up in his own world."

"You're not."

"I'm not the face of my team or the one being featured in *Hockey Today.*"

"You play just as well as him."

Pleasure filled his chest. "I didn't think you noticed."

"Of course I do. If it's not the Wings or Toronto, then Dad's always got the Boston games on."

Oh. Right. The warm satisfaction trickled away. "Your dad, huh?"

"And me. When I'm home."

And not on a date? His chest grew tight.

"Anyway, stop fishing for a compliment." She swatted his arm playfully. "So, what are we going to do?"

"About Brent?"

"Don't you think he needs some kind of intervention? Holly said she's praying for him, which I already do. But I don't think it can hurt to help God a little."

"Holy Spirit's little helper, huh?" His eyebrows rose.

"What's wrong with that?"

"Was that your way of helping before, with that super subtle dig about church?"

Her smile flashed brighter than the disco lights bouncing around the room. "He didn't appreciate that, did he?"

"I think you need to be careful, Bree, and not act in a way that will damage your relationship."

"Please. Give me some credit."

"I know you're smart and caring, and you love your family and want what's best for them. But I also know you can get pretty passionate at times."

"Well, of course I do. That goes along with caring and loving someone, doesn't it?"

He stared at her for a moment, then dropped his eyes. Truth burned in his chest. Was this his moment? "Bree, I, uh, was wondering—"

"There you two are. What are you talking about?" Brent— once more entwined with Chloe—glanced between them.

Mike couldn't very well answer *"You."*

"Just a little project I was thinking on for the new year." Bree shot Mike a mischievous look.

"Is that something to do with your preschool?" Chloe asked.

"No. Another little project. I might even see if Granny Violet is interested in helping me. She's always invested in the best interests of her grandchildren." She raised her eyebrows at Mike.

Yep. He knew what she was hinting at. Granny Violet was

the Karlsson family prayer warrior. He could only smile and shake his head.

"I'd like to meet this grandmother of yours," Chloe said, batting eyelashes Mike was pretty sure were fake. They made her brown eyes look a bit like a Jersey cow.

"One day," Brent said, then turned to his sister. "You eaten anything?"

"Not yet."

"That's gotta be a first." He clicked his fingers celebrity-style, and a server appeared and offered a tray of savory pastries.

Bree hesitated, glanced at Chloe then back at the tray, then snatched one, moaning a little as she stuffed in a mini spring roll. "Oh, that's so yummy."

Somehow, a little piece of sauce-flecked flaky pastry flew from her mouth to land on Chloe's slinky dress, the red spot smack dab on the part of her chest covered by fabric. "Oh, I'm so sorry!" Bree moved to help clean it away.

"Ugh. Get away from me," Chloe said, inching away, her nose wrinkled in disgust.

"Breanna." Brent's eyebrows plunged, his expression as cold as Lake Ontario in the grip of winter.

"It was an accident."

Brent's stormy glance revealed his skepticism, pushing words from Mike's throat. "Come on, man. You don't think Bree did it deliberately?"

"I know you don't like me," Chloe said to Bree, fluffing her hair behind one shoulder as she pushed her lips—were they artificially inflated?—into a trout pout. "I can't help it if your brother wants to spend time with me rather than you."

Bree's mouth sagged. "I beg your pardon?"

"Sooner or later you have to cut the cord and live your own life—and let others live theirs."

"You've got it wrong." Hurt pinched Bree's face.

"Brent, baby, could we go?" Chloe said in a wheedling voice. "I don't feel welcome here."

Brent glanced at Bree and shrugged, then with a "Thanks for coming, man," fist-bumped Mike and walked away.

Bree's breath caught, and she turned to Mike, tears shining in her eyes. "Can you believe that?"

"That was pretty cold." His heart twisted at her shaken expression. How could Brent let his girlfriend insult his sister like that? "I'm sorry, Bree."

Should he wrap his arm around her? Give her a hug? Show her not all guys were cruel?

She blinked rapidly, shook her head, and drew herself up. "See how bad he's getting? He really needs us. *Please* say you'll help me with the breakup project."

God forgive him. But his desire to help Bree had less to do with wanting Chloe out of Brent's life—cold as she'd been to poor Bree—and more with wanting to wipe the bewildered sadness from Bree's face. And if it meant she spent more time with him, then he wasn't opposed to that.

"I'll help you."

"You will?" Her face lit, and his heart gave another painful throb. "Oh, thank you. I knew I could count on you." She grinned, lifting her chin, reverting to that spunky sass he'd always admired about her. "Now." She clutched his arm again, sending tingles up his spine. "What exactly do you propose we should do?"

CHAPTER 2

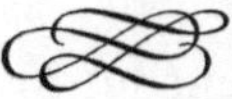

Toronto, Canada

The sound of the Toronto vs Boston game blared through the living room. Bree glanced at the TV, following the play for a little while when Mike's number 78 jersey was on the screen. She watched him defend, working with his partner to stop Toronto from getting a puck in their net. Steady, a calm temperament, trustworthy. The comments from the TV hosts matched what she knew about Mike Vaughan.

His shift finished and she turned away, refocusing on the activity for work tomorrow. Why she had thought color coding nearly a thousand buttons was necessary she no longer recalled. At least the mindless activity meant she could turn her thoughts to more important matters.

She smiled. To know Mike was on her side provided a measure of reassurance, something she was hoping would be further bolstered by the arrival of Granny Violet very soon, when she'd share the plan she'd discussed briefly with Mike a few days ago.

"Bree? Can you help me in here?"

"Sure, Mom." She swept the remaining buttons to one side of the coffee table and moved into the kitchen. Granny Violet was a fan of teacups and scones and all the tasty delicacies that made her visits fun—and made it so hard for Bree to lose her muffin top.

Oh well. Diet starts tomorrow and all that.

She helped dish out the cream into one cut glass dish, then carefully spooned the strawberry jam into another as her mother pulled the trays of scones from the oven. Mmm, scones.

The sound of a car drew her to the window. "She's here."

"Go out and help her, won't you, dear? It's pretty slippery still."

"Sure thing."

Bree hurried to open the door and assist her grandmother inside. "Hi, Granny V!"

"Breanna, darling. How are you?"

"Fine and dandy now. Thanks so much for coming."

"Well, your message made it sound a little urgent." Grandmotherly concern shone in her faded blue eyes as she cupped Bree's chin. "Is everything all right, dear?"

"Everything's okay with me." Bree held open the door. "It's that brother of mine you should be concerned about."

"Really? What is Dean up to now?"

"Not Dean. He's fine. Very happy enjoying married life with Laura. They called earlier. Apparently Vancouver has a chance of snow. No, it's Brent who is the worry. But let me take your coat and gloves, then I'll grab some tea and scones and we can chat in the den. Dad's watching the game, and Mom's finishing up in the kitchen."

"This doesn't concern them?"

"Well, maybe not as much as it concerns me."

She led the way down the hall, past the stairs lined with family photographs, to the room Dad sometimes used as an office but which mostly functioned as a second, more private, living area. "Okay, it's best you get comfy, because this might take a while. I'll be back in a moment." She ducked back to the kitchen, collected the tray and returned to the den.

"What is this about, dear?" her grandmother said, taking a seat in the thick-armed plaid sofa, and accepting the teacup Bree handed her, already prepared the way Gran preferred.

"I need your help with a special project." Bree drew in a breath. "Mike Vaughan—you remember Brent's best friend?— and I met Brent's new girlfriend last Sunday. Remember at Christmas how Brent kept going on about wanting to invite Chloe here? Mom and Dad weren't keen; they've never met her, and judging from my encounter, I don't think they'll be that keen to see her anytime soon."

"Why do you say that?"

Bree recounted the exchange, admitting to her faults—Mike had rightly pointed out her prejudice, something she'd later confessed to God—but expressing her concern. "I think she's leading him astray."

"Brent is capable of making his own decisions, Bree. Are you sure this Chloe girl wasn't right in pushing some of your buttons?" Gran sipped her tea, eyeing Bree from over the gold rim. "What's happening in your life, darling? Do you have a young man who is interested in you?"

What? This conversation wasn't supposed to steer this way. "I—no. There's no one, Gran."

"What about this Michael person, Brent's friend? Is he someone special?"

"No! He's just a friend. Someone equally concerned about some of Brent's recent choices," she insisted, taking her own cup and giving a defiant slurp.

"I see. And what is it you want from me?"

"I want you to pray with me for him."

"I already do, darling. I pray for all my grandchildren, that they would be healthy, happy, and walking in God's purposes."

"But it's that last one—I don't think he is. He's not going to church anymore. Chloe didn't even know he used to." She shook her head as she carefully smoothed on jam and cream and handed a freshly-dressed scone to her grandmother. "You know how I've always had this sense when something's wrong with him? Like that time he broke his hand a few years ago? I knew. It's a twin thing. And I just *know* he's not happy now. He's caught up in being the object of hero worship. It's like a sticky spider web, and now he's struggling to get out."

"Don't you think you're being a little dramatic, Bree?" Mom's voice came from the doorway, holding her pink mug that said 'Teachers have class.'

Bree glanced over her shoulder. When had she come in? "Mom, did you see those pictures of Chloe? How can he think this is normal?"

"Your brother has to learn."

What? They were excusing him too? She took a breath, forced pleasantness to her face, her voice. "And that's what I want help with. I want him to learn he doesn't have to settle for a girl like Chloe. Not when there are so many other lovely ladies out there."

Mom moved to settle on the couch next to Granny V. "So what are you suggesting?"

"I'm suggesting we think of all the good potential girlfriend candidates we know and start mentioning them to him. I mean, I know we can pray, but God helps those who help themselves."

"You know that's not in the Bible, Bree," Granny V said with an indulgent smile.

"Yes, well, it mightn't be actual Scripture, but—"

"In fact, I think the Bible tends to encourage faith and

patience, my dear. We can't twist God's arm simply because we want Him to hurry up and agree with our plans."

"You're sounding a little too much like Mike," Bree grumbled.

"Mike?" Mom pinched a scone from the plate that centered the coffee table. "Do you mean Mike Vaughan? Have you seen him recently, Bree?"

"Yes, Mom. Remember the New Year's Eve party? He escorted me to that."

"He *is* a nice boy. Well, a man, I suppose. Tell him hello from me the next time you chat with him."

"Yes, Mom."

"Are you seeing him?" Mom persisted, studying Bree as she took a ladylike bite of her scone.

"That's what I want to know, too," Granny Violet said, eyes wide with interest, her teacup abandoned.

"He's just a friend. A friend of *Brent's*, and someone else concerned about that brother of mine."

"I've always liked Mike," Mom continued. "Such a nice young man, always so respectful."

Yes, he was that.

"He's been a Christian for as long as I've known him."

True.

"And quite handsome too, wouldn't you agree, Bree?"

Yes, but—"Mom, I'm not interested in him. In fact, I've decided not to date any hockey players ever again. Or at least for this year."

"Oh? Why is that?"

"Because I never know if they like me or just like being linked with Brent's sister."

"But Mike wouldn't be like that."

"Mom!"

Granny V leaned forward to deposit her plate on the coffee

table. "Now, now, Pamela. Don't distress the dear girl. She's obviously made up her mind."

"Thank you, Gran," Bree mumbled, her arms crossed as she studied her mother mutinously. "Can we please get back to the subject here? Brent is the one with the actual relationship. Not that it really is a relationship. It seems comprised of kissing, mostly"—anything more she wouldn't dare suggest in front of her grandmother—"and they've only known each other five minutes."

"So why are you so worried? Surely this will blow over soon."

"Mom, I've seen girls like this before. They sink their hooks in, and before you know it, they're living together."

Granny Violet's breath drew in, and she shook her head. "The state of the world these days."

"Exactly. Which is why I really feel we should do something about it before it's too late."

"Bree, *I* really feel you should leave well enough alone." Mom tsked. "Brent is smart enough and knows what's right and wrong."

Did he, though? He might have the smarts, but he sure didn't appear to be applying any.

"I will pray for him, Breanna. Don't you worry." Her grandmother's eyes held assurance.

"Thanks, Gran. He needs it."

"And I'll be praying for you. I want you to be happy too."

"I *am* happy. I'm just not happy with him right now."

"And if I can think of anyone I'd like to see as part of this family, then I'll let you know."

Bree exhaled. "Thanks, Granny V."

"Now, this Michael person. I would like to see him. He sounds like a catch."

"Gran, we're talking about Brent, not me, remember?"

Her grandmother chuckled. "Yes, yes, I was forgetting."

That mischievous smile didn't look like she'd forgotten one jot.

Mom's brow wrinkled. "I wonder if Hazel's daughter might still be single."

"Mom, she's a doctor. I don't think she'd have much time for him."

"Hmm. Maybe you're right. What about…I don't know, what about Holly?"

"Holly? Please. She's in Australia, Mom. And she's way too sensible to ever fall for him."

"Well, I don't mind putting my thinking cap on and putting out a quiet word to see who's free."

"They have to be a Christian, and we have to like her enough to think she could fit into our family."

Gran nodded. "I'll ask around at the Home, too. You never know who has a granddaughter who might be perfect."

Bree sat back in her chair. Smiled. "Thanks, Gran."

"And while I'm at it, I'll ask around for you too."

What? This wasn't supposed to be about her. "You really don't need to," she stated.

"No hockey players, is that correct?"

"I'd prefer someone who doesn't like sports at all."

"I'll see what I can do."

The door wheezed open, and Dad appeared. "So this is where you all are. Hello, Violet. How are you?" He kissed his mother-in-law's cheek.

"I'm fine. But all this talk has left me thirsty. Now, do you think I could have another nice cup of tea?"

~

Boston

Beantown's skyline twinkled gold and white beyond his apartment windows. Mike sank down into the leather chair—

his one indulgence, which he figured his body well and truly earned—and stared at his reflection glowing against the dark night. Tonight's game had not gone well. Ten goals to two? He winced. Training would be brutal tomorrow if tonight's "pep" talk from the coach was any sign.

His phone buzzed. He glanced at it, found his first smile in what seemed like forever.

SORRY ABOUT YOUR GAME. YOU PLAYED WELL. PS THE PROJECT IS A GO!

Bree.

He tapped his phone to find the picture from the other night, the two of them grinning at the camera like the couple she'd so adamantly declared they weren't. Another wince. How could he get her to change her mind?

Another buzz. Another message. STILL UP?

Brent's ever pithy code for "Do you have time to talk?"

Well, yes. He sure did. He pressed some buttons, and Brent's name was chased by a ringing sound, then Brent's voice. "Yo."

"Hey."

A slurping sound—Brent, like Mike, wasn't opposed to eat-talking—was followed by a gulp. "Man. That was brutal."

"Yeah. Not our best. Finished with a minus four."

"Ouch."

"Uh huh. I bet my agent is hoping I don't get too many more of them before contract negotiations begin again this summer."

"Truth." Another slurping sound.

Sometimes Mike liked to guess what Brent was eating in these calls. "Linguine?"

"Huh? Oh. Close. Leftover spaghetti. Chloe made it the other night."

The casual way he said it sparked concern. "She's staying over?"

"What? No." A beat. "Dude, you sound like that sister of mine."

"Bree cares about you, man."

"Yeah, well, I don't need her kind of care."

Mike swallowed the words he wanted to say. Talking with Brent these days felt like a delicate tightrope of speaking truth and showing grace.

"Hey, don't misunderstand me. Bree's great and all that, but she made her dislike of Chloe pretty plain."

When in doubt, leave it out. Mike said nothing.

"Don't you think? She was pretty rude the other night."

"To be honest, I didn't think she was the only one."

"What? So you don't like Chloe either." Hostility lined Brent's voice.

"Chloe was pretty rude to Bree, and you took her side. From where I was standing, it seemed you barely spoke to your sister all night, when you'd specifically asked her to come. I kinda got the feeling that she only came because you wanted her there, and then you and Chloe barely spoke to her. How did you think that would go down?"

A beat. Another. "You seem pretty tight with her."

"With Bree?"

"At the party you and her practically ignored everyone else."

So said the pot to the kettle. "That might be because she needed someone to talk to."

"She knows some of the guys," Brent protested.

"Yeah, some of the guys who were getting tanked or had half-dressed women draped over them." He winced. Had he really said that last bit aloud?

"Look, Chloe's a model, and just because you and Bree are all conservative doesn't mean we all have to be."

"Wow." Mike couldn't think of what else to say. *Lord, help me out here.* "To be clear, I didn't actually mean Chloe with the half-dressed women thing."

Silence.

"Did you even say goodbye to Bree when we left?"

More silence.

"Brent, your sister loves you. And yes, she's worried that you might be getting in too deep too fast with Chloe, and yet you asked her to meet Chloe and she did. She showed up, man. But —let's be real—Chloe didn't exactly go out of her way to make an effort with her."

Dial tone.

Mike blinked. Seriously? Had the dude hung up on him? This thing with Chloe must be worse than he'd thought. *God, unsnare him.*

He pushed to his feet and snagged a bottle of water from the fridge. Stared at the skyline some more. Wondered where else he'd like to live if negotiations fell through once he hit free agency in June. Glanced at the phone when it rang again.

"Yeah?"

"Sorry about that. Dropped the phone."

Mike's chest eased. "'Kay."

"Seriously? I didn't say goodbye?"

"You did to me, but unless you caught her the next morning, you didn't to Bree."

"Wow."

"Yeah."

"I mean, Chloe was wanting my attention all night, and I didn't realize..."

Mike let that sit in the air between them.

"I should probably apologize."

"Might go better for you," he agreed.

A grunt. "So, you and Bree."

Mike choked. "There is no me and Bree."

"You sure?" Suspicion hung on the words like a dark cloud.

"If you're asking do I like her, then yes, she's a great girl, we get along really well. But I'm pretty sure she just thinks of me as another brother. So we're friends, and that's it."

"You...and her."

"Again, let me reiterate, there is no me and her." Although, now he thought about it, the texts and photos might suggest otherwise. Not that Brent would ever see his phone. Maybe it was time to go on the offensive. "Why? Have you got someone you'd like to see her with?"

"What? No."

"So you trust Bree to choose a man she likes?"

"She's not stupid."

"No, not at all. And she's not likely to pick someone because he earns a lot of money or wears the right clothes." Another wince. Why were all his comments sounding so pointed tonight? He could only hope Brent didn't think he meant—

"Is that another dig at Chloe?"

Maybe. He worked to make his voice sound placatory. "How did you two meet?"

"At a bar. Alex's girlfriend introduced us."

More tightrope walking time. "Does she have any faith? Any church experience?"

"Man, do you have to go on about it?"

"Actually, as a friend who has known you longer than most, I think I have a responsibility to remind you of what you once asked me to say."

A groan. "Here we go."

"You asked me to let you know if you ever started falling away from God, remember? Consider this me letting you know."

Silence.

"I think that's the thing that's got Bree so concerned."

More silence.

He counted to ten. "You need to call her and apologize."

A beat. Two. Three. "Yeah."

Mike yawned. "It's getting late. Tonight's game was one to forget. I'm going to bed."

"Yeah. 'Kay."

The dial tone buzzed in his ear.

Mike blew out a breath and slumped back in his sofa. Well. That had been unexpected. His soul might feel as gnarled and tangled as the abandoned fishermen's ropes in the harbor, but at least he'd finally had the chance to say what needed to be said.

He switched off the lights, moved to his bedroom, plugged the phone into charge.

Changed, slipped under the covers, and closed his eyes.

His phone buzzed. He cracked open an eyelid. Reached for his phone.

DID YOU SAY SOMETHING TO HIM? HE JUST TEXTED TO APOLOGIZE!

He smiled. Tapped out his reply.

I'M GLAD.

A moment later Bree's reply came.

ME TOO. THANKS SO MUCH. YOU'RE THE BEST. SWEET DREAMS X

He swallowed, wishing the X was not usual Bree-ness and might one day be something she actually meant. As for sweet dreams...

He closed his eyes and tried not to think of Bree.

CHAPTER 3

*B*ree glanced up at the hands of the white plastic clock —hands that were moving way too slowly for this time on a Friday night for her to scrounge up enough patience to pretend this was okay. Not that she was known for patience at any time of the day, but on Friday nights it seemed especially hard, as if some people thought their lives more important than others—such as, say, those who had been caring for their children for ten hours already today.

"What is it with parents who think it's okay to swoop in after six with nothing more than a hurried apology?" Sylvie Miles, Bree's fellow Friday night detainee, complained. "Like saying sorry can ever really fix things."

Bree bit her lip, sensing where this was about to go.

Sylvie's grumbling took on a cooing tone as she crouched to play with Max Hammerson, whose father was a perpetual Friday night offender. "If your daddy wasn't such a good-looking man, I'd be very unhappy."

"Sylvie,"—really shouldn't talk like that about the clients —"did you have somewhere you needed to be?"

"I have a date."

"With Jarome?"

"That was last week. Once was enough with him."

"Oh. So who's tonight's candidate?"

"Mark? Mike?"

Her heart tensed. Then she told herself not to be silly. Mike was in Boston. Had another game tonight. And there were millions of Mikes in the world.

"Mack? I can't remember. It's a blind date. My sister set us up. How about you?"

"Nope. No date for me."

"Why not? You're pretty. You could go out and hook up with someone easily enough."

"Hooking up isn't really my scene."

"Too straight and narrow, huh? Oh well, your loss." Sylvie adjusted her fitted black shirt covered in silver-stitched spider webs. Sylvie's usual Gothic-type garb was perfect for Halloween but not always appropriate for general wear in front of small children. But Moira's pointed comments about staff attire seemed to bounce off Sylvie like a spilled M&M tumbling down the street. "Seriously, you should consider a blind date. Or any kind of date. You know Mr. Perfect won't tumble down your chimney."

"I'm fine."

"Are you?" Sylvie's brow wrinkled. "You've seemed a little distracted of late."

"Might be the new diet."

"Ooh, what is it this time? No carbs? No sugar? No flavor?"

Bree laughed. "You might be right about that."

"You need to find a man happy to love you as you are."

"As do you."

"Oh, I'm not settling for anything less, honey. He's got to love all this"—she waved her hands up and down her curvy figure—"and more."

"Hence all the blind dates?"

"It's only been four. But I think I need to go back online and see who else is out there. For a city this large, there seems to be a severe shortage of men."

And even less for a Christian girl wanting a Christian man.

A noise of falling wooden blocks drew their attention to the small boy still awaiting collection.

"Max, are you having fun there?"

The two-year-old smiled and clapped his hands.

"Do you think we need to feed him? It's getting pretty late."

"See if he wants a banana, and I'll try the number again."

Bree shifted to the office, pressed redial on the phone. It went straight through to voice mail, as it had done earlier. She tried his mom's number, earned the same result.

Parents. They had the full gamut of them here—everyone from the over-protective helicopter parents to those whose disinterest in their offspring sometimes made her wonder why they'd chosen to have children at all. She loved all her charges, from those with the bright, sparky personalities to the quiet, more gentle souls, and couldn't wait until it was her time to be a mother. Which would likely be years down the track, seeing Mr. Right was proving so elusive.

She pushed back her shoulders, re-entered the main room. "No answer. Still."

Sylvie's nose wrinkled as she glanced up from playing with Max. "I think he needs a change."

Awesome. Why parents always seemed to have a special intuition to arrive just after their charges needed a change was a mystery she'd yet to unravel.

"Here, give Max to me to change. You can chat to his father while I do so."

Sylvie's eyes lit. "My pleasure," she purred.

Bree frowned at her. "You remember our staff-client protocols, don't you?"

"Of course. But it doesn't stop a girl from looking, does it?"

"He's married, Sylvie."

"I heard their marriage is on the rocks. And really, who can blame him? That wife of his might be an executive, but she's such a royal pain in the—"

"I'm going to change Max now. Please let me know when Mr. Hammerson arrives."

"Mr. Hammerson. Also known as Dave."

Bree shook her head, permitting a small smile at Sylvie's tease. Sylvie didn't really mean anything by it, she knew. She was just as romance-focused as Bree could be.

Bree picked up Max, wrinkling her nose at the smell, and drew him to the change table in the corner. Several efficient moves later he was clean and smelling of baby powder, his fat cheeks wobbling as he gurgled away. "Oh, you're such a gorgeous boy, aren't you?"

He grinned, revealing a row of tiny teeth like chips of pearl.

She stroked his super-soft hair. How wonderful it would be to be a mom, to have her own child. Not that she often admitted to that. People—Holly, mainly—seemed to think wanting to have children and a cozy family of her own was some form of fifties throwback, like Bree had no real ambitions for her life. But she couldn't help it. She had no grand dreams of gold medal glory or clawing to the top of some high-powered executive ladder in a big corporation. All she'd wanted since she was a girl was to have a sweet family of her own—someone she could love and cherish, someone for whom she could be Mommy. Did that make her a dinosaur?

A door slammed, a deep male voice. "…so sorry. Max?"

"Bree is just changing him."

"She's still here? Good. I need to speak with her."

Bree sighed. Looked like her night would stretch on even later. Still, when she'd accepted the assistant director role, this was what she'd signed up for. Moira Bridges had wanted someone who would allow for her to have more days off, so Bree was often in charge.

She picked Max up and moved back into the main room. "Hi, Mr. Hammerson."

"Bree. How are you?"

"Daddy!" Max ran to him, where he was swooped up and cuddled against a wide chest.

Okay, she couldn't deny Dave Hammerson was easy on the eye, with that dark hair and eyes. She could even admit he was the kind of man she'd always thought her type, a bit like Toronto's Daniel Walton, who'd started attending her church occasionally. Tall, dark, and dreamy. But—she harnessed her thoughts back to the present—staff and client protocols were to be considered. Not to mention Dave's wife. *Sorry, God.*

"How is Linda?" Maybe her eyes would pay attention to her ears.

"Well, that's what I wanted to talk to you about." He sighed. "Things have been pretty rough lately, between her work and mine."

"That can happen." She knew of too many relationships strained by distance and odd hours, the pursuit of professional promotion coming at the cost of "I do's".

"Mmm, well." He covered Max's ears, kissed the top of his head, and said in a lower voice, "She's left me."

"Oh, I'm *so* sorry to hear that." Sympathy welled. Poor man. No wonder he was running late. He probably didn't know which way was up, let alone what time he was supposed to collect his son. She tickled Max's jean-clad knee. "Did you want to talk in my office?"

"Sure."

She moved to the room she used on Wednesdays and Fridays and cleared Moira's folders from the visitor's chair. She waved a hand at Sylvie, who stared at her wide-eyed through the glassed barrier, and gave a thumbs up to release Sylvie to her date, but she didn't move. Never mind. If Dave was going to stay, then staff-client protocols said it would be good to have someone else on the premises. She found a set of toy trucks and placed them on the floor for Max to play with.

When he was settled and happily vrooming away she asked, "So, how are things going? How is Max coping?"

"He doesn't know yet."

Poor little mite. "May I ask if you've sorted out arrangements with Linda?"

He sighed. "It's still so new that nothing's been arranged yet."

"Fair enough." She chewed her lip. "Are you planning to keep Max enrolled here?"

"For as long as we can, yes."

"Oh good. He's made such excellent progress in recent months. He barely cries at all now."

"You've done a wonderful job with him." Dave's eyes met hers warmly. "I don't know how I would have managed otherwise."

"The staff here are wonderful. So many years of experience."

"Yes, but not everybody connects with him in quite the same way as you have."

Hmm. A peek at the clock. It was getting much later than she was comfortable with. "I'm truly very sorry about your situation. Was there something in particular you wished to talk about?"

"Not really. Just letting you know that things may be a little tricky over the next few weeks. Linda is leaving most of the Max situation to me, and I'm trying to juggle big projects at work—I'm working on that new tower project downtown."

She nodded like she knew which tower he meant. He worked at one of Toronto's most prestigious architecture firms, so anything he worked on would likely be expensive and striking in design.

"So it may mean that I'm a little haphazard with some of my

hours in upcoming weeks, between juggling work, trying to find new routines, and such things."

"I understand."

He slouched back in his seat and smiled. "You're really understanding, Bree. Far more than Mrs. Bridges."

Something in his voice made her stand, dim her smile back to neutral. "Well, if that's all?"

"Thanks, Bree. You're a lifesaver."

"We like to do all we can to ensure the best outcomes for the children." She gestured to the door.

Fortunately, he took the hint, collecting Max as he preceded her. "Well, thanks again."

"Of course. Now, as it's nearly seven, I'm afraid we must charge you overtime."

"It's that late? Oh. How careless of me. Perhaps I should make things up to you and get you dinner."

"We have places to be, Mr. Hammerson," she said firmly, no smile now. Heaven forbid Sylvie had heard him. "I'll simply add tonight's late charge to your account. Oh, and I'm afraid Max will need dinner as soon as possible. We weren't sure what time you'd get here, so he's had a banana and some milk, but that's all. See you next week."

He nodded, and with another apology and smile, finally left.

"Bye, Max." She waved.

"Bye, Miss Bwee," Max said, settling his thumb in his mouth as he leaned his head on his dad's shoulder.

"Phew." Bree locked the front doors firmly behind him. "Dave Hammerson is not an easy person to get rid of."

"You really want to get rid of him? I think he's so fine," Sylvie said, fanning herself from the door. "Did I really hear him invite you out on a date?"

"No, you did not."

"Um, last I checked, when a man asks a woman out for

dinner, that's counted as a date. So I guess it really is over with him and Linda now."

"It sounds that way." Poor Max. How challenging this would be. *God, be with that family.*

"So, will you take him up?"

"I beg your pardon?" Bree closed the blinds. Did a final check.

"Take up Dave's offer and go out with him."

"No." As far as she knew he wasn't a Christian, and, "There's that staff-client protocol, remember?"

"Oh. That." Sylvie shoved her mass of tight curls into a high ponytail. "He's got that whole swoony Dan Walton thing going on, don't you think?"

Perhaps a diversion in topics would be best. "Did you know he goes to my church?" She'd take any chance to interest Sylvie in God, shallow as the reason might be.

"Who? Dave or Dan?"

"Dan." She had no idea if Dave went to church—yet another reason to throw him in the box marked definitely unavailable. She wanted someone who followed God and tried to live His ways at least.

"Really? Does he go every Sunday? Even after games? Maybe I should come."

"You're always welcome."

"I'll think about it."

"I've met him a few times," Bree continued. "He's pretty down to earth."

"Oh, of course you have." Sylvie's face shifted to something Bree couldn't quite decipher. "All those hockey parties you go to."

"I don't go to that many."

"You go to more than anyone else I know. How was that New Year's thing, anyway?"

"It was okay."

"Okay? Oh, to be you with your lifestyles-of-the-rich-and-famous friends."

Bree eyed her. Honestly, it sounded like Sylvie was jealous. The other workers knew she was Brent Karlsson's sister, but rarely mentioned it. That fact was one of the reasons work had always been a safe space, relatively free from the petty enquiries for free tickets and the like that seemed to exist in most other places she knew. Nobody here tried to take advantage of her connections, apart from the odd parent who liked to talk hockey with her, as if she were some kind of expert and paid attention beyond her brother's games.

"Got any pics? I bet you looked good."

Bree reluctantly fished her phone from her bag. Tapped the buttons until she found the photo Mike had taken.

"Girl, you look so fine!"

"It was one of my better moments, I agree."

Sylvie chuckled, then swiped the screen. "Ooh, now who is this? I didn't know you had a boyfriend. Well, look at you, keeping this one on the sly. Mystery man is hot!"

After a brief tussle, Bree tugged the phone away. "He's a friend."

"Who is very hot." Sylvie fanned herself again. "I'm not surprised you couldn't care less about Dave when you have this one on the side. Who is he?"

"Just a family friend."

"'Just a family friend' she says. Does he have a name?"

"Mike Vaughan."

"Boston's Mike Vaughan?"

She shrugged, working to straighten the finger paintings in the entry hall.

"Seriously? Oh honey, if you don't want him, I'll take him off your hands."

"He's not on my hands"—she frowned at how that sounded—"so you really don't—"

"Come on, spill." Sylvie clicked her fingers. "Give me the goss."

"There's nothing to say. We're friends, and he accompanied me to the party. That's it. He's not interested in me, and I'm definitely not interested in him, and that's all."

"That's all?" Sylvie smirked.

"That's *all*."

"Oh." Sylvie's face fell. "That's disappointing."

She had to redirect Sylvie's too-keen interest. "Honestly, I didn't know too many people at the party and didn't talk to many. Most of the guys had their wives or girlfriends there, anyway."

"Honey, just because someone is taken doesn't mean you can't talk to them." Sylvie rolled her eyes. "Honestly, it's like you're from the Dark Ages or something."

"Why? Because I don't choose to hang around chatting with men who are taken?"

"It's not an affair if you're simply talking, Bree."

"Emotional entanglements usually start that way, however."

"Please." Sylvie's thick-lashed eyes flicked to check out the ceiling again. "It's like you can't separate the two."

"I can separate the two, but I don't think it's wise to intrude in a relationship and be thought to stir things up at a party like that."

"So, are you saying you never talk to a married man? Come on."

"I'm saying I don't think it wise to be in a place where there's lots of media and photos being taken and be seen chatting with a man who others know is not available."

"Hmph." Sylvie straightened the poster board in the foyer, then moved to the staffroom and collected her spider-crowned bag. "I saw a picture of your brother with his girlfriend on the internet. Chloe, isn't it?"

Bree's chest grew tight. "Yes."

"She looks a little—um, how should I put this?—body confident? Trampy?"

Would saying nothing be construed as confirmation? "She's a model."

"Yeah, I bet I know just what she models."

"Didn't you have a date to get to?" Bree asked sweetly.

"Yeah." Sylvie's brow puckered. "I suppose I should go."

"Didn't you say you would?"

"Yeah, but I'm tired now. I could just cancel."

"And stand the guy up?"

"Look, Bree, not everyone is as old-fashioned as you. Sometimes a girl's gotta do what a girl's gotta do, you know?"

"But not if it ends up hurting someone else," Bree countered.

"Look, I don't even know the guy, but already I know he won't be like your hot hockey playing friends."

"Hockey isn't all that," Bree said. "It's a lot of training, a lot of time away, a lot of focus. It's not like you're lying on the couch watching hours of *Pride and Prejudice* together while eating tubs of ice-cream."

Well, sometimes it was like that for her. But never with Brent. He'd as soon shave his legs. She couldn't imagine someone like Dan Walton watching a chick flick like that, either. Or Mike.

No. "Anyway, I've decided this year not to date any hockey players or anyone who says they're interested in the sport. I want someone who is into me, not into any connections I have."

"Good luck with that."

"Thank you."

Sylvie laughed. "I don't think there's a straight man in a twelve-hundred mile radius with breath in his lungs who would *not* be interested in dating someone whose brother is Brent Karlsson."

"Be that as it may, I still believe there's someone out there and hope to meet him."

"Want me to fix you up with a profile on Love Online? It won't take long, and now there's this nice photo of you from New Year's."

"Thank you," Bree said, oddly touched by Sylvie's concern. "But I'd rather do things the old-fashioned way."

"Well, if a hockey player isn't for you, then maybe you should try for Dave."

"Dave?"

"Hammerson? Max's dad? The guy who was just here? You could do worse."

"Remember that staff-client protocol?" Bree followed Sylvie's lead as she stuffed herself into her winter coat, wrapped on her scarf, and grabbed her bag. "It applies to me too."

Sylvie nodded, flicked off the center's lights, and they exited and locked the back door. As they moved to the small carpark out the back, the sensor light switched on, highlighting the recent dump of snow. Great. A cold, slow drive home tonight.

"I hope your date goes well, Sylvie. I'm sorry you'll be late."

"I might not go after all. Work running late is a valid excuse for a no-show." She held up a newly gloved hand. "I'll message him and let him know, don't worry."

"Have a good weekend."

"You too, Bree. Oh, and if Dan's in church, let me know."

"Will do." Bree smiled.

She got in her car and drove carefully through the slush-filled streets, her mind ticking through the various topics of conversation. Was she old-fashioned in wanting to wait for God to reveal Mr. Right? Or was this yet more evidence of the counter-cultural life she was expected to live as a follower of Jesus rather than whatever societal norm seemed to be the flavor of the day?

"God, protect me from the snares. I want the guy who's right for me. Help me be patient for him."

She flicked on the radio. A catchy melody of guitars and

breathy voice filled the car. Words about waiting for love, waiting until it was right, stole through her ears into her heart.

Breath escaped. That was what she wanted. Love prepared to wait until the moment was right.

"And Lord, please help him wait for me, too. Whoever he is, wherever he is right now. Thank You that You hold our world in the palms of Your hands. Help me trust You."

And with a sigh, she turned into her street, ready for another Friday night at home.

CHAPTER 4

Training finished for the day, Mike retrieved his belongings from his locker. His phone had several messages. He glanced at the top one. Smiled.

"What's got you looking so happy?" said Todd Henry, his defense partner.

He shrugged, stuffed the phone in his pocket. "Nothing." He wasn't ready to talk about Bree yet. Not that there was anything to say.

"Sure doesn't look like nothing." Marc Ledinberger, a young defenseman Mike had mentored for the past two years, eyed him. "I bet it's the girl from New Year's."

Mike tensed. "What girl?"

"Maggie, my girlfriend, saw a pic online of you and some chick in Detroit. Don't know why you'd ever wanna go to something there."

"You don't have to," he deflected.

Ledinberger frowned as Todd, fellow defenseman Franklin James, and a couple of others laughed. "Leddy gets burned," Jacques Paviour, their backup goalie said.

"He's friends with Karlsson," Todd explained.

"Didn't he pull some hot model?"

"They've gone out a few times," Mike said cautiously.

"Yeah, if she was my girlfriend, we'd be doing a lot more than going out, if you know what I mean."

Mike shrugged. And this was why he had to be careful. Guys talked, and locker room banter was rarely the holiest of conversations. "Gotta go."

He grabbed his bag just as his phone buzzed again. He pulled it out. Bree. Again.

"He's smiling again."

"Come on. Fill us in. Who is she?"

"No-one—hey!"

Ledinberger held the phone and whistled. "Oh, you've got quite the conversation going on here."

Mike's chest tensed. Quite the conversation he didn't need anyone here reading anytime ever. "Give me the phone now."

"Whoa. Check this out." He flashed the photo from New Year's, the one where he and Bree grinned together. "She's a babe."

"She's a friend." Who was also a babe. But he wouldn't admit that here.

Their captain, Vladimir Josic, tugged the phone free from Leddy, glancing at the screen as he handed it back to Mike, eyebrows raised. "Is that Karlsson's sister?"

"She's a family friend."

"Uh huh. That's why you looked so cozy together, right?" Ledinberger said. "How long have you two been a thing?"

"We're not. It was New Year's. Karlsson asked me to go to it with her."

"Karlsson? That dude is awetastic."

Was that even a word? Mike shrugged. He probably should contact Brent soon, but picking through the landmines of conversation made it a little hard to be motivated.

Conversation shifted to other partners, other hook ups,

some of the details of which made Mike feel as gross as the sweaty shirt he still wore. "I'm heading out. Catch ya tomorrow."

He finally escaped to the parking lot, the chilled air a welcome scour for his lungs and mind, and as he reached the sanctuary of his car, finally reread Bree's latest message.

HEY MIKE, HAVE YOU HEARD ANYTHING MORE FROM BRENT?

A quick reply, then he switched off his phone to concentrate on the snowy drive. Knowing Bree, there'd be a message as soon as he got home. This back and forth between them felt a little like the innocence of high school over a decade ago, the first shots in a game that could escalate into something more than mere words, could ground this flirty feeling into something real. "God, help her see me as more than a friend."

He chewed his lip as he swung into the apartment block's underground parking. One of the perks of living here: reserved parking. He beeped the doors locked and stabbed the elevator button for the next-to-top floor, his thoughts returning to a recent sermon. Was it wrong to pray such a selfish sounding prayer? Or was pleading his case before God simply what he should do?

The doors opened, releasing a gray-haired couple with their Pekingese, a fat yappy thing called Pumpkin that Mike tried hard to like because the Grubers were genuinely kind to him and had been ever since he'd moved here as a rookie six years ago.

"Michael." Beatrice Gruber offered a warm smile. "It's been far too long since you've come for dinner. When are you next free?"

"I've got a thing tonight and a game tomorrow," he said regretfully, "so maybe Thursday?"

"Thursday it is. Leonard's got a wonderful new cookbook, and he's working his way through the recipes."

"So far so good," Leonard said with humble pride.

"I'll definitely be there. You know I love your cooking."

"And we love an appreciative guest."

"Usual time?" They nodded. "I'll bring dessert, then." Something he most definitely wouldn't be baking. "Hey, thanks. I can't wait. Enjoy your day."

"You too. Go Boston."

Mike chuckled, saluted, and moved into the vacant elevator.

Unlike the reserved parking spaces, the elevator's speed was not this apartment complex's best feature. Still, it allowed for more of that transition-of-headspace time between work and home, to shift his thoughts to what lay ahead this afternoon and evening.

First: deal with email. His agent, Phil Mowbray, had passed on a request about whether he'd be interested in being a spokesperson for Mission Possible for Future Generations, a child sponsorship program in the Philippines. He needed to reread the details. He sensed his agent wasn't keen and thought it would prove a big distraction, but Mike had been involved with the organization since he'd earned his first NHL paycheck, and he liked what they stood for, how the money raised actually supported the work of those helping children in slums, and wasn't swallowed up in admin costs. He'd need to pray about that.

Second, tonight was the online pro sports Bible study. He needed to go over the notes and prep a little, seeing as he was supposed to lead some of it, Pastor Josiah having said he'd be late to the Zoom meeting.

And third, he probably should get off his backside and contact Brent again, even if only to invite him to tonight's meeting, which at least would allow him to have something more to report to Bree the next time she messaged him.

The doors opened and he moved down the hall just as another door opened.

His new neighbor, a pretty blonde—Rhianna? Rhiannon?—smiled. "Hello."

"Hey." He nodded. "You settled in okay now?"

"Thank you, yes." She scanned him. Raised an eyebrow. "Been at practice?"

"Yeah." His skin prickled. The way her smile lingered, the way she leaned closer, as if in invitation... Yeah, he needed to get going. "See ya."

"Bye, Mike."

He offered another nod and moved on, feeling her eyes on him as he walked two doors down, taking care not to look as he inserted his key and shut the door. He sighed. Women like that had always made him uncomfortable, like he didn't match the assumed persona his line of work seemed to offer. He knew some of his teammates—even some with a girlfriend—wouldn't mind the conversations and prolonged glances. They only made him feel uncertain and antsy inside.

He threw his bag toward the bedroom, showered, changed, grabbed water from the fridge, and settled in front of the computer. Reread the email forwarded from Phil earlier. Knew a great sense of humility again.

Dear Mr. Vaughan,

As a longtime supporter of Mission Possible for Future Generations, you would know the marvelous work done to help improve the lives of so many children over the years through our education, health, and community programs. We have been truly blessed by God to see hundreds of children's lives improved by the sponsorship of caring partners such as yourself.

Because we know this ministry is something you believe in, we would like to invite you to consider helping us to spread the word by becoming one of the faces of our organization. This would be a voluntary position and would include the use of

your photograph, name, and quote, and possibly some inter-
views in magazines, in order to help the organization find more
sponsors for the hundreds of children still awaiting
sponsorship.
We understand you are a busy man, and would ask you to pray
and seek God's leading. We truly appreciate your support and
encouragement.
May God bless you richly.
Pastor John Ramirez
Director,
Mission Possible for Future Generations

Phil had added his thoughts, which mainly focused on the voluntary aspect of the offer:

Do you really want to put your name to a two-bit do-gooder
organization? Just in case it escaped your notice, voluntary
means non-remunerated, not paid, you'll work for free—is this
really what you want to do?

Mike sat back in his chair, hands folded behind his head, eyeing Phil's words with a frown. No. What he really didn't want to do was to play nice with Phil when it was obvious the man cared more about his bank balance than anything that might require an iota of personal sacrifice. His agent wouldn't appreciate getting a cut of grace.

Mike's thoughts tracked to the children he'd sponsored, whose faces decorated his fridge: Maddy, Peter, Janet, Bella, Alfonso, Ben. All saved from the slums, provided with food, education, and a chance to know Jesus. The program was getting so big now. Maddy had graduated school and was training to be a nurse in one of Manila's universities. How crazy was it to think his spare change could change—was changing—their world so completely?

God?

A sense of peace eased through him.

So, ignoring Phil's comments, Mike clicked on the executive's email address and replied.

Dear Mr. Ramirez,

To say I felt humbled when I received your letter is an understatement. I am privileged to offer you whatever service I can and would love to help promote MPFG to as many people as I can as you see fit....

Five minutes later, he reread it and pressed send.

His lips twitched as he wondered just what Phil would make of that.

A glance at the time and he was soon composing another message.

BRENT, NEXT BIBLE STUDY WITH PASTOR JOSIAH ABRAHAMS IS ON TONIGHT AT 8. BE GREAT IF YOU CAN MAKE IT. DEF WORTH YOUR TIME. LINK IS HERE.

He studied his words, prayed it would find a receptive heart, and pressed send. Then wondered whether he should've just called. Was simply messaging a wussy way out?

He exhaled. Pressed the number. Got an answering machine.

"Hey, just me. Hope you got my message about the Bible study tonight at eight. Sent you the link. Be great if you can join us. Hope to see you then."

He pressed end, prayed again, then moved to the Bible study notes.

This was how he liked to roll: check, check, check. Crossing off the list, maximizing his schedule to ensure he completed tasks on time, that nothing was forgotten. Their parents had always emphasized to Mike and his sister Callie the importance of taking personal responsibility. Callie had taken this on board to such an extent that she'd joined the army and was currently stationed in Germany, working at a medical facility there. He probably should see if she was up for a video call again sometime soon.

Dinner—leftovers, still carefully portion controlled—then some stretches, then it was time for his online meeting.

He checked his phone, unsurprised to see no answer from Brent. Still, maybe the invite had made him think, made the link between them feel like it still had strength.

"Hey." Jai Mullins was a winger for Chicago, as speedy as they came, and usually the first man to show up for these calls when his playing schedule allowed.

Players came when they could, knowing the first and third Monday nights would always find a friendly face and listening ear as they checked in from various parts of North America. Many were based in the north east, several of them part of Original Six teams, but they'd had some players check in occasionally from the west coast, like Vancouver and LA.

Another face: Dan Walton from Toronto, a defenseman, solid through and through. "Forgiven us yet?"

Mike laughed. Losing to Toronto by eight goals had seen Boston chowing down on giant slabs of humble pie. "You're enjoying this a bit too much."

"Nice to finally feel we're clicking."

Beau Nash, a lanky goalie from Carolina, checked in, then a few other guys from Colorado and Texas. The Bible study had started a few years ago when Chicago-based church minister Josiah Abrahams's love for hockey had led him to want to encourage and support the Christian players within the sport.

After a few minutes more of catch up and tease, Mike brought the meeting to order. "Jo said he'd be a little late, so we can start without him. So let's pray."

He bowed his head, glad for this time and space to relax and be real with guys who understood the pressures of playing in this sport that so often glamorized lifestyles the Bible didn't agree with. Men who might play hard but had soft hearts, were willing to both give and take advice, whose offers to pray meant he could count on God hearing prayers. None of them were saints by any stretch of the imagination, but he knew he could trust them. And in a world where guys could get traded on management's say so, where his teammates might be his opponents the next day, it was good to have forged some friendships deeper than the jersey he wore.

Tonight's study: the rise and fall of David, and how a man who'd committed adultery could still be called a man after God's own heart.

They read through the passages emailed earlier and conversation began.

"I always struggle with this," Jai confessed. "I hate how it seems David gets away with stealing a man's wife."

Mike knew Jai's dad had left his mom years ago. No wonder he struggled.

"What do you think, Dan?"

Dan shrugged. "I'm still kind of new to all this. Sorry."

Fortunately, Josiah soon joined them, and he steered the conversation through some at-times turbulent waters. "Because really, who are we to judge? We can think we won't fall, but David's story shows us how even those who are close to God can be blind sometimes and end up putting someone before God. I think the beauty of this story is that it shows God's forgiveness. David knew he'd sinned, he acknowledged his sin, and God in His mercy saw David's broken and contrite heart and ultimately redeemed him, thus showing God's grace."

"But it still doesn't mean David got away with things scotfree," Beau said. "What about Absalom?"

"You're right. He had to live with Absalom's treason and dramas with his other children."

Thank God for husbands and wives who chose to love

through thick and thin. Thank God for Mike's own parents, who kept their vows even though his dad's work took him away from home, sometimes for weeks at a time. Mike wanted to be that kind of man, committed to loving his one-day wife no matter what challenges came their way.

The time ended with prayer, with each guy sharing one or two prayer points. Most of the time it was family stuff, occasionally relationship-focused, as nearly all the guys were single. Sometimes it was about wisdom regarding contracts and work things.

Mike shared about the sponsorship ministry opportunity, which drew a chorus of "awesome" and "sign me up," which meant he'd send them links tonight. "And if you can pray for me regarding my next contract, that'd be great."

"You're unrestricted from July?" Dan asked.

"Yeah. It'd be nice to stay here in Boston, but I don't want to feel undervalued, which I kind of do."

"You trust your agent?" Beau asked, his Southern accent thick as molasses.

"Sometimes," he replied honestly.

There came a series of nods. Not all agents were created equal, some apparently way more interested in their bottom line than in working for the best interests of their clients.

A few more prayer points, a bit more talk and tease, and it was time to go. With a round of farewells, the screen went black.

Mike emailed the guys the links to the mission organization then glanced at his phone. It was getting late, but she might still be up...

HEY BREE. INVITED BRENT AGAIN TO TONIGHT'S BIBLE STUDY. HE DIDN'T COME, BUT LET'S HOPE IT MAKES HIM THINK. HOPE YOU'RE DOING OKAY.

He pressed send. Waited a moment. A moment longer. Then,

MIKE, YOU'RE SUCH A STAR! SO APPRECIATE YOU. SWEET DREAMS. B X

Heart full, he switched off the phone. Sweet dreams? Oh yeah. He knew what he'd be dreaming of tonight.

~

"BREE, HAVE YOU GOT A SPARE MINUTE?" Moira asked. Her flyaway graying curls were barely restrained by an Alice band, the vintage of which was suspiciously 1980s given its plastic gloss.

"Sure." Bree placed the coloring sheets to be photocopied on the spare table near the door, a spare table designed to be a catch-all for whatever projects, paperwork, or forgotten craft projects the staff—or children—left behind. Today being Thusday morning, Moira hadn't cluttered it too high, given Bree's clear out last night.

"What can I help with?"

"Oh, I do like that about you," Moira said. "Always so obliging, nothing too much trouble. Unlike some young people working here, who seem to think they're doing me a favor rather than the other way around."

Bree nodded. She didn't need to think too hard about whom Moira was referring to.

"So, I've been looking over the planned activities for the year, and as you know we have a number of important fundraising events that families love to get involved in. I was wondering—hoping more so—that you would take these on this year."

Bree blinked. "You mean things like the Easter egg hunt, the Fall festival and the Christmas pageant?"

"Exactly so." Moira sighed. "I'm getting older, and my energy —and I'll be honest, my enthusiasm—levels just aren't where they used to be."

"You know me, Moira. I love to organize such things." How exciting! Especially if she could finally implement the ideas she'd had for years. "But are you giving me the entire responsibility, or am I simply to follow what we've done in previous years?"

Moira waved a hand. "At this point, I don't care. I'd rather have something organized by someone guaranteed to make it happen, which may mean it's easier to simply continue with similar types of activities to what we've done previously. But you're young and enthusiastic. Perhaps you've got some other ideas we could explore."

Mom had long said that Bree's middle name should not be Jane but Enthusiasm. She smiled. "When would you like such ideas?"

"Oh, as soon as you can. We'll need to start preparing for the Easter egg hunt, so perhaps you'd like to keep that much the same."

"I think that's wise," Bree said with a nod. "But you'd be happy for me to look at some other events and see if there are some aspects we could tweak?"

"Yes, yes. Let me know in February what they are."

"Speaking of February, are you open to a Valentine's Day event?"

"Well, I suppose I could be. It's rather soon though, isn't it? Might be a bit of a rush to get something happening in only a few weeks."

"Leave it with me, and I'll get back to you by the weekend about whether we can arrange something."

"Very well." A scream came from the older children's room. Moira exhaled, shook her head. "Oh dear."

"I'll go check what that is."

"Sounds like it's just young Felix up to his usual tricks."

Bree nodded and made her escape to where Fiona was holding the small boy as his mother hovered near the door. It wasn't Felix's issues so much as his mother's insecurities that meant every parting was like Felix was here for the first time. But if he was to attend school later this year, then he really needed to learn how to deal with separation anxiety now. As did his faint-hearted mother.

"Good morning, Rani," Bree said, moving to cut the line of sight between mother and small boy. "Please say goodbye to Felix so he can get settled for the day."

"Oh, but he needs me."

Brent had often accused Bree of being soft-hearted through the years. But she was a tough chick of Holly standards compared to timid Rani.

"What he needs is for you to go so he can get settled with his friends," Bree said kindly but with firmness. She gestured for Fiona to draw Felix closer to the plush dinosaurs he seemed to love, then turned back to his mother, whose attention remained fixed on her son as she moved around Bree to wave at him. Fortunately, Fiona's skill at distraction—learned from long experience—meant Felix was now focused on talking to Miss Steggy, the green-and-purple stegosaurus, and away from the agitations of his mother.

"Felix, do you want to say goodbye to your mommy?" Fiona asked, her Irish accent bringing a smile to Bree's heart. Maybe she should ask God for an Irish boyfriend, one whom she could happily listen to for hours.

"Bye, Mama," Felix said, not looking up.

Rani gave a small sob. "Oh, he didn't even look at me."

Bree gently steered her to the foyer. "It's good he's quietened now, isn't it? We want him getting used to such routines so he's ready for big school later. You wouldn't want Felix being teased or ostracized by other children because he hasn't learned to cope with being away from you."

"Oh, but you do not understand. How can anyone under-stand when they are not a mother?"

"I know it's hard, but—"

"He is all I have."

"I'm sure that's not true," Bree said softly. "You have family and friends."

"But my husband still is in detention. I do not know how long it will be until I see him again."

"Oh, Rani. I'm so sorry." Bree's heart twisted with compassion. "Is there something we can do?"

Rani shook her head, tried to peer past Bree's shoulder, then sighed. "I should probably go."

"Felix will have a wonderful day, don't you worry."

"You must think me very foolish, but I get so scared for him. I want him to be safe and happy, unlike his poor father."

Bree gently touched her on the arm. "I will pray and ask God to help your situation." Technically she wasn't supposed to mention her beliefs while on the premises, but she'd always thought that was a rule that God's ways naturally precluded.

She chewed her lip, her mind spinning with possibilities as she watched Rani trudge to her small Mazda. Surely there had to be something she could do to help this situation. *Lord, what can we do?*

Back in the older children's room, Fiona's smile of reassurance suggested all was well, so Bree knocked quietly on Moira's partially opened office door, waiting as Moira tapped away at her computer while chatting on the phone. Moira soon ended the call and beckoned her in. "Yes?"

"Quick question: Rani and Felix—what do we know about their situation? She mentioned just now her husband is still in detention. Did you know that?"

"What? I thought they'd released him."

"Do you know how Felix's position here is being funded? He's a subsidized place, isn't he? Surely there are extended family who are helping them."

"I thought you said this was a quick question."

Bree shrugged. "I'm wondering if maybe we could do some extra fundraising for families such as theirs."

"What are you thinking?"

"I haven't thought it all through yet, but I would like to do something for refugees like Rani's husband and others in her community. It's easy to assume everything's finalized once they've settled here, but it seems like that's not the case at all. Whatever we do, we'd need to be subtle about it, to not embarrass them, but I'm sure there's something we could do that would be of benefit."

"Perhaps. Think about it some more and let me know what you come up with. As sad as that situation is, they're not the only ones with family challenges."

Bree nodded. "Have you heard anything more about Diana's treatment?"

"I'm afraid the radiation isn't working."

Bree bit her lip. "Poor Diana. Those poor girls." Hannah and Grace were two of the sweetest girls to have ever attended the center. Twins of the most gentle natures, they were little sunshiney angels. She'd been praying for their mother ever since she'd learned about Diana's breast cancer diagnosis. They'd thought she'd beaten it, but now it appeared to have spread to her lymph nodes and lungs. This new treatment was—barring a miracle—her last chance.

Heaviness weighed on Bree. "I best get back."

Throughout the morning and into the afternoon, she fulfilled her duties: mopping up juice, picking up toys, reading stories, encouraging naps. Work was never boring. But behind the smiles and quick assistance, her heart was troubled, ideas and plans drifting in for consideration before being discarded as either too hard, too expensive, or just plain infeasible.

But she just *knew* she had to do something. This project, seeking to bless struggling families with an appropriate fundraiser, suddenly seemed so much more necessary than the project concerning her foolish brother. Speaking of…

She fished out her phone. Saw another text from Mike. Smiled. At least here was a guy she could count on, someone dependable, honest, and strong.

An idea flashed through her mind. Before she had a moment to think, she tapped out the words:

HEY MIKE, ARE YOU FREE FOR VALENTINE'S DAY?

CHAPTER 5

*B*oston in winter wasn't everyone's destination of choice. But it was warmer than Toronto, at least. And a rare day off was never to be spent entirely indoors. Mike sucked in a breath of bitter coldness, the ice carried on last night's wind still in the breeze. He liked this feeling; it seemed to wake his soul, blow the cobwebs from his mind.

But as he walked down near the harbor, along freshly shoveled sidewalks with the few locals brave enough to trudge through snow, he couldn't help but wonder how he'd spend such days if he had a girlfriend. Inside watching movies, a cozy restaurant or coffee shop, maybe visit the museums he'd passed by since he'd first visited as a newbie, when he'd been all shiny-eyed wonder. Seeing things like that on his own hadn't been much fun.

He tugged his scarf closer, huddled deeper into his thick jacket, this morning's emails still running through his head. MPFG was thrilled, would appreciate the chance to talk online at his earliest convenience, etc, etc.

Phil: nothing to report regarding contracts.

Then there was that text from Bree.

A ripple unrelated to cold raced along his spine, and he turned from the broken windowpane-like ice shards lying along the edges of the harbor and hurried through the slush to the row of stores whose lights suggested they were open.

He stopped in at Bob's Coffee, slamming the door against the cold. "Hey, Bob."

"Mike. How you doin'?"

"Nice to be inside. Be even nicer once I'm caffeinated."

"Usual?"

"Thanks." The booths were near empty, save for an elderly man reading the paper in the back. "George."

"Mike." He tapped his paper. "Gonna win against the Flyers?"

"That's the goal."

"Ha." He tapped the side of his nose. "I see what you did there."

Mike grinned and turned back to Bob. "Glad you're open."

"Glad you're here. Was wondering if I should close, but figured Mike Vaughan might appear."

"You know me well."

"Oy, what am I?" George called. "Chopped liver?"

"You're part of the furniture. Always here." Mike winked.

"That's enough out of you, young Michael. Go win a game or something."

"I'll do my best." He saluted George, then collected his coffee, slipping a bill larger than needed to Bob. "See you next time."

"Sure thing."

He exited, popped off the plastic lid, and savored the scent before taking his first sip. That was better. Coffee truly was a gift from God. And the way Bob made it, smooth with none of the bitterness so many places seemed to offer, meant he didn't need it flavored or sweetened. Bree, he knew, was always up for whatever was new or in season—the sweeter and foamier the better. He grinned, remembering she even seemed to hold a preference for the abomination that was a pumpkin spice latte. Yeah, according to his taste buds, that was barely coffee.

Bree. His heart scampered as he recalled her text. He'd not answered yet, unsure how to reply. How weird that he could face down men the size and speed of locomotives, but this girl had him second-guessing himself all the time. Maybe he should just call her.

By the time he reached his apartment building, he'd determined to do just that.

Once in the foyer, Mike sipped his coffee as the elevator took its usual sweet time. The building's glass doors opened, admitting a frosty blast and his new neighbor. What was her name again? All he could remember was that the first part sounded a bit like Bree—beyond that, he hadn't paid attention.

"Well, hello, neighbor."

"Hey." He stabbed the elevator button again.

"Great minds, huh?" She held up her coffee. "Where'd you go? I've tasted this, and it's okay but not what I'm used to."

"Bob's. Down near the harbor."

"You ventured that far? You really are a tough guy, aren't you?"

What was he supposed to say to that?

"I must give it a go next time."

He nodded. Tugged out his phone. He didn't want to appear rude, but neither did he want to give the impression he was available. Bree. What would he say to Bree?

"So, I thought I'd try to come to the next game. Who are you playing?"

"Philly." *Come on, elevator.*

"Who do you think will win?"

He raised an eyebrow.

She laughed. "I should've thought that through. How not to win friends, right?"

Right.

Finally, the elevator doors made their clanking shudder as they opened. He gestured her in first. Realized the error of his ways as she smiled.

"Aren't you the gentleman?"

Another comment for which he had no reply.

"You don't talk much, do you?"

He glanced up from his phone, where he was pretending to type. "Sorry, a little busy here."

"Oh, right. Didn't mean to intrude."

He swallowed a sigh. Maybe he was coming across as rude. "I'm just texting my girlfriend."

Her eyes widened. "Oh! Sorry, I didn't know."

He felt an internal ping at his lie. Was it wrong to call Bree his girlfriend? She was a girl and a friend, so technically it was true. And it wasn't like anyone would be hurt by his pretense.

Girl-whose-name-he'd-forgotten was silent the rest of the ascent, and he heaved another sigh of relief when the doors opened onto their floor. He let her out first, keeping his steps slow, still acting distracted so as not to walk at her pace. He passed the Gruber's door, which opened as if Beatrice had been lying in wait. "Mike! You haven't forgotten about tonight, have you?"

"Looking forward to it, Beatrice."

She smiled, then peered past him to see their new neighbor. "Oh, Rachel. You're here."

Rachel?

"I'm sure Mike wouldn't mind, but it seems Leonard has cooked enough for an army. Would you like to join us for dinner too?"

Rachel—seriously, how had he thought her name rhymed with Bree's?—glanced at him. "I don't wish to intrude."

"Oh, nonsense. Mike won't mind, will you?"

Actually—

"And you're still new. It'll do you good to get to know some other residents. And Mike here is such a gentleman."

When described like that, he could hardly refuse. "Be good to have you," he said politely.

Her face shone. "If you're sure your girlfriend won't mind?"

"Girlfriend?" Beatrice's eyes rounded. "Why did we not know? Is she here too? Oh, you must invite her as well. I'd love to meet the woman who has stolen your heart."

"Yeah…" *Come on brain, think.* "She's out of town."

"Oh. Well, be sure to let us know when she's next around. We'd love to have you both here for dinner."

"Sure." That'd probably be never. Although that text message implied otherwise… "Thanks for the kind offer."

"So, tonight? Six? See you both here then."

"Thanks, Beatrice," said Rachel.

"See you then." He nodded to both women before escaping into his apartment. Awesome. How to explain…

"Sorry, God," he muttered, moving to the window. From here, the harbor he'd just seen close up seemed more serene, the plastic-wrapped boats that housed the "live-aboards" in the harbor bobbing like restless toys in the gray sea. Now that was a life he couldn't imagine.

A knock came at the door. He peered through the peephole —uh oh—then opened the door. "Rachel."

"Hi, Mike." She pushed her hair to one side. "Look, I really don't want to make things awkward for you, so I'm just going to tell Beatrice that something has come up and I can't make it tonight."

Guilt creased his stomach. "It's no problem. Really."

"Your girlfriend won't mind?"

He shrugged. "I'm about to call her and explain."

"Oh. Okay. Well, sorry to intrude. See you tonight?"

"Sure."

She smiled at him, and he nodded and closed the door. Looked like he'd be making that call after all.

But when he rang, there was no answer, and after psyching himself up to speak, he couldn't figure out a message to leave. So he hung up. Shook his head. Well, Bree would see he'd tried to call. Maybe that would inspire her to call him back. Regardless, the hope of her message stole through him like the scent of his morning coffee—stirring his senses, breathing life into his dreams with the promise of something sweetly addictive.

IF ONLY SOMEONE could invent an unsend function for messages. Ever since she'd sent that message Bree had known unease. But seriously, Mike wouldn't think anything of it. How could he? They were friends. Even so, uncertainty gnawed at her careless words, causing her to switch off her phone and get her head in the right space for work.

The morning passed smoothly, lunch time—always one of the more hectic parts of the day—going tears-free. She met with Moira for a quick chat during naptime.

"So, how are things progressing with your Valentine's Day fundraiser? We don't have long until we would need to advertise."

"I'm still working out the details, and when I have something more definite, you'll be the first to know."

"Hmm. Very good."

Bree smiled and moved back to the room where Sylvie was rostered on again today.

"What did she want?" Sylvie tucked her black hair behind an ear, showcasing her giraffe earrings, as they began a quick tidy up of the toys.

"Oh, just to discuss the Valentine's Day plan."

"The Valentine's Day plan? Do tell."

"Well, that's it. There's nothing to tell at this stage." Bree collected the sturdy plastic Noah's Ark animals, and placed them on the boat. "I need to iron out some more details before I can share anything."

"Do you really think people will want to do something that day?"

"I can't see many of our parents here getting dressed up and going out for dinner, so they might see it as a pleasant change, especially when they know it's for a good cause."

"Hmm. I think you might find you're in for a challenge." Sylvie snagged Noah and handed him to Bree. "Aren't you trying to find a nice person for yourself?"

"But I'm not."

"Oh!" Her eyes rounded. "Is that because you already have a nice someone?"

"But I don't."

"Come on, girl. What are you doing? Let me set you up with someone, please."

"I'm not interested in casually dating. I want him to be someone who can be the father of my children."

"Whoa." Sylvie leaned back on her heels, her palms upright. "What happened to just plain having fun?"

"I've done plenty of that over the years, and it always leaves me feeling a little blah. My hopes always get dashed, and I end up feeling worse than before."

"Girl, I'm talking about going out for dinner with a handsome man. When was the last time you did that?"

New Year's? Or did that not count? "Look, I don't go in for casual flings. I'm not wired that way."

"Bree, I suspect you don't know what way you're wired until someone sets that motor running. Know what I mean?"

Bree doubted she wanted to know exactly what Sylvie meant, but nodded anyway.

"What are you doing tomorrow night?"

Friday night? Probably watching a game with Dad, hoping the camera would catch Dan Walton smile, as he sometimes did, and daydreaming that he smiled at her. Was that lame to admit?

"I'll take that as nothing. So, consider yourself booked." Sylvie stabbed a navy-polished fingernail in Bree's direction.

"What?"

"You, me, dinner. Seven sharp."

"But the game—"

"You would consider standing me up for a game that you can watch as a rerun?" Sylvie made a 'are you kidding me' face, her curls suddenly terrifying in their bounciness.

"Dinner sounds fun," Bree said meekly.

"That's more like it. Make sure you dress cute."

"Why?"

"Because you're one of the best-dressed women I know, and I don't want my reputation falling because you don't live up to what I've said." Sylvie reached to grasp the tiny gray elephant that would complete the set.

"What *have* you said?"

"Oh, nothing you need to worry about. So it's a date?"

Bree withheld a sigh. "I'll book it in."

The afternoon passed with the usual activities followed by the mad rush of pick-ups as families collected their children before the after-care fees kicked in at six. Dave Hammerson flashed Bree a megawatt grin as he scooted in at 5.59pm. "I'm getting better, I promise."

"Good." She smiled. "Max seemed a lot more settled today."

Dave glanced around him, then dropped his voice. "Things have been a lot better at home. Linda is a lot more calm."

"I'm so glad." Wait… "I thought you said she had left."

"Yeah, well, she's left me but is still around for Max's sake."

Oh. That made sense. "You say she wasn't calm before?" That was a red flag that childcare workers might need to report, given government mandatory reporting guidelines.

"She has not been happy, I'll say that much. I know I haven't always been the best of husbands, but I wish she wouldn't show her temper in front of Max. I can't help but feel some of it rubs off on him."

Bree nodded slowly. Sounded like another conversation to have with Moira. "Well, as I said, Max seems quite good today. But if ever there are issues, there are counseling services that can help."

"You're so kind to be thinking about me."

Hold on—"To be thinking about what's best for Max, yes. Now, I'd better go."

"See you tomorrow?"

"Yes. Please be on time." She added a smile to temper her words.

"You have a date?" He raised an eyebrow.

She blinked. "That's none of your business. See you tomorrow."

She turned away, pretending to busy herself in picking up abandoned scarves and gloves before moving away.

"Bye, Miss Bwee."

She turned, smiled at Max—and only Max—and waved. "See you tomorrow, Max."

"Bye, Miss Bree," Max's father echoed with a faint caress on her name that made her shudder and wonder whether he'd misconstrued her friendliness.

Maybe she should have a word with Dave Hammerson.

Back at home, she was happy to find Mom serving dinner, to feel the warm cocoon of security and love as she tucked into hearty lasagna and steamed vegetables. Maybe the heated rabbit food would negate the calories of the delicious, gooey carbs.

"How was your day?" Mom asked.

Bree swallowed a mouthful of crusted cheese sauce, her favorite part. "Fine. Mostly."

"What is it, sweetheart?"

"Oh, nothing." She sipped her water. "Just a weird feeling I got after talking with one of the dads."

Her own dad looked up, a faint crease between his eyes. "What happened?"

"Nothing I can put my finger on. Just a sense that he might be interested in more than just childcare for his son."

"Perhaps Moira can have a quiet word with him," Mom said.

"Maybe. But I feel this is something I should handle on my own. I don't want to go running to Moira each time something is wrong. How can I be an assistant director if I can't solve things myself?"

"Yes, but you shouldn't take chances. Especially not when a child's father is involved. Things have the potential to get messy."

Bree nodded. Fair enough. Mom knew what she was talking about, having worked in HR for many years. "I'll talk to her soon."

She checked her phone. Oops. Four missed calls. Three she cared little about, but one… Her heart tensed.

"Anything important, Bree?"

"No. Just something I forgot to do earlier."

"That's not like you."

"I've been a little busy working on some fundraising project possibilities."

"For the center?"

"For some families connected to the center, actually." She mentioned—without names or specifics—some of the challenges Rani's family was facing. "And I hope to do something for Valentine's Day to raise money."

"What are you thinking?"

"You remember how we made those chocolate hearts last year? Well, I thought it would be fun to do something like that again, seeing they sold well, but this time do an auction as well."

"What sort of prizes would you offer?"

"I hope some local businesses might sponsor us, especially given it's a good cause, so we'll see." More than that—and exactly who she'd asked to consider being involved—she couldn't admit to yet. Not until she'd talked to the man himself.

An hour later, having cleaned up, sorted washing, and replied to an email from Holly, she finally tackled the missed phone call. She could only put things off for so long.

She dialed the number and waited. It seemed to take forever. Then he finally picked up. "Hey."

"Hi, Mike! How are you? I hope you had a good day and it's not too chilly there. I can't believe how cold it is here. It seems the wind and snow will never stop, and I'm forever telling the children to remember their scarves and gloves, and—" She grew conscious of some background noise, the tinkle of glasses. "Oh, I'm sorry. Are you out?"

"Yep, dinner with my neighbors."

"Oh. Okay. Maybe this is bad timing." There came the sound of feminine laughter, and she wondered about the age and attractiveness of his neighbor. "Are…are you on a date?"

"Just dinner. Look, can we talk later? Maybe tomorrow night?"

"Um, I'm out tomorrow night."

A beat. Two. "Okay then. Maybe sometime this weekend?"

"Sounds good."

"Great. Well, I'd better go."

"Okay. Sorry to interrupt your evening."

"It's okay. I'm always happy to hear your voice."

The sincerity in his words eased a knot of concern. So they couldn't talk tonight. She'd explain things to him soon enough.

But she still couldn't help but wonder about the woman he was dining with.

CHAPTER 6

Sometimes Bree wondered if she were a Jane Austen character in a weird time-slip reality, more comfortable with the social conventions of two hundred years ago in Regency England than with the randomness of dating of today.

She studied the restaurant—really more of a bar, given the amount of alcohol being consumed—and wished, not for the first time, she'd checked what dinner with Sylvie would actually involve. Her gaze drifted to the two men who had magically appeared, beers in hand, as soon as Sylvie claimed their table.

"Bree, Jack. Jack, Bree." Sylvie didn't mention the other man's name, or if she had, Bree hadn't heard it over the sound system's thumping bass.

Drinks—she'd settled for a lemonade—and carbs in the way of poutine: French fries loaded with cheese and gravy, with a bowl of sour cream and sweet chili sauce on the side. She wondered whether they served anything not deep-fried here.

"So, Bree, Sylvie mentioned you work together," Jack said after a swig of beer.

"Yes." She should probably be polite. "And what is it you do?"

He said something, but she barely heard his reply. "Sorry?" She gestured to the music. "It's so loud in here I can't hear you."

He nodded, but didn't repeat himself, so she wondered just how much he'd heard.

She sipped her lemonade, noticing how his eyes kept lowering to her chest. Ugh. She leaned closer to Sylvie. "Does this place serve salads?"

Sylvie handed her a menu, her attention fixed on the man she was with. O-kay.

Bree looked over the menu. Nope. Seemed to be nearly all burgers, fries, and deep-fried everything. Enough to mask the flavor of whatever had existed before.

Her phone vibrated on the table. She turned it over, saw a missed call from Brent. Finally. "Excuse me." She pointed to the phone, slid out of the booth. "I've got to take this."

Sylvie frowned, but Bree didn't care. This wasn't her scene. Jack was most definitely not the one, so there was no point in pretending. She grabbed her bag and apologized. "So sorry, but this is urgent." She gave Sylvie some cash. "Catch you next week."

Sylvie shook her head and turned away, but Bree didn't feel too bad. Her workmate had obviously made these arrangements without Bree in mind.

When she reached the relative quiet and cool of the foyer, she tried her phone. "Brent? At last. How are you?"

"Look, I haven't got long. Chloe is here, and I—"

She closed her eyes. Ugh. "Brent, I just wanted to know if you thought you'd be free on that date."

"To be honest, I'm not sure. I doubt it. I'll probably be doing something with Chloe," he added in a lower voice.

Hopefully not proposing. She shuddered. "How's church?" she asked, forcing brightness into her voice.

"Have you been talking to Mike lately?"

Mike? She stilled. "Why?"

A beat. "You have been talking to him, haven't you? Man. What is it with you two?"

"I really don't know what you're talking about," she said primly. "All I asked was how church is. I didn't realize I'd be subject to an inquisition." A couple walked in, admitting a blast of wintry air. She probably should phone for a cab. "Have you got anything else to say? Actually"—she might get hammered by her brother, but at least she'd know and not lie in bed later, wondering—"what did Mike say?"

"He's just been doing the same, asking me to come to things."

"Like what?"

"Bible study."

She gave an inner cheer. Good for Mike.

"I swear it's like you two don't think I'm able to make my own decisions."

"Oh, we know you can. We just don't like some of those decisions you've been making."

"So you have been talking then."

She bit her lip. How to answer? "We talked at New Year's, but haven't really since then."

"Right."

"No, really. I mean, I talked to him yesterday, but that was simply to ask him if he'd consider coming along on that day too. So really, brother dear, you sound like you're a little paranoid. Perhaps the sign of a guilty conscience?"

The phone died, and her jaw dropped. Really? Had he hung up on her? Hurt arrowed through her. She pressed her lips together to stop a wobble.

"Miss?"

Bree looked up at the restaurant employee.

"Are you all right?"

She nodded.

"Can I call you a cab?"

"Yes, please."

Half an hour later she was huddled in her PJs in the living room next to her dad, watching Toronto demolish the Islanders, ears pricking each time Boston's score was updated. She still didn't know exactly what she'd say to Mike about the Valentine's Day dinner. Hopefully it wouldn't be another messed up phone call like the one with Brent.

"You okay, Bree?" Dad asked.

She nodded.

"You're very quiet tonight. Did your date not go well?"

"It wasn't a date. I thought I was going out for dinner with a friend, but it seemed she thought dinner would be better with two guys."

He winced. "A surprise double date, huh?"

"Super fun to get blindsided like that."

"Never mind." He wrapped his arm around her shoulders. "The right guy will come along when it's the right time."

"Will he, though? I appreciate your confidence, Dad, but sometimes I wonder just how long I'm supposed to wait."

"Did you like the man tonight?"

"No. I'm sure he's a very nice guy and all, but no, not like that."

"What do you want?"

"A Christian. Someone who's kind and strong and makes me laugh. Someone who wants to make a difference in the world."

"He's out there, hon. Don't give up."

The muted advertisements shifted to one for feminine hygiene products, which seemed to remind Dad of the need to do something in the kitchen. A moment later, Mom came into the room.

"I just got off the phone with Regina."

Mike's mom. "How is she?"

"She's well. She was just telling me about Mike's exciting news."

She hoped it wasn't that he had a girlfriend. *Sorry for being selfish, God.* "Really?"

"Did you know he recently accepted a role as a spokesperson for that children's charity in the Philippines we sponsor children from?"

Bree straightened. "Wow! Good for him."

"Someone who's making a difference in the world?" Dad said, reentering the room with a cup of coffee and a Cheshire-cat grin.

"Ugh. Dad, how many times do I have to tell you, we're just friends. Besides, he plays hockey, and I've decided not to go out with anyone who plays hockey all year."

"Is this another of your New Year's resolutions?" Mom asked with a tolerant smile.

Something about the fact that no-one believed her, that they all expected her to fail—so what if she'd already broken her bonus vow not to eat chocolate?—dug determination deep. "Mom, he's my *friend*, and I would really appreciate it if you don't tease me about it anymore."

"Can I tease you?" Dad asked.

"No!"

She joined in their laughter, but was conscious of a strange feeling of discontent, a hurt, like a soul bruise, that her nearest and dearest didn't trust her to keep her word—and were so blind about what they thought was best for her that they couldn't see their teasing stung.

MIKE WOKE to a groan of aches and pains, legacy of last night's bruising encounters with the Flyers. At least Boston had managed a win, scrappy as that win may have been. He sipped his morning coffee, waiting for Bree's call, his stomach tightly coiled in anticipation. Valentine's Day? With Bree? At her initiation? It seemed like his wildest dreams had come true, and he didn't want to do anything that might spoil the illusion.

The memory of their stilted conversation from Thursday night flitted through his brain. He didn't want to know what she might have thought about his dinner out—probably exactly what he'd thought when he'd learned she was going out on Friday. Yet it couldn't be that serious if she wanted to spend Valentine's Day with him...

Valentine's Day with Bree. His heartbeat skittered. Imagine being with her, holding her hand, kissing—

No. He exhaled. Restrained his thoughts from going there. Focus. He had to focus on other things. So he completed the week's laundry. Cleaned the kitchen. Emailed his sponsor kids. Took a call from Beau where he spent every second hoping Bree wouldn't call. Wondered whether she had actually said she'd call or if he'd implied he would amid the awkwardness of Thursday's conversation. Maybe he should man up and call her instead?

"Gotta go, Beau. I'll pray for you. It's pretty awesome if Montreal are keen."

"Thanks."

Mike smiled. He didn't know anyone else who could make one syllable sound like two in just that way.

He hung up the phone. Five seconds later it rang. His heart leapt at the displayed number. "Bree. Hi there."

"Hello to you! Gosh, it's good to talk to you—"

He smiled.

"—to someone normal."

"Um, who exactly have you been talking to lately?"

"Oh, you know, the usual people. Mom had some ladies from church drop in this morning for a ladies' breakfast, and all they could ask about was whether or not I had a boyfriend. I mean, honestly."

"And do you?" he dared.

"Mike! Please, for the love of everything that is good in this world, don't be like them. I count on you to not be like them."

"Gotta admit, it's not my goal to be like the ladies from your church."

She laughed. "Let me assure you, Mike Vaughan, that you are nothing like the ladies from my church. Speaking of, your mom called my mom lately and mentioned that you recently took on a spokesperson role for the kids' mission. That's so awesome!"

He loved her energy, loved this natural excitement of hers. "They're a great group and definitely deserve as much attention as they can get. I'm just amazed they asked me."

"Of *course* they asked you. Who better? And they'd know just how committed and dedicated you are."

His heart glowed. Did she know the effect her words had on him? Breanna Karlsson's words super-charged his heart, inspired and motivated him. She had the gift of encouragement—and enthusiasm—for sure. "It's pretty humbling that people might want my help. I'm just glad to use whatever profile I have to help others."

"Oh, I'm so glad to hear you say that."

He paused, wondering what she meant exactly. "I know there are others who could probably speak better than me, but I'm happy to do whatever I can if it turns the spotlight on them and means another dollar raised for such a worthy cause."

"Did you just hear yourself there? And you worry about not being able to speak well? You'll be great."

Bree was like sunshine in his life, her joy contagious. "It's good to hear your voice," he said softly.

"Oh, it's so good to talk to you."

Was this the moment to turn the conversation in a more serious direction, to admit that he missed her? He opened his mouth to say—

"Speaking of talking, I spoke to Brent last night."

Oh. His heart jerked at the change in subject. "How is he?"

"So you haven't talked to him lately?"

"I left a message on his voicemail. He's proved a little hard to reach lately."

"Probably the influence of she-who-shan't-be-named."

And here they were. Again. "Bree, I—"

"I asked him how church was."

"And how'd that go?"

"Yeah."

His lips twitched at the wealth of emotion in that one word. "If it's any consolation, I asked him to join us for Bible study, but he didn't reply."

"He mentioned that. To be honest, I don't think he's appreciating our efforts. So we'd best keep at it, then."

He chuckled.

"And keep praying," she continued.

"That I do."

"You're so sweet."

Another hungry rush of gladness at her praise.

"Mike?"

"Bree?"

She laughed. "Stop mocking me. I have something very important to ask you."

He drew in a breath. "About Valentine's Day?"

"Yes."

He heard her intake of breath, told his pulse to settle down. Really, he should be the one making this call, asking her out. Why hadn't he done it years ago? "Sure. I'd love to. What time?" He'd make it work. It wasn't that far from Boston to Toronto. Or she could come here. And then they could—

"But I haven't even told you about it yet."

She didn't have to. Have dinner with her? "I'll do it."

"Really?"

"Of course."

"Oh, you're such a lifesaver! Thank you so much. I'm so glad. You won't regret it."

He smiled. Yeah, he didn't think he would.

"I've taken on this new role with work and I'm doing all this work to fundraise, and it's honestly a lot harder than I realized, because you have to be so careful not to over-share, and we both know that I can be inclined to over-sharing a teensy bit, and then I had this great idea and thought you'd be perfect, and so—"

He smiled at her usual Bree-ness as she continued talking about some refugee family and how she wanted to help the father through some auction idea. He loved her heart for the poor, loved her heart for family, could see a future where she was a mother herself, the mother of his—

"—and asked Brent, but he has a game so couldn't do it."

He blinked, struggling to recall what she'd just been saying. Why were they back to Brent?

"So that's why I'm so glad you can."

He shook off the uncertainty. He had a date with Bree, and that was all that mattered. "Tell me when and what you'd like me to do."

"You don't have a game scheduled that day, do you? I checked, but do you have training?"

"I can get out of it." He'd get out of anything in order to spend Valentine's Day with her. "What time do you want me to come? Or did you want to come here?"

She laughed. "Oh, you're funny. No, you come here. The earlier the better."

His heart kicked. Wow. She was that keen?

"I'll be there as soon as I can get a flight. I…" He swallowed. "I can't wait to see you."

"Oh, you too."

He smiled, phone against his ear as he shifted to the leather couch, propped up his feet. He could spend hours listening to her, sharing with her, imagining what a life together could be like.

"It'll be so good."

Her happiness seemed to match his. Could it really be possible?

But wait. How did this correlate with her going out last night? Should he ask? How could he not? Not when he'd spent half the night wondering about who she'd been with. "Hey, uh, how did your date go last night?"

"Oh, that. Please. That wasn't a date. That was simply me thinking I was going out for dinner with a work colleague. Turns out she didn't think my company was quite enough."

"What do you mean?"

"Oh, it was dreadful. Not five minutes after we arrived, along came two guys. She set me up, Mike. What kind of friend does that? Let's just say I got out of there as soon as I could."

His chest eased. But what could he say? *I'm sorry?* He wasn't.

"Everything was bad. The music was too loud, the food was all deep-fried—not that I don't mind some deep-fried in my life, but it's nice to balance it out with something healthy."

"I hear you." Maybe this was his chance to find out what sort of restaurant he should book for Valentine's Day. "So what would you prefer? What kind of date would you like?"

"Well, call me old-fashioned, but I'd love to visit a tea house —you know, the kind that do fancy high teas?"

He chuckled. "Can't say I really do." But he'd soon learn.

"There are some lovely ones here, and I'd love to visit one with a man secure enough to take me."

"Noted." He'd add that to his must-dos.

Silence stretched between them.

"So, um, how about you?"

"My perfect date?" *Is you*, he almost added, but didn't.

"No, silly. How was your date the other night?"

"Date? Bree, it wasn't a date," he rushed to reassure. "Just dinner with some neighbors. There's a couple here who basically adopted me when I first moved into the building, and I have dinner with them on a semi-regular basis."

"Oh, how lovely of them. I'd love to meet them."

"Maybe you should. You could come visit sometime, maybe in the summer."

"Ooh, I've never visited Boston. You could be my tour guide."

"There are a lot of places I haven't yet seen, despite having been here several years."

"How shameful of you."

"Scandalous."

She laughed. "Well, I'm very happy to be your chance at redemption."

She was his chance at so many things. He swallowed, truth burning on his tongue. "Bree, you know Brent won't be happy."

"Brent? Like he can talk right now."

True, that. "I just don't want to cause you any problems."

She sighed. "Mike, I want this. I think you'll be perfect."

Huh? He'd take it, but—

"And I really don't care what he has to say. And I don't think you should worry about him either."

He exhaled. "Okay then."

"Okay then." He could hear the smile in her voice. "So you're still happy to come then?"

He drew his laptop closer, opened up the internet. "I'm booking a flight right now."

"Oh, I so appreciate you."

"I can't wait."

"Me either. Thanks so much for doing this, Mike."

"My pleasure. If I'd known you were interested, I'd have done something about this a long time ago."

"Really? Oh, okay." She sounded puzzled. "Well, thanks again. I should probably let you go."

"Go book my flight, you mean?"

"That"—she chuckled—"and other things. Hey, thanks again for doing this. It's been so good to talk to you."

"It's been my absolute pleasure," he assured.

"Bye, Mike."

"Bye, Bree. Take care of yourself, okay?"

"You too. Bye!"

He waited until she ended the call, then sat on the sofa, mind spinning at the wonder of it all. How long had he prayed? Who'd have thought that would go so well? God really did give His kids the desire of their hearts. *Thanks so much, God. I'm so grateful.* He finished booking and paid, noting the details with a wince. They were in the same time zone, so that was something, but it'd mean he'd have to scramble to get to the practice before the game the following day. Still, she was worth it. And if this went the way he hoped, it'd be the first of many more dates.

Speaking of... He clicked on a website, found a list of Toronto's olde-worlde tea shops, and made a note of which ones were open on Valentine's Day evening. He rang the first: booked out. Rang the second. Made a booking. Exhaled. Grinned. Valentine's Day would be a day she'd never forget.

<h1 style="text-align:center">CHAPTER 7</h1>

The next weeks passed in a blur of busyness for Bree, the organizing for the auction requiring many hours phoning businesses and families connected to the childcare center to seek donations. As wonderful as the prizes offered were, none were as keenly talked about as the chance to have dinner at a fancy restaurant with one of Toronto's home grown NHL stars. God bless Mike. Not every guy would be so willing to give up an evening to have a meal with a random stranger, but he'd always had a heart of gold.

"I can't believe you got someone like him to agree," Sylvie said, studying the picture Bree had placed on the noticeboard, the photo taken at New Year's. Some creativity had photoshopped her out of it, so the focus was entirely on Mike's big smile, cool hair, and blue eyes. Really, Bree thought, studying his picture a little more closely, if she hadn't sworn off hockey players, it would be fun to go out to dinner with him herself. Not that she could rig things to work that way. But in other circumstances, in a different year, maybe...

She shook her head out of her stupidity. Mike was her friend. Just because they got on so well, it didn't mean anything

82

more would happen. Besides, she could imagine the heart attack Brent would likely have. He'd always had a thing about his friends and her, which was weird, because a normal person might think he'd be glad to have vetted any potential boyfriend. But hey, there was little normal about her brother. Especially at the moment.

"Mike is a good guy," Bree said, straightening the notice. There'd been a flurry of interest, word spreading far and fast as soon as they revealed the big ticket items.

Muskoka Shores, a fancy resort two hours north of the city, had offered a weekend accommodation and dining package. Various attractions in the city had also come on board. But the chance to dine with an NHL star was the most anticipated.

"Did he say where he'd take the winner?"

"No. But knowing him, it'll be great."

"I can't believe you know all these people."

"I don't know that many, and it's really only through my brother."

"He wasn't interested in getting involved?" Sylvie asked. "I would have thought something like this was right up his alley. He's always been popular with the ladies."

"I don't think his girlfriend would approve," Bree said, sourness filling her mouth.

Brent had proven even harder to reach lately, her phone calls ignored, text messages unanswered, emails not responded to. The feeling that things were not quite right with him refused to dissipate, upping her prayers. Perhaps she should visit him.

"Girlfriends. Seriously. So needy all the time." Sylvie rolled her eyes. "Jack was asking about you again."

"Jack?"

"From the wine bar?"

"Oh, Jack. From that time I thought you and I were going out for a simple meal and it turned out to be something way more than that."

"I thought you Christians were supposed to be forgiving."

"And I have forgiven you," Bree said with a smile. "Just haven't quite forgotten."

"Apart from Jack," Sylvie said.

"Who?"

Sylvie laughed. "So how is the guy hunt going, seeing you're not a fan of the man I found?"

"I'm not exactly hunting," Bree admitted. "Between work and church and organizing this fundraiser and preparing for the next, I've been too busy to find someone I might want to go out with, let alone actually go on a date."

"There're no prospects in your church?"

"Does Dan Walton count?"

"Ooh, you keep dropping his name. Maybe I should come sometime."

"He's got his own crowd and isn't there as much as some ladies would like. Then every summer he disappears for months to his cottage in Muskoka."

"Maybe we should go visit his church up there."

"Maybe. Or maybe we should just focus on the real world and not get caught in fantasyland."

"So he's not really a prospect then?" Sylvie sounded disappointed. "False advertising, Bree."

"Yeah. Sorry about that."

But such was the only false advertising. Everything else—apart from Brent, of course—was coming along smoothly. How wonderful to see so much support, especially as people knew the money raised would go toward those in need. To avoid specifics, such as Rani's husband's situation, Bree had simply advertised the Valentine's Day fundraiser with a "Love your neighbor" tagline and listed a variety of local charities, of which the refugee support group was one. Of course, the bulk of the money would go there, but no one apart from the accountants need know the specifics of which group got what funds.

She finished cleaning up, only to encounter Max Hammerson's dad again.

"Hi, Bree."

"Hello, Mr. Hammerson. Max is ready to go home now."

Dave had been around a bit lately, stopping by to chat, always friendly, but sometimes his gaze lingered a little too long. She'd mentioned her concern to Sylvie, who'd simply laughed her off, and Moira, who reminded Bree that she could make an incident report, or at least record her concerns if his attention became more uncomfortable. Bree appreciated the support, mild though it may be. It de-escalated her concern and made her wonder if maybe she'd been making more of this than necessary.

"How has Max been today?"

Her heart eased. *Focus on the child.* "He's been very settled. Oh, look, here he is with Fiona now. Please excuse me."

"Uh, before you go, I was wondering if I could have a quick word."

She bit back a sigh, willed her expression to pleasantness. "Sure."

"I'd feel more comfortable talking in your office, if that's okay."

It wasn't, but, "Okay." She'd keep things professional: make sure the door was open, that Max was front and center of the conversation and in the space. She gestured Mr. Hammerson inside and rolled her eyes at Sylvie's curious expression.

"I'm sorry, I can't talk long. What is it, Mr. Hammerson?"

"I, that is, we, well, Linda and I are trying to reconcile."

"Oh, that's wonderful!" And a relief. "I'm so happy for you. And especially," she added, noting his eyes had lit, "especially happy for Max. He really needs stability in his family life now."

"Yes, well, that's what I wanted to talk to you about. I really need someone to look after Max on Friday nights so Linda and

I can attend counseling together. And I was wondering if you could suggest someone."

Silent exhalation. For a moment there, she'd thought he was going to ask her to babysit. "Have you not had a babysitter in the past?"

"Not one we can rely on." He sighed. "Maybe that's what has contributed to our problems. Linda always wanted to go out, and I've been so cautious about who we leave Max with."

"Of course," she murmured.

"So if you have any names of people you could recommend, I'd be very appreciative."

"Right. Well, I'll give it some thought." Something about the way he looked at her goaded her to test him. "Have you talked to Mrs. Bridges about this? Was she unable to help you?"

"It's been rather a new development, so no." He sighed again. "Besides, you and I both know she doesn't always seem to be aware of what's going on."

Bree's eyebrows rose. "I beg your pardon?"

"Oh, I don't mean to sound disrespectful. Simply that to know a potential young babysitter isn't her department so much as yours."

"I don't exactly feel like it is my department, but as I said, I'll give it some thought. I'll contact Linda with a name as soon as I can. How is she by the way?"

"Oh, she's so busy, and stressed with all that's going on. She's really regretful of what she's done, and I don't want to put unnecessary burden on her."

"A phone call is hardly a burden. Especially when it's one you seem to think quite necessary."

"And it is," he said. "Counseling is supposed to start this Friday night."

In two days. She knew a niggle of guilt for not offering her services. She was free; she could offer. Wasn't helping a marriage reconcile better than sitting at home watching a game?

But something inside whispered she should refrain. "I hope you'll find someone by then. Perhaps the counseling service can offer space for Max to play nearby. Now, I really must go."

She stood, waiting for him to leave, offering a smile for Max that faded when Dave Hammerson drew near. "Good night."

She turned back to the desk, pretending to be busy with shifting papers, until she heard his footsteps leave. Then she turned around. Only to encounter his gaze through the glass, like he knew what she was doing.

A shiver prickled up her spine. She grabbed her phone, stabbed the numbers, her charade continuing as she faked her call being answered.

"Hi! Just thought I'd see how you are." Her ears filled with the rush of her heartbeat. Dave was still watching. She lowered the phone and raised a hand and said, "Excuse me a minute— Goodbye, Mr. Hammerson." Her voice was loud enough to carry beyond the room. She pretended to talk on the phone again. "I really miss you and can't wait until I see you again. Uh huh." Fake laughter. "Yep, that sounds great! See you then. Love you."

Her breath released as she saw him leave. Okay, first thing tomorrow she'd be talking privately with each worker and ensuring none of them were left alone with him. Her internal radar with guys might not be foolproof, but there was definitely something off about that man.

"Who was that?" Sylvie said.

"Dave Hammerson. He's kind of creeping me out."

"No, not him. Who were you talking to just now?" She gestured to the phone.

Bree glanced down. "Oh no." Her pretend message had been left for real on Mike Vaughan's phone.

~

MIKE STARED AT THE PHONE, the message just left stunning his senses like a puck to the heart. Had she really just said what he thought?

"Mike?"

He blinked, refocused on the video call with the director of MPFG. "Sorry. I didn't mean to get distracted." But Bree's last words would captivate him for the rest of his life.

"If you need to return a call, that's okay."

"No. Let's sort out the details now. Trying to find another time might be as challenging as this was to arrange."

"Okay." John talked more about the project, what the board thought Mike could offer through interviews and the like.

"Ideally we'd love to actually film you in the slums, but we know you're busy."

"My season finishes in June, probably earlier. I might be able to swing a quick trip to south east Asia."

"Really? You'd do that? Oh, that would be wonderful."

It wasn't like he didn't have the money to fund such a trip, and he had no other plans this summer. Apart from Bree's proposed visit to Boston. And who knew if that would take place. But after that last call…

They discussed further details, and he finally hung up. The Philippines looked like a go.

He shot Phil a quick email to give him a heads-up, then turned on his phone, heart dancing in anticipation. He listened to Bree's message again, felt his heartstrings tense, then ease. She loved him? Oh, he knew she was exuberant, open with her feelings, but this seemed a new level of candor even for her. But he'd take it. He'd take anything she offered.

And surely such a message deserved a response from him. He dialed, anticipation rushing through his veins. But when he rang, her phone was switched off, and he couldn't even leave the message he'd begun composing in his mind.

Frustration surged. Should he text her? That wasn't quite the same as talking in person, but at least she'd understand.

HI BREE. THANK YOU FOR YOUR SWEET WORDS. I HOPE YOU'VE HAD A GOOD DAY. CAN'T WAIT TO SEE YOU SOON. I LOVE—

His phone rang, startling him into dropping it. It was only when he picked it up that he realized he'd accidentally pressed send. Meanwhile, the phone kept ringing. Brent.

He answered. "Hey, stranger."

Dial tone.

Huh? Weird. Or was that Brent feeling oversensitive about the fact he'd ignored Mike for the past few weeks. Maybe he shouldn't have teased him with the stranger comment.

And maybe he should stop second guessing himself. He dialed. Left a message on Brent's voicemail. "Dude, I don't know if you pocket dialed me, but anyway, I'm returning your call. Hope you're doing okay." A strange sense made him add, "Praying for you."

He pressed end and frowned down at his phone. Something wasn't right. He knew a weird and urgent sense to pray for Brent's protection, for his soul, for his life. There was a heaviness within that kept him praying until he felt a release.

Whoa. Weird. His prayers continued in fits and bursts over the next hour as he fixed a quick stir-fry, as he cleaned up. He wanted to call again, but something held him back. Whatever that weirdness had been earlier, he sensed God was doing something in Brent's life.

He wondered if Bree had felt it too.

He tried her number again. Still not available. It was enough to make him wonder if she'd been embarrassed by her message before and didn't want to talk to him.

Bree. Bree. Bree. He really needed to focus on someone else, on something else. This trip to the Philippines might well be an answer.

He flicked on the TV. Watched the news, then caught a game.

The Wings were playing Calgary, and to his relief Brent was on the ice. Mike followed Brent's shifts, but he seemed to play as skilled and hard as ever. The camera caught a glimpse of his face. No joker in that stony expression tonight.

Mike prayed again. Checked his phone. Nothing more from Bree, so he settled in to watch the rest of the game, analyzing plays, critiquing what he'd do differently. Brent was playing well against Calgary's hard pressure, but he wondered if there was a certain robotic element to his moves.

He checked his phone again. Still nothing. Exhaled. Watched the rest of the game as it progressed to overtime, saw Brent score the game winner.

But he didn't stay for the usual interview, which again made Mike wonder just what was going on with his best friend.

He sent a text. DUDE. HAPPY TO TALK WHENEVER IF YOU NEED ME. CALL ME ANYTIME.

He flicked off the lamp and went to bed.

THE PHONE RANG in the darkness. Mike reached out and grabbed it from the bedside table. Glanced at the screen. Knew a moment's disappointment followed by relief. "Finally."

No answer.

"Brent?" His ears strained for any trace of sound. "Are you there?"

A noise like shaky breathing met his ears.

"Brent? What's going on?" Concern ratcheted up as another sniffling sound twisted his heart. Was the dude crying? "Hey. It's okay. Whatever it is will be okay."

More ragged breathing.

"Do you want me to come see you?"

"No."

"Is it Chloe?"

A sound like grunted affirmation.

"You two over?"

Loud exhale. "I've been so stupid."

"We all are sometimes."

"I...I can't talk about it right now."

"Whenever you're ready, I'm here."

"'Kay."

What should he say? "Hey, I'm sorry this sucks right now."

"Yeah."

"I'll call you tomorrow, 'kay?"

"Thanks."

Dial tone in his ear.

Whew.

He shot up another prayer and glanced at his phone. It was too late for Bree to be up, but she might appreciate the heads-up, anyway. He'd never normally share about someone else's pain, but she was Brent's sister...

SORRY ABOUT THE HOUR. BRENT CALLED. HE'S NOT GOOD. PRAY FOR HIM. GOODNIGHT.

And he switched off his phone and prayed some more until he fell asleep.

CHAPTER 8

The memory of her utter stupidity the previous night faded when Bree woke, turned on her phone, and discovered five missed calls and two messages from Mike. She winced but was glad to see he hadn't left a voice message.

Bree scrolled through the messages, wondered what his unfinished one meant to say, but her attention was snagged by the next. Brent wasn't good? Needed prayer?

She tried to call him, but there was no answer. Ignoring her strange reluctance, she tried to call Mike. Nada.

Would Holly be up? She glanced at the clock. Sent her an invitation to chat online. Smiled as her message was received and Holly's face met hers in the box on the computer screen. "Hi. I didn't think I'd reach you. I didn't wake you?"

"I wasn't expecting to be up, but all this travel makes it hard to settle into sleep."

"Remind me where you are."

"Tokyo."

Envy tugged. Holly of the skinny bod and her travels around the world. Bree pushed the feeling down. "Your next competition starts in a few days, right?"

"Yeah." Holly yawned. "Sorry. It's kind of late here, or maybe it's really early. I don't know anymore. Anyway, how are you?"

"Busy. Working on these fundraisers for the center." She grinned. "We're doing a Valentine's Day auction where people bid on different prizes. I thought I'd cutesy it up a little by placing the winning vouchers in handmade chocolate hearts."

"You're so clever at organizing that sort of thing," Holly said, propping her head in one hand, long hair swinging around her shoulders. "So what are the prizes?"

Bree explained before finally sharing, "The best one is the chance to win dinner with an NHL star."

Holly's eyebrows rose. "Did you convince Brent to do that? Wow."

"Well, you'd think he would, seeing he's such a hit with the ladies, but no, it's Mike."

"Mike?"

"Mike Vaughan, remember?"

"I didn't think that would be his cup of tea. Good for him."

"He's such a sweetheart to do it. Although…"

"Although what?"

"I, well, I might have accidentally given him the wrong idea."

"What do you mean?" Holly gave another yawn.

Bree explained about her voice message fail and the reason behind it. "And I didn't realize I'd actually called his number!"

Holly laughed. "I wouldn't worry about it. He probably just thought it was you being your usual effervescent self. It should be easy enough to explain."

Bree chewed her lip.

"Has he given you any sign he's interested?"

The more she thought about it, the more… "Maybe."

All those flirty-feeling conversations—had she misconstrued those too? Oh, her guy radar was so broken if that truly was the case.

"Talk to him, Bree. I'm sure it'll work out fine." Holly's face grew serious. "But the other thing is something you need to sort out quickly. Have you told this dad person he makes you feel uncomfortable?"

"Not in so many words. To be honest, I don't really want to. It makes me feel like he'll then know he has power over me, and I don't want that."

Holly nodded. "Maybe you can phrase it differently. Maybe say something like you're concerned that others may misconstrue his words and behavior and you'd hate for things to get complicated for his son."

"You're so clever." How did she know these things?

"Workplace harassment isn't something to ignore. We just had some training about this, as we come across weird customers at the supermarket occasionally. Remind him of the policies of the center, and make sure others know about it and that you keep detailed notes."

"Thanks, Holly."

"No worries." Holly yawned again. "Sorry, but I really need to sleep."

"Okay. Take care. You know I worry about you with your competitions?"

"Yes, Bree, I know. But remember, I love this sport, and we keep pretty safe." She smiled. "It's just so exciting to finally be competing here."

"You deserve it."

"Well, pray for me, and I'll pray for you. Have a good day."

"Good night, Holls."

Holly smiled, then the screen went dark.

Bree sucked in a breath. Okay, she had things to do. Best get them done and out of the way. She glanced at the time. Tried to call Brent. No answer. Tried to call Mike. Still nothing. Ooh, the frustration!

She rubbed sleep from her eyes and trudged to the shower.

Maybe she'd be better off with a bit more time praying so she could clear her heart and head.

~

"Sorry. It's just been crazy."

"Dude, that's the third time you've apologized. I don't mind the hour, I'm just glad you called."

Brent sighed. "I still can't believe it. I could barely sleep last night."

Mike waited, eye on the time. He had a road trip that left in two hours. He didn't think Brent would be that long, but you never knew. "So what happened?"

Another heaved-out breath. "So, yesterday I was having my pre-game nap when something woke me. It…it was Chloe. She, uh, well—"

Mike so didn't want to know. "I think I get the picture." One he wanted out of his brain ASAP.

"I didn't know she'd gotten a key and definitely didn't expect her to climb into bed with me. We've never, I've never—I…"

Mike knew a ping of relief, then felt a ping of conviction for having assumed the worst. What kind of friend was he?

"It was like this fog had lifted, and I could see she didn't care about me. I've told her a million times I didn't want to take things further and that I need to rest before a game, but she's always been at me, saying she doesn't feel loved, saying I don't spend enough time with her, that it proves I don't love her."

Mike winced. How manipulative. *God, thank you that Bree is never manipulative.*

"Not that Chloe ever does much, anyway," Brent continued. "She's not really a model. She just goes to lunch with her friends, and they go get fake tans and stuff, then she hopes to get photographed. We got into this huge argument"—Brent's voice dropped—"and I basically told her to leave."

"You broke up?"

"Yeah."

Fist pump. *Thanks, God.*

"When I got home from the game, she'd scrawled her lipstick across all the apartment's mirrors, thrown my clothes across the floor, tipped the pot-plants into the sofa. She made it pretty clear she didn't like me anymore. Man, I didn't know just how crazy she'd be."

"Whoa." What else could he say? Saying "Yes, your ex sounds like a psycho" probably wasn't helpful. *God, give me wisdom.*

"I've got the cleaners coming later, but this place will never be the same. Good thing it's just a rental."

"I'm sorry, man."

"Yeah. I didn't realize just how messed up all this would be."

Mike hurt for the pain he could hear in Brent's voice. It was one thing to have a trashed apartment, quite another to feel you'd trashed your heart. "Chloe can't have really loved you if she treated you this way."

He heard Brent's breath hitch. Winced.

"Yeah." Brent sighed. "Seems she didn't."

"She was pretty, but seemed pretty interested in herself more so than anyone else."

"You got that right. I feel like she was only into me to boast to her friends."

"You need someone who cheers you on, who's an encourager." Like Bree. *Stop it.* He rushed on. "We were talking about this last time at the Bible study group, about being unequally yoked. It's one thing to have the same beliefs, it's another to hold different values or be with someone who can cope with the pressures of our work. Hold out for a Christian girl who understands the demands of sports."

"Yeah, I think I'm gonna avoid any relationships for a long while."

"Probably wise. Gives you time to focus on God and sort

yourself out without being distracted by someone looking for you to fix them—or to fix you." He paused. "Gives God time, too."

"Yeah." Silence, laden with brokenness and hurt, filled the line. Then, "I never thought I'd get into such a mess."

"I don't think anyone does."

"You know the worst thing? Bree is going to say I told you so."

Mike chuckled. "I hardly think that's the worst thing. But knowing your sister, I think she'll be so relieved that you're free of obsessive Chloe, she just might not say that after all."

Silence stretched.

Had calling Chloe obsessive been too much? Was he offended? "Dude?"

Cleared throat. "How well do you know Bree?"

What? "Dude, there's nothing to say except we're friends." Right now, anyway. Admitting his Valentine's Day plans and that he hoped for more might not be wise. "Anyway, this isn't about your sister but about you. You know Bree loves you and wants your best. And leaving Chloe sounds like you're getting back on track."

"I'm gonna have to talk to someone."

"You know Pastor Josiah is a huge fan of yours."

"Don't know how much of a fan he'll be when he hears my sorry story."

"He's heard a few. You can't shock him. He's a good guy."

"When's the next Bible study thing?"

"Next Monday. I have a game, but I'll send you the link."

"Thanks, man."

Mike glanced at the time again. He'd need to get ready soon. But this talk was too good to interrupt.

"I think I'm gonna have to move," Brent continued.

"Wow. But yeah, maybe. Start afresh, find a new apartment with no memories."

"Yeah, I'm so sick of apartments. I wonder if I should buy a house."

"Sounds like your contract will mean you'll be staying a while there in Detroit."

"The no-movement clause means I'm here for a good few years, so a house could work. Maybe a fixer-upper. I could get out the work tools again. That'd keep me busy."

"I've heard demolition is a great stress reliever."

"Yeah. I might need to demolish a city block the way I'm going." Brent rasped out a chuckle. "Hey, how about you? Any word on contracts or team movements?"

"Have to wait and see. There are rumors of some guys getting traded, so it'll be interesting to see who they get in and what that means for me. I'd like to stay another year at least."

"Where would you want to go if you had to leave?"

"Toronto or Ottawa would be awesome." And would mean he could see Bree way more often. "Anywhere in Canada would be nice, especially if it means I don't have to cross the border anytime I want to see family. But I don't really have to think about it until June if Boston doesn't make me an offer."

"They'd be stupid to pass on you."

"Right?"

Brent laughed. "Hey, I better go. You have a road trip today, don't you?"

Huh. Brent really must be feeling better if he was noticing what was going on in other people's lives. "Yeah. Just a quick trip to Buffalo and New York."

"Good luck."

"You too. Stay in touch, okay?"

"Yeah."

"And if you want to talk with Pastor Josiah, I'll send you his number."

"Yeah, that'd be good. Thanks."

"'Kay. Later."

"Later. And thanks again."

"No problem."

Mike hung up, heart at ease. Well. Who'd have thought? God, obviously. Which might be why he'd felt that sudden urge to pray at precisely when Brent's nap time was happening. *Thanks, God.*

He glanced at his phone. Saw Bree's missed calls. Felt his heart lift again. He listened to her messages, which were all along the line of "Hope everything's okay. Please call me when you get a chance."

He glanced at the bag still needing to be packed. Knew if he didn't do it now he'd be late. Well, in that case, he'd just find a quiet corner of the airport, and then maybe they could have the conversation he'd waited years to have.

THE SHRIEKS and hollers of two dozen small children were making Bree's head ache. Why she'd thought free play was necessary on today of all days, she could not recall.

Her phone buzzed. She glanced at it. Mike. No. She shouldn't answer now. She was the chief supervisor, and it wouldn't go down well if she took private phone calls when policy stated that those on supervision had to be actively supervising.

She slid the phone back into her jeans' pocket as two trikes collided and wails the volume of planes filled the space.

"Benjie, Manu, you're both okay." She crouched and wiped away their tears. "A little bump on your heads, that's all. Like you've been kissed by the ground."

"Don't like the gwound," Benjie said. "Gwound is naughty." He swung his foot and kicked, then let out another howl as he stubbed his toe. "Gwound is very naughty!"

Poor pet. Bree stroked his hair as he sobbed into her shoulder. Seemed someone might benefit from a sleep.

"Shall I put him down for a nap?" Fiona asked.

"Would you be an angel and watch the kids while I do it? My head is killing me."

"Of course." Fiona's green eyes held concern. "Maybe you should have something for that headache."

"I think I will."

She held Benjie's hand and moved inside, taking care to tuck him in on the little cots they used for nap-time. She watched him for a while, stroking his hair until he dropped off to sleep, thumb in mouth, face relaxed. Her heart grew soft. How wonderful to be a mother, to have the chance to tend a little human. *Lord, one day I'd love to do this. Could you please send Mr. Right soon?*

When Benjie's tiny snores suggested he was in deep sleep, she tiptoed to the office, found the painkillers, popped two, and had a drink of water. She clutched the edge of the desk as a wave of dizziness passed. Whew.

Her phone buzzed. She fished it from her pocket. Glanced at the number, then glanced around. Well, she could always say she was finalizing details for the auction if questioned.

"Um, hi, Mike."

"You're finally answering. I only have a few minutes because our flight's about to board, but I thought you'd like to know the latest."

"About Brent?"

"Look, I don't want to be a gossip, so all I'll say is this: when he calls, don't say I told you so."

She gasped. "They've broken up?"

"Smart cookie."

"Really? This is wonderful news. Mike, you've made my day!"

"He's not feeling too good about himself, so tread carefully."

"Of course. Oh, thank you."

"No worries. Hey, just curious, did you happen to feel some great need to pray for him yesterday?"

"Pray for Brent? To be honest, I've barely stopped, and yeah, I've sensed in recent days some escalation of things for him. Why do you ask?"

"No reason."

"Come on. You can't say such a thing to me and not explain yourself. Why did you ask?"

"Well, er, I felt an urgent need to pray for him yesterday afternoon, and it turns out that was when—look, let's just leave it at that."

"That was when he came to his senses?"

"I'm sure he'll explain himself when he's ready. Hey, look, I need to go. Hope your day goes well."

"It will now. Thank you *so* much for telling me. Oh, I hope your flight and games go well."

"Thanks. Catch you later?"

"Looking forward to it. Bye."

She hung up, her smile as encompassing as her earlier headache had been. What wonderful news! Oh, God bless Mike for telling her.

Dear Mike. What a good friend he was. What a good friend he was to Brent, praying for him so faithfully. And what a good friend he was to her, to let her know of this.

Mike. Oh, how thankful she was for him. She smiled. Glanced at the poster with his face on it. And knew a new throb of concern.

She shook her head, felt another wave of dizziness. Blinked it away. Next time. She'd explain things properly to him next time. And everything would be okay, especially now Brent was out of Chloe's clutches.

Oh, thank You, God! You are so good. Thank You for saving Brent. Please protect him and guide him, and restore his relationship with

You. She moved out of the office, her hand clutching the doorway to stay balanced. Felt an urge to pray for Chloe. Rejected it. Then repented. "Okay, sorry, God. Please help Chloe too. Help her find a relationship with You. She really needs it."

Really? That was the best she could do?

Contrition for how she'd thought and spoken about Chloe panged, forcing her thoughts to slow, to deepen in sincerity.

"And I'm sorry for being so quick to judge her. Forgive me, Lord. Help me not be so quick to judge in the future." Like with Dave Hammerson. Or Sylvie. Or anyone.

She moved to the foyer, saw the poster about the Valentine's Day fundraiser. Her heart smiled. *And God bless Mike, too.*

CHAPTER 9

"*Y*ou've done a marvelous job, Bree."

"Thanks, Moira." Bree smoothed her hands down her long red skirt and glanced around the room decorated with paper hearts the kids had drawn—or scrawled—on. Every family had taken at least five hearts to distribute to their extended family and neighbors, each heart inscribed with the message *You are loved*. Some families had requested twenty more, which had necessitated Bree staying up late again last night to prepare them for today.

But—she nodded with satisfaction—the place looked beautiful, the chocolates were ready to be brought out soon, and this happy glow in her chest assured her that all was progressing as it ought.

"If you can't feel the love here today, you're probably dead," Sylvie said. In deference to the day, she'd swapped her usual Gothic attire for a fifties-style dress patterned with hearts and skulls. When Bree had asked about the skulls, Sylvie had simply shrugged and said, "Love always dies, one way or another."

"How depressing."

"True, though."

Well. Maybe. At least Sylvie wore hearts.

The other staff members had gladly worn shades of reds and pinks in honor of the day. Dress up days were always fun, and today's auction at four would be the cherry on top.

She glanced at the clock. She'd asked Mike to come a little earlier than the prescribed time in order to mingle a little and hopefully cause a bidding war when the ladies—or possibly some of the hockey-focused men—realized just how nice a guy he was. Not that she'd told him about wanting a bidding war. The busyness of recent days had barely allowed for sleep, so she'd hadn't had a chance to speak to him apart from confirming his times and asking him to wear a suit. After today, her attention would switch to the Easter egg hunt, then Mother's Day in May, where she hoped to host a special pampering session for the moms—like poor Diana—who needed a special day to remember. Plans were already spinning around her brain, waking her in the night. She loved to do this, to have plans and goals and see her hard work come to fruition. To see everyone coming together for such a good cause, even those flying in from Boston to help her dream come to life. Oh, Mike was good to do this. She owed him big time.

Rani drew near, her pinched face brighter than normal. "I come early, bring sweetmeats." She pointed to a tray on the table set up in the eating area.

"How lovely. Thank you." She should probably find out what ingredients were used, whether there'd be any allergens that might mar today's celebration.

"They have allowed my husband visit from lawyer. We hope to hear something positive soon."

"I'll continue to pray," Bree promised her before asking about the ingredients used and feeling reassured that Rani's special offering could stay.

Her phone buzzed. She glanced at it. Smiled. JUST LANDED. SEE YOU SOON.

Oh, God bless the man. She couldn't wait to see him.

"You look happy," Fiona said.

"I really feel like it's going to go well."

The redhead nodded. "I heard some mothers talking about the dinner. They wanted to know what restaurant it might be."

"It's a surprise, but Mike said it would be somewhere fancy." *Somewhere you'd like* had been his exact words, but more he wouldn't say. How nice he was entering into the spirit of all this, too.

"He's certainly a catch."

"Let's just hope these mothers remember that they're married."

Fiona laughed. "They might get competition from some of the fathers. I don't think they'd mind how basic the restaurant if they get the chance to talk to a real life NHL player. Even if he does play for Boston."

"To be honest, I never expected the level of interest." Which was dumb, especially considering how many times Sylvie had called Mike hot, fanning herself each time she walked past the poster of him. But he was still only Mike. Her childhood friend. Hard to believe people really saw him that way.

"Moira was saying she was getting phone calls, people wanting to bid on the phone."

"Seriously?" How crazy was that? Bree waved at Diana, looking gaunt yet defiant against disease in her shiny blonde wig as she sat beside her daughters.

"Look, here she comes." Fiona slipped away.

"Bree, what do you want me to do about all these phone bidders?" Moira hissed, holding out the center's two phones. "We can't keep the phone lines clogged up in case there's an emergency."

Bree thought quickly. "How about we ask each person who enquires what their top price is and lodge that as a formal bid?"

"Yes. That could work."

"Maybe add that if they don't want to do that, then they can nominate a friend who is here, then call them and instruct them to bid on their behalf. But they need to know that Mike is only here for dinner tonight, so they need to be ready at six to go out. There won't be a raincheck." How many times had she explained this? Perhaps the excitement meant people forgot such details.

"I'll let them know." Moira looked around at the bustle of excited children and adults. "I never expected to see such a wonderful turnout."

"I never expected we'd be like Christie's and fielding phone bids."

"Well, Mike Vaughan is a rather handsome young man."

Bree nodded. Yes, he was.

A stir in the corner drew her attention to a clutch of mothers, several of whom had also taken the encouragement to dress in Valentine's Day colors to heart, some even dressing matchy-matchy with their daughters.

She knew her own outfit had raised some eyebrows from the more fashion conservative among them, but she kind of liked how the red skirt clashed with the hot pink long sleeve top with its scattering of white kisses. As the auction's emcee, she'd wanted to look stylish yet wear something practical enough to work with children for several hours. When it had become apparent that many parents were coming earlier than the usual 3 p.m. pickup, she'd tugged the red skirt over her black leggings, swapped her oversized-heart sweatshirt for this cute long sleeve top, and exchanged her pink sneakers for stylish boots. After fixing her hair and makeup, she thought she now owned a certain elegant but edgy look. She hoped Mike liked it.

"You look great."

Ugh. She turned, forced a smile. "Mr. Hammerson. I didn't see you come in."

"Good to know you were keeping an eye out for me."

"I keep an eye out for all the parents." She stepped back. Suddenly wished she were wearing the oversized sweater rather than this top that now felt a little snug. She'd really have to speak to him soon and make it extremely clear just what the boundaries were. "Excuse me. I'm very busy."

She rushed past him, ignoring his plea to talk to her, and engaged some newer parents in conversation, taking care to introduce them to others. Perhaps they should organize a get-to-know-you supper when the weather warmed up a little. Another thing to organize down the track.

Her phone buzzed. BE THERE IN TEN.

She smiled. Texted back. CAN'T WAIT!

"Is that your boyfriend?" Mr. Hammerson's voice slid into her ear.

"Our special guest is on his way. Please excuse me." She threaded through the parents and moved to the kitchen area, where the chocolate hearts lay in the fridge, chilling until time. They still looked fine. As they should. Mom and Granny V had been so wonderful in helping her prepare them in recent days, their care and creativity ensuring each heart looked a picture of delectable perfection. And she knew they were delectable, having accidentally sampled one too many last night.

A taxi pulled in to the drive. She peered out the window. Grinned. He was here!

A quick smooth of her hair—she hoped her lipstick hadn't smudged—and she was moving through the foyer ready to welcome him at the front door.

"Mike!"

He grinned and she rushed toward him, clasping him as she usually would Brent in a hug that defied any air getting between them. Oh, how good it was to see him!

Mike stilled, then relaxed to hold her close in a way most unlike Brent ever had or would. He pulled back, studying her for a moment, heat filling his eyes as his head tipped to kiss her cheek, lingering in a decidedly non-brotherly way.

Her tummy tipped into flutters. Breath halted in her lungs. Oh. Dear. She pulled back, willed her expression to look welcoming and not stunned.

"Bree, you look amazing."

"Thank you." Okay, she was tired and had simply misinterpreted that look in his eyes before. That must be it. They were just friends, after all. Her gaze swept him up and down. Had he always filled out a suit so well? And was that a new haircut? "You look incredible."

"You told me to dress up. I wanted to impress."

"It worked. Not that I wasn't impressed before."

He reached out a hand, touched one of the kisses decorating her sleeve. "Is this a sign of things to come?"

Uncertainty filled her. "Do you mean are you expected to kiss your date tonight?" And why did that thought knot her insides?

"Just trying to understand the expectations."

"Well, no. It's just dinner." She patted his arm, ease returning to her heart. This was more the Mike she'd always known. "I don't want you feeling obligated to do anything you don't want."

His gaze lowered to her mouth, then moved back up again. "What if it *is* what I want?"

What? Disappointment creased her chest. She'd never thought he was like so many other men, happy to kiss and run. She'd always thought kisses should be reserved for someone special, not like a try-before-you-buy perfume sample in a store, to see if this one happened to suit. She swallowed. "Um, well, if the lucky lady wants you to, then I guess you could. But it's totally up to you."

His gaze kindled, his lips pulled to one side, and she knew a sudden stupid wish to be that lucky lady. But he was her friend. She must be exhausted indeed for her brain to have stopped working properly. And even if Mike wasn't just her friend, as the organizer of today's event she couldn't very well waltz away with the top prize on offer. Anyway, she'd vowed not to date a hockey player. And Mike, while not a player in the romantic sense of the word, was definitely into hockey.

Maybe she should have an early night tonight, and hopefully her brain would track normally again tomorrow. "We'd better go inside. There are dozens of people waiting to meet you."

"Then we'll have dinner?"

"You booked for six, right?"

"Yes." He smiled. "You can't know how much I've been looking forward to this tonight."

"I have some idea, seeing as you've mentioned it, oh, a few dozen times."

He chuckled, wrapped an arm around her shoulders.

Oh, she liked his scent, liked how his bigness made her feel protected and less tall than usual. She knew a strange desire to press closer to his side, so much so she had to fight against it. How ridiculous. She must be going insane. With a big few hours ahead, she'd better get these stupid feelings under control. Now.

She slipped out from under his arm and hurried to open the door. "Are you ready?"

He smiled. "Ready as I'll ever be."

"Better brace thyself then. Thy army of devotees awaits thee."

"Army?"

She tugged him forward into the melee of waiting fans.

When Bree had first mentioned Valentine's Day, he'd known anticipation. But for days now his entire body had hummed in excitement, preventing him from sleeping much last night, preventing him from eating today. Then, when she'd appeared all gorgeous and whimsical in her red and pink outfit, like some sixties movie star, he'd wanted to kiss her senseless, and finally say what he'd longed to for years.

He'd save that for tonight. Besides, outside was pretty cold.

But here, inside the foyer as he stepped through this portal into Bree's working life, the crush of bodies, noise, and excitement made him tense. Why were there so many people here? Was this usual or just some special Valentine's Day thing? Maybe all these people were here to collect their kids to drop at babysitters before they celebrated tonight.

A deep breath and anticipation thrummed again. He hoped Bree would like the place he'd chosen. He probably should've eaten more earlier—a tea house suggested cakes and delicacies that weren't exactly man-hunger satisfying—but the nerves had held sway.

He liked the fact she wanted him to know more about her world and the people in her life. Maybe that was another sign she was willing to tip this friends thing into something more. Of course, saying "I love you" should be something on which he could pin his hopes. But with only brief text messages since— and certainly nothing of that magnitude—tonight would be a great chance to clarify just what this relationship could be.

"You're so popular," Bree said with a red-lipsticked smile.

She really didn't need to wear lipstick for him to pay attention to her lips. "Are there always this many people?"

"We're not visited by many NHL stars, so no, this is all you."

Huh. His heart settled back into confidence. Maybe this was how some of the real NHL celebrities felt. He'd take it. As he would the fact that she wouldn't have told all these people about him if she didn't care about him.

She drew forward an older lady with graying bird's-nest hair. "This is Moira Bridges, my boss."

"Oh, Mr. Vaughan, thank you ever so much for agreeing to this tonight."

Agreeing to a date with Bree? "No problem."

She clasped his outstretched hand in both of hers, bangles clanking. "It's such a wonderful turnout. Hasn't Breanna done a marvelous job?"

Turnout for what? The question faded as he glanced down at Bree. "She always does well."

Bree glowed.

"Thank you for giving up your time," Moira continued. "You are very good."

"Uh, sure." He glanced around. Women smiled and nodded and waved. The surprising number of men—apart from one with a creased brow and crossed arms—did the same. "Like I said, I'm happy to be here. I've been looking forward to it for a while."

His gaze shifted from Bree's boss to Bree. She was bending, listening to a child, her attention absorbed. He imagined her engaged in a similar way with their child and felt his chest constrict. *God, one day, please.*

He breathed out. Glanced around some more. Stilled. Felt himself grow lightheaded. Knew his heart begin to pound. Maybe he should see a cardiologist. Or maybe he should've clarified exactly what today was about. He reread the poster on the opposite wall.

Valentine's Day Charity Fundraiser.
Win a date with NHL star Mike Vaughan!

What? Cold dread trickled through his stomach. No.

"Bree." He tried to get her attention, but a gaggle of parents surrounded her, many of them dressed in pink or red.

"Mr. Vaughan?" A young woman with wild curly hair, who

looked a few years younger than Bree, smiled up at him. Wait—were they skull earrings?

"It's Mike." He felt numb.

"Oh, it's so good of you to do this. And so brave! Not that we expect people in your line of work to be afraid, but you haven't met some of the mothers here."

Dear God. No. This wasn't what he thought it was, was it?

"Mike?" Bree's grin drew another painful throb of his heart. "I want you to meet some more people."

No. No. He didn't want to meet anyone. "Uh, sure."

A plate of savories was thrust at him, and he blindly picked something and shoved it in his mouth. Maybe eating would help calm this dizzying sensation.

Bree introduced him to various people, and he caught the stares, the smiles, the speculation as various women scanned him from head to toe. Brent might be comfortable with this, but this was totally not his scene. He did his best, though, gritting out smiles that probably looked like those reserved for the dentist, acting interested when they talked at him, when really he was desperate to talk to one person and one person only.

"Bree." He snagged her sleeve as she glided past. "I really need to talk to you."

"Um, sure. We're starting in a few minutes. Can it wait until after the auction?"

"No, it really can't."

"Oh." Her brow puckered. "Okay then, let's go to the office. It should be a little quieter there."

He followed her, nodding as people greeted him, as they sent him smiles that made him shudder and wonder just what he'd agreed to. How had he not known? Why had she not said?

"Oh, Mike. Honestly, this is just amazing."

He was amazed all right. Shocked. Alarmed. Upset. How had he not known? "Yeah, about that. I'm glad you look like you're going to raise a lot of money tonight, but I just wanted to clarify something about tonight."

"You mean the dinner? Oh, the ladies are so excited! Honestly, I almost find it a little concerning, given they're married, but it seems the men are just as keen—"

What?

"—and want to pick your brain about the NHL—"

Phew.

"—and I'm sure wherever you have picked will be suitable."

Yeah, maybe not for the guys. He cleared his throat. "Um, I feel like this is a bit late in the game, but I really thought..."

"What?" She gazed at him patiently.

"Tonight. I thought..." Words halted in his mouth. How could he explain without sounding like the world's biggest fool?

"Oh. Did I not explain things properly about how tonight would work? I'm sorry. I really thought I'd explained it during that first conversation, but then Holly said I should clarify things, but between one thing and another it just didn't happen, and I'm so sorry."

She placed a hand on his arm. He had to shift his arm away. He knew such a sense of hurt and betrayal that even her touch stung. How could she have said she loved him? How could she hold him like she had outside? How could she use him in this way?

Bree was still talking. "...so exciting to see such a great turnout. We have a lady here who's a refugee, and her husband is having such trouble, so it's wonderful to think we'll raise money to help him out."

Maybe there was still a glimmer of hope. "Are you bidding?"

"Me? Well, as nice as it would be to hang out with you, I can't bid even if I wanted to. I'm the organizer, and that just wouldn't look right or be considered fair. Besides, I don't think I told you, but I decided at New Year's I wouldn't date any hockey players this year."

What? Talk about a sucker punch to the heart. "Why?" His voice sounded strangled.

She sighed. "Oh, it's a long story."

One he'd *love* to hear. *Dear God, help me.* How had he allowed his stupid imagination to get the better of him? He really needed to eat something. Or sit down. Or call a cab and fly away.

"Oh, Mike. Don't look like that. I know some ladies look a little intimidating, but I promise there won't be anything to worry about. In fact, I'll give them all a heads-up that the winner needs to behave herself with you, otherwise they'll have me to deal with."

He couldn't admit his disappointment. Had he really misunderstood all this time? And even if he'd misunderstood tonight, she wanted nothing deeper than this friendship with him? Nausea crawled across his gut.

"Mike? You really don't look good. Do you want to sit down? I need to go out now to kick things off, but you could stay in here until it's time for you."

It would never be time for him. She'd made that abundantly clear. Still, maybe he could save face. He cleared his throat. "So, just to be clear, I'm taking out tonight's auction winner to the restaurant I've booked, we eat, then she or he goes home and I fly back to Boston."

"That's it precisely."

No wonder she'd kept going on about how amazing he was. He amazed himself at his blind stupidity.

"Bree?" The man of crossed arms from earlier frowned at Mike from the door. "Moira's calling you."

"Okay. I'm coming."

The man nodded, his smile sliding from Bree into a glare for Mike as he moved back to the room.

Mike's chest grew taut. Was this the kind of man she preferred? Someone who looked like he worked in an office, probably had a kid here who she was all soft-hearted about? Someone safe—who didn't play *hockey*?

"So, you're all good now?"

Nope. He doubted he would ever feel good again. Bree didn't want him? He wanted to curl up in that pile of kiddie cushions in the corner and smother away his pain.

"Sure." He dredged up his pride, plastered a smile on his dial. "Let's get this show on the road."

He'd fake it and make sure she never knew how much this auction of hers had cost him.

CHAPTER 10

"*O*h, it was so good, Mom. Thanks for all your help. You too, Granny V." Bree kissed their heads before slumping into a dining chair, the night's events a parade of glittering stars. "We must've raised close to twenty thousand dollars."

"That much?"

"Well, about half of that was for Mike."

"My goodness." Mom put down her cup of tea. "That man certainly surprised me by agreeing to do that. I know Regina was shocked, too."

"Yeah, that makes three of us. In fact, I think he surprised himself."

After a moment's uncertainty in the office, when she'd wondered if she had ever explicitly explained what today's proceedings would involve, he'd seemed to take on a new persona, becoming someone more like Brent, with his glad-handing and cheering, before he took the stage and smiled and bantered and urged the bids higher. She was so proud of him.

"So, who was the lucky lady?"

Bree chuckled. "Well, we had a number of phone bids, can

you believe? It honestly felt like we were in some fancy auction house with a Van Gogh painting up for grabs."

"I've never liked Van Gogh." Granny V sniffed. "Give me a good Monet anytime."

"Anyway, Mike is a little more handsome than those Van Gogh portraits," Mom said.

Bree's pulse fluttered. Yes, he was. She rubbed at her eyes. Oh, she was tired. "Well, one of the mystery phone callers obviously thought so. It turns out that Francine, one child's grandmother, bid for her daughter, but the daughter was tied up with work and couldn't go, so Francine ended up going in her place."

"So Mike went out with a grandmother?" Mom's eyes widened. "Was he okay with that?"

"He didn't seem to mind. And—get this—he'd arranged to have dinner at the Gaugin Tea House. Isn't that amazing? Most men would've picked the nearest steak house, but Mike had booked it weeks ago." How sweetly romantic was he? "I bet it was so busy on Valentine's Day. I've always wanted to go there. We'll have to go sometime, Gran."

Granny V nodded and slid a look at Bree's mother.

Bree's gaze followed. Her mother's brow had knotted. "What is it?"

"Are you sure Mike wasn't expecting to have dinner with you?" her mother asked.

"Me? No. I made that very clear." Especially clear tonight. "And made it very clear I'm not dating hockey players."

"And how did he receive that?"

She shrugged. "He's just my friend, Mom. He was cool."

But something about the way her mom and grandmother exchanged another glance made her chest tight. No. Mike *was* cool. He'd expected nothing else. Hadn't he?

"Well, I'm very glad it was so successful," Granny V said. "You should feel proud of yourself, Bree."

"At the risk of sounding arrogant, I do." Bree exhaled. "But I'm glad it's over now. Now I can focus on the next event."

"The next one? Bree, you need to be careful not to overdo things." Mom clasped her arm. "You've seemed a little tired of late."

"I've been busy, that's all. Anyway, I enjoy planning events like this. We have Easter in a few weeks, and we'll do our Easter egg hunt for that—that's always so popular with the kids. Then it's Mother's Day, and I thought we could do a pampering day. Poor Diana looks so tired, and I want her to feel special, because"—emotion clutched Bree's chest—"who knows how many more she'll be here for? And tonight I was reminded that we should have a get-to-know-you supper for some of the new parents—"

"That all sounds lovely, Bree," Mom said, "but what about your boss? Is Moira responsible for any of this, or does she leave all the organizing to you?"

"I enjoy this."

"I know. But you have spent an awful amount of your own time devoted to these things. You need to not push yourself to exhaustion."

Bree nodded, pinned a smile on her face she hoped her mother would believe.

"Is Mike travelling back to Boston tonight?" Mom continued.

"I think so." She dragged out her phone. Checked for a message. There was none. "I should text him and say thanks once again." She bent her head, quickly tapped out: THANKS AGAIN FOR COMING TONIGHT. YOU'RE THE BEST!

"I'm sure he'd appreciate that, dear."

Something about Granny's V's tone made Bree's gaze shoot up to meet her grandmother's too-innocent eyes. "What?"

"Nothing." She sighed. "It's getting late. I should probably go."

"I can drive you home," Bree said. "I need to catch you up on the latest with our project."

Ten minutes later she was doing exactly that, sharing what Mike had told her a week or so ago. Brent she had yet to talk to at any length—he'd been on a road trip, and she suspected he was glad to not have the reminders of his life with Chloe constantly pushed in his face—and away games always made it tricky to know whether it was safe to call or not. Still, he'd replied to her messages—she'd prided herself on being gracious with her comments, no snarkiness or "I told you so"s from her —and she was happy to relay this to her grandmother.

"Well, I'm glad that's done. So, now Project Breakup is done, does that mean we can focus on you?"

"On me? Oh, Gran, there's no point."

"Well, there doesn't seem to be when you waste perfectly good opportunities."

"What do you mean?"

"Bree, I may be old, but I really do not understand your reluctance to foster something more with this Michael person."

"Mike is just a friend."

"Who goes to extraordinary lengths to help you, even going so far as to book a restaurant you would like to go to."

"That's just because he's nice."

"Is it?"

Bree's stomach clenched. No. Surely he didn't like her. But there'd been that look in his eye, that lingering hug, that moment of uncertainty in his face as she'd explained how things would work tonight. Did Mike like her? Her chest grew tight. No. He couldn't. She shook her head. "He doesn't feel that way about me. He's never said anything—"

"I would have thought tonight's actions spoke much louder than any words would need to."

No. *No.* Gran didn't know him like Bree did. Gran didn't know Mike was just her friend. That he'd always been, would only ever be, her friend. She swallowed, tried for nonchalance as she said, "Well, if that's so, then he's no longer going to be feeling that way after tonight."

"Yes. I think that's very true."

Hurt writhed inside, tugging at her emotions until she wanted to cry. Surely she hadn't lost Mike's friendship over a stupid misunderstanding?

"It sounds like you were very clear."

She blinked hard, pressed her lips together, steered the car into Granny's drive.

"I'm sorry if I upset you, dear."

Bree pinned on a smile. "I'm not upset. Tonight was a great success, and the money raised will go to several excellent causes."

"Well, that's good then. And I shall continue to pray for that brother of yours."

"Thanks, Granny V."

"And for you too, my dear, that your Prince Charming comes along soon and sweeps you off your feet."

"He'd have to be exceptionally strong to manage any sweeping off these feet," she mumbled.

"Someone strong like a certain hockey player, perhaps?"

"Granny V! I don't want to go out with a hockey player."

"Why not?"

"Because…because I want to be known in my own right, not because of who I'm with or who I'm related to." Moisture pricked her eyes. She blinked it back. "All my life I've been known as Brent's sister, and people only ever see me as that. I don't want to be pigeon-holed anymore."

"Do you really not see how others see you? Breanna darling, you are a wonderful, caring, beautiful young woman, full of vibrancy and love. People see that, not your connections to others."

"You don't hear them, Gran. Even our cousins ask me for

tickets to Brent's games—I think they've given up on asking him —and I'm just so tired of feeling like people don't see me."

"Bree, if a young man pays enough attention to book a restaurant you've always wanted to visit, don't you think he sees you?"

"He might've just wanted to go there himself."

"Please, Breanna. Don't demean my intelligence. No man since the Garden of Eden has ever voluntarily chosen to attend a tea house for himself."

But if Mike had thought he was taking her out, he certainly wouldn't want to now. Tears renewed. Oh, she must be tired. Coupled with the usual letdown after a big event. That was all, wasn't it?

"Good night, darling." Gran pressed a kiss to Bree's cheek, the same cheek Mike had gently touched hours earlier, and whispered, "Don't let a silly ideal trick you out of what is ideal for you."

She nodded. Pasted on a smile. "Good night, Gran. Thanks again for all your help."

"I love you, Breanna Karlsson."

"Love you too, Granny V."

Bree waited until Gran's inside light flashed, the signal she was inside and safe, then drove away, her smile faltering before slipping away entirely.

As great as tonight had been, as wonderful as it would be to hand the checks to the charities and hopefully see Rani's husband's situation soon improve, she couldn't help but feel a sweeping sadness, like something irretrievably precious had been lost, something she hadn't even known she wanted had slipped between her careless fingers. Gone. Broken. And it was all her own fault.

Tears spilled, and she pulled the car over and cried.

~

MIKE WOULD NEVER SPEAK of the disaster that was Valentine's Day again. He felt frozen, numb, stiffly moving around his apartment like the old man he wasn't. He'd barely managed to string more than two words together with his own mother when she'd called him this morning after training, wondering how his date with Bree had gone.

"It didn't," he'd said flatly.

"You mean you came all this way and she didn't go out with you? What—was she sick? Too busy?"

"I...misunderstood a few things." Try a lot of things. Try everything.

"But I thought—"

"Yeah."

A beat passed. Another. "I'm sorry, son."

His throat cinched.

"I know reservations at Gaugin are rare as hen's teeth on Valentine's Day. Did you go out anyway?"

"Yep." With a large old lady who never stopped talking while he sat there like a dummy with nothing to say. How could he say anything when all his words had been stolen by disappointment and all his energy used up in acting like he didn't care?

"Was that nice?"

"Nice enough." If you liked food that barely scraped your sides, and cups so dainty you were scared to take a sip. Look at him, big tough NHL star. Not.

He knew his mom and Bree's were tight, so more he wouldn't say, couldn't say. Admit Bree seemed to prefer one of the dads from her work? Mom was a safe deposit box of secrets, trustworthy as a grave. But the sting of sympathy was something he couldn't bear. Who wanted to own up to being the world's biggest fool?

His teammates, knowing he'd gone home for a date, had asked him about it too. He'd fake-smiled his way through the post-training interrogation to where he was almost sure they believed him.

But he couldn't reply to Bree's texts. He wasn't sure he'd cope with seeing her anytime soon. Maybe this misunderstanding had been compounded by his massive disappointment, but he still felt a little exploited—used up and spat out—and needed time to lick his wounds, to recalibrate his soul. He was pretty sure the sound of the plane flying east last night had covered the cracking of his heart.

He was glad for the game scheduled against Washington tonight, gladder still for the road trip that would take them south for ten days. Maybe in Florida's warmth he'd find the coldness inside ease and figure out what to do with the broken pieces of his heart.

THE ROAD TRIP south took in New York, Carolina, Florida, then back to Nashville, one of their longer stretches. Mike didn't mind exchanging Boston's cold for the southern warmth, nor that each time he went he enjoyed sampling Southern food. Grits might not be to everyone's taste, but the shrimp and grits he'd tasted in Nashville were second to none. The change of scene helped, as did the fact his days were filled with travel, training, games, and time with the guys. Time away also meant less time alone to think, to regret, to wallow in the pain of his own stupidity.

His phone buzzed, and he glanced at his phone again. Bree had left another two messages, this last one asking how he was. At least it made a change from before. But he still wasn't sure whether to reply or what to say if he did. He knew he needed to unhook his heart from her, and the only way that could happen would be to not talk or spend time with her.

Well, he knew that was what he *should* do. Didn't make it any easier to *actually* do.

"Mike, wanna come to the Jack Daniel's place tonight?"

And watch his teammates drink beer and tell jokes he wondered if he was too young to hear? He'd always liked Boston for its club history and proximity to home, but finding people who understood him, who would share jokes that didn't leave him wanting to wash out his ears, who didn't try to big note through alcohol and old-town roughness like they had boulder-sized chips on their shoulders—they seemed few and far between. But was hiding away in his hotel room pretending to talk to family and friends any better?

Maybe he'd have more friends if he made more of an effort. "Sure."

Franklin looked surprised but pleased and gestured for Mike to join him. Baseball cap on, a light jacket, jeans. This hotel wasn't as fancy as some, and they weren't required to wear their suits as they were when on public display.

His heart eased. Maybe tonight would be okay. Would at least get his head out of his own thoughts. Besides, they'd talked about opportunities like this at the Bible study group online. Talked about how Jesus didn't shy away from hanging with those the religious called sinners, that he must've enjoyed a drink, given the culture of the day. "Opportunities only come a certain amount of times," Pastor Josiah Abraham had said, "then you either build a reputation as someone others want to hang with or someone they just know not to ask. Ask yourself what kind of person Jesus was and what kind of person you come across as, and then ask Him how those two could better line up."

"So..." Mike struggled to remember who was in Franklin's life. "Your parents, where are they based?"

"Calgary. Been there a while now." Franklin pressed the elevator button. "Shame it's so far. I like the city."

That's right. Franklin was a prairies boy, Alberta born and raised. Calgary was about as big a city as he liked—Toronto too big, while New York gave him anxiety. Boston, with its much smaller population, was about a perfect team to play for.

"Been there much?" Franklin asked.

"Apart from games, rarely," Mike admitted.

"It's a great place to kick off into the wilderness. Banff isn't too far, and there's great skiing nearby."

Skiing that their contracts forbade, along with most extreme sports.

The elevator opened. Franklin got in, turned to face Mike, his expression wry. "I don't mind admitting I wouldn't mind a trade there one day."

"You're not loving the East Coast?"

"It's different, but it doesn't feel like home."

Mike nodded as the elevator continued its downward journey. Toronto was his home, but if he had to move, he wouldn't mind going further west. Vancouver, where Brent's older brother Dean lived, looked nice. Calgary, a plane trip four hours west from Toronto, could also be an option.

The doors opened, and they found the restaurant strip attached to the hotel, their teammates already sucking down a few cans at a long table in the back. Team management usually recognized the end of a trip as a time when the rules about alcohol could relax a little, and given they were heading back to Boston tomorrow and had two days off before their next game, he wasn't surprised to see a couple of staff at a table nearby.

They weren't the only ones, though. Several girls—unrelated to anyone's official status, as far as he knew—sat interspersed among his team. Yeah, this. This was why he struggled at times, not wanting to give the wrong impression. Not that he needed to worry about what Bree thought, apparently.

He joined his teammates at the end of the table, happy when the server soon arrived and he could order his meal without too much fuss. Maybe God was giving him the opportunity to be a light in this place and possibly even deepen these ties into friendship.

Halfway through his order of a cheeseburger with a side of shrimp and grits, his phone beeped. He checked the message. Heart twisted. Bree.

"You gonna get that?" Franklin asked, as it started to ring.

"Who's calling you?" Ledinberger asked, snatching up his phone. "Hey, it's your chick from before."

"Dude, give it back."

Ledinberger glanced at Mike, smirked, and pressed a button. "Mike's phone."

Mike's chest tensed and he reached across and snatched it back. Pressed end call. Switched it to silent.

"Whoa." Ledinberger held up his hands surrender-style. "Someone's a little touchy."

"Cool it," Todd said, looking at Leddy like he might a flea.

As soon as Mike got a minute, he'd delete his text messages from Bree. He should've done so already. Just hadn't wanted the utter finality of erasing Bree's words and the spark of hope they represented.

Vlad glanced at Mike, eyebrows raised. "How's that going?"

He shrugged. *It's not* wasn't an answer he could admit. "It's going." Much the same as before, anyway. His stupid, stubborn attraction. Her utter obliviousness. Yep, much the same as before.

Ledinberger started bragging, his story soon making Mike feel as nasty as the bar's sticky floor. Man, he was getting tired of how Leddy spoke about women. Vlad might be the captain, but he seemed deaf to half the stuff that spewed from Leddy's mouth. Or maybe it was his English-as-a-second-language deal that meant he didn't understand it. Would that Mike didn't understand it either.

He sighed. "Leddy."

The young defenseman paused his conversation. "What?"

"Do you have a sister?"

"Huh?"

"Do you have a sister?"

"Yeah."

"How would you feel about guys describing your sister the way you just described that girl?"

"What are you on about?"

Franklin coughed, Todd guffawed.

Mike narrowed his eyes as Leddy looked at him with confusion. "You're crass, man. Nobody wants to hear you talk like that."

"At least I have women."

"Yeah, we're not talking about ones you have to pay," Todd said, arms crossed as he finally acted like the assistant captain he was.

"Don't talk like a jerk, man," Franklin added. "If I heard someone talk about my sisters the way you talk about women, I'd want to beat the bo-jingles out of him."

Thankfully, the arrival of food proved a welcome distraction, and Mike could dig into something good. Shrimp and grits. If he ever moved to Nashville, he'd have to up his training regime. This stuff was way too good.

Mike took a sip of water. His phone buzzed again. He glanced down. Bree. Again.

"You going to answer it?" Franklin asked.

If he didn't, there'd be questions about why. "Excuse me." He collected his phone and exited, finding a quiet corner where he could finally take the call. "Bree."

"Oh, thank goodness you're answering!"

He waited, studying the poster of an upcoming show at the nearby Grand Ole Opry as he tried to ignore the kick in his heart at the sound of her voice. *God, help me deal with this. I don't want to feel this way anymore.*

"Mike? Are you there?"

"I'm here. What's up?"

"Are you okay? You…you haven't been answering my messages, which is why I'm surprised you have now, and—don't get me wrong, I'm very glad you're talking to me now, it's just—"

"What is it, Bree? I left dinner to take this call. I thought it was important." He winced at how harsh that sounded.

"Oh." A beat. "Are you…are you on a date?"

He exhaled, not wanting to admit to the boring truth. "Bree, if you have nothing to say, I'm going to hang up before my food gets cold."

"Oh." Disappointment laced that word.

"No? Okay. Well, have a good night then."

"Mike."

His finger hesitated above the end button. With another sigh at his utter lameness, he lifted it to his ear. "What?"

"Can…can we meet up the next time you're in town?"

"Why?" He winced. Did he really want to know the answer?

"I…I feel bad that you came out to help me, and I maybe didn't explain things as well as I could have. I'm really sorry. And I'm really sorry that I barely spent any time with you."

But spending time with her when she only wanted to be friends wasn't healthy for him. "We don't play Toronto for a while." Thank goodness.

"Oh. Well, um, would you mind if I came to visit you? We sort of talked about it before, and I'd love to see Boston, especially with you."

"Yeah, I don't think that's a good idea." Not for the state of his mental wellbeing, anyway. "You're pretty busy, and so am I, and…yeah."

"Oh."

Disappointment weighed that word. He hardened his heart. "Look, I gotta go."

"Of course. I…I hope you enjoy your night out."

No way was he admitting it was just a meal with the guys. "See ya."

"Bye, Mike."

Her voice, breathy in his ear, squeezed his throat. He rasped out a "Bye" and quickly ended the call.

This was just how things would need to be played now. Distant. Cool. The breakup project that had shattered his dreams and broken this friendship in two.

CHAPTER 11

The next weeks passed in such a blur of work, organizing the Easter and Mother's Day events, that Bree craved her times of rest on Sundays—church followed by lunch with family or friends, which usually involved an online catch up with Brent if he was available.

Things with him seemed to have settled into a new kind of ease. Unlike things with Mike. She still couldn't get their last phone call out of her head, would go to bed wondering who he'd been out on a date with and what she could do to ease this fractured friendship into something that felt more whole.

She moved through the double doors of the church auditorium, smiling, waving to acquaintances, and dropped her handbag to secure the seats where her family usually sat. A quick hello to some kids heading out to the kids church—she wasn't rostered on today—then she resumed her seat.

The musicians—an eclectic mix of old, young, African, Asian, Anglo—moved to the stage, Jordan's blond dreadlocks bouncing as he sat behind the drums. Josie Miller, the dark-haired music director, moved to the front and smiled. "Welcome, friends. Let's stand and give thanks to our great God."

Bree stood, closed her eyes, and exhaled. This was where she needed to be. To let the worries and frantic chaos of her life be put on pause. To be. To hear. To worship. To breathe. Music, songs designed to get her focus back on God, to remember He was large and in charge. *Sorry, God, for living in my world so much. Help me be aware to live in the rhythms of Your life and grace.*

Several songs later, Bree's heart was more at rest and the service moved to announcements, then communion, then a sermon from today's guest preacher, John McPherson, who, together with his wife Angela, had led the church for many years before health issues led him to take on a quieter role at a small church in Muskoka.

Her heart pricked in anticipation. His sermons were always challenging and resonated long after Sunday.

"'Trust in the Lord with all your heart and lean not on your own understanding; in all your ways submit to him, and he will make your paths straight.'" He glanced up from his notes. "It's a familiar enough couple of verses for many Christians, is it not? Proverbs chapter three, verses five and six. You can look it up in your Bibles—you brought your Bible, didn't you?"

Bree smiled, remembering the question as one he'd always ask. She flicked her Bible open to the correct page.

"Sometimes I wonder if we read this and simply think it an add-on to what we've already determined in our hearts to do. 'God, bless this plan of mine,' we pray, or 'God, make this thing work out for me today,' like we look to Him as some kind of magical Santa Claus who dispenses good gifts for our enjoyment and pleasure, like His sole interest in us is to make us happy." He glanced around the room. "Do you really think that God is interested in merely making us happy?"

Bree bit her lip. Well, no. But…

"Don't get me wrong. Our Heavenly Father does delight in giving His children good gifts, but I wonder if sometimes in our modern society we look too closely at those gifts and weigh their value according to our feelings. And some of God's good gifts will not be ones we might enjoy."

Bree swallowed.

"If we truly are trusting God to direct our paths, then we need to be willing to see past the immediate, to take a step back and see the bigger picture and trust God to work situations out for our good, just like it says in Romans eight, verse twenty-eight. Let's read it together. 'And we know that in all things God works for the good of those who love him, who have been called according to his purpose.' It's a good one, isn't it?"

Various nods and murmurs of assent.

"We know God loves us, so we can trust Him to work for our good. *For* our good. Not just that He will do good, or make rainbows and lollipops fall from the sky. No, I believe God is interested in something far deeper than whether or not we're in a good mood. He wants us trusting Him. Trusting Him unswervingly. He wants us to be people who can look back on our life and see the times, the many times, when He's proven faithful. When He healed you. When He saved your child's life. When He provided finances when you were down to your last dollar. These times of faithfulness are the times He grows us to trust Him more. So when we face difficult circumstances, we can say to those difficult circumstances, 'I know my God, and He has proven faithful throughout the years. I will trust Him now and trust Him in my future.' This, my friends, is faith. Gritty, hard-won faith."

Bree knew the sear of conviction. How often did her faith seem to rest upon her feelings? How often was she content to drift along and not let God in all the way with her decisions?

"Yes, God has good plans for you. Yes, we can trust Him to work things out for our good. But what we think is for our good and what God knows is for our good can be different things. So my challenge for you today is to let God be God in your life. Ask Him what He's wanting you to learn from the trying situations you face today. And ask the Holy Spirit to remind you of the many ways God has helped you in the past, to give you courage for what you need today. Friends, God is working for your good. You can trust Him to direct your paths. Let's take a moment now to listen to what God has to say to each of us. Come, Holy Spirit, have Your way."

Bree bowed her head, allowing the truth of John's words to wash through her, as the Holy Spirit's conviction penetrated inside. And repented of her selfishness. Asked God to make His plans clear and give her wisdom and strength to walk in His ways.

After a few moments, John prayed, and she echoed his amen. Wiped underneath her eyes. Knew herself challenged. She would trust God with all her plans, with all her hopes. No matter what the cost.

The service concluded with a final song, and she placed her offering in the small velvet bag that passed around.

"He's always such a good preacher, isn't he?" Mom said.

Bree nodded, collected her bag and Bible, and stood, only to be enveloped by a clutch of Mom's friends.

"Breanna, how are you?" Suzanne Blainey, a pianist with a gray pixie cut, smiled at her. "We've heard such wonderful things about your recent fundraiser. You must feel so pleased."

"Yes, thank you. People were extremely generous."

"I'm sure the charities you partnered with are very grateful."

Bree nodded. "They were very pleased." Rani's husband's advocacy group had been stunned. Grateful hadn't even begun to describe it.

"And Pamela says you're right back to working on the next one?"

"Easter isn't too far away."

"And will this be for a charity too?"

"We always have an Easter egg hunt for the children, which the kids really enjoy, and it raises some money for the center.

I'm hoping our Mother's Day event will help some of our moms who have been struggling lately, and we'll definitely aim to have more charitable fundraisers in the future."

"Oh, I just love how the young people of today are so outward-focused. Regina was telling us about young Michael and his work for the Philippines charity. I think that's just wonderful, don't you?"

Mike. She swallowed. "He's very generous."

"Mm. And very handsome, or so my twins always say."

Bree stiffened, then forced herself to ask about the Blainey twins, currently studying in London. They exchanged a few more words, then Bree moved away only to come face to face with Mrs. Vaughan.

A jingly-jangly awkwardness filled her. She tried to cover it with a bright smile. "Hello."

"Hello, Bree." Her smile seemed smaller than usual.

"Oh, Regina," said Mrs. Blainey, "we were just talking about your wonderful son, weren't we, Breanna?"

Bree swallowed. "Yes. Um, about his charitable endeavors."

"I do think it's most encouraging to see Michael working with his charity there, Bree working with her charities here."

"Oh, I'm not really doing much," Bree felt the need to say.

"Oh, nonsense. You do more than you think."

Bree knew her smile must look as strained as it felt. She turned to Mrs. Vaughan as Suzanne turned to answer a question from a student. "How is Mike?"

"He's well."

"I...I tried to call him recently, but he was pretty busy."

"He got in from his road trip two days ago and plays Buffalo tonight."

Bree nodded. She kept tabs on his schedule and knew that. "It...it was good of him to come to our Valentine's Day fundraiser."

"It was."

The flat response, the pique in her expression, made Bree's heart wither and told her his mom knew. She'd always liked the Vaughan family and got on well with Mike's mom, but this stiffness...

"Breanna?"

She turned, grateful for the distraction provided by another of Mom's friends. "Hello, Mrs. King."

"I wonder, Pamela here said you're not seeing anybody these days. I wondered if you were free Friday night. My son Boyd should take you out."

Her stomach roiled. Oh no. Why had Mrs. King said this in front of Mike's mom?

"Bree?" Her own mother prompted her.

"Um, I might be a little busy Friday night—"

"Nonsense," Mom interrupted. "It'll do you good to get out of the house. You've been so busy planning and organizing and programming. You need a chance to enjoy yourself."

"My son is just the same. Boyd thinks life is all about work, work, work. It'd do him good to go out with a pretty girl."

But it might not be so good for him if he knew his mother was organizing this. "Um, does he even know about this?"

"Oh, sometimes mothers need to arrange things for their children."

Yes, but she'd rather a man be man enough to organize something himself. She couldn't very well say this, especially as Mrs. King was beckoning her son near. Bree looked for Regina Vaughan. She'd moved away. Her heart dipped.

"Boyd, come here. You've met Bree Karlsson before?"

"Hi," Bree said lamely.

Boyd's dark hair and height held a faint echo of Dan Walton, one of his friends. But that was where the resemblance ended. Dan was built, and Boyd was...not. Neither did he have Dan's open countenance or easygoing manner. "Hi." He turned to his mom. "Yeah, we've hung out before."

Somehow Bree found herself agreeing to a date that Boyd hadn't needed an auto-cue to invite her on, so she smiled and pretended this was a great idea. And maybe it would be okay. She was trusting God to direct her paths. And Boyd was an accountant in one of the city's major firms. He was employed, wasn't horrible to look at, and was friends already with Dan Walton, so he wouldn't be looking for any hockey-related favors from her.

If only it hadn't happened in front of Mike's mom.

"I TRUST IN YOU, I trust in You, I trust in You, with all my heart."

The music rang through the modern building as Mike closed his eyes, working to relax and let the challenge sink into his bones. He needed to trust God, needed to keep his hope fixed in the One who anchored his soul. Trust God with his future, trust God with his hopes and dreams. He would do all he could, but would ultimately trust God to open and close whatever doors needed to move.

His mind flicked to their back-up goalie, who'd been traded away just yesterday. Poor guy. Gets home from a road-trip only to get a call from his agent to say *sayonara, Boston, hello, LA.* Paviour had called Mike on the way to the airport, mentioned he was meeting his new team on their road trip in Dallas and that the teams had arranged movers to ship his stuff as soon as possible. Talk about life moving fast.

He prayed a moment for his friend and refocused on the sermon.

"We sing these songs about trusting God, but do we really? What if God asked us to give up our dearest dream? Would we truly submit that to Him? Or would we be more inclined to want to hold that thing tight in our hand and say, 'Lord, you can have Your way in every part of my life—except this one.'" The pastor leaned over the pulpit. "Come on. Let's be honest. Who here hasn't done something like this at some point in their life?"

Mike chewed his bottom lip. The pastor seemed to have had too much coffee this morning. This sermon was hitting pretty close to the bone.

"So I dare you to ask God what it is you've been holding onto tightly and give it up to Him so He can truly be Lord over all of your life. Let's take a moment to pray about that now."

Mike bowed his head, unclenched his fingers, and joined the pastor in his prayers.

Did he hold anything too tightly? Was there a dream that he refused to let go? He'd never been as ambitious as some, but he did hold secret hopes. Did his stubborn hope of a future with Bree count? What if God asked him to give her up because God had something, someone, better for her? His chest tightened. No. God wouldn't do that, would He?

Would He?

"Those things we're struggling with, help us, Lord, to release them into Your care. You see our various situations. You know what is for our best. Help us give these things to You, so You truly can be Lord over all in our lives."

No. He couldn't pray that. He didn't want to pray that. Give up his stubborn dreams of a life with Bree?

"In Jesus' name, amen."

He mouthed an amen and wondered if God would take that as assent. His heart felt a little shaky, like there was something he was supposed to have done but hadn't. It led him to make a fast escape from the service before the pastor or anyone else could come and commiserate with him after last night's poor result, which, after the abysmal game of three days ago, had him questioning his ability and wondering how long it would be before they snapped this losing streak.

He made it outside and was unlocking his Chevy when his phone beeped a message.

He got inside, turned on the engine for heating, and returned the call. "Hey, Dad. How's Manitoba?"

"Cold. Wish I was home with your mother, but that's the way business goes. Hey, you free to talk?"

"Yeah. Just left church, heading back for a quick nap before tonight's game."

"I just felt to encourage you. I caught your game last night."

Mike winced. Five zip wasn't a score line anyone liked to see.

"I know the past few haven't been great, but just be patient. A couple of bad games do not make a bad player."

"Thanks, Dad. It's not been fun this past little while, that's for sure."

"You've done okay, though. Apart from that missed block against the Sabres."

"Not my finest hour," Mike admitted.

"Distracted, were you? Looked that way from the TV angle."

He thought back. "Nope. Just a missed shot."

"Might need to work on that then. Any news on your contract yet?"

"Phil's been very quiet."

They talked some more, then his dad had to end the call. But it was nice to have reconnected. His father's work took him on the road fairly often, so Mike didn't see him as much as he did Mom.

He thought some more on his dad's comments about contracts after he ended the call and drove home, the unsettling in his spirit picking up in pace.

Phil Mowbray, Mike's agent since he'd first signed as a rookie, seemed to devote more time to his bigger name clientele and only talked to Mike when contracts really needed nailing down. But he didn't mind the one-way conversations. Well, he hadn't. But lately the chatter in the locker room was about some other players' multi-million dollar efforts, and it was enough to make Mike wonder whether he was being short-changed. He'd never been envious of Brent—had always admired him as a true five tool player, with the skating, shooting ability, puck skills, smarts, and physicality on a level Mike knew he himself simply didn't possess, and recognized that such qualities deserved a pay packet nearly twice Mike's own. But Ledinberger? How could there be talk of him earning more than someone of Mike's experience and years?

The inner agitation only increased when he returned home to find his reserved parking spot stolen. Great. Normally he'd just let it slide, but today he didn't want to go searching for a spot on a different floor. There was a reason he'd chosen this apartment complex, and the reserved parking space was one of those reasons.

By the time he finally entered his apartment, his time for a nap had reduced significantly. He searched the fridge for food, ate a quick sandwich, slipped off his shoes, closed the curtains, lay down on his bed, and begged God to help him sleep.

Deep breathing helped. Fixing his mind on good things. He consciously relaxed his shoulders, relaxed his torso, unclenched his fingers as he stretched. Sleep. He needed sleep...

A phone buzzed. He felt around on his covers. Forced blurred eyes to see. Sat bolt upright. Seriously? That was the time?

The next five minutes were a frantic rush to do all those things he needed to do before he got to the game, things he usually allowed a minimum of thirty minutes for. He bolted downstairs—the lift would take too long—and unlocked his car. The drive shouldn't take long, and he might just squeeze in before the official pre-skate began. Never had he *ever* missed a pre-game skate. Coach Matthews would be furious.

And...he was. Mike clenched his teeth at the catcalls and comments but hoped his stellar record would excuse his tardiness now. Matthews was not buying and made it very plain

Mike would be demoted to the third line if he should be so cavalier again.

"Sorry, coach." He gritted his teeth. He'd need to prove himself and then some to make up for today.

Three hours later Mike trooped back down the tunnel, sweat-drenched, shoulder aching from where Jai Mullins, Chicago's winger, had slammed him into the side—part of the fun of yet another loss.

He bore the dude no malice—they were friends, after all—but it seemed a fitting end to everything else today. He showered, changed, listened to the instructions before their road trip south the next day, and kept his mouth shut as he endured some more good-natured ribbing from the guys about his absence.

"You finally got yourself a girlfriend?"

Bree's face flashed through his head. "Nope. Just overslept."

"You well?" Vlad asked, his Slovakian seriousness radiating in his lowered brow and stern expression.

"I'm fine. I don't know what happened. I must've slept through my alarm. It won't happen again."

"It better not," grumbled Todd. "I hate playing second string."

"I don't mind if it does," Ledinberger said with a grin. He'd played well today. Really well. Maybe that talk of money would be worth it after all.

Mike's drive home was usually short, but tonight road work meant it took longer, and in trying to follow the detours he took some road heading out of the city and got lost. Great. He needed to turn around.

His phone buzzed. Another text message. He pulled the car into a space near a park overlooking the harbor. Bree. Heart lifting, he read the message.

HI YOU. JUST THOUGHT I'D SEE HOW YOU'RE DOING AND WHETHER YOU'VE HEARD FROM BRENT LATELY.

He stared at the message, disappointment seeping through his chest. That was all? He rested his head on the steering wheel.

What had he thought—that she might want to ask him something personal? He hadn't heard from her since Nashville but still had dared hope she might care. Seemed she didn't. More fool him. Again.

Agitation twisted his heart, and in keeping with his mood, he tapped out a terse reply.

NO.

He switched it off and tossed his phone to one side, watching as it bounced on the passenger seat once, twice, then landed with a small cracking sound on the floor. Really? He unclipped his seatbelt and leaned over to pick it up. Yep. Figured. Smashed screen. That'd make the third since he'd upgraded his phone last year.

Whoever thought him patient probably didn't know *that* about him.

A heavy breath rolled from him as he plunged his hands through his hair. Everything seemed to be going wrong today. Not kids-he-sponsored-in-Asian-slums bad, but the splintery kind of discontent that seemed to fracture across his soul, much like the screen's multitude of webbed cracks.

Loneliness arrowed into him. He knew he wasn't alone, but sometimes he wondered whether Boston was the best fit for him after all. Where had all this started? A memory sparked. That's right. This morning, when he'd felt challenged in church about Bree. Was he guilty of putting his hopes for her ahead of God's desires?

He swallowed, watching the golden white lights rocking gently across the harbor. Maybe God was right and this foolish fancy of Mike's was getting in the way of God and His plans for Mike's life.

"Hey, God, I'm sorry." He shook his head, noting that despite the car's heater being on high, his breath was wisping white. "God, please steer me in Your paths and lead me." He swallowed.

"And be with Bree. Protect her, Lord. Give her the man she truly needs and deserves."

Even if it wasn't him. Emotion cinched his throat. "God bless her future husband, whoever he may be."

Words had never tasted so raw in his mouth.

CHAPTER 12

Bree's Friday and Saturday nights seemed to have taken on a surreal quality. Ever since that first date with Boyd—one which left her underwhelmed and wondering whether he was the kind of guy who watched budget-night reports on TV—she'd said yes to a variety of dates offered by various men, or their mothers, connected to her church. Along the way she'd learned that she didn't like super spicy chili, that she had a low tolerance for men who sneezed—extremely loudly—ten times in a row, and that she much preferred going out for a meal than watching a guy play on his X-box, or whatever today's computer game equivalent was.

Someone sweet, someone Christian, someone who understood her—she knew it would take time. But all these dates with men made her wish again she had someone with whom she could be a friend, relax with, and not go through the pressure of applying makeup and clothes she hoped made her look slimmer and available but not *too* available.

"It's amazing," she said to Holly via FaceTime one Saturday morning, "how some of these Christian men seem to have very different standards to me. You'd think some of them have never left a cave, the way they carry on."

"You mean they treat you like a princess?"

"No." Bree readjusted the pillows behind her. "Unlike you, I have absolutely no problem with a guy holding open a door or wanting to pay for my meal. It's what some of them expect as a reward for doing such gentlemanly things that I have a problem with. I mean, I'm not about to kiss a guy if he can't keep his eyes on mine and his hands to himself. Ugh."

Holly straightened, her eyes narrowing. "Is there someone I need to hurt for you? I can come over there and do it now my season is done."

Bree laughed. "Thank you, but no. I might not be as tough as you, but I'm tough enough to swat a hand away. Besides, Brent is more than protective of me."

"He's taking an interest again, is he? That's good."

"Yeah, it's good, but he's still not good, if you know what I mean."

"I hesitate to ask."

"No! I don't mean that. I mean, he's still not quite himself. He's pretty quiet and broody, not quite the relaxed joker I grew up with. I never thought I'd say this, but I miss my brother's tease."

"I'll continue to pray for him."

"Thanks, Holl." Bree smiled. "He's at least attending church again, which is awesome. And he tells us he's going to a pro sports Bible study." With Mike. But she'd not mention his name. Her cluey friend would latch on and say—

"Is that the one Mike goes to? I think you've mentioned it before."

"Uh huh. Hey, Holly—"

"Wait, what is that look for?"

"What look?" Bree feigned innocence.

"That look. Is this Mike related? What's happening with him?"

"Nothing's happening." And therein lay the sting.

"Do you want something to happen?"

"He plays hockey, Holl. So no, thank you."

Why was Holly's gaze so piercing even ten thousand miles away?

"So, the hunt goes on," Bree rushed to continue. "Now, tell me, is there any news on the man front with you?"

"Nope. Nothing to report. Same old, same old. I think God will have to drop Mr. Right into my lap somehow, one day. But I don't care. I'm focused on making the squad for Vancouver, and training doesn't allow time for relationships, let alone finding someone who can understand what I do."

"You need a professional athlete, Holl. I should ask Brent if he knows anyone who would suit you."

"Yeah, I suspect your brother and I have very different opinions on what would suit me. So thanks, but no thanks."

Bree laughed. "He's not that bad."

"Yeah, considering all you've told me about Brent and his hordes of female fans, it'll take me a while to believe you."

"Maybe you and Brent could one day get together. He's a Christian, so are you, you both love sports—"

"Yeah, no. He's not my type, we live on opposite sides of the world, and he's too tall anyway."

Bree grinned. "It's just that the more I think about it, the two of you could really work—"

"Bree, no. Just no. If you want to remain friends, then you best not ever say that again. Okay?"

"Sorry. I probably sound as bad as all these mothers from church who try to fix me up with their sons. Way to make a girl feel desired, to have a mom ask on their behalf."

"You should take it as a compliment. Those mums obviously think you'd be a great match for their son."

Huh. Well, all except one.

"Maybe you just intimidate the men a little bit. You're so pretty and vivacious and funny and smart. I can see some guys not knowing what to do about that. Or maybe that's just the Australian men I know."

"Pretty sure it's a worldwide thing."

Holly laughed. "Well, good thing we've got God to guide our paths."

"Amen."

"Hey, thanks for calling. I love the charm you sent, too."

"The maple leaf is a sign, Holly, that Canada will be in your future."

"It already is, given I have you as my best friend."

Bree's heart glowed. "Happy birthday, Holly."

"Thanks. I hope work settles down for you soon, now Easter is done, and you can relax a little more."

"Thanks, you too."

Holly grinned. "Yeah, off season means double shifts at the supermarket, so not too much relaxing here. But there is today, at least."

"Enjoy the day with your family."

"I will. Take care, Bree. Bye!"

The screen went dark, and Bree exhaled, knuckling at the pain deep in her forehead. The headaches had increased of late, the dizziness she'd first noticed back in February making its return. She was never sick, so it wasn't that. Just probably the stress of organizing so much stuff to do with the center.

Or maybe it was the stress of knowing Mike would soon be back in town. Boston hadn't made the playoffs—unlike Brent's team—and she suspected he'd soon be home. Soon be attending church. Soon be back in her world.

She still sent him the occasional text message, but he rarely responded, save for something that might count as the bare minimum of politeness.

Her eyes blurred, and she once again knew regret at how Valentine's Day had gone. She wanted him as her friend, not this distant stranger.

"God"—she sank her hand into her hair—"I really need Your grace. Help me be patient, help him know that I'm his friend, and please help me trust You. Amen."

She shifted the phone to her bedside table and slowly disentangled herself from the sheets. Shoved a hand through her hair again. Ah, who cared if it looked like a scary mop today? She wiped a hand over her eyes and yawned again. Probably should've cleaned off the mascara last night after the date with a high school science teacher who seemed to think she wanted to know all about some volcano in Indonesia that had erupted nearly two hundred years ago. Why were all these guys she went out with so boring? Hard as she tried, she really had little in common with them. It was enough to make her want to stay at home to watch hockey on TV. Maybe then they'd have something to talk about.

Oh well. She got out of bed, staggered. Felt the wooziness again, this time accompanied by a rapid pounding in her heart. Whew. Mustn't have had enough sleep last night. A car door slammed outside. She yawned. Obviously some people didn't believe in sleeping in on Saturday mornings.

She began the slow trek down the stairs to the kitchen. Mom and Dad were used to seeing her without the makeup armor she wore to work and church. Her skin and hair needed a day off from all the primping. And these PJs were definitely not fit for being seen by anyone outside of the family. She paused on the bottom step and yawned again loudly. Opened her eyes. Stared. Oh no.

"Hi, Bree." Jordan's dreadlocks bounced around as he grinned.

Her mouth dropped open as she glanced around the kitchen filled with men for the bi-monthly men's church breakfast Dad had mentioned last night. The men's breakfast that she had clearly forgotten.

"Hi." She crossed her arms—why had she thought to wear her stupid daisy-print PJs with "I'm a Dazy Lazy Daisy" printed on the front?—before noticing someone else, sitting at the far end of the dining table, as a smile—or smirk?—tugged at his lips.

Heaven help her. She swallowed. "Excuse me." And whirling around, she raced back up the steps.

SOMEHOW, the sight of Breanna Karlsson looking as stunned as Mike felt made the torture of coming here almost worthwhile. When Dad had suggested it, Mike hadn't wanted to but figured it would only be a matter of time before he'd have to see Bree and pretend everything was okay.

Seeing her in her cute PJs—what had those words said?—made it a little more okay. But trying not to remember how curvy cute she looked would likely prove a nightmare.

The past weeks had been torture. Mom had not exactly been backward in coming forward about Bree's various dates. He glanced around the table now, wondering who else apart from Boyd had been lucky enough to take her out. Wondered why she wasn't interested in him doing so.

Exhale. *Focus.* Today wasn't about Bree. It was about encouraging these men of faith right here, right now.

"Pancake?"

"Sure, thanks." Mike helped himself to a pancake and some bacon, splashing on a good amount of maple syrup, food he normally didn't allow himself during the season. He shoved in a mouthful, taste-buds roaring at the flavors he'd deprived them of for months. He forked in more. Carbs added up—a little here, a little there, and life would be even more tricky when preseason training recommenced. Not that he'd assume he'd be training in Boston. Not until the end of June and his agent finally got the offer.

Who knew where he'd be. Guys could get traded at a moment's notice, and someone he'd roomed with could be on the opposite team the next day. Pro hockey was a business, but a harsh business sometimes.

But that was something to think about another day. Right now, he just needed to focus on contributing to the conversation and not thinking about work or his future or what Bree might be doing right now, in her room right above where he sat—

"Mike?"

"Sorry, what?"

"We're ready to hear about the Philippines project."

Oh, that. He pushed aside his nearly empty plate—he'd eaten that quickly?—and fished from his Bible the brochures that had arrived the other day. Ten young Filipino men, all aspiring to higher education but deprived because of circumstances beyond their control.

He shared a little about the program, mentioned he was booked to visit the Philippines in June, and asked if anyone who was interested in sponsoring some of these boys would take a brochure and either contact MPFG or let him know straight away. "I really believe our little can mean a lot for them. The money we can easily spend without even noticing—a cup of coffee here, a newspaper or subscription there—can mean the difference in whether a family of five can eat." He gestured to his plate. "I'm more conscious now of how much food I can waste, so I want to encourage you all to consider supporting this good work and helping our brothers and sisters in Christ who live in other parts of the world."

He handed the brochures around, pleased they were all

taken, making a mental note of those who wanted more information.

The morning progressed, but he fought to stay focused. Awareness of Bree seemed to hum through his veins. He leashed his thoughts—tried not to imagine her in the kitchen, smiling at him as she'd done a hundred times before when he'd visited, tried not to recall her smile, her tease, her voice—but he was struggling, a lone man against an unstoppable force. The helpless longing wound his nerves tight as a bowstring, and he shifted restlessly on his seat. Exhaled. Fought to regain control. Saw his dad glance at him, raise his eyebrows.

Mike shook his head. He'd be okay. If he could just hold on. Pretend. Fein disinterest, put on calm. Coming here today had been a terrible idea.

ONLY A FEW MINUTES more and Bree could finally escape. She watched from the window as men departed, one man, another, another...There! The tension lining her heart ratcheted up several notches higher as Mike left with his father, Mike's shoulders hunched, gaze on the path, a far cry from the easygoing man she'd always known him for.

If only she could set this friendship back to ease. If only they could go back to being friends. This horrible awkwardness between them weighed so heavily on her soul, pounding in her head, her heart, chagrin knotting her chest, guilt tying her tongue. What could she even say to make things better?

Moisture pricked her eyes as the Vaughan men got into Mike's car and drove away, Mike not glancing back, as if he didn't care. Oh, how wretched was she?

"God," she whispered, forehead pressed against the glass, "please fix this. Help Mike forgive me. Help us be friends once again."

. . .

BREE PROPPED her head in her hand as she finished the last of the paperwork. She was so tired, the words seemed to blur, and she had to blink to focus again. Oh, her head ached. And these palpitations never seemed to go away.

She braced herself at the desk, forcing herself to concentrate, the center lying dark and still beyond Moira's office, as if resting from this week's chaos and child-filled chatter, just as she longed to do too. These past weeks had proved exhausting.

The Easter egg hunt had proved popular as always, and the pre-Mother's Day pamper session last night had been fun. She'd loved the chance to connect with moms like Diana and Rani and encourage them as she painted their nails, and then they'd been treated to foot massages from professionals. Her handmade cards—never as good as Holly might make them—reminded the mothers they were loved and valued, and the special bits and bobs she'd worked on to fill their gift baskets had been well received.

All in all, she could count this year's Mother's Day events a success, even if it had felt like a lot of work. Not that she'd admit to anyone just how tired she felt. Fatigue seeped strength from her bones, much like disappointment was doing. And she'd never admit to anyone how sad she was that despite Mike being back in town, he'd still not talked to her.

Of course she knew—via the grapevine that was Brent and Mom—that he'd gone to Detroit last week to watch Brent's Conference semifinal playoffs against San José. If she hadn't been so busy preparing for last night, she would've accepted Brent's offer and attended with her parents too. Oh well. In just a few moments she'd be done, and she could watch tonight's game from home as the Wings took on Anaheim in the first game in the Conference Finals best-of-seven, the winner to play in the Stanley Cup.

A smile pushed past the weariness. How wonderful for Brent to finally be living his dream. Detroit was playing awesomely well, and Brent's renewed focus meant he was often on the scoresheet. How thankful she was that the drama of Chloe seemed left behind.

"What's that smile for?"

She jumped, gladness sinking faster than her no-chocolate resolve. "Mr. Hammerson, I thought you'd left." Hadn't she locked the door? She was forgetting all kinds of things these days. She glanced around the space. It was silent—she'd sent the others home a little early, figuring they'd liked to spend as much time as possible with their families this Mother's Day weekend. Should've figured the man who'd said he was working to reconcile with his wife didn't really mean it.

"Why are you here?" she asked wearily. Every week it was one thing or another.

"I came back because Max forgot his sunhat."

"Seeing it's supposed to rain all weekend, I didn't think that would be a priority."

"You're right." He moved closer until he was blocking the exit from the office. "But it's my wife. She gets so angry. I was simply trying to defuse the situation—"

"Mr. Hammerson—"

"Why so formal, Bree? I thought we were friends."

"You are the father of one of our students, and there are protocols around such things. Now"—she clenched her fingers at the sudden stab of pain in her head—"I really must ask you to leave."

"Why? Are you going out tonight? Do you have another date with that hockey boyfriend of yours?"

She blinked. This headache was making it hard to understand. "I beg your pardon?"

"The guy who was here on Valentine's Day. Big boofy kind of guy, with more muscles than brains."

"Well, you can't be talking about Mike Vaughan. He's not like that at all." She straightened in her chair, willing herself to look authoritative. "Now, I need to ask you to leave."

"So you are going out with him."

"That is none of your business. Now please—"

"So you're not?"

"Mr. Hammerson—"

"It's Dave."

"Mr. Hammerson, if you stay, I will be forced to report your behavior to Mrs. Bridges." She glanced at her phone, lying on the desk.

"Oh, Moira won't care." He slouched nonchalantly against the door, his gaze too intent on her.

"Mrs. Bridges is well aware that there have been several times when your actions have bordered on inappropriate, and it has raised questions about the future of your son's attendance at this center."

"What? You can't do that." His face flushed.

"According to the contract that both you and your wife signed when you first enrolled Max here, failure to adhere to the code of conduct will mean the termination of your child's position at this institution. If you don't wish for that to happen, then I suggest you leave now."

"But we're friends, aren't we?"

"Friends do not treat each other like this." Bree mustered strength to speak more firmly. "Please leave."

"Just one more smile? For old time's sake?"

"Goodbye, Mr. Hammerson." She returned to the papers, drew her phone closer. She flicked it on, saw the battery charge was low. Glanced up. Saw he now had hands on either side of the doorframe, was eyeing her the way a toddler would an ice-cream.

Her heartbeat escalated, pounding erratically. She pushed back her chair and rose unsteadily. Another wave of wooziness hit, and she clutched the side of the desk. So tired. So achingly tired.

"Bree? Are you okay? You look pale."

She felt wretchedly awful. But nothing that a good night's sleep wouldn't fix. "I'm fine. Or I will be as soon as you leave."

He sighed. "Back to this again? I just want to talk to you."

How she'd ever thought he was not a concern she didn't know. Her faulty guy radar at work once again. "I'm busy, as you can see. Leave now or else I'll be forced to call 911."

"What? You wouldn't do that to me, would you?"

"I most definitely will." She picked up her phone. Pressed the numbers. Held it to her ear. "Move away from the door now."

"Fine." He held up his hands, shifting, but only so much that she'd be forced to brush against him to exit. Ugh. The man made her feel so uncomfortable. No way did she want to touch him.

"And leave." The phone was answered. "Hello? I need police. I have a trespasser on the premises who refuses to leave."

"I'm going," Dave Hammerson said, shifting to the exit.

"What's your address?" The voice in her ear sounded tinny. "Miss? I need the address."

Bree gave it, watching as Dave finally slunk away. She exhaled in relief. The pain in her head sharpened, and she stumbled to the front door, fumbling to lock it behind him.

But her limbs seemed made of water, the stars swaying in front of her eyes bending, twisting, pinpricks of light in darkness, until she joined her dropped phone on the floor.

CHAPTER 13

Mike glanced at the text, sent less than fifteen minutes ago, and steered the car down the street. He'd wondered whether this was a fool's errand, but the sense of urgency only increased. Brent's message, sent while Mike had been sitting down to dinner with his mom, had propelled him to an apology, his feet, and then his car.

PLS CHECK ON BREE. SHE'S NOT ANSWERING HER PHONE OR AT HOME. TWIN THING. WORRIED.

It was those last three words that worried him. Bree and Brent had long held this weird connection where they knew when something was wrong with the other. For as long as Mike had known him, Brent had never admitted worrying about anything. And they were both such professionals Mike knew Brent would never message him half an hour before a Conference Finals playoff game unless it was really urgent.

He turned down the street where the Karlssons lived. Nope. Her car wasn't here. The lights were off. It didn't look like anyone was home. Which would mean—her work?

The sense of alarm grew. Yes, her work. He steered through the back streets, wondering if this was the route Bree took each day, and pulled up in front of the place he'd vowed never to return to. Unlike Bree's house, the lights were on here. He hurried out, glimpsed her car. Seemed she hadn't left for the day yet.

He knocked on the front door. "Bree?" He knocked harder. "Bree? Are you in there?"

A push and the door inched open, and a scene from his worst nightmare lay before him.

"Bree!" He rushed to kneel by her side. "Bree, honey, can you hear me?"

She stirred, blinked long blinks, seemed to focus on him. "Mike?"

"Bree, you're on the floor. What's happened?" He quickly checked her face and limbs for any sign of injury. Nothing apparent, save for the sheen on her forehead and a trembling that worried him even more. "Bree, I think you need a doctor."

She pushed his hand away, but it was more intention than strength. "No."

Her phone lay on the floor. "Bree, I think you fainted. Look, your family is worried. I'm just going to call them."

She closed her eyes. Her head lolled.

"Bree? Wake up. Come on, Bree, you need to wake up."

"I feel awful," she groaned.

"You don't look great."

"That's not nice."

A smile escaped as he wondered what to do. She was awake —sort of—but definitely not herself. He reached across her, grabbed her phone, and pressed the missed call.

"Brent? It's Mike. I've got her. She's fainted or something. I'm taking her to the hospital. Don't worry, she's in safe hands. Talk to you soon."

He ended the message and scooped her up in his arms. He lifted her higher, caught a whiff of something sweet and airy. Bree.

"What are you doing?" she murmured drowsily.

"I'm taking you to the doctor. Or the hospital. I'm going to take you to the car and call your mom and see what she thinks."

She leaned her head against his shoulder, her face tipping into his chest. "I'm fine," she mumbled. "Just so tired."

"Honey, you're not fine. Not if you've fainted. Now, I'll take you to my car and get you settled and then—"

Red and blue flashing lights outside halted him before he made it through the door. He drew Bree closer as a uniformed police officer exited the vehicle, one hand raised, one hand on his holster.

"Excuse me, sir. I need you to put the young lady down."

Seriously? "The young lady just fainted. I'm taking her to hospital."

"I repeat: put the young woman down. Don't make me ask you again."

He sighed. "Sorry, Bree. I think they mean business."

"Who?" She shifted. "What's going on?"

He gently returned her to the ground where she curled into the fetal position, her head lying on an outstretched arm. Mike took a step away, hands raised in the air. "I can explain—"

"We received reports from a young woman that there was a trespasser on site a few minutes ago. Miss"—the officer moved closer to Bree, eyes still watchful on Mike—"are you the person who called 911?"

She blinked, rubbed her head. "I don't know."

"Bree?" Mike crouched beside her. "Did you—"

"Sir, I'm going to have to ask you to step away from the young lady."

"Seriously, there has been some kind of mistake. I'm not a trespasser. I'm her friend. Look"—he dug out her phone—"you can see as much here."

If she hadn't deleted his contact details. Or that picture from New Year's. The one he'd yet to delete from his screen.

"Slide the phone across, and get back with your hands up," the officer continued. "Don't make any sudden movements."

The second officer now approached, eyes intent on Bree. "Miss? You don't look well. Has this man hurt you?"

"Mike?" She pushed up slowly, shook her head as if the very effort cost her. "No. No. I hurt him."

What?

"Miss, I'm afraid I don't understand. Are you the person who called in the report about a trespasser?"

"Yes."

Mike felt a chest twinge, then realized she couldn't mean him. "Who? Bree, who has been bothering you?"

"Mike," she murmured, before slumping on the ground again.

He hurried to her side. "Bree? What is it?"

"Move back, sir." The officer held up a hand in warning.

A warning Mike ignored. "Can't you see she's not well?" He wrapped an arm around her shoulders and eased her upright, then stroked her hair, her face. "Come on, Bree. Wake up."

"Sir, what is your name, and why are you here?"

"My name is Mike Vaughan. I'm a family friend. Look, I'm going to give you my wallet." He withdrew it slowly, slid it across the cold tiled floor. "I'm best friends with Bree's brother, Brent Karlsson, and he asked me to check in on her as he's in Detroit and has a game, and—"

"Brent Karlsson? Not *the* Brent Karlsson who plays for the Red Wings?"

"Yeah. And I'm Mike Vaughan."

The officer flipped through his wallet. "Wait—you play for Boston, right?"

"Yeah. And Bree is a family friend and is sick and really needs a doctor."

"But the report of a trespasser..." The officers conferred

among themselves. "Wait here," said the first one, "and I'll check the premises."

Mike drew Bree close under the watchful eye of the second officer. "Bree, honey, we'll get you help soon."

"Miss?" the officer said. "Miss, can you confirm this man is not the trespasser you called about?"

Bree opened her eyes and smiled up at Mike. "Mike is the best."

Her eyes drifted closed as his chest glowed. He raised his eyebrows at the officer.

"Huh." The officer coughed. "Well, perhaps we were a little hasty."

"But not if she really saw an intruder," Mike said. "Bree, who was the trespasser you rang up about before?"

"Dave. Hammerson. Max's dad. Always 'round. Doesn't like you," she said, eyes opening again, her gaze meeting his. "Likes me. He's married. Bad man." She closed her eyes again. "I like you, though."

The officer's chuckle turned into a cough. "Mr. Vaughan, can you please remind us of how you came to be on the scene?"

"Brent texted me. Look, you can check my phone." He pulled up the messages. "I came here and found her slumped on the floor. Which is why I'm really keen for her to see a doctor as soon as possible. I've never seen her like this before."

"Of course. Here, let me help you up, miss."

But Mike didn't want this man touching her. Instead, he scooped her up again and moved to his car. "I hope you understand she needs to see a doctor right away."

"Of course. Here, let me get that." The officer opened the passenger door, and Mike carefully loaded her inside.

"No sign of anyone else," reported the other officer, returning into view. "Just a blue Toyota out the back."

"That's Bree's car," Mike said. "Look, she needs to get seen by a medical professional. Is it okay if we leave?"

"I'll secure things here," said the first officer. "Is there someone we should call?"

"I've called her family, but you might need to call her boss. It's Mrs. Bridges, first name starts with an M, I think."

"Moira?" the officer said, pointing to the sign at the front door. "I'll check inside for her details and lock up."

"And I'll call the Market Street Clinic and let them know you're coming," the other officer said. "It's an after-hours clinic with pathology on site. They can transfer Miss Karlsson to a hospital if necessary, but you really don't want to wait around in emergency on a Friday night."

"Thank you," Mike said. "Actually, we'd better get her bag with her ID."

"How about we lock up and escort you there ourselves?"

And this was why he liked being Canadian. The police service lived to serve, not just use force.

"Thanks."

It was a few minutes more before the lights were switched off, doors locked as best they could before Moira arrived. Mike rang Bree's mom, then rang his own, filling them in on what had happened.

"I'll be in touch as soon as I know anything more," he promised.

And the strangest night of his life continued, Bree in his car, slumped against the door, as profound concern wrestled with intense joy that he'd at last been able to help her.

LIGHT DRAPED across her face in strange ways. The bed, while soft, did not have the same dips and indents as she was used to. And there was a soothing scent, like pears and magnolia. Her eyelids lifted. Closed. Then opened again. This room. Where was she?

"Bree, you're awake."

Bree forced her eyes to focus. "Mrs. Vaughan?" She peered around the space. "Where am I?"

"You're in our spare room. Do you remember anything from last night?"

Last night? She still retained glimpses of some nightmare of flashing lights and shadows and fear and machines and needles. She shook her head, winced.

"You fainted and Mike took you to a medical clinic, and now you're here."

Movement came from outside the door. "Mike?" his mother called.

The door inched opened, and Mike appeared, dressed in a T-shirt and shorts. "Hi, Bree."

She smiled but confusion still swamped her brain. "Hi." Her voice sounded raspy.

"How are you feeling today?"

"Not great, but not as bad as yesterday." That much she at least remembered.

Mike nodded, leaned against the doorframe. Another memory sparked. Clenched fear.

He straightened. "What is it?"

"Last night. Did they find him?"

"Who?"

"The police. Did they find him?"

"What police? Mike?" His mother looked between them.

Mike winced. "Don't worry about the police, Mom. I'll explain that later."

"You can explain it now, seeing as Bree has mentioned it."

He huffed out a breath. Bree's lips twitched. Really, it was quite fascinating seeing how such a diminutive person as Mike's mother could whip him into line.

"Fine. Apparently one of the dads has been harassing Bree

for a while. Bree called the police, and they came just as I found her."

Regina's eyes widened. "Someone had been harassing you, Bree? Oh, my dear."

"There was a mix up for a little while," Mike continued, "but then it got sorted."

"What, with the police?"

He nodded.

His mother's jaw dropped. "They tried to arrest you?"

"It didn't get that far." He crossed his arms, his biceps bulging. "Anyway, it meant we could get to the clinic and get Bree sorted quickly."

"What happened?" Bree finally asked. "I can't remember what's real."

"You were coherent enough to give consent for them to take your bloods, and you were under observation until the results came back." His brow furrowed. "You really can't remember?"

"It's all such a blur."

"They put a rush on things and found you have extremely low iron. You're really anemic, Bree. Apparently your iron count is so low it's a miracle your organs haven't started shutting down."

What?

"Have you been feeling lightheaded lately?"

"Yes."

"And had heart palpitations?"

"How did you know?"

His lips pulled to one side. "The doctor mentioned this last night, but I'm not surprised you've forgotten. There was a lot going on."

"Anything else happen?" It was like seeing an alternative version of herself, a secret life she'd lived that she couldn't remember.

"That bandage on your arm? It's from an iron infusion."

"A what?"

"They pump iron compounds into you intravenously. It gives your bloodstream the kick-start it needs to get your red blood cells working properly."

How did he know all this? "Were you there the whole time?"

He inclined his head.

She bit her lip, glanced at his mom. "Thank you. I...I can't remember any of this. I'm so sorry to have been such a nuisance."

"It's no problem at all." Mrs. Vaughan patted her hand. "Now, are you feeling like you're ready to eat something?"

As if waiting for the invitation, her stomach growled, prompting a smirk from the man at the door. "Apparently I am."

He nodded. "I'll leave you to it."

Wait. That was it? "Are you going somewhere?"

He paused. "Your mom is flying back from Detroit. I'm going to go meet her, bring her here."

"Oh, but—"

His eyebrows rose as he waited. She swallowed. How could she explain just what she wanted from him? She wasn't even really sure what she wanted. All she knew was that when Mike Vaughan was around, she could breathe, she could relax, she could trust him.

Her eyes filled with a rush of tears.

"Breanna?" His mother leaned closer, handed her a box of tissues. "What is it?"

Bree blinked rapidly, but it didn't work, so she scrubbed a hand over her face to hide the emotion. Mike still waited by the door.

"Mike," his mother said, "perhaps you could stay and look after Bree while I go. Now I remember I have something I need to do, so it would actually be easier to do it today." She glanced at Bree. "If that's okay with you, Breanna?"

Bree nodded, barely knowing what she was agreeing to. But if Mike was near, then it felt like everything would be okay.

Mike glanced at his mother and sighed.

He didn't want to? Her heart grew sore. "You don't have to," she murmured. "If someone drops me at home, I'll be fine by myself."

"Yeah, the doctor didn't think so," he finally said, managing to flick a glance at her before eyeing his mother again. "Fine. You do your mystery shopping and collect Pam, and I'll take Bree back home."

Her chest eased. Mike shot his mom a raised-eyebrow look, glanced at Bree, nodded, and closed the door behind him.

"Now, let's get you changed, then you can have some breakfast and go home."

Bree nodded, pushing wearily upright. Clasped Mrs. Vaughan's hand. "Thank you. Thanks for being so gracious."

"Bree, you know we've always thought of you as part of our family. I...I hope you know how much we all care about you."

Bree nodded, sensing something deeper in the words. But right now, her brain felt too stuffed with wool to unravel the threads of intention.

She got changed, realizing she wore her own PJs. "Where did these come from?"

Mrs. Vaughan gave an embarrassed-sounding laugh. "Mike went over last night. You told him where to get your things."

Embarrassment shivered over her. He'd been in her room? "That was nice of him."

"He cares about you, Bree."

She swallowed. Yes, she was starting to see he did.

Twenty minutes later she was seated at the Vaughan's kitchen island, watching as Mike cooked scrambled eggs while she worked her way through a small bowl of the iron-fortified granola he'd foisted on her. When she'd said she didn't normally eat such a large breakfast, he'd raised an eyebrow. "Maybe it's time you did. Eggs are good to help boost iron."

So she meekly succumbed, idly wondering whether his muscles resulted from such things, all the time appreciating the sight of such a strong man fussing over her, asking her how she liked her eggs.

He turned and motioned to her empty glass. "Want a refill?"

"Mike, I'm sure I've never drunk this much orange juice in all my life."

His lips tweaked. "Orange juice is good to help absorb iron."

"How do you know all this?"

He shrugged, turned back to the stove, and started plating up. Besides her eggs on toast, he'd cooked mushrooms and tomatoes, carved an avocado, and presented the plate like something she might find at a fancy café.

"It looks beautiful," she said, wondering how she would do his hard work justice. "But you didn't have to go to all this trouble."

"Breakfast is the most important meal of the day."

He retrieved knives and forks, checked if she wanted tea or coffee, then served himself, seating himself on a stool beside her.

Awareness grew of the intimacy of this, eating breakfast together like they were a normal married couple, subtly inhaling his just-showered scent of sea-salt and spice, knowing he'd collected her PJs from under her pillow—had she really admitted such a thing to him? How tired had she been?

She peeked at him again. How could he tumble out of bed and look GQ ready, while she needed at least half an hour to feel decent enough for others to see? She cringed. Given the lack of time she'd spent on her appearance this morning, she couldn't wait to get home and mask up with her makeup.

"Are the eggs not seasoned enough?"

"What? No, they're fine. They're way more than fine. They're really delicious. I didn't know you were such an excellent cook."

"I have my talents."

He sure did. She shoveled in a mouthful of eggs—perfectly seasoned—and peeked across, saw his brow had furrowed again, and wondered what was bothering him. "Are you okay?"

"Yeah."

"Um, I don't really need a babysitter if you had other plans for today."

He finished his mouthful. "I don't mind."

She glanced at her plate, wondering again how she would fit it all in.

"You don't have to finish it all."

She glanced up, met his gaze. "But I don't want you mad at me."

"I'm not mad at you."

"You sure? You've barely smiled at me all day."

Both ends of his mouth twitched up. "Better?"

"Hmm. I'm still not one hundred percent convinced, but if it's the best you can do…"

He gazed at her with that same serious look he'd leveled at his mother, then returned his attention to his breakfast.

If only she could figure out what was going on inside his head.

ike had to get away. Sitting here next to Bree on the Karlsson's sofa, watching a film with her... Once upon a time this was all he'd hoped for, all he'd dreamed.

But now she'd dug her way even deeper into his consciousness, and this was torture. The past twenty-four hours had proved a crazy mix of highs and lows. Highs: the greedy pleasure of holding her in his arms, cooking her breakfast like they were a couple, wondering how she still looked so pretty when sick, her heavy-lidded blinks daring his heart to wonder if she woke like that in the morning. Lows: the fear when he first saw her, the frantic rush of medical procedures, the heavy-lidded blinks daring a scared part of him to wonder which blink might be her last.

She could've died. The doctor hadn't minced words, but it seemed she'd forgotten. But Mike never would. Her internal organs, left without a sufficiency of red blood cells due to a lack of iron, would soon have stopped functioning. They didn't know why her iron was so low. She hadn't asked, Mike hadn't pushed. The doctor had assured him they'd need to take her bloods again in a few weeks and see if the infusion had taken hold, that they could conduct more tests.

He'd hoped to explain some of this to Pam when he picked her up from the airport, out of Bree's hearing and concern, but his matchmaker mom had apparently had other ideas.

His lips pushed to one side. Not that he minded hanging out with Bree too much—apart from the torture of wishing she was his and he had the right to hold her hand and snuggle instead of pretending to watch a chick flick with people who dressed in mighty uncomfortable-looking old-fashioned clothes and rode around on horses in front of big fancy English houses. He hoped she never mentioned this to Brent.

Bree yawned, inched closer. Smiled. "Are you coping?"

"With this?" He gestured to the screen.

"I bet it's not your usual Saturday fare."

"You got that right."

She chuckled, leaned her head against his shoulder. "Thanks so much for staying with me."

He swallowed. Fought the instinct to wrap an arm around her shoulder. That moment had passed. But he'd not forget it.

An hour later, she was snoozing as the credits rolled when he heard a car outside. He gently shifted Bree back to the other end of the couch and moved to open the front door.

"Mike." Pam Karlsson rushed up the path. "How is she?"

"She's fine. Just fell asleep watching a movie."

Pam hurried inside, bent to caress her daughter's face. "Oh, Breanna."

Bree stirred with that same sleepy-eyed blink that caused his gut to clench, then her face brightened. "Mom!"

Mike knew a moment's envy at the sight—he wished she'd greet him with such joy—and turned away. His own mother had entered, her expression one that said she knew and sympathized with his situation.

He plastered on a smile. "Well, I don't want to be in the way here." He spoke to Pam. "The doctor's instructions are on the dining table, along with some medications. He thinks she'll be pretty raw the next few days, so she's not to push things, just rest as much as she can. And"—he reached into his back pocket and withdrew a folded paper—"here's a list of foods she should try to eat. Eggs, red meat, green leafy vegetables, nuts and dried apricots and so on. It's all there." From his desperate midnight googling when fears hadn't permitted sleep.

"I'm so grateful to you, Michael," Pam said, her eyes filling with tears. "I don't know how I would've coped if you hadn't been there or been so thoughtful in letting us know how things progressed through the night."

"Glad I could help."

Pam hugged him, and he patted her back, then, seeing Bree's smile, ducked his head.

"I'd better go. If there's anything else I can do, please let me know."

"Oh, would you be able to drive me so I can get my car?" Bree asked.

"You're not supposed to be driving, the doctor said. Not yet."

"But—"

"Breanna, listen to the man. We'll get your car later. It's not like you're going anywhere today anyway, young lady." Pam picked up the DVD cover, glanced at Mike with a smile. "I see someone has been far more tolerant than my own sons would be."

He shrugged, heat traveling up his neck. It was *really* time to leave.

"I'll see you later. Bye, Pam. Bye, Bree."

Mother and daughter smiled, matching dark hair, light eyes, wide smiles. "Thanks again, Mike, for all you've done," Pam said.

"Thanks, Mike," Bree said. "You're the best."

He dipped his chin, promised his mom he'd see her soon at home, and hurried away.

But even as he drove back, Bree wouldn't leave him alone. Her scent filled the car, the memory of her slumped against the passenger window twisting his heart. The kitchen, too, the sweet tease and warmth as he imagined what it would be like to share life with her, share breakfast with her every day. Even his room held traces of her, the papers beside his laptop holding the scrawled notes from the frenzied searches through the night. He'd never admit he'd stayed up half the night, googling potential causes for her illness as he prayed it wasn't cancer or something he was helpless to fight against. The list of foods was the one thing he could offer her mother that seemed practical and would not invoke fear.

As for his memories: seeing her in their spare room, sleep-tousled and so sweet; remembering that visit to her bedroom to get her stuff, finding those PJs he'd wondered over, smiling at the Dazy Lazy Daisy, wishing he featured in her dreams like she did in his. She'd trespassed into his thoughts, planting herself there as if she'd never leave.

She'd imprinted herself everywhere—in his house, his life, his heart—and now all he could do was see her, smell her, his gut tightening with longing for what he couldn't have.

He had to get away. A city of two million was way too small for him.

The garage door clanked up. Mom had returned.

He braced himself, met her in the kitchen, switched on the kettle, counting on her usual need for tea. She nodded at his question, settling at the bar stool Bree had used earlier as Mike used yet another of his talents to make the perfect cup of tea.

His mom sipped, smiled, sighed.

"Thanks for all you did, Mom. I know it wasn't exactly the Mother's Day weekend you planned for. I'll make it up to you tomorrow, I promise."

"Poor Bree needed some mothering, especially with Pam out of town. I'm glad we could help." She eyed him. "But are you?"

He shrugged. "I'm okay."

She sipped again. "But…?"

"But I can't help but wish it was easier."

"I'm sure she's very grateful."

"Yeah, it's not her gratitude I want, Mom. And I've tried and prayed and struggled against these feelings. I can't do it anymore. I need to get away."

"My sweet boy."

His throat tightened. What a wuss he was turning out to be. Must be the aftereffect of watching a Jane Austen movie. He was turning into a girl.

She patted the stool beside him, and he sank into it obediently.

"What will you do?"

"Brent's given me tickets to see more of the playoffs, so that'd get me out of town at least. Then the Philippines trip is in June."

"That will definitely be a change of pace."

Yeah. A month out of his usual routine, out of his usual comforts, getting grounded in the realities of life rather than wallowing in what-ifs and regrets, might be the very thing he needed.

Hope flickered. "I can't wait." The sooner he was gone, the sooner he might lose this addiction, absence a kind of rehab for his soul.

Whatever. He had to get away. Bree was too addictive for his heart.

WHOEVER ORIGINALLY THOUGHT HAVING an iron infusion was a good idea probably hadn't had one. The next days passed in a welter of concerned phone calls—Dean, Brent, Moira, Holly—and exhaustion, where Bree's muscles seemed at odds with her bones, like her body had decided that with the doctor's diagnosis she had permission to be tired. She could barely concentrate on conversations, so it was little surprise Moira had insisted she take an extended break.

Just as well. She could barely stand upright long enough to take a shower, let alone deal with the rough and tumble of small children. This—taking a break—seemed so decadently wasteful. But when she fell asleep during the day and still felt tired enough to go to bed at eight each night, she guessed it was wise not to push it.

She watched Brent's team play on TV, glancing at her mom every so often, feeling guilty that her mother was here with her instead of watching her son play.

"But what would you have me do?" Mom had protested when Bree had admitted her regret. "What kind of mother would I be to leave you here alone?"

Mike had not returned. She had a sense that she'd—once again—not treated him as he deserved and he'd stayed away. Truth be told, so much of that evening was a blur, although a few memories had surfaced.

The feel of his arms around her and the security she'd known in that moment. The way he'd stayed by her side through the evening, holding her hand as the IV drip was inserted. And that moment when she'd thought he called her honey. Her heart spasmed now just thinking about such an endearment falling from his lips.

And spasmed again as she recognized a deep, deep sense that she wanted to be that sweetness for him.

"Oh, here he goes."

Her mother's words blinked Bree back to reality, and she refocused on the game. The Ducks were leading three goals to one, and Brent had the puck and was swerving with his usual flair between the opposing defensemen. At moments like this she could see he really had a gift, and it was with a new appreciation she watched him play.

"He shoots, he scores!"

They matched the jubilation of the Detroit commentators on the TV. Brent had texted before the game, and she'd called him back straightaway, wishing him well. He seemed to have a new solicitude for her, which was sweet. It still amazed her he'd had that sense to check if she was okay. It amazed her even more that Mike had been so willing to trust Brent and follow his hunch.

Mike.

Her eyes blurred.

"Bree? Are you okay?"

She blinked fiercely, summoned a smile. "Sorry, just getting a little emotional. It's so good to see him playing as he was born to do, don't you think?"

"Absolutely. It's wonderful when your children are walking into their destinies."

Bree snuggled closer to her mother, leaned her head against her shoulder. "I wish I knew what my destiny was."

"Oh, Breanna. You must know your gifts include warmth and hospitality. I think that's why you got away with doing all that extra work for the center for so long. You were operating in your natural giftings, so it was easy. But it was also easy for Moira to take advantage of that, seeing as it was something you enjoyed doing." Mom sighed. "I might be a Christian, but I do not find it easy to overlook her negligence in this."

"But I wanted to do it, Mom."

"Hmm." She patted Bree's knee. "Is that father still there?'

"He was asked to withdraw his son." A fact that grieved Bree. "I feel so bad. Max was making good progress and would still be there if his father hadn't fixated on me. I don't know what I could've done differently."

"You can't blame yourself. People need to take responsibility for their actions, even if that means there are consequences for others."

Still, it hurt that she'd not had the chance to say goodbye to Max. Of course, if saying goodbye meant another encounter with Dave Hammerson then she was glad to have skipped that.

Sylvie had visited yesterday and explained that Dave had lied about the whole situation—that it was he who had left Linda after she'd threatened him with divorce when she learned he'd resumed having affairs.

"What a sleaze," Sylvie had said.

"I always felt uncomfortable around him," Bree admitted.

"Second sense, huh?"

"I think God gives us little warnings like that so we can steer clear of danger."

"Hmm. Maybe. Or maybe it's your gut instinct, woman's intuition."

"Which maybe is also God giving us a little nudge," Bree countered.

Sylvie laughed. "Fine. Call it what you want."

"I hope Max is okay. It's so hard when kids are part of your life and then they suddenly disappear."

"I overheard Moira talking to Linda, and it seems she's wanting to put as much distance between Dave and Max as possible."

"I don't blame her," Bree said. But what a horrible way for a marriage to end. And vile as he was, Bree sensed Dave had a love for his little boy that greater distance would increasingly strain. Not to mention the love Max had for his father. Her eyes blurred. It was such a mess.

"Hey, they'll be okay," Sylvie reassured.

Bree nodded. *Lord, be with that family. Heal them, help them know the peace that's found in You.*

"So, enough gloomy stuff. What's going on with the manhunt?"

"What manhunt?"

"Your hunt for a man."

Bree managed a raspy laugh. "Yeah, you may have noticed I'm not exactly up for dating at the moment." And she had no real desire to date anyone, either. "To be honest, getting to know someone is kind of exhausting, and the only romance I feel up to is on my DVDs."

"That's so sad. But understandable. I, on the other hand..." She paused, lashes fluttering like a diva.

Bree took the bait. "What's happened? Who is he?"

"Oh, he's a chef in a little French place near where I always get my groceries. We bumped into each other reaching for the same cheese, and boom, it was love at first bite."

"Sounds like a vampire movie."

"It does, doesn't it? Move over, Edward Cullen."

Bree laughed. "Yeah, that's not exactly my scene."

"No. You're such a hopeless romantic, you want it all—the whole Cinderella deal, huh? The handsome prince who sweeps you off your feet."

Bree's thoughts flicked to Mike. Breath hitched. He'd done that.

"You've got to admit those kinds of guys don't really exist, Bree. I mean, can you imagine a guy sitting through one of your old movies?" She waved a hand at the ever-growing Jane Austen DVD collection. "The guy would have to be a saint."

Bree swallowed. Maybe Mike was some kind of saint. She'd known the film wasn't his style, but he'd not complained, instead patiently enduring watching it. For her.

"Like, seriously, how many modern guys would treat a woman the way these gentlemen did? Giving with no expectation in return. They don't. That's just too good to be true."

"Maybe. Or maybe some guys are just good."

"Come on. Tell me someone who is like that."

She didn't want to say Mike's name. Admitting he was like a

personal Prince Charming would invite more of Sylvie's speculation, and she didn't have the strength to deal with that. But
how many times had he showed undeserved kindness to her
and not once suggested he wanted anything in return?

"See? You can't. Ergo, they do not exist."

"I still believe there are good men out there," Bree said
stubbornly.

"Hmph. Well, I've yet to meet one."

"What about your chef?"

"Francois?" She giggled. "Well, he's not exactly good."

Bree smiled, but her heart hurt for her friend. "I hope you'll
find someone who makes you happy and encourages you to live
your dreams."

"Ah, you too." Sylvie had squeezed her hand. "I hope you find
a man that you deserve."

But, Bree thought now, watching the rest of the hockey
game blindly, the man who had done so much for her truly
didn't deserve someone as blithely self-centered as her. He
deserved someone a million times better.

CHAPTER 15

Mike glanced out the plane window at the string of green jewels far below him, the archipelago punctuated by occasional cone-shaped volcanoes that hinted at the history and danger of this country. Twenty hours in planes was no picnic. His subsequent dazed state as he entered breath-stealing humidity and tried to follow the bird-like chatter of those around him made him wonder if he'd taken too many pucks to the head. But the welcome at the airport from John Ramirez, the director of Mission Possible for Future Generations, was so friendly and enthusiastic that Mike had no doubt this was indeed the right thing to do.

Everywhere was loud, bright, and tropical. John drove him from the airport to the hotel along an avenue of waving palm trees and hibiscus, the congestion and sights so foreign that Mike was glad he wasn't driving. Brightly decorated jeepneys, motorized tricycles, and motorbikes that carried entire families, the noise and pollution and crazy zig-zag maneuvers of locals who seemed to go where they wanted at their choice of speed—he sure wasn't in Boston anymore.

On John's advice—"less culture shock this way"—Mike had

booked himself into a fancy hotel, but even with the delicious dinner and comfortable bed and amenities, he slept poorly. Time zone differences and jet lag made it hard to sleep, let alone the tiny geckoes scampering up the walls, with their blue and orange skin and calls of "to-kay" and the *snap* as they ate marauding insects.

He went downstairs for an early breakfast of toast and tropical fruits whose flavors sang on his tongue—pineapple, papaya, pakwan, and mangoes that tasted so much sweeter than any he'd tasted before—then explored the facilities a little, the wide, breezy atrium and open windows demonstrating how warm it could get here.

Back in his room, he flicked on the TV, the channels showing the usual: news, weather, dramas, sport. There was a brief recap of the hockey, the Ducks looking like they'd beat Ottawa for the Cup. He still hoped the Senators would pull out some magic, but it didn't seem likely.

He watched the highlights for a while, thinking back to the last live game he'd watched a week or so ago, when Anaheim had just pipped Detroit by a goal to reach the Stanley Cup finals. He'd caught up with Brent later, who had been disappointed but realistic. The Ducks had been dominant throughout the Western Conference final series, so it was good having played their best to lose to a superior team.

Brent had also said he planned to return to Toronto to keep an eye on his sister, which had brought Mike a sense of relief. He didn't want to have the burden of Bree in his mind anymore.

The sports report turned to football, so he switched it off, drawing in a breath of heavy, humid air. He wondered what this, the first actual day meeting the MPFG team and visiting their work in the city's slums, would entail.

A flick through his email saw another from the online Bible study. The guys had been so encouraging, using their various networks to promote MPFG, and the sponsorships had kept rolling in. He smiled. He hoped the team he'd meet today would have enough resources for all those who had already pledged support.

Knock knock.

He flicked off the TV and answered the door. "Good morning, John."

His host was a slight man with a deep tan, dark hair, and the kindest eyes Mike had ever seen. "Are you ready for your day?"

"Yes. We start with the breakfast program, right?"

"That's right. You will meet my wife, whose original vision this program was, then we will eat with the children, then visit some of their homes."

"Excellent." Mike grabbed his baseball cap, phone, digital camera, and wallet, then followed his host downstairs.

The heat seemed to soak right through him as they passed from the concrete porte cochere to the parking lot beyond. John led him to a minivan decorated with Jesus stickers and painted with smiling faces and the logo and name of MPFG on the side.

"We use this van to pick up the children who come from far away."

"How long does that normally take you?"

"It can take nearly an hour, depending on road conditions. And parents."

"I would've thought the parents would be glad for their children to come."

"Most are, but some think we take too long. They cannot see the benefit of education and training their children for better jobs. They'd rather their child earn money today."

"What kinds of jobs would a child do here?"

"Pick through garbage heaps. Sell bananas to tourists. Sell other things to tourists." His lips tightened.

Mike blinked. "You can't mean they encourage their kids to sell themselves?"

"They do not encourage but can turn a blind eye when it occurs."

Nausea rippled. "But why?"

"Money. Or the lack of." He steered around a motorbike holding the largest bunch of bananas Mike had ever seen. "I know it's shocking, but it's true. There are many tourists who come to Asian countries like ours wanting depraved things, and children are trafficked into sex or slavery or smuggled out as babies to western people. Crimes like these against children cannot be easily stopped. The perpetrators are like cockroaches that slink into the shadows, and the children are often too scared to say anything. Even the police cannot always be trusted. Which is why if we can break the cycle of poverty and convince parents that their children and communities are better off with an education, then we will."

How could Mike not know this? How could he live such a charmed existence when humanity suffered like this? "I...I didn't know."

"But now you do."

Yes. Now he did. And he'd do whatever he could to help this important ministry.

Rose, John's wife, was a slight, soft-spoken woman who radiated kindness and energy. Her face lit as she drew near, two hands outstretched. "Mr. Vaughan, it is so lovely to meet you. Thank you so much for coming all this way. Welcome to our home."

He clasped her hands in his. "Thank you for your hospitality. I'm excited to be here and hopefully shine a light on some of what you do." He glanced around the small room of the lean-to. "Is this where you minister from?"

"Yes. We are very glad to have such a large space for our meetings."

In a room smaller than his apartment's dining area. Emotion

clamped his throat. He swallowed. "I'm looking forward to finding out about what you do here."

"My wife started a school for the poor children of the slum area. They cannot afford to attend school, so my wife teaches them here."

In the dimness he saw a small chalkboard and a collection of books and pencils and paper. "How many children do you teach?"

"It varies, anything from ten to thirty, depending on the day."

"How do you fit thirty children in here?"

She smiled. "We don't. Those days we take them outside and work there."

He nodded, thoughts flicking to Bree's fancy childcare center. She'd love to see this. He bet her heart to help would beat faster over ways to see things flourish here.

Rose shared about the work they did, about the lives impacted through the ministry. Like Carlos, whose father used to beat both him and his mother. He'd come into the program and learned to read and write and was now leading his class in high school. Or Michelle, a little girl with big dreams, whose mother had been killed in a category five hurricane several years ago. She wanted to become an engineer and build safer buildings to protect people.

Mike thought back to his privileged life and wondered about the worth of his dreams. How had he thought trying to beat a younger teammate in contract money a worthy ambition? This was gut-searing stuff. Life held so precariously made it so precious.

"We want to film you walking through some of the work we do here. Show you meeting some people, taking part in the activities, attending some church services too."

"Anything. You tell me what you want and you've got it."

"You don't mind what we film?"

"Turn the camera on and keep it rolling. I'm yours. Put me to work."

That morning he met the children in the free breakfast program, an opportunity to feed hungry bellies to help hungry minds. He felt ridiculously large and pale and overfed in relation to the thin and tiny bodies—the contrast between those who had too much and those who had too little.

Rose soon settled the children into a circle and introduced him to the class. He smiled, lifted a hand. "Hi. I'm Mike."

"Mike is from Canada in North America."

"America!" One boy clapped. "Coca Cola."

"Basketball."

"Michael Jordan!" A taller boy asked, "Do you play basketball, Mr. Mike?"

"Not very well." The boy looked disappointed. "But I'm happy to give you a game if you like."

The boy's face lit, and Mike resolved to purchase as many basketballs as he could find. "You be Michael Jordan, Mr. Mike."

He chuckled. "Yeah, I'm pretty sure I'll disappoint you."

John laughed from his corner of the room. "They don't care how well you play. They just love the chance to play against someone like you."

"A westerner?"

"A man who pays them attention."

As the days passed, Mike soon realized it wasn't just small children who were interested. Several times Rose had to speak quietly to some young ladies present whose smiles and prolonged glances his way seemed to denote interest he'd done nothing to encourage. He tried to explain this to John one night at dinner. John just nodded. "It is customary, unfortunately. You are white, have blue eyes—you're very handsome to most Filipina girls."

"I wasn't expecting this. I...I actually came here hoping to clear my head about a girl back in Toronto."

"What happened with this girl?"

"She doesn't want me, and I'm trying to come to terms with that."

"Ah, it is hard, trusting God to lead you into His purposes, especially when disappointments come."

Sure was. "You must have faced a few challenges along the way. How do you maintain your faith?"

"We have struggled," John admitted. "Both Rose and I grew up elsewhere, so when we moved here our families could not understand why we'd give up our good education and opportunities to serve people in the slums. But we felt God's hand in this and have seen His provision many, many times. This has strengthened our hope for the future."

"Can you share about some of those occasions?"

"Let's see." John templed his fingers, glanced up at the ceiling, smiled. "You see above us?"

Mike glanced up at the dusty rafters and simple tin roof.

"A while ago, my dear wife and I paid for a poor boy who had been hit by a car to go to the hospital. It was the last of our money. We had no food, not even any rice, as we had given it all away. But still, my wife here"—he gestured to Rose—"she stubbornly believes God will provide. So we sat down at the table with our two girls and held hands and thanked God for our meal."

"The non-existent meal?"

John nodded. "There was no food. But then, as we prayed, we heard a scurrying across that rafter"—he pointed to the beam across the ceiling—"and a twenty peso note floated down, right onto the table."

Mike's skin chilled. "What?"

Rose smiled. "God is faithful. He provided."

Mike couldn't wrap his head around it. "But where did it come from?"

"A rat?" John shrugged.

"What was a twenty peso note doing up on the rafter? How'd it get there?"

Another shrug. "My daughter thinks it was an angel."

Moisture clogged Mike's throat, his eyes. What faith these people had. "I don't know what to say."

"God is good."

"God is so good." And as soon as he got back home, he'd set up a direct deposit to fund these faith-filled servants. How could he live so extravagantly, basically seeking his own pleasure, when these people living for God's purposes struggled to eat? This world was so broken.

"Are you okay, Mike?" John asked quietly.

"I'm just trying to comprehend how messed up this world seems to be. I come from a place of so much, and yet here people seem so happy with the little they have. And the faith of people is so real and raw and…and I don't know how I'll go back and think that's normal again."

"It is a big world, with many challenges and differences to comprehend. But the God who cares for us in the Philippines is the same God who cares for you in North America."

Mike nodded.

"I wonder if it is because we have so little that we depend on God so much," John continued. "We really know Him as Jehovah Jireh, our provider."

That was for sure.

"We have friends who work with the Chinese underground church. They ask us not to pray that God would cause the government's restrictions to ease, but that God would cause their faith to grow and spread, like the Bible talks of the planted mustard seed. Sometimes ease and comfort can be to the detriment of dangerous prayers."

"I want my faith deepened like this too," Mike admitted.

Faith that could believe the impossible for all aspects of his future.

He heard more stories that seemed impossible. Visiting ministers who'd seen the blind and the deaf healed and heart conditions fixed. A man who'd been pronounced dead had returned alive from the morgue after being prayed for. An Australian pastor who'd ministered in a remote jungle church with no lights had had a firefly land on his lapel for the exact length of his message before it disappeared into the night. John's pastor friends, who'd arrived to speak at a church only to discover the translator hadn't turned up, had found God filled their mouths with the relevant language so the locals understood.

Mike felt his faith stretched, confounded, reshaped into something deeper. This was a land of possibilities, God's world one of deep challenge and immense reward.

The time of ministry continued. Mike met his sponsor children and some of their families, their heartfelt thanks doing even more to break him inside. How crazy that his little bit of change had changed their world so much. He took them out for a special meal along with John's family, wishing he could honor them the way they'd honored him. What an extraordinary privilege to be here, to serve them simply by using the trappings that came with his love for sport.

He spoke during a church service, offering greetings from his church and friends, praying, sharing a brief message he'd felt God impress upon his heart. He was no minister, that was certain, but he still felt God minister through him and to him. Perhaps the point of trips like these wasn't for Mike to change their world but for God to change Mike's. He knew his life would never be the same.

The initial two weeks weren't long enough, the relationships formed ripening into genuine friendship. He asked John if it was okay for him to stay, and John agreed. "We can take you into the mountains, and you can visit some of our friends who have a church up there. I had planned to go this week. They need encouragement."

"You're the right man for the job then."

John shrugged. "Rodel and Elise have been disheartened, as the church they were hoping to build has had its building work delayed again. The money they had raised had to go to special medicines for their daughter."

"How much money are you talking?"

John mentioned an amount, and Mike nodded. "Do they have the materials or do they still need to be purchased? Can we buy them here and take it with us?"

"You would do it?"

"In a heartbeat." He didn't want to be like a white savior, but honestly, if he could help these people focus on what really was important, then he'd be glad to serve in this way too.

John and Rose's generosity was contagious. Such a contrast to Phil, who, when Mike told him he'd delayed his return for a while, insisted he return stateside. "We have contracts to sign."

"So there's interest?"

"Boston is talking re-signing you, yes."

Thank you, God. Maybe one of his paths was being made straight.

"I'll be back in time to sign," he promised.

"I don't want you lost in a jungle somewhere and unable to give me a yes or no at crunch time."

"It'll be fine," Mike assured. His time here in the Philippines was working deeper faith for the future.

So he joined the little cavalcade that led into the highlands, met the pastors who had seen the miracles John had mentioned before. Rodel and Elise lived and ministered from a small lean-to, the holes in the tin plugged by what looked like wads of chewing gum.

He asked John about this privately. John admitted they were

poor in funds, but rich in faith. Still, Mike knew he'd be giving money to support these pastors too.

They'd been astounded at the supplies carried up from the city. "Too much, too much," Rodel said in his broken English.

But when Mike met their daughter, Esther, a small wide-eyed girl barely the height of his knee, he knew whatever he gave would never be enough. Forced to choose between their daughter's health and funds for a church building? He felt sick.

"You feel strong today, Mike?" John asked the next day.

"Sure."

"Let's build the church. From the ground up."

They spent the next two days digging holes, dropping posts, placing poles, lifting sheets of metal, working hard before the clouds threatening in the distance dumped rain.

"This is typhoon season, so to do this now means that services can continue in the wet."

He was thankful to do something practical and use his muscles in helping them construct a basic open-sided church. The floor was dirt, the lights battery-powered, the chairs simple planks on large tin cans. Along the way they sang songs and told stories—not all of which he understood—and shared in fellowship that said it didn't matter what language they spoke, it was enough to be ministering and serving in love.

And along the way he found their faith-enlarging lives and stories, and his acts of service, ministering and healing his heart, too.

CHAPTER 16

Bree wandered past the living room, her ears pricking, her feet stopping at the voice. Brent was on Skype, and that voice…

"It was so funny. John and I were waiting by the bus when the other guy went into the cane fields to do his business. One guy from Rodel's church got sick of waiting and yelled at him to hurry up. As a joke, he then picked up a rock, hurled it into the cane fields, which were, like, an acre wide, and would you believe—"

"He hit him?"

"On the shoulder. He was okay, but—"

She smiled, listening to Mike's deep chuckles, a sound she hadn't heard much before.

"—honestly, what are the chances?"

"Sounds like you're having fun."

"This place has been unreal. I've taken so many photos. John and Rose are awesome. I've been so challenged. Man, the stories I could tell you."

"Maybe you can. We booked a lake cottage for a week around my birthday. You'll be back by then, won't you?"

She stilled, waiting with suspended breath. To have Mike join them for *her* birthday, too. *Thanks, Brent. Thanks for asking if I'm okay with it.*

"I'll be back, but I don't want to intrude."

"It'd be great to see you. I know Bree will want to catch up with you too."

Wait—what?

She must've made a noise because Brent turned and saw her. Waved her over. "Look, here she is now. Hey, Bree, you don't mind if Mike joins us for a few days up in Muskoka?"

She crossed her arms, hiding the PJ top she'd yet to change from. No more Dazy Lazy Daisy from her. "I don't mind."

"Hi, Bree," Mike said. "You're looking better."

"Feeling better, too. That iron infusion kicked in a couple of weeks ago, and now I'm feeling much stronger."

"Iron woman, huh?"

His smile twisted her heart. "Sounds like you're having a ball."

"It's been so good. I've met so many wonderful people that I don't know how I'll manage coming home."

She nodded, smile pasted on, and wondered if he had anyone in particular he was reluctant to leave.

He lifted a hand, which seemed to be her cue to leave, so she said goodbye and moved to the door, out of sight from both Brent and the computer screen.

She slid down behind a couch and eavesdropped. Yes, she knew it was juvenile, but something within *craved* to hear Mike's voice. To hear more details than the mere sketches in his emails to the MPFG sponsors.

"...can't believe the stuff I've seen. So good to be here and know my minor efforts can be multiplied and made into more."

He was so humble. So generous.

"So, anything else I need to know now my sister isn't here?" Brent asked.

Mike coughed. "Dude, if ever you want to feel like Mr. Popular, you need to come. I've been propositioned, proposed to—you name it, I've heard it. It's crazy."

What? Her chest grew tight.

"But even with stuff like that I've enjoyed the space, the chance to clear my head about a lot of things. The stuff I thought important back home really isn't so much anymore."

"Like?"

"Like my contract. I mean, I get that more money means more opportunity to help others, but the tension about that seems to have faded."

That was good, Bree thought.

"The tension about other things I thought I wanted too."

Her heart caught.

"You mean—?"

Another sound, like an embarrassed chuckle. "Are you going all Oprah on me? I don't need a psych."

Oh, she wanted to know what—who—he meant. To know: did he mean her? Did he not want her anymore? Her eyes filled.

"Look, I need to go. It's getting late."

"Hey, great to talk with you, dude."

"See you soon."

"Later."

There came a sound of tapped keys, then the creak that suggested Brent had risen.

She huddled into her space wondering, hoping, wishing, praying that the man she'd once inadvertently rejected hadn't meant to sound like he'd finally given up on her.

"Thanks again for all you've done." Mike hugged his host and hostess. "I think the footage you showed me will be awesome."

"It's been a real blessing to have you here," John said. "Rodel has barely stopped talking about it."

"It was nothing—like, truly nothing—compared to what you and he do every day. I really think I'm going to struggle when I go back."

"That's called reverse culture shock. Just remember, the God we serve here is the same God you serve there, and He plants people where He wants them to accomplish His purposes in His timing."

Mike nodded. Gave them both another hug. Then moved through security in order to board the plane.

His time here in the Philippines had blessed him so much more than he suspected he'd blessed them. God had stretched him, caused his faith to grow, to deepen, like he could feel the roots of his mustard seed of faith extending deep into God's promises. But how could he reconcile the have-nots he'd seen here with the haves of home?

Even Brent's offer, as well-meaning as it was, seemed a waste of time and resources. Didn't people know the money used for a week in Muskoka could pay the wages of three Filipina pastors for a year? What about the food they ate and wasted while ten percent of the world's population starved? How could he return to his decadent lifestyle of luxurious modern living and providing entertainment for the masses when he'd met people whose lives were truly making an eternal difference in this world?

Conviction chased him the whole return flight, guilt spearing him interspersed with bouts of anger when he saw passengers leaving their bread rolls. Didn't they know that food could've gone to someone who'd truly appreciate it? Why was this world so unfair? Why were people so greedy and selfish and caught up on stupid things when there was a world of people going to hell who needed to hear about Jesus?

Still. He'd do what he could. Try to shine a light on MPFG, try to encourage others to consider their actions so they'd live less wastefully, more purposefully. So they'd make this brief dash of life between their birth and death as meaningful as God intended.

His flight landed in Boston, his chosen destination just in case Boston reconsidered and he had to clear out his stuff in a hurry. He'd make UFA status in a day or two, and as an unrestricted free agent, he'd have the chance to test other teams and see what they were offering—unless Boston decided they'd keep him after all. It was a weird time, and he was glad for the monotony of chores like washing and cleaning off the dust accumulated from a month's absence. Good thing he didn't have houseplants or a goldfish counting on him to survive.

He checked his phone. Still nothing from Phil. Oh well. He checked through his email. But the jetlag that had plagued him mildly on his trip west seemed to have tripled in impact here. He was so tired.

His phone buzzed. A text message.

Brent: WELCOME HOME.

He replied, wondering if he should accept the offer to stay with him in Muskoka. Sure, the lakes in that part of Canada were awesome, and it would be great to hang out with Brent, but the niggling questions about the ethics of doing so when so much of the world suffered persisted. How was it right to enjoy such things?

Another message. He flicked it open. Beau had sent him a friendly text. He'd been traded—not to Montreal, as he'd thought, but Phoenix. Wow. Talk about polar opposites.

GOD KNOWS WHAT HE'S DOING. WE CAN TRUST HIM. YOU'VE GOT THIS, he texted.

Beau replied: AMEN and Mike shifted to look out across the harbor. Prayed for his friend and all this move would mean. Prayed for John and Rose and their ministries. Prayed for his own future, that he'd be content with whatever direction God had for him. Prayed for his sponsor children, that God would bless them. Prayed that Phil would hurry up with an offer so he'd not need to keep distracting himself. A face flashed into his mind; he rejected it. He couldn't pray for her. He'd done a stellar job getting her out of his system, which was why the invite from Brent felt fraught with danger. Because if he was there while she was there, he might very well fall back in—

His phone rang. Phil. He snatched it up.

"Mike? You got your contract there?"

He hurried to the coffee table, flipped open the contract from Boston he'd read a dozen times already. "Yeah."

"They want you. Got you an extra hundred K more. But with an option to trade down the track if necessary."

"Trade options being?"

"Same places we talked last time. Canadian cities and Detroit, Chi-Town, Ohio, Buffalo, New York. All you have to do is sign and the deal is done."

"The extra one hundred grand?"

"I'll get them to email you a new copy now. But you'll need to sign it and fax or email it back."

"Or I could just drive over to the office and do it there."

"You're in Boston?"

"I told you that." Like, five times in the last email exchanges.

"Huh. Must've forgot."

Or he was too busy chasing other clients with bigger pay packets, which meant he'd get a bigger cut.

"I still need a copy," Phil said.

That was, if he signed it. Was it worth holding out for more? Playing hardball a little? More money would mean more opportunities to help John and Rose.

"Mike? You there?"

"Yeah, just thinking."

"What's there to think about? This is a great offer. You won't get a better offer. You—"

"Why not?" Tiredness sharpened his voice.

"Pardon?"

"Why wouldn't I get a better offer?"

"Well, uh, um…"

"Have you tried chasing offers from other clubs, or did you just stick with Boston because it's easy?"

Phil coughed. "I'm going to overlook that comment and put it down to jet lag."

"Truth is, Phil, I get the impression you're prepared to overlook a lot of things with me."

"Excuse me?"

"You heard me. Now, have you asked any other clubs or not?"

"I, er, I thought you didn't want to leave Boston."

"That's not answering the question, Phil. Can you answer it?"

"Wow. Going to Asia really knocked you around."

"I'm going to take that as a no, then."

"Now, Mike—"

"I understand you might prefer things to be easy, but frankly, I'm tired of paying for you to not do much at all."

"What are you saying?"

"I'm saying that if nobody comes to the party tomorrow, then I'll sign with Boston and this season is done. But I want to make it very clear that any place I get traded to is gonna have to be offering a lot more."

"How much more?" Phil asked.

Mike told him.

Phil whistled. "I didn't think you were so mercenary."

"It's not being mercenary to know what you're worth. And I have commitments that mean I'm looking for the best deal for me, not the easiest one for you. And if you don't like it, then maybe we've reached a parting of the ways."

Phil choked. "Are you threatening me? You'd better have another look at that contract you signed with me all those years ago and we'll have another conversation about this."

"I will. And when we have that conversation, you better believe I'll be considering other agents who might work *for* me rather than shuffling me off so they can focus on their bigger-name clients."

There was a beat of silence. Two. "Mike, I think you've misunderstood."

"I don't think I have. Another deal on the table would convince me you've tried, but if not, then I guess we know where this may head."

"I'll be in touch," Phil said tersely.

A dial tone rang in Mike's ear. Had he been too forceful? Or had his previous willingness to go along with things simply meant he'd been too soft?

His phone rang. Thank goodness. "Hey, Dad."

"Any word yet?"

"Phil just called. They're offering an extra hundred K, but…"

"You're not sure you'll take it?"

"I suspect he's not pushing me anywhere else."

"You asked him to?"

"I made it very plain."

"What are you going to do?"

Mike explained about his wish to see an alternative offer to know if Phil was doing his job or not. "And if nothing happens, then I guess I'll sign with Boston and see what happens before the next trade deadline."

"You have any other agents in mind?"

"I'll talk with Brent. He's doing okay for himself."

"Hey, you never know, you might get another offer. But even

if you don't, you don't mind staying in Boston another year, do you?"

"No. I'm settled here. As long as I'm not being short-changed. I hate wondering whether I'm being ripped off." Was Phil right and Mike was being greedy?

"Your mother and I will be praying, son."

"Thanks, Dad."

"And I hear you're heading up this way again soon?"

"As soon as this is done. Be good to hang out with you and Mom."

"She also mentioned you'd received an invitation to spend time with the Karlssons."

Hope flickered. Maybe there was still time to arrange for his parents to stay nearby. Then he could hang with Brent on his terms without wondering if he'd be seeing Bree in those cute PJs he'd been unable to forget. He frowned. Had she been wearing them the other day when he'd Skyped Brent?

"Mike?"

"Oh, sorry, what were you saying?"

"Your mother mentioned something about Muskoka. You planning to go?"

"Maybe. It'd be good if you and Mom could come too."

"Unless the place they've rented is a small palace, I can't see it working out. But maybe we can head up for a day."

"That'd be great."

His dad grunted affirmation and soon ended the call with a repeated promise that he'd be praying.

"Thanks, Dad. Love ya."

Mike hung up. Checked his emails. Sent off a quick text to Brent: REMIND ME WHO YOUR AGENT IS?

His phone rang. "Dude. Are you thinking of firing Phil?"

Mike explained the situation, listened as Brent offered his thoughts and prayers.

"Thanks. It's good to know there might be some options."

"There are always options," Brent said. "Hey, I'll pray, get Bree to pray too."

"Nah, don't bother her."

"Why not? You know she's always interested in what's going on with you."

His heart flickered. He tamped it down. "Still, I'd rather—"

"She was always asking about your emails, wondering why you hadn't included her in the stuff you sent to everyone else."

"That was just to the Bible study guys and my folks," he protested.

"Yeah, well, I think she took it a bit more personally than that."

New guilt writhed. He hadn't emailed her more for his own protection, to guard his heart.

"Hey, had any more thoughts about coming with us?"

"You mean Muskoka?"

"It's big enough that you needn't see my sister if you don't want to."

"It's not that."

Mike's phone beeped to let him know another call was coming. "Sorry, better check this other call."

"Later." Brent dropped out.

Mike switched to take the new call. "This is Mike."

"It's Phil. The Sabres are playing."

Huh. "Good to know."

"But their price is a little lower."

"How much?"

"Two hundred grand."

"Got a contract?"

"What? You want to sign with them?"

More, he didn't really trust Phil to be telling the truth. "Send me the contract. Tell Boston there's another interested party. Don't tell them how much and let's see if they want to go higher."

"Fine," Phil said, releasing a huff.

"Thanks." Mike ended the call.

Well. That was something. Maybe Phil could work his way back into Mike's good graces.

All would be revealed in tomorrow's wheel and deal trade lottery.

CHAPTER 17

The slam of a car door pulled Bree's attention from her magazine. She peered through the sheer white curtains draping the wide French windows of the cottage. Her heart bounced. Mike. After all the dramas of recent days, he'd come after all. She shot to her feet, fluffed her hair, then resumed her seat on the cream leather lounge. Casual. She needed to look casual. She ran her tongue over her teeth. Hopefully no poppy seeds from the muffin earlier decorated her mouth. She didn't want to look *that* casual. She rose, raced to the mirror. Wiped at the crumbs next to her mouth. Winced.

"Bree? Is something wrong?" her mom asked from the hall.

"Nope." She hurried across polished wooden boards back to her seat, snatched up the *Muskoka Living* magazine from the glass-topped coffee table, and assumed nonchalance.

"Did you want to go into town a little later—"

A door knock.

Bree jumped.

"Oh, I wonder who that—oh, Michael! How wonderful you decided to join us."

A soft murmur.

"No, it's so good to have you come. Now, Brent's out with Rob fishing, but Bree is in the living room. Look, here she is."

Bree glanced up. Smiled. Instead of playing this cool, maybe she should act as if nothing was wrong. Nothing *was* wrong, she told herself. Besides, playing things cool had never been her style anyway. She bounced to her feet. "Mike!"

"Hey, Bree."

Nothing being wrong meant treating him as she ordinarily would, which meant rushing over to hug him. "Oh, it's so good to see you."

But when she'd given him hugs in the past, she'd never experienced this tug low in her stomach. Had never noticed the delectable scent of his aftershave, which sent her pulse racing. Or his swift inhale and stiff arms that said he really wasn't into this as much as she was.

She pulled back, hiding her chagrin with a bright smile. "How are you?"

Despite the tan, he looked tired, his lips tight, his eyes disillusioned. What was wrong?

"I'm fine."

"I'm sure Mike would like a chance to sit down, Bree. Would you like a cup of coffee or a cool drink?"

"Thanks, Pam. I probably should go get my bag and put it somewhere."

"Oh, Bree can show you to your room while I make us all a cup of coffee. Or would you prefer iced tea?"

"Coffee would be great, thanks."

"Bree?" Mom inclined her head.

Bree followed the summons while Mike went back to his car to get his bag. "What is it?"

"I sense from what his mother said he's still a little weary after his time away. So you might need to give him some space."

"When have I not?" Honestly. Mothers.

Bree met Mike in the hall, then conducted him to his room

right at the end, next to Brent's. "So, we thought you might like this room. It has a view of the lake—see? Isn't that beautiful?—and should be pretty quiet, except you are next to Brent, and we all know he can snore sometimes, so I hope you brought earplugs. But if you didn't, I'm sure there are spares somewhere, or we can buy some. What else? Um, the bathroom is just two doors up, there are towels on the end of the bed, Dad and Brent will be back in a few hours—hopefully with a boatload of fish, or at least a few we can cook for dinner—and the Wi-Fi code is next to your bed."

His lips turned up. "The perfect hostess. You enjoy doing this, don't you?"

"I love it," she confided. "I think hospitality is one of my gifts, and I love to make people feel welcome. Especially when it's someone we all know and love."

At his startled, swift look, she felt heat rise in her cheeks. "Okay. I will leave you to freshen up, then meet you back in the living room. Unless you want to rest."

Another twitch of his lips. "I'm not an old man, Bree."

"I know that. Any red-blooded woman with eyes would." Wait. Had that truly come out of her mouth? "Uh, I'll see you soon."

She hurried from the room, refusing to look at him. Oh my goodness. What was wrong with her? Maybe coffee would spark sense to her brain.

But later, as she sat with her mother in the living room on the couch opposite Mike, looking for all intents and purposes like a Jane Austen heroine entertaining a suitor while a chaperone looked on, she realized coffee would not stop these strange feelings. Her eyes wanted to soak him in, draw in every little detail from the curl in his hair to the way his fingers seemed to play piano on his thighs restlessly, like he was nervous.

She glanced back up. His gaze shifted away. Her heart

thumped erratically. Not like the iron-deprived condition of a few months before. No, this feeling was far, far different.

"So, Bree." His attention returned to her. "You look a lot better."

"I…" *sound like a strangled cat!* She swallowed. "I feel a lot better."

"Good." His features seemed to ease slightly. He took a sip of his coffee.

"Bree has been very good at taking her supplements and eating her green vegetables."

"Mom, I'm not a child." Bree rolled her eyes, caught a wisp of Mike's amusement. Her heart eased. Maybe she could make him smile, make him laugh, and he could relax from this strange tension she saw. He'd always been the most relaxed and easy-going person she knew. Which was why she'd always loved his company. He seemed the opposite of her. Mr. Perfect.

Mr. Perfect? She coughed, which swiftly became a choke as she wheezed for air.

"Bree? Are you quite all right?" Mom asked.

"I'm fine," Bree eventually managed to say. "Some coffee must've gone down the wrong way."

Mike raised an eyebrow.

"Carry on," she said, waving a hand. "Ignore me."

She pasted on a smile to ease their concern.

After another reassurance from Bree, her mother turned to their guest again. "So, you enjoyed your time away?"

His features lit, then dimmed again before he answered politely, "It was great."

"Do you have photos?" Bree's voice had settled into normalcy now. "You sent some to Brent, but I bet you have many more."

"You really want to see them?"

"Of course! I'd love to know all about your time there—what you did, who you met…"

She waited. The chances of him telling her—and her mom—about the girls' interest in him were pretty low, but you never knew.

"I have some photos on my camera. I can get it if you like."

"Yes, please."

He studied her, nodded slightly, then excused himself.

When he returned, she patted the space between her and her mother, and after a moment's hesitation, he sat between them.

Then he started sharing, showing pictures on his digital camera, and any awkwardness faded as she lost herself in wonder at his time away.

SITTING NEXT TO BREE, taking shallow breaths so as not to inhale her scent, trying not to notice how her hair swung near to skim his skin to prickle his senses to even greater awareness, was like the ultimate in cruel torment by a James Bond villain. He'd thought he'd got her out of his system, could manage the torture of staying here for a few days, but in the space of a few seconds—even before she'd flung herself at him in a hug that roared his heart and body to need, even before she'd said, *dear God*, she loved him—she'd proved to be as enticing and desirable as ever.

"And what about this one?" Bree leaned close, her arm touching his as she pointed to a scene when he was at Rose's tiny school in the slum.

He swallowed, subtly shifted his arm away. "That's the school for kids too poor to go to regular school."

"You mean they don't normally go? The poor kidlets," Bree added in a whisper.

"It's a slum. Many of the kids have to work so their families can eat. Education is a luxury."

He could see her compassion as her eyes sparkled, and she bit her lip. "I knew this would move you," he murmured.

"What can we do?" She gestured to the picture, placed her fingers on his hand. "Oh, what can *I* do?"

"This is where the sponsorship program comes in. The money goes directly to helping support the children, making sure they have enough food and materials and ensuring they have fewer barriers to receiving a good education." He eased his hand from hers. "When the parents see their child is being fed and they don't need to do it, then they're motivated to keep them attending."

"I need to sponsor another child. Will you give me more details?"

"Sure."

"Rob and I will sponsor another child too," said Pam.

"Thanks. Every bit helps."

"How many kids require sponsorship?" Bree asked, pulling her knees up as her body angled closer.

"They have hundreds on their waiting list. John and Rose said there might be even thousands, but they need time to contact parents, to ensure authorities see everything is aboveboard."

He moved to other pictures, other memories from his time heading to the mountains, and they oohed and aahed over the blue hills, the vivid greens, the bright flowers and birds of the tropical scenes.

"What's this one?" Bree asked him, hand upon his arm, prickling new awareness.

He knew it didn't mean anything—it was just Bree being Bree. But it took a moment before he could answer. He cleared his throat. "That's when we went up to the mountains. Rodel and his wife pastor a church and have a little girl who's been quite sick. We helped build a church for them." He flicked over to show them, scanning through until Bree's hand paused him on a picture of him holding Esther, his gaze on hers as they smiled at each other.

"Oh, how adorable," Bree said, leaning her cheek against his shoulder. "I don't think there's a nicer thing than seeing a big tough man holding a tiny child with such tenderness."

His heart glowed. "That's Esther. She was the cutest little girl."

"What a picture of trust," Pam said, smiling at him.

"You'd make a good father," Bree said, her eyes meeting his then bolting away.

He drew in a deep breath to steady his heart. Caught a whiff of her fragrance. He couldn't do this. Couldn't stay here. Had to leave.

He rushed through the next few pictures, but Bree kept interrupting, her sweet interest fueling his heart and frustration.

"You literally built the church?" She squeezed his bicep. "So strong."

"Bree, stop teasing the poor man."

"I wasn't teasing," he thought he heard Bree mumble before she pointed at another picture. "What's that?"

He explained about the chewing gum blocking the rain, and again her swift inhale showed the depths of her compassion.

"Oh, what can we do for them?"

Try as he might, he couldn't help but love this girl. "I gave John some money for them," he muttered. John's eyes had nearly fallen out of his head before they'd swum with tears, and he'd thanked Mike profusely.

"You're such a good man," she said, patting his arm.

He glanced up to catch Pam's odd look at Bree before excusing herself to clear cups and mugs.

The extra room on the couch permitted him to surreptitiously ease away. Bree's presence was too distracting, her nearness all-absorbing, every nerve ending shifting to her like those plants that turned to face the sun.

"Bree, perhaps you should let our guest have some space," Pam said from the door.

"Oh, you don't mind, do you, Mike?" Bree said, snuggling close again. "How many more to go?"

"We're almost there," he rasped. Thank goodness. He was almost at the end of his self-control.

He quickly flicked through the last photos, his skin tingling as he paused at the image of the river. The sound of a car pulling up outside pushed him to his feet.

"Sounds like they're back."

Bree didn't sound excited, but he couldn't help but feel relieved. Bree had always been a touchy-feely person, but today she'd seemed much more so than usual. It was a miracle he'd made it this far without exploding from the torment.

Brent entered. "Hey, Mike, you're here!" Man hug. "Wasn't sure you'd make it."

"You didn't sound like you'd take no for an answer," Mike said dryly. Brent's persistent efforts had dragged Mike's sorry butt up here.

"Did you catch any fish?" Bree asked, a tease in her voice.

Brent shot her a glance. "Sometimes it's more about the journey, not the destination."

She chuckled. "I take it that's a no then, brother dear."

"Breanna."

"Brent." She crossed her arms, eyes blinking innocently.

"Let me know if I'm in the way here," Mike said.

Bree shook her head. "I'll leave you to it. Thanks so much for showing me your photos." Her smile tugged a painful throb from his chest.

"No problem," he muttered.

"Catch you later." She swatted Brent's shoulder and exited the room.

Mike could finally breathe more deeply now.

Brent moved to sit on the coffee table. "Good trip up?"

"The roads were clogged with tourists, but then I guess I'm one too."

"So, how's it all going with the contracts?"

"It's signed."

"You don't sound excited."

Mike shrugged. "To be honest, I'm not super excited, but at least it's work." Work that could help support others doing far more meaningful work.

"I can still have a chat with my agent if you want."

"Thanks, I'll let you know. Phil seems to at least be trying now, not taking me for granted."

"That's something."

"Yep."

"At least you're here and can forget some of that stuff and focus on relaxing."

Mike inclined his head. Probably best to shift the focus. Talking about himself so much was exhausting. "So, how goes the house hunt?"

"I saw a good option up in Grosse Pointe. Thought I might put in an offer."

"Wow. No waiting around, huh?"

"It needs a bit of work, but I had a building inspection and everything looks pretty good. When it's right, you know, right?"

Mike nodded. Except when the person he'd always thought was right for him, but had then surrendered to God, dared to tease that she was right after all.

CHAPTER 18

"*Happy* birthday to you!"

Bree settled back on the lounge, smiling as Holly finished singing. "Thank you. I love the card, by the way. You're so clever." She picked up the handmade birthday card Holly had sent all the way from Australia.

"You know I love to do stuff like that, especially for the special people in my world. So, what's your plan for today?"

"It's been pretty fun so far. Mom cooked us a big breakfast, then we're spending the day on the beach, then we're going to a nice restaurant tonight. Should be really good."

"Any waves with that beach?"

"Not like what you're used to."

Holly sighed. "Training has started, and already I'm missing the beaches of home."

"Where's your first competition?"

"The Desert Classic in Utah, then there's a comp in Asia. Then if I qualify, I'll finally get to compete at the world cups."

"How exciting! You'll make it. You're awesome."

"Well, yeah, I'm awesome"—Holly rolled her eyes—"but

whether I make it remains to be seen. I've told you about Kate Jenkins before, haven't I?"

"The mean girl with an ex-Olympian as a father?"

"So that's a yes. Yeah, well, she's taking up so much training time, gets so much more help than I do. I don't want to sound like I'm a whinger, but I can't help but wonder if my other roommate, Jess, is right. If I didn't have to work as a supermarket check-out chick and could spend my time training, then I'd be so much better. But hey, wishing doesn't change anything, does it? Only hard work."

"And you're such a hard worker, Holl," Bree said loyally. "You'll make it."

"And you're such a good friend. Thanks for believing in me."

"Hey, what are besties for?"

Holly smiled. "Well, I'm glad you liked the charm."

"I always like your charms. And the Sydney Harbour Bridge? We'll have to visit someday."

"That'd be awesome."

"One day," Bree promised as her mom moved near.

"Careful, I'll hold you to it." Holly lifted a hand. "Oh, hi, Mrs. Karlsson. How are you?"

Bree shifted back as her mom and Holly briefly shared. It still amazed her how some of her high school friendships had faded while this bond with Holly had stayed strong. Maybe it was the intention behind it that kept them both invested. She glanced at the silver charm from Holly, sitting in its velvet box that she'd sent from Australia. She couldn't wait to add it to her bracelet.

"Good to see you too, Holly," Mom said. "I'll leave you to it."

Holly waved, her attention shifting back to Bree. "I like your mum."

Bree's mom smiled as she picked up some magazines. "I like you too, Holly," she called before exiting to the kitchen.

Bree joined in Holly's laughter. "She's pretty popular at the moment. Brent and Mike are doing full justice to her cooking."

Holly blinked. "Mike is there?"

"Didn't I mention it before?"

"No, Breanna Karlsson, you did not. Are you going to tell me *why* he is there?"

Bree hoped her shrug conveyed disinterest. "He's Brent's best friend. He needed a break."

"Wasn't he just having a break in the Philippines?"

"Yeah, from the way he was talking it wasn't exactly a break. Did you know he helped build a church? Like, literally helped build it? And I overheard him this morning telling Brent about this flood that happened, where he saw a family's house flood in the city. Apparently nobody would help them. All their neighbors ignored them, so Mike asked if he could help, and the flooded family were so happy, even if it meant all their neighbors were pointing fingers at him and laughing."

"He's a good guy, huh?"

"*So* good. He's just so sweet, and strong. Oh, you should've seen the pictures of him holding this little girl, like she was his own. The expression on his face! Anyway, it's been so great to have him here, and—" She broke off, conscious Holly was looking at her with a smile Bree couldn't quite decipher. "What?"

"He's *so* good, and so strong and muscly, and so kind—oh, and he's a Christian." Holly's eyebrows shot up. "Is he still playing hockey?"

"What? Why?"

"If I didn't know you better, I'd be thinking you had feelings for the man."

"Don't be ridiculous. We're friends, that's all."

"*Really* good friends I'm hearing."

"Look, just because his family has been friends with mine for forever doesn't mean anything will happen. That's as silly as thinking you'll end up with Brent because you get on with my parents."

"Please." Another eye-roll. "Spare me."

"Anyway, this is my year for not dating hockey players, and I've made it this far, so I won't stop now."

"Sticking to a silly resolution at the price of a potential relationship isn't wise, Bree."

"Look, I like him, but not like that," she said firmly, ignoring the twist in her heart.

"You keep telling yourself that, Bree. Anyway"—Holly yawned—"I'd better go. It's really late here, and I've got training at six tomorrow morning."

Bree winced. "Stop swearing at me. It's hard enough watching Brent go off with Mike and train while I sit here and feel guilty about how much I'm eating."

"You could join them," Holly suggested with a sly smile.

And embarrass herself in front of Mike? "No, thank you. Hey, thanks for calling."

"Hope you have a great birthday. Bye!"

The screen went dark, and Bree sank into the lounge.

"Who was that?" Brent said, walking into the room trailed by Mike.

"Holly."

"Who?"

She rolled her eyes. "My Aussie friend? The short-track skater?"

Brent shrugged.

His indifference sparked indignation, and she held out her wrist. "Holly came and stayed with us on exchange? You know, the one who sends me charms each year for Christmas and my birthday? Remember her?"

"Barely."

Mike glanced at the velvet box. "Did she send you something this year?"

She nodded. "She sent it to me back in Toronto, and I saved it until today to open it. Look, isn't it beautiful?" She held it up, forcing him to come closer to inspect it. "It's the Sydney Harbour Bridge."

"Huh. That's a place I wouldn't mind seeing someday," Brent said, giving the charm a cursory glance and nod.

"Me too," Bree said, fiddling to unclasp her bracelet so she could add the charm.

"Can I help?" Mike asked.

She nodded, surprised at his offer. Ever since his arrival he'd been so careful around her, never getting too close, barely glancing at her, as if he wanted to avoid her. To have him draw near made a nice change. But then his fingers brushed the delicate skin of her wrist in a goosebump-raising moment. Or were such tingles the result of inhaling his scent as he unhooked the clasp? Or maybe it was the awareness of his head so close to hers that all she'd need to do was lean in a little and know his kiss. Breath rushed in, expanding her chest.

"Thank you," she murmured, glancing up to meet his eyes. Oh, he had nice eyes. So clear and calm, like the lake sparkling outside the window, and fringed with thick sandy lashes.

He glanced away. "Happy to help," he muttered, stepping back, hands in his back pockets.

Brent looked between them. "Everything okay here?"

"I'm good." Bree stroked her charm bracelet with shaky fingers.

Mike shrugged. "I'm fine."

Brent's gaze narrowed. "You sure?"

"Yes, brother dear."

"Yeah." Mike's gaze touched hers then immediately veered away, crumpling her yearning for more.

Still, there was no way she was going to let her brother know the topsy-turvy feelings his friend stirred in her chest. "So, are we going to the beach, or did your pre-breakfast run drain all your energy?" She smiled sweetly at her twin. "I mean, I know not everyone here has been spending the off-season helping build churches and such things, so I quite understand if some people aren't feeling up to it."

"You're a brat, you know?" Brent said, tousling her hair.

"Hey, you're the brat. In fact, I'm pretty sure our big brother would say that you being my twin means you're equally bratty. Actually, because you're so tall, I think that means you're even more of a brat than me."

Mike chuckled. "She's got you there, man."

Brent rolled his eyes. "I thought you were supposed to be on my side."

"You shouldn't complain that you have a friend who's so honest," Bree said, hooking her arm through Mike's before glancing up at him. "Should he?"

His gaze met hers. He swallowed. "Uh, no."

She smiled, and his lips slowly lifted to echo hers.

"This has just been the best birthday ever." Bree's face glowed like the candle she'd blown out earlier as the chatter of restaurant patrons around them contributed to a happy atmosphere Mike simply didn't feel.

"It's a shame Dean couldn't get the time off work to join us, but it was good to talk to him earlier," Pam said.

Mike nodded, pretending interest as the conversation at the table shifted to the remaining days in Muskoka. Time with the Karlssons had proved equal parts pleasure and pain. It was good to spend time with Brent—training together, spending time doing activities that got him out of his head. But time with Bree remained torturous. He'd heard some of what she'd said to Holly—hadn't meant to eavesdrop, but Pam Karlsson had insisted on fixing him a coffee, and Bree's voice had carried through the open-plan rooms. His senses remained on high alert wherever she was concerned. The upshot? She didn't like him in the way he wanted. And even if she did, she was still holding to her "no dating hockey players" resolution.

He exhaled, picking at the remains of his cake—the special birthday cake Pam had ordered from a fancy bakery in Gravenhurst—and did his best to avoid Bree's gaze. It didn't help that she'd chosen the seat opposite him. And it definitely didn't help that she wore a summery dress that showed enough tanned skin to bring back memories of their time at the beach today, when she'd worn a white shirt over a green bikini that made him beg God for help as he wrestled with his thoughts and did his best to keep away. Which was kind of hard when she kept drawing close and smiling at him and including him in conversation.

"What do you think, Mike?"

He dropped his fork with a clatter. "Sorry, what?"

"What do you want to do tomorrow?" Rob Karlsson asked. "Seeing you're only here another day or so, you should probably pick how you'd like to spend tomorrow."

"Are you leaving so soon?" Bree's pink lips pushed into an adorable pout.

What would it be like to kiss—? *God, help me.* "I don't mind." Anything that didn't involve him seeing Bree in a swimsuit would help. Probably should've thought that through before agreeing to come to Muskoka's lakes in summer.

"Sounds like we'll be hitting the beach again."

He hitched up his lips. "Great."

He noticed a tweak in Bree's forehead as she studied him, and he ducked his head, not wanting to encounter her concerned gaze. He'd noticed it a few times lately and couldn't bear trying to explain his thoughts. Not when so many of them concerned her.

But it wasn't only thoughts of Bree that made him feel detached and dismayed. He still couldn't reconcile the easy luxury he was living with the hardship that he'd seen mere weeks before. But how to explain?

Later, they returned to the rented cottage and enjoyed the firepit for a time until it grew cool. They moved inside and played board games that often had him a few seconds too slow to make his moves or contribute an answer. How could he when he listened to Bree's laughter and wished she laughed with him? How could he laugh when he'd encountered misery firsthand? His smile felt like that of a creepy clown—garish, painted on. Never had he been so glad as when goodnights were called and he could escape the cheer he couldn't join.

Eventually, when the house had grown quiet, he stole back outside. He sat in one of the Muskoka chairs positioned by the firepit of glowing coals next to the small strip of sand that made up the cottage's beach. Sank down, gazed up at the stars.

The spray of heavenly lights seemed bigger out here, away from the light pollution of the city, and sitting, gazing, being still as he listened to the noises of the night, brought an ease to his inner restlessness.

God, I'm so messed up. I don't know what to think or feel anymore. Forgive me. Help me. I want to trust You, but this is hard.

He breathed in. Breathed out. Breathed in. Breathed out. God was still God, no matter where Mike was. God's plans were still good, no matter whether they met Mike's hopes. God was still faithful, as certain as the stars, as sure as the sun that rose each day. Mike could trust Him—he knew that—but it seemed a little easier in the deep velvet of night.

A stirring of pebbles drew his attention. Someone was coming. He hoped it wasn't— "Bree."

"Oh, hi! I, um, didn't mean to disturb you. I can, um, go back if you don't want company."

And reject the girl who'd only been kind to him? It might be torture, but, "You can stay."

Still she hesitated. "Are you sure? I don't want to interrupt you if you're in the midst of some God time or something."

He swallowed. How did she know that? "It's okay."

She moved to the other seat, zipped her sweatshirt up to her throat. "Only if you're sure." He caught a flash of her smile in the dim light from the house. "I…I sometimes get the impression you don't really want to hang out with me."

Guilt writhed. "I'm sorry. It's not you"—well, okay, it was, but it was also a bunch of other things, too—"it's just I'm trying to sort some things out."

"Like your contract?"

He shrugged. "That's sorted. I'm at Boston for another year, but hey, they might trade me away, so we'll have to see."

"So uncertain."

"Yeah." He paused, wondering if he should share some of the deeper stuff. He'd tried to with his mom and dad, but he sensed they'd been so relieved to have him back safely they hadn't really heard his heart. Brent, too, seemed more focused on Mike's contract than any deep, life-altering revelations Mike had had while overseas. But something about Bree's keen interest in his photos, in her persistent efforts to talk with him, suggested she might be a safe listening ear.

"Is it about the Philippines?"

How did she do that? Was he such an open book?

"Your time there sounded so amazing. I bet it wasn't all a picnic, though."

See? This was why he loved her, despite her not loving him. She got him on some deeper level, as if they spoke a heart language only the two of them understood.

"Yeah, it relates to that. And coming back. And trying to reconcile the poverty I've seen with this." He gestured to the luxurious cottage, the boats bobbing in the water.

She was quiet for a minute. "It seems so wrong that pastors there have to use chewing gum to block the holes in their roof."

"Exactly."

"Or that they don't have church buildings, and yet here we complain about the volume of the music in church, or whether our seats are comfortable enough."

He nodded. "We have it so easy, and they have it so hard. But honestly, there seems to be more faith there than what I've seen in a lot of churches here."

Her head bowed. "Maybe it's easier for us here to seek answers in things apart from God."

"Yeah."

"Is that what's been troubling you?"

She'd noticed? He can't have done a great job of hiding things. He hunched deeper into his jacket. "It's one thing. I came straight back into contract negotiations, and I slipped straight back into the usual pressures of 'Am I being paid enough?' and 'Should I seek more money elsewhere?'" He sighed. "I hate it. I hate that I'm so mercenary, especially when I've now seen how others live."

"Oh, Mike." She dragged her seat closer, placed her hand on his. "You're not mercenary at all."

"No?"

"No." Her voice held conviction. "If you were, you would've insisted on MPFG paying for your flights and accommodation, and you didn't, did you?"

"Of course not."

"If you were mercenary, you'd never offer to help others unless there was a reward for you." Somehow her fingers slipped between his, and she squeezed. "You're not mercenary, Mike. You're the most unselfish man I know."

His throat cinched. He blinked away moisture.

"I wondered if maybe you were finding it a challenge being here. It is a lovely cottage, but I totally see what you mean."

"I'm such a mess. I hate feeling so guilty, and that now seems to have colored my experience there, but at the same time, I feel like my guilt means I can barely enjoy it here."

She gently squeezed, her lack of words spilling more of his.

"The Philippines was so amazing, Bree. Amazing, heartbreaking, overwhelming."

"It sounds it."

The lake gently lapped. Somewhere a bird called. Breeze hushed through tall pines. The world around them: beautiful, mysterious, awe-inspiring.

He closed his eyes, thankful for the darkness that meant he could escape her too-observant scrutiny. Thankful that she listened and seemed to understand his pain. Even describing his conflicted feelings as pain felt so self-indulgent. But it was like his time away had shown him life from a new perspective—a kaleidoscope of fragments of his life, who he thought he was—and nothing fit the pattern of what he'd always known.

"I wonder if God allows our hearts to be broken so we can empathize more deeply with the hurting," Bree mused.

"You mean God is into breakup projects too?" he tried to joke.

"Maybe." Her smile flashed in the moonlight. "Or maybe it's breaking down our preconceived ideas. I…I know I can be pretty judgy at times, but then God shows me something good and sweet about that person. I think we all have times when we feel a little broken." Bree released his hand, drew her knees up, wrapped her arms around her knees. "But surely it's how our hearts are put back together that's important. And you won't be much use to MPFG if you're resentful of your circumstances here."

Her words held an echo of what John had said before. "John calls it reverse culture shock."

"So it's a thing. Well, if that's the case, then you can let yourself go through this process and know it's fairly normal. You're not wrong to feel confused, and you're not wrong to want to be paid fairly. Just think how many more lives you can help if you earn more money."

"I have thought that," he admitted.

"So don't feel guilty. God, who is the God of those in the Philippines, is also the God of us here. I know you spend your money and time wisely, sowing into God's kingdom. It's not like you're off wasting money having Botox because you're afraid to look old when you're seventy."

A chuckle broke the intensity. "Who does that?"

"Oh, some of the grandmothers of the kids I work with seem to want to look younger than me." She waved a hand. "Be thankful there weren't too many of them at your auction."

He shuddered, his spirits dipping once more in remembrance of the awkwardness of that whole sorry episode.

Maybe she felt it too, because she hurried on. "But really, you should know God is using you to help others, and that's something to remember when you feel you have too much."

Her words continued to resonate deep within his soul. She was such an encourager.

"Thanks, Bree."

"I hope you know how proud we are of you."

We are, or she was?

"I loved seeing your pictures before," she said. "It really helped to get some idea of what life was like and what you did."

"I can't even begin to share all of what happened while I was there."

"Tell me a story you haven't shared with others then."

He glanced at her. Her face was turned to him, her eyes big and expressive and focused on him. Should he? Why not? But would exchanging something so deeply personal bond them closer in a tie he would be wiser to forgo?

"Please?"

How could he deny her? "Okay." He shifted in his seat so he

faced her more. "This happened when we were coming back from Rodel's church in the mountains."

"Rodel was the pastor with the gorgeous little girl you held?"

She remembered? "Yeah."

"Go on."

"So, we stopped at this river. There'd been a storm before, and the water was moving really quickly. We needed a break—"

"Like when you stopped by the cornfield?"

The cornfield?

"I heard you telling Brent about that."

Oh, the cornfield. Uneasiness crossed his chest. What else had she heard him say from that conversation? "Um, anyway, we were waiting for someone, skimming rocks and so on, when John's wedding ring flew off into the water."

"Oh no!"

"Exactly. Every time we moved, the pebbles shifted underneath, and there were three or four of us there looking. We must've been searching for the ring for a good twenty minutes when I got frustrated. We'd just come from this place where people had been healed of blindness, and here we were searching for a ring. So I prayed and said, 'God, help us find John's ring,' then put my hand down in the water and straightaway found the ring."

Bree gasped. "How awesome."

"Right? I felt like a miracle had taken place. We'd searched and searched to no avail, then I prayed, and boom. God answered."

"That's so amazing, Mike."

"God is so amazing," he said softly.

Her fingers slipped through his again and tightened, and he knew the desire to ask her about her comments to Holly earlier today. Maybe God could do another miracle.

But she squeezed his hand and released it. "I'd better go. It's getting late."

"Hey, thanks for talking. And listening."

"I hope you feel a little better now."

"I do."

"Good." She smiled. "Then that makes my birthday complete."

He'd nearly forgotten it was her birthday. "I should've got you something other than flowers."

"Why? I was so pleased to get your flowers. I'm rarely given flowers, but I love them, and daisies are such happy flowers, aren't they? I did wonder if it was some oblique reference to my PJs, but I figured you were too much of a gentleman to say anything about that—"

He smiled. He wasn't. They had been.

"—and anyway, I was glad to get flowers and not that hat you brought back for Brent. I mean, I'm sure it will look fine on him, but it's not exactly my style if you know what I mean."

His lips twitched. "I know what you mean."

"Anyway, all that to say thank you. It was the perfect gift. And you can give me flowers anytime you like." She gave an embarrassed-sounding chuckle. "On that note, I'll let you enjoy the serenity." Her smile tugged at his heart. "Good night, Mike."

It was now. "G'night, Bree. And thanks."

And Mike settled in to watch the distant lights reflecting on the water and thanked God for Breanna Karlsson and her gift of joy.

$\mathcal{A}$nother day of swimming had left Bree's skin a little wrinkled, so she took the chance to read on the chair where she and Mike had shared their conversation last night. She smiled, thinking back to how his spirits seemed to have lifted. It was nice to feel like she'd encouraged him a little at least.

She turned the page of the Georgette Heyer book. The Regency novel was one Granny Violet had given her for her birthday before they'd come north and was so witty she was constantly explaining herself to Brent when he asked her why she was chuckling. He didn't get the humor, but that was no great surprise.

"Hey."

"Oh, hi." She grinned at Mike. It was so nice to be back to this feeling of ease between them. He seemed happier today, more at peace. "How did the fishing go?"

"Don't tell your brother, but I don't think he's cut out for fishing. He has the patience of a gnat."

She chuckled. "You've noticed?"

"How can I not? Especially when I have the patience of a saint."

"Now, that I *have* noticed."

"Discerning person that you are."

"You know it." Gosh, he had a nice smile, and it was so good to have seen it more often today. "Hey, I was thinking, now that you're back in Boston for another year—"

"Making the most of it for as long as they want me."

"You don't think it'll be forever?"

He shrugged, took the seat next to hers. "Not like Brent in Detroit. He's a poster-boy for the team. I'm more a stop-gap."

"You shouldn't say such things about yourself," she protested. "People want you." She paused, her comment sounding uneasily like something more. "So, um, anyway, I was wondering, can I still come to Boston?"

"Well, yeah. It's a free country. You're not on any FBI watch list or anything, are you?"

"No, I meant come and see you. In Boston." At his startled look, she hurried on. "It would just be nice to visit. I haven't been there, and I'd like to see it with a friend while he's still there."

"A friend, huh?" He glanced away. His lips flattened. "Sure."

Her heart panged. It didn't seem she'd expressed things well.

A crunch of gravel from behind drew her attention. "Hey, Brent."

"What are you two talking about?"

She slid a look at Mike, swallowed a smile. "Mike was just telling me about what we'll do when I go see Boston."

"I was?" said Mike.

"You should be," she said slyly.

"You're going to Boston?" Brent asked, eyebrows shooting high.

"You could come too," she said, then instantly wished she hadn't.

"Depends on when it is. I might be busy with my house."

"Your offer got accepted?"

"Just found out."

"How exciting!" She leapt up and hugged him. "Although, I still can't believe you bought a house without showing any of us."

"Yeah, well, I didn't want anyone else getting it ahead of me."

"So, details please."

He shared about the house and yard's features, the commute time to the arena, the renovations to be done. "I hope to get a start on those before the season begins. Rip out the ugly kitchen, get something a little more modern installed."

"You're not exactly into patience, are you?" Bree said with a sideways glance at Mike. He smiled.

"Like you can talk," Brent retorted. "How many times have you started new year's resolutions only to fail?"

What? Offense heated her chest. "I don't see what that has to do with anything."

"No?" He grinned. "How about the 'no eating of carbs' or the 'don't eat chocolate' promises you've made only to fail within a week or two?"

"I really don't see what relevance that has—"

"Is it lack of patience or lack of self-control?"

"Brent!" Tears pricked her eyes. He might be teasing, but his words still stung. She *would* keep this resolution if it killed her.

"Dude." Mike straightened, eyeing Brent with a frown. "Stop picking on Bree."

Thank you, Mike.

"What? You two have a thing going on?" Brent's glance shot between them, his brow lowering. "Don't you remember what I said? Bree can't keep any of her resolutions. Her latest resolution was to not date any hockey player this year. Have you forgotten?"

He'd told Mike she couldn't keep any of her resolutions?

How embarrassing. She wanted to crawl into a ball and disappear.

"It's a good thing we're just friends, then, isn't it?" Mike said. His gaze found hers again. "We *are* friends, aren't we?"

"You and I are friends. Brent and I are only siblings right now."

Mike chuckled, and her heart's tension lifted a smidge. God bless him for trying to ease the friction.

"Brent, you can consider yourself uninvited," she said to him. "I think I'd prefer to see Boston without you."

"So you'll just go there by yourself? And see him?" He jerked a thumb at Mike. "Your non-boyfriend?"

"Why not? As you say, he's not my boyfriend, so I don't see what the problem is. This isn't Jane Austen's time, Brent. I don't exactly need a chaperone."

"But—"

"But nothing. I'll stay in a hotel and Mike will stay in his apartment, and you can stay and do the renovations of your awesome new house in Detroit, and it'll all be good. At least I'll go see Boston with someone who cares about others and is never mean."

"Wait, I didn't mean—"

"No. You've always been a little self-focused. Maybe you should realize how you come across to others." She pushed to her feet. Ignored Brent. Smiled at Mike. "Please let me know what weekend works best for you. I'm only working four days a week now, and I suspect Moira will be very obliging if I say I need an extra day or two off. I can't wait to see Boston."

"Uh, sure." Mike slid a glance at Brent, who had crossed his arms and now studied Mike and Bree with a scowl. His lips twitched. "And if your big brother decides he wants to come too, well, I'm prepared to overlook his rudeness if you are."

"Seeing as he's my big brother by only fifteen minutes, I feel no obligation to overlook his rudeness anytime soon."

Mike's smile peeked out as Brent snorted.

"Well, you must excuse me, gentlemen. Or gentleman," she said, smiling at Mike. "I have a date."

"With who?" Brent asked.

"With *The Quiet Gentleman*," she said, holding up her book. "My preferred kind of gentleman." Her eyes found Mike's again, her gaze lingering before another snort from her brother reminded her she needed to go. Before she said anything else she'd regret to her brother. Or before she exposed anything more of her heart.

EVEN IF BREE WAS—BY some miracle—to one day admit she liked him, Mike knew he'd never admit that to Brent. The sight of Bree's glistening eyes and trembling lip fired new protectiveness and a determination to prove Brent wrong, even if it came at personal cost. Which it wouldn't, he told himself firmly. She'd made herself very clear the other day, even if she seemed to send mixed messages at times—holding his gaze, his hand, for longer than necessary, if still not as long as he'd like.

"What was that?" he asked Brent.

"What was what?"

"One minute you're all excited about your house, and Bree, your sister who loves you, is excited for you. The next you're drilling her on stuff that's really unkind."

"I was just teasing."

"Didn't sound like it. And she sure didn't think it did. You might need to fix things up with her."

"You seem to take a big interest in her."

Mike willed his features to impassivity. "I've known you both for years. And I'm not used to you treating her like that. Anyway, don't try to turn your rudeness to Bree onto me. What was it about?"

Brent shrugged. "Sometimes I worry about her."

"You have a funny way of showing it."

"Look, she doesn't have the same goals as you or I do. She's kind of just drifting when she could do so much more."

"I beg your pardon?"

"You and I have always had the NHL to focus on, and now you've got this charity you're involved in. What's Bree got? Nothing."

"She's got a great job doing what she loves, that's what she's got."

"But she's working for someone else and almost wore herself out doing so. I just don't want her to look back on life and think she wasted it."

"Wow." Mike narrowed his eyes. "Do you hear yourself?"

"What?"

"Who made you the person who determines whether a life is wasted? It makes you sound like you think you're God."

"I'm not saying I'm God. I just want the best for her."

"But surely Bree is the best judge of what's best for her." He heard an uneasy echo of his words to Bree from months ago. Guilt softened his tone, even as his heart rumbled with protectiveness for her. "I don't think a person's value can be measured by the standards we so often think are important. It's not about how much money or how big a house we have or how many degrees or friends we have. Life isn't a popularity contest."

"I know that."

"Do you? Maybe it's time you trust Bree and her future to God and not make her feel you dislike her."

"I didn't do that."

Mike raised an eyebrow.

Brent crossed his arms. "Why do you keep defending her, anyway?"

And they were back to this. He bit back a sigh. "Bree loves

you. Maybe you should show her that you love her too." He pushed to his feet. "I need to go."

"Are you leaving because of this?"

"I'm leaving because I said I was going today. I've got stuff to do in Toronto, and then I'm driving back to Boston." He glanced at his watch. "I better go thank your mom and get my stuff."

He made his way back inside the house only to have Pam beckon him to the living room. "Mike, I couldn't help but overhear some of what was said earlier."

Uh oh.

"I just wanted you to know how much Rob and I appreciate you standing up for Bree like that," she continued in a quiet voice. "Brent has a tendency to be a little overbearing at times, so it's good when a friend can pull him into line."

"I don't know that I did much."

"Well, if it makes him think about how he treats her, then that's good."

"She didn't hear, did she?"

"I don't think so. But even if she did, she'll know she has a loyal friend in you."

"That's me. A loyal friend." His lips twisted with wryness.

She studied him a moment, then tilted her head. "May I offer you a piece of advice?"

Uh oh. He didn't think he'd want to hear this, but, "Sure."

"Be patient with her. I suspect it won't be long until she recognizes her heart."

Heat traveled up his neck. "I don't think I dare ask what you mean."

"And I thought a man as brave as you would never shy from learning the truth." She chuckled. "And that truth will be something you and Rob and I will be very glad to see."

Wait—was she saying what he thought she was?

"One day," she added with a small smile. "Like in the new year."

He swallowed. She knew? About his feelings and Bree's resolution?

"Bree needs a chance to prove herself," she said with a nod.

"And be seen by Brent to keep her resolution," he said slowly.

"You are a wise man, aren't you?"

He shrugged, but her words threaded great pleasure with a tiny piece of hope through his heart. To have Bree's parents' blessing was something he'd never looked for today. Now to learn if he could ever help Bree see him as something more than a good friend.

MIKE THOUGHT and prayed about it on the drive back to Toronto. He thought and prayed about it while at his folks'. He thought and prayed about it on the eight-hour drive to Boston as he passed through Niagara Falls and Albany and along I-90 through Massachusetts. He knew a measure of peace about Bree's proposed visit to Boston. Knew that this might be a time when they could connect in a more meaningful way than having her brother on guard might allow. Not that there'd be any connecting on a level he'd be ashamed of. But enough to hopefully show her she could trust him as more than a friend.

So, in between bouts of training and organizing things with MPFG, he texted her ideas about what to do in Boston. Enjoyed her swift replies and smiley faces. Enjoyed replying with his own. His time in August was pretty free—apart from working with his trainer he had no real commitments until preseason training camp mid-September.

So he asked her about her availability, learned she'd mentioned the visit to her grandmother, who had instantly expressed a desire to go too, and Bree—kind-hearted creature that she was—wanted to know if that was okay with him.

I DON'T WANT TO BE A NUISANCE, BUT GRANNY V IS OLD AND

WANTS TO VISIT CONCORD BEFORE SHE DIES, SO I WONDERED IF THIS MIGHT BE OKAY WITH YOU. IF NOT THEN I'LL ARRANGE IT FOR ANOTHER TIME. I DON'T WANT TO IMPOSE—TOO MUCH!

Bree coming to Boston and spending time with him by herself was one thing. Having her grandmother there only further reiterated Bree's lack of interest in him. Which was okay, he reminded himself. Her mom certainly seemed to think there was something to work with there.

NO PROBLEM. BE GREAT TO SEE HER TOO. WE CAN MODIFY STUFF SO SHE'S NOT TOO TIRED.

A few seconds later came her reply: YOU'RE THE BEST! THANK YOU.

CHAPTER 20

The flight to Boston wasn't long, but being responsible for an elderly lady had a way of making it feel longer than one hundred minutes. Still, Bree thought, looking eagerly around outside the airport, they were here now, and any minute now she'd see—

Her heart double-thumped. "Mike!"

He straightened from his slouch and grinned, lifting a hand, and she raced to him, suitcases banging against her legs. "Hi!" She wrapped him in a hug, and after a second's freeze, he returned her embrace. She buried her face in his neck, taking the moment to inhale his scent, to pretend this was real. Oh, his arms around her felt so good, so reassuring, so much better than the last time they'd hugged on that too-awkward goodbye in Muskoka. If only she could hug Mike forever.

"Ahem."

His arms fell. Bree eased back. Heat rose in her face. Okay, so this wasn't exactly the way she'd intended to re-introduce Mike and her grandmother.

"Granny Violet, you remember Mike Vaughan, don't you?"

Her grandmother smiled, and when Mike held out a hand

and said hello, she pulled him down. "No, I want a hug like my granddaughter got."

He chuckled, and with a "Yes, ma'am," hugged her until she squeaked and swatted his arms to release her.

Granny V exhaled, fanning herself. "Well, it's certainly been a while since I've had a hug from such a strapping young man."

"Brent doesn't count?" Bree asked.

"Relatives never do."

Bree laughed and hooked her arm through her grandmother's. "I'm sure he'd love to hear that." Relations with her brother had improved after his apology and a quick visit to see his new house near Detroit. But she was glad his house renovations meant he'd be busy for a while longer and couldn't come here now.

"I have my car nearby. I can take your bags and then drive to meet you out the front, or we can walk there together."

"What do you feel like doing, Gran? Walk to the car or be collected?"

"Oh, I'm quite happy to wait here. You go with Michael, dear. I'll wait just there." She pointed to a seat.

"I'll wait with you," Bree said. "I'm not taking no for an answer."

"But darling," her grandmother said when Mike had taken the bags and moved beyond earshot, "I don't want to get in the way of you spending time with your young man."

"He's not my young man, Gran."

"No, that's obvious from the way you hugged him and the way he can't stop looking at you."

"He looks at me?"

"All the time," Granny V confirmed. "Now, it's not my intention to be a third-wheel, so you let me know when you want some time alone with him."

"Gran."

"Yes?" Her grandmother turned big, overly innocent-looking blue eyes to her. "What is it, dear?"

"We're here to see Boston, that's all. Not to see if anything else will happen."

Her grandmother sighed. "Well, I have a feeling I'm going to need some quiet time in the hotel room. A woman of my age, you know."

Bree laughed. "You didn't come all this way to sit in a hotel room, Gran."

"And pretend as you might, you didn't come all this way just to see Boston, did you?"

Bree looked away, refusing to acknowledge the truth in her grandmother's eyes. Okay, so what if she liked Mike? She wasn't going to do anything about it. She might've forgiven Brent, but it didn't mean his words hadn't stuck. And it was awfully hard to forget that some people seemed to view her as a kind of flake.

"Oh, look, here he is." Bree stood and offered Granny V her arm as Mike pulled up beside them, jumped out, and opened the back door. "Your chariot awaits, Gran. Now, front seat or back?"

"Back, of course. I'll let the handsome chauffeur lead us on." She pushed away Bree's attempt to follow. "No, you need to sit in front. Michael needs someone to talk to."

"You're incorrigible," Bree whispered.

"That is true," her grandmother said with a regal nod.

Bree meekly obeyed, surprised when Mike moved to open her door. "Um, thanks."

"You're welcome."

His gaze caressed her face for a moment, his smile flickering, then he closed her door and moved back to the driver's position, allowing her a moment to exhale.

He seemed so much happier than the last time they'd met, the tension gone, a relaxed ease in his smile and manner that made her heart skip a little faster. The August air seemed to hold anticipation, a bubbling expectancy that this time together might lead to something in her future rather than just visiting places connected to the past. She hoped so, anyway.

"So, you're staying near Seaport, right?"

"Yes." The hotel she'd booked had water views and a couple of comfortable restaurants she thought her grandmother might like.

He steered through traffic smoothly, and Bree found herself once again admiring his calm, the way he never seemed to let anything faze him. "Thanks for doing this," she said.

"No problem." He shot her a quick grin. "Nothing I'd rather be doing."

Another heart palpitation. But her iron levels were good. She'd received the results of her latest blood test just a few days before. No, this heart condition was caused by something else entirely.

"You are such a dear to look after us like this," Granny V said from behind. "It's such a comfort to know we'll have someone who is almost a local showing us around."

"I've been here a few years now, but I suspect it takes a life-time before someone's considered a local."

"Oh, I understand. Some people can be very parochial when it comes to newcomers."

Bree ducked to glimpse the skyline, then they drove down into a tunnel.

"We're going under the harbor now."

"Ooh, the harbor where they dumped the tea?" her grand-mother asked.

"I believe your hotel is near the museum and tall ships," Mike offered.

"I cannot understand a waste of good tea," Granny V continued.

"I suppose they had a point," Bree said. "No taxation without representation and all that."

"Be that as it may, it's still my intention to find a place where they do a proper afternoon tea while we're here. Michael, I hope you're not averse to a nice pot of tea."

He slid Bree a look that said he wasn't exactly enamored by the idea but was amused as well. "I don't mind."

"Oh, good. I know Bree had a schedule arranged, didn't you? What day did you plan for our Boston tea party, dear?"

"Friday afternoon, I think?"

"I can't wait. Nothing says fancy like having cucumber sandwiches with the crusts cut off, don't you agree, Michael dear?"

He coughed, and Bree swallowed a giggle. Judging from his fleeting look of dismay, he could think of nothing worse. "It's okay," she said, patting his arm. "We can let Granny V eat your share of cucumber sandwiches."

"Promise?"

"Absolutely."

He shot her a smile and steered onto the offramp. From here they could see the modern skyscrapers interspersed with older heritage buildings.

"Where's your apartment?"

"It's nearer TD Garden. I thought I'd take you both there for dinner, if that's okay."

"Way okay." Bree grinned. Finally, to see a glimpse of his life, to learn more of this man.

"I should've checked. Did you want to go straight to your hotel or have a city highlights tour now?"

"Oh, I'd love the chance to freshen up," her grandmother admitted.

Mike shot Bree a look, and she nodded. "Hotel it is, then."

Within twenty minutes they had gained their room and the promise from Mike to collect them in two hours. "You can go now if you like, Bree," Gran said. "I know you're probably not nearly as tired as me and would like to start exploring with this handsome young man."

Bree refused to look at him. "I'm okay."

"You sure?" he said. "I really don't mind. I've cleared my afternoon."

Put like that, it sounded uncharitable to ignore him. Not when he'd given up his time already. She straightened her shoulders, turned to her grandmother. "Are you sure you don't mind?"

"Oh, my dear." Her grandmother placed a hand over her mouth and delicately yawned. "I am quite done in. In fact, I think I'll have a little rest. I'm not used to all this travel."

"We'll be back in a couple of hours," Bree promised, collecting her handbag.

"Oh no. Best make it three or four. I'm sure I won't be awake until then."

Bree exchanged amused glances with Mike before shifting her attention back to her grandmother. "Three hours then."

"Better make it four. I'm sure I'll be ready for dinner by then."

"You don't need anything now?"

"I had a little bite to eat at Toronto, and I'm sure this place does room service if I get peckish, yes?"

"I'm sure they do." Bree shifted the hotel phone and TV remote control nearer Gran.

"Well, how about you go now, then come and get me around five. If that works for you and your dinner plans, Michael."

"I thought we'd eat at six so it's not too long a day, but we can make it later if you like," he offered.

"Oh, you're such a thoughtful man. Isn't he a thoughtful man, Breanna?"

"Very thoughtful," Bree murmured, not trusting herself to say anything more or to look at him. Could Granny V be any more obvious?

"I shall be most comfortable here." Her grandmother chose the bed closest to the window. "Now, off you two go and have fun."

"Bye, Gran," Bree said, kissing her cheek.

"See you in a little while," Mike said with a smile.

They closed the door, glanced at each other, and chuckled. "Sorry," Bree said.

"I think she's pretty cute," Mike said as they headed to the elevator. "My grandparents would never think to leave their little town, let alone go off to have adventures with their awesome granddaughter."

"Awesome, huh?" she said, looking up at him.

"Very awesome," he said, eyes intent on her.

She drew in a shaky breath, relieved when the doors opened and the moment of intensity passed. "So, um, what did you want to do?"

He pressed the button for the ground floor. "You had nothing on your schedule?"

"Are you mocking my scheduling ability?" She placed a hand on her hip.

"Me, mock? Not at all. I think it's very impressive."

"Why does that sound a tad condescending?"

"I have no idea," he said meekly.

She swatted his arm, and he laughed.

The doors opened, and they moved to where he'd parked his car. He opened the passenger door for her. "So, did you have a plan for today?"

"I didn't. I knew you were talking about dinner, so I didn't want to interrupt your plans for that. What are those plans, by the way?"

"It's a surprise."

"Will it matter if it's put on hold for a bit?"

"It'll be fine," he assured her. He leaned against his vehicle. "So, thanks to your grandmother, we have four hours to kill. Do you want to look at anything or walk around here, get something to eat?"

"A walk around here sounds nice. And maybe something to eat."

He glanced at her. Nodded. "Then I know the perfect place."

~

WALKING around Seaport on a gorgeous summer afternoon was no great hardship. Walking around Seaport on a gorgeous afternoon with a beautiful woman by his side—no hardship at all.

Something seemed to have shifted between them, shown in the way Bree's gaze grazed his then danced away, shown in the way her earlier exuberance seemed to have found restraint. Perhaps her grandmother's cheeky comments had stirred something. Mike could only hope.

They walked up along Seaport Boulevard, enjoying the sunshine, the buzz of a Wednesday afternoon where everyone seemed to have taken time to relax. Maybe he should do this more often.

"What a glorious day," Bree said, neck tilting to look at the sky. Man, even her throat was pretty.

"So, there's a bunch of fish markets and things nearby—"

"Hence the name Seaport," she interrupted with a playful smile.

"Hence the name Seaport," he agreed. "We can stop at a fish place and get something to eat, if you like."

"Oh, that'd be great. I'm getting hungry." As if to confirm this, her stomach gave a savage growl.

"Best we feed that dragon, huh?"

"If you want things to go well for you, yes."

He smiled, heart lifting at her easy banter. She was so easy to be with, her smiles and laughter adding as much sunshine to his day as that huge star in the sky above them.

They crossed the bridge dotted with old-style lamp-stands,

and she snapped photos of the view looking south toward the Tea Party museum with its tall ships.

She exhaled on a note of happiness. "You couldn't have picked a better day if you'd tried, could you?"

"I ordered it especially for you."

She laughed. "Ooh, look!" She pointed to a small trailer with the name James Hook & Co. "Can we go there?"

"Uh, sure." It wasn't the restaurant he'd imagined taking her to, but he'd heard good things.

Inside the shack were aquariums of live fish, crabs, and lobsters. They ordered lobster rolls and cups of clam chowder and sat outside at the square tables under fixed umbrellas, sipping water as they waited for their number to be called. The food was delicious, the rolls packed with meat, the buns buttery soft, the clam chowder as good as Bree's ecstatic sighs implied.

"This is so delicious."

"It's pretty good," he agreed.

She swallowed another mouthful. "I can see why you might want to stay here. Great views, great food, lots of history and culture."

"It's pretty nice, especially in summer."

She wiped her mouth with a napkin. "But if you get traded, where would you want to go?"

"Canadian cities, or those close to the border."

"Original six?"

"Doesn't matter. It'd be nice, but hey, I've had the chance to play here, and it's been awesome."

"So you want to be close to home?" She sipped her water.

"I think if I get traded I'd like to make my home there for a while, to settle down a bit. And it would be nice and a whole lot easier to not have to deal with lots of travel or border issues each time I want to see those I care about."

She met his gaze with widening eyes, then glanced away, a blush on her cheeks. Yeah, she was reading this right.

"Vancouver would be nice," she said eventually. "I've visited Dean a few times and always thought that a nice place to live."

Was she hinting?

"Anything with water like this"—she gestured to the gleaming harbor—"would be good."

"Guess that rules out Calgary then."

She eyed him. Took another bite of her roll. "This is so good."

He nodded, swallowing his disappointment at her change of subject. He'd hoped she'd say something like "Anywhere would be good with you," but the wacky feelings of today must be misfiring his brain.

"You know," she said, looking out at the water, "I wonder if you appreciate this sort of thing more when you only see it rarely. It's like people who live somewhere but never visit half the local attractions tourists do." She sipped her water, gaze still fixed on the harbor. "I think you could easily live in Calgary and enjoy places like this each summer." She faced him. Smiled. "Don't you?"

He almost choked on his roll. "Uh, sure."

"And really, it doesn't matter where you live, as long as you work somewhere where you feel valued and"—her gaze shifted away again—"you have loved ones near."

"Yeah." He waited, watching her until her gaze found his again. In that moment, something seemed to pass between them, something real, deep, true. "Without someone to love, what's the point?"

She nodded slowly. "Whether that be family or friends or… someone special."

"Someone special," he echoed, studying her, until her lips lifted and she glanced away.

"Whew." She reached for her bag and retrieved sunglasses, then plonked them firmly on her nose. "It's getting rather warm, isn't it?"

"Yeah." And it had nothing to do with it being summer.

"Are you almost finished?" She gestured to his red-and-white-checked box.

He ate the last of his roll. "You keen to go exploring?"

"Five days, Mike. I've only got five days. I need to make the most of it."

He disposed of their trash, and they moved along the Harborwalk, which took them nearer the tall ships. "Granny V really wants to do some of the historical things, such as see Paul Revere's house and the historical trails and so on. I think we're scheduled to see this museum tomorrow, so I'd better not do it now."

"Anything in particular you want to see?"

"Well, call me quirky, but there's really only one place I want to see. Apart from TD Garden, I'd really like to see this place where they have a stained glass map of the world."

"Really?"

She shrugged. "Told you it was quirky."

"I'm happy to do quirky with you." He glanced at her hand, wondered if she'd object to his holding hers. Probably best to let her take the lead on that. "So, tell me more about this famous schedule."

"Look, when you only have a limited time, you need to make the most of it, which means plenty of research. So I've researched."

They found a place that sold gelato and sat outside, enjoying the tangy sweetness as she explained about the sightseeing plans. They ate and she shared, he listened and smiled, and they laughed until it was time to go collect her grandmother.

"This has been fun," he said.

"I know, right? Aren't you glad you invited me to visit you?"

He laughed. He didn't care who'd invited who. "Really glad."

She grinned, and he smiled.

That night he took them to his apartment. He'd wondered

about the wisdom of cooking for them but suspected Bree would enjoy the views and hoped she'd like this insight into his world.

They caught the elevator only to have it pause at foyer level, where the Grubers entered.

"Oh, what a sweet dog," Bree's grandma said, giving it a pat.

The Pekingese growled. Beatrice apologized. "I'm sorry. We've been at the vet's, and poor Pumpkin here isn't feeling herself."

At her raised-eyebrow enquiry, Mike caved and introduced everyone.

"Oh, so you're the mystery lady," Beatrice said to Bree, tossing Mike a wicked grin. "Well, it's lovely to finally meet you."

His skin prickled. Could the elevator go any slower?

"Nice to meet you too," Bree said.

He felt her glance at him. Tried to act cool.

"Perhaps we could get together for a coffee and exchange stories," Beatrice said, still with that evil glint in her eye.

"I really don't think—" he began.

"What a marvelous idea," Bree said with her own wicked glint. "I'm most curious to hear all about how mysterious I'm supposed to be. You don't mind, do you, Mike?" she asked, batting her eyelashes playfully.

"You're the ones with the busy schedule. But hey, it's your visit, so I'm happy if you're happy."

"We're hoping to take in a high tea while we're here," Violet said. "Perhaps you could join us."

"That sounds delightful."

Mike offered a strained smile. Fortunately, the doors opened, and he waited for the others to exit before farewelling the Grubers and taking Bree and Violet down the hall to his place.

"It's just down here." And if he could get there before—

The door two up from him opened. "Hi, Mike."

"Um, hi." He wished he could recall her name.

"I'm Rachel," she said, giving Bree the once-over. "Mike's neighbor."

"This is Bree. And her grandmother," he hastened to say. "We're having dinner, so you'll have to excuse us."

"Dinner, huh? Well." Her brow puckered as she glanced between him and Bree. "I thought you were an illusion."

"Bye," he said, gesturing his guests forward.

"Nice to meet you," Bree offered, glancing up at him with her own raised eyebrows as he opened the door and she and Violet passed into his apartment.

Mike exhaled and closed the door. Leaned against it as Bree moved to the window.

"No wonder you like it here. Look at this view, Gran. Isn't it great?"

Violet nodded. "Very pretty. Especially at this time of day with the lights coming on like that."

"It's only a few minutes from the stadium, and I can walk to practice if I need to. Not that I do very often. There are a lot of fervent fans here."

"And is your neighbor one of them?" Violet asked.

"I don't know."

"She seems a fan of you, anyway."

He shook his head at her and looked at Bree. She was wandering about his space, moving to the kitchen. Studying the pictures on the fridge. "Are these some of your children?"

"Your children?" Violet said, with raised inflection, peering at him like he was a naughty child.

Bree laughed. "His sponsor children. Wow, you have so many." She glanced up at him. "Such a good man."

Mike flushed. "Um, are you hungry? I have some cheese and crackers here." He hid his embarrassment by fixing a plate of different cheeses, crackers, and grapes, placing it on the coffee table in front of where Violet had settled. "Can I get either of you a drink?"

"Water is fine," Bree said.

"I'd like a gin and tonic if one is going."

"Grandma!"

Mike laughed, catching the twinkle in the older lady's eye. "Sorry, Violet. I'm all out of G and Ts. But I could get you a lime and soda."

"That will do nicely, thank you."

He chuckled. Fixed their drinks. Made dinner: steak, salad with loads of dark green vegetables, and a potato salad he'd made yesterday that he reheated in the oven as he cooked the steak.

Bree set the table, and he marveled at how well they worked together, the sense of harmony she brought to his space. He soon served their meals, thanked God for the food and their company, and they tucked in.

"Oh, this steak is so delicious," Bree said, her fork suspended in the air. "Cooked to perfection."

"I wanted to make sure you got some iron into you."

"So considerate," Violet said, her look one of approval.

"You're eating well?" he asked Bree. "Eating lots of iron?"

"I'm certainly going to be doing so tonight," she said, gesturing to the spinach.

"Knowing how many activities you have planned, I don't want you collapsing from exhaustion," he said, refilling their glasses.

"I don't think I'll collapse, unless it's from eating all this deliciousness."

"Well, I hope you've left room for dessert." He rose, collecting plates.

"There's dessert, too?" Bree helped clear the table. "I didn't think you athletes believed in such a thing."

"I normally don't, but I know you do and suspected Violet here might have a sweet tooth."

"Clever man," Violet said, nodding approvingly.

"So, what's for dessert?" Bree asked, as she retrieved bowls and spoons like she'd lived here all her life.

"I wanted to give you a sample of one of our specialties, so it's a Boston Cream Pie, made right here in Boston." He presented the dessert with a flourish.

"What? You bake as well?"

"'Fraid not. This is one I bought from the cousin of the guy who runs my favorite café. She bakes the cakes Bob sells there."

A few minutes later they were tucking into the chocolate ganache-covered vanilla cake with custard filling.

"So good," Bree said, playing with the half-melted remnants of her ice-cream. "I don't think I can eat another bite."

"I couldn't have you going home hungry."

"I might go home obese, though."

"You look great to me." His eyes held hers until she looked down.

Violet glanced at him, her smile widening. "Oh, you are a charmer, aren't you?"

"I try," he said meekly, to her and Bree's laughter.

Happiness soared within. He suspected these next few days would be a lot of fun.

CHAPTER 21

The next days passed in a blur of historic sites such as Old North Church, Paul Revere House, Faneuil Hall, and other places on the Freedom Trail. They ate cannoli from Mike's Pastry, visited the stunning Mapparium with the world in stained glass, sailed the swan boats in the Public Garden, walked through Boston Common and saw the *Cheers* bar, and ate a decadent amount of biscuits and cucumber sandwiches—which Mike swallowed manfully—at a fancy olde-worlde hotel. Beatrice Gruber had declined to attend—because of a cough, or so Mike said—and Bree couldn't help but think him relieved.

"She'll have to explain the mystery later," Bree said.

Mike met her gaze over his cup of tea, a delicate cup that looked far too small in his large hands. "There isn't really a mystery," he admitted. "It's just I don't get many visitors."

Her heart panged.

"And certainly no female visitors," he added. "And I—" He swallowed, glanced away. "I may have once suggested that I had a female friend who lived elsewhere, which is why Rachel made that comment the other day."

"About me being an illusion? Right, well that now makes sense."

"It's easier if people think I'm not available."

She knew a surge of gladness that the pretty blonde neighbor didn't seem to be high on his radar. Which made her wonder—

"Would you like more tea, Michael?" Gran asked.

"Thanks, but I'm good."

"Are you looking forward to continuing our literary connections tomorrow?" she continued.

"Can't wait," he deadpanned.

Bree swallowed amusement. "Do you mean to tell me you've always been a big fan of *Little Women* too?"

"Huh? No, I prefer women who are taller."

Her heart glowed, even as Granny V chuckled. "You've made your preference very plain, my dear boy. But no, Breanna refers to the book by Louisa May Alcott. We're going to visit her house in Concord tomorrow, then see Salem in the afternoon."

"Right, of course."

Bree patted his arm. "But it's good to know you don't mind my height."

He shrugged and offered a good-natured grin.

On Saturday they visited the Hallmark movie-worthy town of Concord, then Orchard House, the Alcott home, followed by the Sleepy Hollow cemetery. A short drive took them to Salem, with its year-round decorations, and inside Nathaniel Hawthorne's house and various historic locations, followed by a meal at a restaurant under Tiffany lamps before Gran's admission of tiredness led them back to Boston and their hotel.

On Sunday they attended Mike's church, visited TD Garden, where Bree imagined Mike playing, and had coffee at Bob's, where they met some colorful locals who spoke with the distinctive New England accent, before Gran once again complained of tiredness and insisted Bree go out for dinner with Mike alone.

"I'm an old woman, and you've worn me out with all this gallivanting, Breanna."

"But Gran, you said you wanted to go to all of those places."

"Well, yes, I did, didn't I?" Granny V sighed. "I'm sorry. I thought I had more energy than I do, and now all I want to do is stay here and complete my brand new jigsaw puzzle. But it has been rather fun seeing all these places I've wanted to see for so long."

"We can stay, if you prefer," Bree said, already knowing the answer.

"Oh no, my dear. You young people go have fun. But not *too* much fun, young Michael."

Bree swallowed a smile at his look of chagrin.

"Of course not, Violet. I'll ensure that only a moderate degree of fun will be had."

Gran laughed and patted his arm. "Now, did I hear you telling Breanna you planned to visit a lovely restaurant?"

"Well, yes." He slid Bree a look. "It's pretty nice, which I thought would be a great way to cap off your visit."

"See, Gran? Mike arranged this for us. For *both* of us."

"Yes, and it's such a shame I truly don't feel able to manage it."

"We can stay here, Violet," Mike said kindly.

"No, no. That's very sweet of you, but I insist. Truth be told, there was something on the room service menu I wanted to try out, and I didn't want to have to admit to it, but now, alas, I've been forced to."

"If you're very sure?"

"Oh, I'm very sure," Granny V said, looking up at him. Wait —did she just wink?

The amusement tugging at his mouth smoothed away as he glanced at Bree. "I'm sorry. It looks like it's just you and me."

"However shall we manage?"

"Well you, my dear, will manage by putting on that very nice dress," her grandmother instructed. "You didn't bring it all this way just to leave it in the suitcase."

Mike stage-whispered, "Probably best not to upset your grandmother, Bree."

"And you," Gran said to him, her lips twitching a little, "had best go home and return in an hour or so dressed in a nice suit."

"Yes, ma'am," he said, kissing her cheek—to her fluster.

"Oh, go on with you now."

His smile caught Bree. "I'll see you in an hour, okay?"

"Okay."

An hour later, having scolded her grandma affectionately, showered, and changed into her dress—a knockoff Ralph Lauren black number that made the most of her figure without revealing too much—Bree fixed her makeup and was just fussing with her hair when the knock came at the door.

"Oh, Bree, you look wonderful," Granny V said.

"It's not too much?"

"Oh, it's just enough. If that young man can't see what he's missing, well, he's not the young man I thought him to be."

"It's not a date, Gran," she insisted.

"Of course not."

"No, truly. It's—"

"Are you going to open that door, or are you going to stand there talking and force me to get up on my creaky old legs and—"

"I should make you answer it," Bree said, laughing as she opened the door. "Mike."

Wow. She swallowed. Looked like he'd made an effort too.

His face softened as he looked her over. "You look so beautiful."

"Thanks." The way he looked at her—like she was a dream—

made her feel suddenly shy. Or maybe that was the knowledge that Gran was avidly listening.

"Hello, Michael," she called.

"Hello, Violet," he said, waving to her from the door.

"My, don't you look dashing."

"I tried."

She chuckled. "Well, look after my granddaughter, won't you?"

"You don't have to ask," he assured her.

"Enjoy your date now," Gran called as Bree collected her bag and light jacket.

"It's not a date, Gran," Bree said from the door.

"Okay. Enjoy dinner with your handsome young man, then."

"He's not—oh." She exhaled, shaking her head. "Honestly."

Mike chuckled as Bree shut the door. "I like Granny V."

"She's a card," she muttered.

"She cares about you and what's in your best interests."

"And that's you, is it?"

He lifted his hands, waiting for the elevator. "Hey, I don't want to presume."

She laughed.

Thirty minutes later they were being escorted to a lounge area, the hostess assuring them that their table would be ready soon. She encouraged them to take seats that had a superb view and took their drinks order.

Bree's insides felt as if they were lit with twinkly lights. It didn't matter she was drinking a mocktail; the dizzying height and wondrous views created enough buzz, and alcohol couldn't heighten this experience. And the fact that she was here with Mike, who'd dressed like a movie star and caused more than a few women's heads to turn, elicited a sparkly feeling inside—one chased with uncertainty, like she wasn't sure what would happen.

This was *not* a date. Mike was only her friend.

"If you would both like to follow me this way, your table is ready."

Mike—gentleman as he was—held her hand to help her rise, and they followed their hostess past the bar that backed onto a window and into a corner seat that offered sunset views of the river, sea, and cityscape stretching from Cambridge to the North End.

"This is amazing," Bree whispered as the waiter left them to their menus and dinner selections.

"You know, if Brent was here, he'd probably think this looks like a date."

Dressed up? Check. Fancy restaurant? Check. She swallowed. "But it's not. It's just dinner. Isn't it?"

AND THAT WAS the diamond ring-worthy question, wasn't it? A date or not a date. "Tonight is whatever you want it to be," he finally said, meeting her gaze.

She bit her lip, her violet eyes searching his for the longest time. "Well, you know about my new year's resolution."

He nodded. "I don't understand it, but I respect you for wanting to keep your word."

Her eyes filled, and she blinked rapidly. "Thank you," she replied in a squeaky voice. "Everyone else thinks I'm being silly, but I really want to prove Brent wrong."

"Prove him wrong, or prove something to yourself?"

Her gaze shifted out to the view, and it was some time before she said, "I think it's both, really. But the fact you even recognized it could be the latter just shows"—she swallowed—"just shows how good you are to me. You get me."

His heart filled with pleasure. Yes, he did. He'd made a science of paying attention to Breanna Karlsson for many years. He understood her. Well, except for one thing.

"Why do you want to avoid dating hockey players?" he dared.

Her gaze dropped, and she spent a moment fiddling with her linen napkin, like she was collecting her thoughts. "Because I…I want to be liked for me," she finally admitted. "Not for who my brother is. Not for any connections I might bring. To be honest, and don't take this the wrong way, I don't actually want to talk hockey all the time."

"Neither do I."

"Shh, don't let anyone here hear you say that." Her smile faded as she touched her water glass, played with her knife and fork, her gaze avoiding his even as he patiently waited for her to look up. "I just want to be seen for being me, Mike."

"I see you," he said softly.

She glanced up and bit her bottom lip.

"And I like—I've always liked—what I see."

Her breath drew in quickly.

"Now, have you decided what you'd like for starters?" the waiter intruded.

What? It took a moment to refocus, to think about the options for their meals. They ordered, bread was delivered, and the quiet between them resumed.

She'd grown pensive, avoiding his eyes again, so he contented himself with wondering about the softness of her skin.

"So." She finally looked up with a tentative smile. "This is getting very serious."

"I can't help but be a little glad your grandmother isn't here to hear this," he admitted, lips curving to one side.

"Oh, me too. She kept going on and on, and…" Her voice trailed away, and she looked at him again. "So what was the last date you went on?"

He tore apart his bread roll, his actions deliberate as he slowly buttered it. "I don't date, Bree."

"What? Never?"

He thought back. "There might've been one girl in high school who I went out with when I was told the girl I liked would be impossible to date."

"Impossible? For you? Who'd dare say such a thing?"

"Brent."

"What?"

He waited until her eyes met his again. "There's only ever been one girl for me."

The restaurant seemed to drain of all sound and movement as the intensity of the moment mushroomed.

She wet her bottom lip. "Who?"

"You know who, Bree."

The server drew near again, and the weighty moment dissipated like a spent soap bubble. "Okay, here we have the salad"—the server placed a plate of greens in front of Bree—"and the chowder for the gentleman. Would you like cracked pepper, sir?"

"No, thanks." All Mike wanted was to resume this all important conversation.

After a few minutes of their starters being sampled and exclaimed over, they grew quiet again, and he wondered if she'd refer back to their previous conversation. He was a patient man and would wait for as long as it took. He was just so pleased to finally have the opportunity to say what he'd ruminated over for so long.

"So..." he began.

"So." She met his gaze again.

"Are you enjoying yourself?"

"This is great. Thank you for bringing me here."

"I've heard a lot of the guys say how much they've enjoyed it."

"But you've never come?"

"Not to this part, no."

"Why not?"

He eyed her. "A special place deserves special company, don't you think?"

She swallowed. Nodded. Took a deep breath. Exhaled. "So you, um, never said who it was who was the only girl you ever liked."

"Who I still like," he corrected.

"So, um, who is she?"

"I think you know."

"Maybe you should spell it out. Make it really obvious so there's no confusion."

Very well, then. "It's you, Breanna Karlsson. It's always been you."

"Oh." Her eyes filled.

His heart sank. She didn't want his admission of affection?

He concentrated on scooping out the rest of his soup, suddenly unable to look at her. He might be able to face down a puck zooming at him at one hundred miles an hour, but this felt too raw, too personal, and he had no idea what he'd do if she rejected him. Fake a sudden illness. Pretend to get an urgent phone call. Maybe visit the bathroom and somehow call her grandmother to pretend she was sick and needed Bree home right away.

"Mike."

He finally met her gaze.

"Why?"

Why? He took courage in both hands and finally admitted the deep recesses of his heart. "I...I can't help it. You're everything I think wonderful and true. If I wasn't captivated by your heart and compassion for others, then I'd be captivated by your joy and laughter and your smile and beautiful eyes."

Those beautiful eyes widened, seemed to hold a sheen.

He hurried to finish. "And Bree, I don't know if you could ever feel the same way, but I understand that even if you feel that way too, you've made a promise and can't do anything about it. Like I said before, as frustrating as that is, I understand and can even support it. Even"—he swallowed—"even if you can't ever consider dating me one day for real."

There. He sat back in his seat, feeling drained of emotion. He'd put his heart on the line, and now it was up to her.

"May I remove your plates?"

Man, this waiter had a crummy sense of timing. Mike waited as their plates were cleared, wondering what Bree would say. He internally braced. *Lord, give me strength to cope with rejection.*

Another waiter came and refilled their water glasses, asked about wine. Bree shook her head, and Mike refused for both of them.

"Why do you say that?" she finally asked.

"Say what?"

"*If* I can't consider dating you, like"—she wet her bottom lip again—"like I haven't already considered what dating you might be like."

What? His heart leapt. But no. He needed to calm down, to play this cool, to not get carried away by hope rather than what she really meant. "What are you saying, Bree?"

Her gaze finally met his again. "I'm saying that, dumb as my reasoning might be, if you're prepared to wait a few more months, then I am too."

The air seemed to hold a dizzying weight that threatened his breath. "I think you need to spell it out so there's no confusion."

"Okay then." She leaned an elbow on the table and propped her chin in her hand, her violet eyes sweetly uncertain as they reflected candlelight. "Michael, if you're prepared to wait until New Year's Day, then I hope you'll ask me out."

A thousand hallelujahs took flight inside, begging for release. He wanted to fist pump, to yell like he'd won the Stanley Cup. But the fancy restaurant meant he'd have to settle for a grin.

Her gaze was shy. "I know it's dumb—"

"It's not dumb. It's a yes."

"Really?"

"Yes." Oh, yes. A heaven-load of yes. *Thank You, God.*

His cheeks were getting sore from all the smiling when a thought struck. Best he ask rather than spend all night wondering. "But I have to know, will you date anyone else in the meantime?"

"No, of course not." A beat. "Will you?"

"Bree, how can you ask me that?"

She smiled. "I'm just making sure, so there's no confusion."

"Good."

"Good."

Their mains interrupted his heart-zinging euphoria, and he had to settle for stealing glances and smiles from Bree while the waiter did his thing. Finally he left.

"So."

"So." She glanced at her chicken. Then back up at him. "Just so we're clear—"

"It's important to be clear."

"I think you should know I haven't dated anyone since April. Or was it March?"

"No?"

"No." She smiled, picked up her fork and cut into her chicken. "And just so we're really clear—"

He swallowed his mouthful of steak. "Yes?"

"I don't actually really count it as a date unless there's two things involved."

"What's that?"

"Well, first, you have to intend for it to be a date."

"So that means tonight is out. It's just dinner, right?"

"Right."

"So you haven't broken any resolution or anything, have you?"

"Exactly." She grinned.

"And the other thing?"

"Well…" Her gaze met his. "I don't count it as a proper date unless…unless there's kissing involved."

He grabbed for his water glass and drained it, his heart a tumult of emotion.

"Mike?"

"Yep?"

"What is it?"

He had to know, otherwise he'd die a million deaths. "Does this mean you've been kissing on all these other dates?"

"No! Oh. I guess that means they weren't really dates then. I haven't kissed anyone since…I don't know." Her attention returned to her food. "Can't have been very memorable."

His gut tightened, whether at the thought they were even having a kissing conversation or in envy at the guys who had kissed her, he didn't know. But one day, judging from the way her gaze dipped to his lips, he might also know. One day. Like January first.

Later, after decadent desserts, their hostess took them downstairs to the observation deck, where they could see the city landmarks glow in the last of the twilight. Mike wrapped an arm around Bree—something he'd done a hundred times before, but never had it felt so un-brotherly or so tenderly precious, like a long-awaited dream had come to life.

She exhaled and snuggled closer, a little less exuberantly than she might otherwise have done, which made him wonder if she, too, felt the magnitude of their earlier conversation.

He experienced something similar on the elevator ride downstairs, when a bump pushed her closer and he was forced to steady her by holding the smooth skin of her upper arms. "You okay?"

She shivered. "Yes."

But her eyes were lit like stars, and the way her gaze shifted to his mouth made him wish—hard—it was January first and he could finally learn how soft her lips were.

And as he drove her back—the long way—and they sat in his car talking about a million things as they overlooked the harbor lights as he'd done six months ago, he couldn't help but thank God for this chance to be with Bree, like God had given him permission to hope and dream once more.

"Bye, Mike. Thanks for inviting us to Boston."

Mike's eyes danced. "You're very welcome. I'm glad you could come."

They'd agreed last night to temper things, to not stir up Granny V's suspicions any more than they already had. But in the easy hug he gave her, the way his breath danced along her cheek, Bree knew a million sensations she'd never noticed before as well as a crazy impulse to seal her lips on his.

She exhaled, stepped away. Managed a smile. "I guess I'll see you in a little while."

He inclined his head. "I hope to be back in Toronto soon. But training ramps up now, and the team selection tryouts are soon, so it might take a while."

"I look forward to when you do. I—" She shot her grandmother a swift glance; she looked way too interested. "I'm sure your parents will be very glad to see you."

His lips twitched, but he simply nodded again before farewelling Granny V with a kiss to the cheek, provoking stupid envy of her grandmother. How did Granny V know his kiss while Bree still was without?

"Thank you for coming, Violet. I hope your rest last night helped."

"It was later than I expected when Breanna finally got back, but I suppose some dinners can take a while."

"That they can," he agreed solemnly.

Bree bit back the urge to laugh. How had she not noticed just how droll the man was? As well as muscly. And his aftershave scent was so divine. Good thing they would be spending time apart.

"Take care of yourself," he said to her.

"You too."

Suddenly the brief hug from before didn't seem nearly enough, so she rushed to envelope him as she usually did. "I'll miss you," she whispered into his neck.

"Miss you too," he said before kissing her brow. "Hope that's not against the rules."

Her breath was shaky. "It's not." She pulled reluctantly away. "I better go. They're calling our flight."

"Bye, Bree." He gave her a special smile. "Bye, Violet."

Bree waited until her grandmother's back was turned, then blew him a kiss.

He smiled and placed his hand on his heart, causing her own to skip a beat.

"Well, that all went very satisfactorily," Granny V said a short time later when they settled in their seats on the plane.

"It has been fun, hasn't it?" Bree said with a happy sigh, still hugging her emotions to herself. Everything felt so new and sparkly and filled with possibilities. How had things shifted so dramatically? It felt as if a curtain had lifted and she could suddenly see how life could be. But the advent of these new feelings meant it already seemed too long until she'd see Mike again.

"Yes. This little project has gone very well," Gran said, pulling out a magazine.

"What project? The breakup project was about Brent."

"Of course."

"So what project are you talking about?" Bree asked.

"Shh, dear. The flight attendant wants us to pay attention."

"But—"

"Shh!" Gran turned to face the safety demonstration with fixed attention.

Bree paid attention too, mind humming over the possibilities, but when the demonstration concluded and she went to ask Gran to explain her comment from earlier, Gran yawned and said she needed to sleep. "I think you forget how wearying such adventures can be, Breanna. I don't know how you'll manage at work tomorrow."

Bree wasn't sure how she'd manage either. The past days had been filled with so many fresh sights and tastes and emotions that trying to settle back into life as she'd always known it felt like an old jigsaw piece trying to fit into Gran's brand new puzzle. Would she need to bend and squeeze into her old life, a life that had already adapted to allow her extra days off to accommodate her illness, or would she begin to see a new picture of what her life could be if this unfurling of a potential relationship with Mike should one day come to be?

What *could* it mean? Yes, she was probably dumb to leap ahead into the ramifications, but what girl raised on romance didn't wonder about such things? If they did get together and one day got married, would she leave her work? Probably. Unless he got traded to Toronto. Where might they live? He'd mentioned Calgary—presumably he'd be okay with Edmonton too. She'd tried to sound positive and encouraging yesterday, but honestly, cowboy chic wasn't her cup of tea. It'd almost be better to be based in the US than move to Calgary. It did at least have the benefit of being close to Banff. But was that enough to pick up her stylish city life and move there?

"This is ridiculous," she muttered.

"Did you say something, dear?" her grandmother asked sleepily.

Bree shot her a quick look. Okay, so maybe she hadn't been feigning sleep to get out of talking to her. She patted her arm. "It's okay. I'm just thinking."

"About your handsome young man?"

"Yes—I mean, he's not my handsome young man," she said sternly. "That's ridiculous."

Granny V gave a slight chuckle. "The fact you keep denying it is what is ridiculous, my dear."

Hmm. Bree hunched away.

"Now don't be offended. You need an advocate for your cause, especially with that twin of yours."

Brent. Her spirits dipped. "Please don't say anything to him."

"You can trust me, Breanna."

But the way her grandmother eyed her made Bree wonder just what Granny V might say.

"So, how did things go with my sister?"

Mike leaned back in his seat, watching the computer screen as he and Brent caught up before the others joined tonight's Bible study conversation. He fought to keep the smile from bursting all across his face. How'd it go? Fantastically well. So much better than he could have expected. All his hopes and dreams hung on the turning of the calendar from December into January. Bring on the new year.

"Yeah, it was good."

"Good?" Brent raised a skeptical eyebrow. "Is that all?"

Okay, so maybe he wasn't buying what Mike was trying to sell. "We went places, saw things. Your grandmother seemed to enjoy it too." Pointing out Violet's attendance might help soothe some of Brent's apparent fears.

"Huh. I forgot she went."

Mike filled him in on some of the exhilarating activities, like the visit to Concord and Salem to see the homes of authors he vaguely recognized but had never read. "High tea is something I don't plan to do again." At least, he might if Bree wanted to. As long as it didn't involve cucumber sandwiches. "I had to get a burger on my way home," he admitted. "Not that I told them that."

Brent laughed. "So you had to do some girly stuff."

"Your grandmother is fun."

"And Bree?"

More feigned nonchalance. "Yeah, she's fun too."

"So you and her—?"

"Aren't together"—yet—"if that's what you're asking." But God willing...

"You're sure? Bree apparently mentioned something to Mom about a dinner last night."

Mike swallowed. What else had she said? "Do you think dinner together has to automatically mean a date?" he finally asked.

"It does if it's in one of Boston's most expensive restaurants."

"Well, if it makes you feel any better, I'd planned for both Bree and Violet to go. Your grandmother said she was too tired. Does that mean I planned to double date them? Seriously, man, you need to calm down. Don't you think men and women can be friends?"

"No."

Mike shrugged. "Well, I've been friends with your sister for as long as I can remember, so I think you're wrong. Maybe one day you'll be able to appreciate a girl for more than her looks."

Brent's eyebrows shot up. "Seriously?"

"Yeah. Now tell me how the renovations are going."

Brent seemed to struggle between being offended and wanting to share. He finally blew out a breath. "The old kitchen is ripped out, and I'm installing new tile before the cabinets get delivered next week."

Mike encouraged him along this vein until a ping of new notifications alerted them to the time and the fact that there were others waiting to join them for the pro-hockey group tonight.

Tonight was more a general catch up than specific study, and as it had been a few weeks since their last meeting, there were some guys with whom Mike hadn't yet shared his adventures in the Philippines. The fact they asked seemed to hit him almost like a surprise, like he'd lived a different existence for a month, then slipped too easily back into his usual way of life.

"So when do we get to see this amazing video?" Beau asked.

"John's latest email suggests it should be ready by the end of the week."

"Cool." Jai nodded. "I noticed there are a few big storms heading through that way."

Guilt struck. Jai had noticed while Mike had been off dreaming of a future with Bree.

"Will that affect any of the work they do?" Jai continued.

"It's hard to say. But there's so much potential for natural disasters in that area—like active volcanoes, mudslides, tsunamis, and storms—that anything we can do to help will make a difference."

The conversation turned to more practical ways to offer support, reminding him of the need to focus on what he could do right here and now. As far as his future with Bree was concerned, he had to trust God with it all. As far as MPFG, he'd have to do the same.

"So, how is everyone's training going?" Dan asked.

The guys shared, reminding Mike again about the need to up his intensity. His first game might still be a month away, but training camp would sort out those who'd slacked off over the summer and those who were hungry for success. There were always newbies keen to prove themselves, and as he was now someone who'd be trade bait for other teams, he'd need to give the coaches plenty of reasons to keep him around. Especially now he knew how much Bree liked it here.

"How goes the hunt for a place in Phoenix?" he asked Beau.

"The team's been great in helping me get things sorted. It's nice, but a little different."

"Yeah, North Carolina and Arizona aren't exactly the same," Brent said dryly.

"I thought I was used to heat in Raleigh, and I was looking forward to the milder summer temperatures of Montreal, but hey, I guess God knows what He's doing, right?"

"Desert heat sure is a different heat, isn't it?" Jai said.

"So much drier," Beau said. "I read somewhere that Phoenix gets the most sunshine of any major city on Earth."

"You can work on that tan of yours," Brent suggested.

"Yeah. When temperatures top 110 degrees, I can't see much outside action happening."

"I guess you'll appreciate the difference in winter," offered Dan. "You'll notice the milder climate then."

"It's gotta have something going for it."

"Is your family planning to visit you there soon?" Mike asked.

"Yeah, soon. I'm hoping to get Mom to help me set things up, but I know this kind of heat knocks her around, so it might be a little longer until I'm entertaining. But hey, if any of you dudes are looking for something to do, I've got plenty of things needing attention anytime you're free."

"Might need to sell the place to us a bit more," Jai teased.

"I'd come," Brent said, "but I'm fixing to have my renovations finished before preseason begins."

"Yeah, I figured you'd be a tough crowd. It's okay. Mom's an interior designer, so she'll whip things into shape before I know it."

"Hope she makes it soon," Mike said.

"Thanks. This place is doing my head in. I'm used to trees and green hills, and this is just so dang different. I was sitting in my apartment the other day and saw this dust storm rolling in. It was like a scene from an apocalyptic movie. I thought the end of the world might come."

"Dude, not the way to get us to come," Jai said, shaking his head.

Beau laughed. "Yeah. I better work on my appreciation before we start. But hey, this is the circle of trust, right?"

"It's okay to be honest," Mike said.

"It's not easy moving teams," Dan said. "When I moved from Pittsburgh to Toronto, it took a while before I felt like it was home, which seemed ironic considering I grew up half an hour away from where I now play. But it takes time to adjust, to find your groove."

Mike listened, wondering if he'd soon be in a similar position. The uncertainty was something every player had to deal with—except for those like Brent with an iron-clad "no movement" clause in their contract. But this sport was a business, and when they signed their first contract, they signed up knowing that money would dictate their futures, even if they didn't understand all the ramifications of that signature.

"Be praying for you," Mike offered, an offer echoed by the other guys.

"Thanks." Beau shrugged. "I know I sound like I'm on a downer, and hey, maybe in all honesty I am. But I'm sure things will work out when I know the team routines and the guys a bit more. I know some of them, but we never really hung out. So I might be leaning on you all a little."

"That's what we're here for," Mike said, determining he'd go visit as soon as he could. No point advertising it here, though. He'd send Beau a message and arrange it on the quiet. Poor dude.

He waited until the call ended, then tapped Beau a message, offering to come.

Beau sent back his own. BRENT AND DAN JUST SENT MESSAGES OFFERING THE SAME. YOU COULD ALL COME TOGETHER OR SEPARATE. LOVE THE COMPANY IF YOU'RE STILL GAME.

He glanced at his calendar, the schedule marked out with booked training times and those planned with MPFG. He had a few weekends free before the season started. Of course, it'd mean he wouldn't be getting back to Toronto to see Bree. But what was the point when she'd made it perfectly clear that there would be little date-worthy interaction until the new year? At this time, Beau needed him more.

He texted back: I CAN MAKE ANY WEEKEND FREE. LET ME KNOW WHAT WORKS FOR YOU AND I'LL MAKE IT HAPPEN, WITH OR WITHOUT THE OTHERS.

A minute later his phone pinged with a new message: a date in two weekends' time and a THANKS DUDE, APPRECIATE YOU at the end.

He nodded, the last words an uneasy reminder of what Bree had said previously. He wondered what she'd say when he chose to help a friend over helping connect with her in a deeper way.

CHAPTER 23

"*H*e's going to do what?"

Bree shrugged as Holly leaned closer to the screen. "He emailed to say he's going to help a friend in Phoenix and won't be back this summer."

"Well, good for him for wanting to help a friend."

"Yeah." She pasted on a smile, but couldn't help the renewal of disappointment since his email yesterday. Gran had been right. Getting back into work had proved harder than she'd expected, the fizzing hope of future possibilities dying a sudden death at Mike's message. Not that she wasn't glad he was helping, but it would be nice to know he thought about her.

"So, does this mean Bree and Mike are a thing?" Holly asked.

"No."

"Then why look so woebegone?"

"Do I? I think I'm just tired. Work is a little crazy now with all these parents suddenly deciding they want to enroll their kids for the coming school year, almost like they haven't known that little Johnny will need an extra year because he's not quite ready for big school yet." She shrugged. "I love little kids, but I'd forgotten how intense they can be."

"Must've been a pretty good break to forget so quickly."

"It was. Boston is awesome. I'd love to go"—live there, she almost said, but swallowed it to say—"visit again sometime."

"Sounds like you had fun with Mike."

"Yes, but not too much fun." She smiled, remembering Granny V's similar comment.

"Uh huh. So the 'no dating hockey players' resolution?"

"Is still in operation. One hundred percent."

"And does that mean dating others?" Holly asked, way too perceptively.

"I really think I'm going to be a little busy over the next few months. I'm covering a few shifts for my friend Sylvie, and between that and these enrollments and a special cookie fundraiser in September, then Thanksgiving and Halloween and the lead up to Christmas, I'm trying to manage my time better so I don't get exhausted like before."

"Your iron levels are okay? You're eating well?"

"Honestly, you sound like"—Mike—"Mom. She's always checking on me, feeding me red meat and greens."

"Hey, I study sports nutrition as part of my course, so I'm gonna be asking my best friend how she's doing, understand?"

"Understood." Did Mike's similar concern mean he had ascended from friend to good friend status—maybe more? Her stomach fluttered. Would she one day consider him a best friend too? How she'd like to know how this would all play out. And preferably know it now.

"So, enough of me. How is life going with you?"

"After this weekend I head back to Australia to prepare for the championships. Honestly, I just want to beat Kate at something. I wonder if that makes me selfish or just motivated."

"My vote is for motivated," Bree said with raised hand.

"And that's why I love you."

"It's tricky, isn't it, balancing hopes and dreams with expectations and other people?"

"Like with Mike, you mean?" Holly said slyly.

"My life goals don't revolve around him, thank you very much."

"Good. Women should be able to stand on their own two feet if they can."

"You're such a feminist, Holly."

"I just don't think a woman should depend on a man for her happiness." Holly shrugged. "So, what *do* you want?"

Bree sat back in her chair, thinking. "To be honest, I don't really know. I want to be happy, to have a family, a simple life." For a moment she wondered about Mike as a father. He was so good with kids. "I know that our personal happiness isn't God's primary goal for our lives, so I'm trying to not live so self-focused." She heard her own words, and they dug deeper into resolve. *Lord, forgive me my self-centeredness. Help me live for you and others.* "I guess I'm not like you, with Olympic-sized dreams. I just want to live life well."

Holly nodded, her expression gentle. "I hear you. That should be the goal for all of us, shouldn't it?"

Bree nodded, they prayed, and the conversation soon ended.

To live well and not be so self-focused. That was living well indeed.

"Miss Bwee! Miss Bwee! Come see the pwetty butterfwy!"

Bree hurried to Hannah's side, where the yellow-and-black-winged insect flapped its wings. She loved the children's enthusiasm for noticing little things, finding beauty and excitement in the details so many others missed. Something she could afford to do a little more of instead of wishing life away. Her conversation with Holly last week still rang in her ears.

"Look," she said, pointing as the butterfly danced in the air, "there are always special things to see, especially when we use our eagle eyes. Who has their eagle eyes on today?"

"Me!" they chorused, which sent the tiny visitor flying away.

"Aww, look what you made him do," Benjie complained.

"Butterflies can be very shy, but if we're patient and don't move, he might return. Let's hold our hands out very still and see if he wants to give our fingers a kiss."

The children held their hands out obediently, but their special guest wasn't playing, flitting away in a huff as a child sneezed.

"Oh well." She smiled. "Perhaps we could go inside and draw some pictures of butterflies."

"I likes drawing," confided little Park Lee, slipping her hand into Bree's.

"And you're very good at it."

She ushered the children inside, and they took their places at the drawing station, a collection of desks with crayons and fat pencils for little children still learning to grip. The noise subsided into occasional requests—polite or otherwise—as children shared colors and opinions on the drawings involved.

"That doesn't look like a butterfly."

"That's because I'm dwawing Miss Bwee."

"Miss Bree doesn't have wings."

"But Miss Bwee is a fairy."

Bree swallowed her laughter. These kids were sweet.

"A fairy, or an angel?" a voice said.

She turned. "Sylvie! How was New York?"

"Awesome. Hard to come back to this."

"It's not so hard when you're a fairy," Bree said smugly, tapping the picture.

"Or an angel. Thanks for covering my shifts."

"No problem. You covered lots for me when I was sick a few months ago."

Sylvie glanced around the room. "How are things going here?"

"It's settled down a little now that the school year's begun. We have the cookie fundraiser this week."

"Your work again?"

"Well, I had some help. Fiona and my grandmother and Mom. It was quite the production line, but the bags look great, don't you think?"

"Elegant as everything you do."

Pleasure filled her chest. "We haven't sold as many as I hoped, so I sent a few to friends and family." Like Brent. She'd even dared send one to Mike. "I hope they arrive in one piece."

"Did you freeze them first?"

"Yep. I hoped they'd stay fresh a little longer that way too."

"Then you should be fine."

"They taste good."

"So modest."

"Just speaking the truth here."

Sylvie laughed. "I better go see Moira. See you soon."

"Miss Bwee, Miss Bwee!"

Bree waved good bye to Sylvie and crouched beside Hannah. "Oh, your picture is amazing." And a little hard to see how it related to either a butterfly or herself. "Can you tell me about it?"

She listened as the little girl explained the horn looking thing on the head was actually a fairy wand, and the puffy sleeves were actually her wings. "I'm so glad you explained it to me. These colors are so beautiful."

"You're so bweautiful, Miss Bwee."

Oh. It was hard sometimes to not have favorites. "How's everyone going with their pictures?"

There was a collection of hastily finished drawings, which varied in expertise. When Park Lee began pointing this out, Bree thought it best to intervene. "I know a wonderful story about a special butterfly. Who would like me to read it?"

"Yes pwease!"

She encouraged the group of four-year-olds to carefully replace their crayons and pencils into the correct containers, then move to select a cushion from the pile in the reading corner. She herself chose two books, sat on the chair—which saw Grace instantly shift to place her head on Bree's knee—and began to read aloud *The Very Hungry Caterpillar*.

"I wuv that story," Hannah said sleepily.

Hopefully the next would be enough to encourage them to sleep. She pulled out the *Sparkly Wing Butterflies* book and read it aloud, showing off the pictures, answering questions. The children were still curious, but their questions came slower, the blinks became longer, and she soon judged it was time to rest.

They might normally move to the napping section, but they'd be comfortable enough here. She motioned to Fiona to turn down the music, then drew a breath. These extra shifts hadn't exhausted her, and baking and preparing the cookies last weekend had been fun, but she'd be glad to enjoy some time off this weekend and have next Monday off. She wondered if Mike would return this weekend to see his family.

See his *family*. Not her. She sighed. Being thankful and living unselfishly was so hard sometimes.

"BREANNA MADE THESE?" Beau said, biting into a cookie. "Oh, good gravy. I might need to marry the girl."

Mike slid a look at Brent. Swallowed amusement as he bristled.

"Just because she can cook doesn't mean she's marriage material," Brent muttered.

"Is she taken?"

Mike's chest tightened as he waited for Brent's reply.

"Not as far as I know." He slid Mike a look that bordered on suspicion. "But she's made a commitment to not date any hockey players this year."

"What? Why?"

Brent shrugged. "Who knows with her? Not that I can see her keeping that commitment."

"Why not?" Mike felt to ask.

"She never does."

Mike's hackles rose, then, conscious Beau was glancing between them and that Brent was hardly going to have his suspicions eased by Mike getting defensive on Bree's behalf, chose to de-escalate his offense and offer a shrug instead. No way was he going to admit that Bree had sent him a pack of the same delicious cookies that Brent had brought to Phoenix, or that he'd wolfed them down in one sitting while thinking thoughts much like Beau's. *He* had to marry this girl. Beau definitely did not.

The past two days had been fun. Beau's delight in seeing friends had seemed shaded with desperation, hinting at his own frustration. "Mom can't come until next weekend, so to have you two here, and Dan and Jai come in a few days, is awesome."

And it had been pretty good—catching up, unpacking furniture, moving things, going to the gym. Brent had been Mike's training partner since they were kids, and while neither of them were in their usual routine, the chance to train together was something.

Preseason started in two weeks, and then life would be full pelt as he worked to prove his worth. This would be the last break he'd have for a while.

"I hope she cooks some more this weekend," Brent said, picking at the crumbs.

"You're going home?" Mike asked.

"Yeah."

"Hey, do you think I can come?" Beau said, licking chocolate off his fingers. "I want to meet your sister."

No! Mike forced his hands to unclench. Getting possessive like this wouldn't do anyone any good. And wasn't he trying to trust God with his future with Bree anyway?

"Did you forget?" Brent asked Mike.

"Bree?"

Brent's brow lowered. "The last chance for a weekend home before training camp begins."

"Must've slipped my mind."

"You could always change your ticket."

"For tomorrow? At this late stage? I don't do spontaneous like you."

"Hey, it's better that than missing out." Brent eyed Mike as if he could see what was running through his head. Yes. A quick trip to Toronto could also mean seeing Bree, something he hadn't anticipated. But now that his heart had started anticipating…

"Sure," he said as nonchalantly as he could. He pulled out his phone and checked flight availability.

But at this late stage, the only available was a first-class seat with Delta, which would mean he'd get in at ten at night. Still, it was better than nothing. And while it'd be great to see his family, it'd be even more awesome to see Bree.

THE POST CHURCH crowd didn't linger today, most families seeming to want to make the most of the great weather. Bree was glad to have Brent back from his jaunt in Arizona, even though he'd looked at her a little funny a few times this morning when he'd finally made his way downstairs. Still, he hadn't mentioned Mike, so that was a plus.

Bree was itching to leave the church auditorium when she saw Regina Vaughan out of the corner of her eye. Maybe she'd know if Mike was planning to be in town.

Her breath hitched as a figure with dark-blond hair rose from a seat beside Regina, turned, and faced her. Smiled.

She grinned back, everything inside her wanting to run into his arms, but she simply nodded and turned away. Brent was watching her again.

"Who is it?"

As he turned to scan the crowd, Bree slipped past to talk to Granny V. Her grandmother often preferred a different church service, claiming the ten o'clock was too loud. It would be good to have a buffer should Brent make his thoughts on her interest in Mike audible.

"Gran, can I steal you away for a moment?"

Bree made it look like she was busy talking to Gran when Brent finally met them, Mike in his wake.

"Here you are," Brent said to her.

"Here I am." She smiled sweetly. "And Mike! There you are. How are you?"

"Fine, thanks. Good to see you." His eyes twinkled, as if he understood her reluctance to admit more. He turned to her grandmother. "And Violet. How are you?"

Granny V turned her cheek, and Mike dutifully kissed it. Granny V glared at Brent. "This young man knows how to treat an older lady, while my own grandson refuses to give me a kiss."

Bree exchanged smiles with Mike as Brent sighed and bent to kiss Granny V's cheek.

"Now, how are you two getting on?" Gran said, glancing between Bree and Mike. "Have you been on any more dates?"

"I knew it!" Brent said, eyeing Mike with suspicion. "You said it wasn't a date," he accused.

"And it wasn't," Mike insisted.

Bree coughed. Well, this was a bad idea. "It was a dinner, Gran. That was all. The one you were invited to, remember?"

Gran looked at Bree, then looked at Brent, uttered an "oh" and nodded. "Of course. My mistake. I imagine that's a no then."

"It's a no," Mike confirmed. "We haven't seen each other since Boston, have we, Bree?"

"Nope." At Brent's skeptical look, Bree hurried on to say, "It's nice you can be here this weekend."

"Brent encouraged me to come, make the most of time here before training camp begins."

"He's so thoughtful that way," she said, linking her arm through her brother's. "Always wanting the best for others, seeking to help wherever he can, aren't you, brother dear?"

Brent frowned down at her. Bree swallowed a chuckle, returning her attention to Mike. "Well, I hope you enjoy your day with your family. What are you going to do?"

"Maybe see if there's a restaurant free and have lunch."

"Or you could join us for lunch," Granny V said.

"Gran," hissed Bree through a clenched-teeth smile.

Mike's smile widened. "Thanks, but I really don't want to impose."

"But—"

"Really, Violet, it's okay," Mike said, his gaze lifting to meet Bree's ever so quickly before darting away. "I messaged my sister, and Callie's planning to Zoom us if she gets time."

"Well." Gran looked disappointed. "I hope you'll stop by at some point today. I'd love to catch up with you again."

"Yes, ma'am," he said. "I'll try to do so." And he glanced up and winked at Bree.

CHAPTER 24

That evening, Bree had just finished cleaning up in the kitchen when a knock came at the door. She heard Brent answer it. Heard Mike's voice. Smiled.

She'd been looking forward to his visit all day. Couldn't wait to see him and see if maybe she could sneak in a hug. But not in front of Brent. He'd not seemed convinced after Granny V's unfortunate slip of the tongue earlier.

"Bree."

She turned at the sound of her brother's voice, her big smile fading at the sight of Mike's pale face. "What is it?"

"You got a few minutes?" Brent said.

"Sure." She wiped her hands, moved to touch Mike's arm. "What is it?"

"We can talk in the den." Brent led the way, and she followed soberly, wishing she could hold Mike's hand or do anything to alleviate the distress she saw in his face.

They sat. Brent closed the door, switched on the TV, and muted it as he scrolled through channels.

"What's happened?" she asked again. "Mike?" She grasped his hand.

He glanced up, and she recognized anguish in his eyes.

"Here." Brent unmuted it, glanced back just as she released her hand from Mike's.

There was a TV report about mudslides and a giant storm in Asia.

"...and early reports suggest that thousands are missing, presumed dead. The many islands of the Philippines have been particularly hard hit."

Oh no. Her heart wrenched. "Is this where you were?"

Mike jerked his head. "The island has faced the brunt of the typhoon. These pictures are from a few days ago. This afternoon I got an email from John, the director of MPFG, to say a number of the kids we've sponsored, that I sponsor, are missing. Or"—he swallowed—"dead."

"Oh, Mike." She grasped his hand again, threaded his fingers through hers as the reporter continued.

"There is now great concern that the excessive rain will trigger mudslides as devastating as when Typhoon Durian killed close to fifteen hundred people," the newsreader continued.

She had no words. Could only squeeze Mike's hand and pray aloud. "God, help them."

"Amen," Brent echoed, followed a moment later by a raspy-voiced Mike.

She turned to him. "Mike." His gaze slowly met hers. "What can we do?"

"I don't know. I feel so helpless watching this, knowing this, but what can we do?"

We. She liked how he said that. She glanced at Brent. "We can raise awareness. We can spread word about this tragedy via email, on Facebook and Twitter. You both have connections. Now is a great time to use them and ask for support."

"What did John say specifically?" Brent asked.

Mike pulled out his phone and tapped it, then started reading aloud.

She listened, her heart twisting a little more at each sentence. It appeared really grim, but while there was the shock of such devastation, it seemed there was only one confirmed death—a little boy connected with MPFG—though scores of others remained missing.

"But John points out that communications have been bad," Mike said. "That suggests the death toll will rise as reports come in."

"Or it might just mean that nobody has had a chance to report they're safe," Bree said.

"Such an optimist," Brent murmured, ruffling her hair.

She squirmed away, turned to face Mike more fully. "Mike, would you like me to put together a newsletter for the sponsors here in North America? We can ask them to pray, and maybe put in a reminder of the bank account so they can contribute."

"Would you?" he said, finally looking at her.

"I'd be happy to. Well, not happy about this situation, but I'm happy to help you in whatever way."

"And I'm happy to get in touch with whatever media wants to listen to share more about this if you like," Brent offered.

"Thanks guys. I...I don't know what I'd do without you."

"Come on," Bree said. "Let's pray, then let's get this newsletter sorted."

LATER THAT NIGHT, newsletter sent, phone switched off, Bree tried to watch some dumb sports movie in an attempt to distract Mike from worry. Her heart hurt. She knew he was seeing faces and people he'd talked with, laughed with, eaten with. It was different for her. She might sponsor and pray for three children, but really, they were little more than photos and statistics to her. And it was the emotions, the stories of these people, the time he'd spent with them, that made this tragedy so very real.

She peeked at Mike, seated near her on the sofa. He glanced at her, lips tweaking to one side in a wry smile that made her hand shoot out and envelope his fingers in hers. He looked surprised, glanced down, then over at Brent with raised eyebrows. She shrugged and gently squeezed.

This man. This tender-hearted, compassionate man. She'd do anything to help him feel better.

Brent left for a drink, and she leaned over. "Are you doing okay?"

"Better," he admitted, giving her hand a squeeze.

"If there's anything I can do, you'll let me know, won't you?"

"Thanks, Bree."

She smiled and released his hand as Brent returned to the room.

She would simply pray and ask God to guide her, then do whatever He led her to do.

HOURS LATER, after Bree had cried herself to sleep thinking on Mike's lost look, wondering how she could possibly help, she woke suddenly, brain on high alert. She glanced at the clock. It was too early. Way, way too early. But maybe he'd be up. If she sent a message and he responded, then she'd know it had been the right thing to do.

HI. HOPE YOU GOT SOME SLEEP. HAD A GOOD IDEA - MAYBE EVEN A GOD IDEA. CALL ME WHEN YOU CAN.

She lay back on her bed, watching her phone. Nothing. Nothing.

A light flashed, signaling an incoming message.

ARE YOU SURE YOU'RE AWAKE?

She laughed and pressed to call. "Hi, Mike."

"Bree. Do you know what time it is?"

"I couldn't sleep. Well, not much. But anyway, I had a great idea."

"And this couldn't wait until daylight?"

"Oh." Disappointment crossed her chest. "I'm sorry. I should let you sleep—"

He chuckled. "I was awake too. What's your great idea?"

"Well, you know how you took all those awesome pictures while in the Philippines?"

"I know I took photos, but I didn't think they were that great."

"Oh, but they are! Listen to you, all humble. Mike, some of your photos are truly beautiful. And I was thinking, perhaps we could use them to help raise money."

"What do you mean?"

"We could make a calendar—pick twelve photos, thirteen if you want a different one on the cover, and with a little explanation and a Bible verse or two, it could be a reminder for people to pray for the ministry of MPFG and the people involved."

He was silent for a long, long moment—so long that she wondered if he'd gone to sleep. Eventually he said, "How do you come up with these ideas?"

"Don't you like it? I really thought it might be a good, practical reminder, but if you don't think it'd work—"

"I love it, Bree."

For a moment she misheard him, and her heart started to race, then she realized he'd said "it" not "you" and settled down. Exhaled. "Do you think it'd work?"

"I think we should check with John, but I don't think he'd have a problem. We might need to clear some privacy issues if we're using people's pictures."

"You have so many that you don't even need to include those that show people's faces." Her heart hummed with hope. "I really feel this could work."

"What are you doing tomorrow—well, later today?" His

voice held excitement. "We could look over them, make a selection that you think might work, then I could email John and get the ball rolling."

"I'm free whenever. It's my day off."

"And you wouldn't mind helping me?"

"Of course not. Like I said, anything I can do."

"You're the best, Bree."

She smiled into the darkness.

"I should let you go so you can catch some sleep," he said.

"Or we could talk some more. I don't think I'll be able to sleep."

A chuckle. "I don't think I will either. But all the same, if you get some sleep now, at least one of us can function with all we have to do tomorrow."

"Or later this morning," she said, glancing at the clock.

"Come for breakfast? Whatever time suits you."

"Is now too early?"

Another chuckle. "G'night, Bree."

"Goodnight, Mike."

And she ended the call praying he'd find sleep—praying she'd find sleep—as another part of her wondered if he snored.

WHEN BREANNA KARLSSON set her mind to something, heaven forbid anyone who got in her way. She reminded Mike of Brent in that way, the steamroller effect of persistent determination, only she wore clothes better and he'd never wanted to kiss Brent.

She'd turned up on his doorstep at precisely 7:00a.m., an hour that surprised his mom, as he hadn't had a chance to tell her about their visitor or their plans for the day. But when she heard about Bree's idea, she cleared off the dining table, which became their war room as they discussed photos and Bible verses, composed and sent emails and messages, and watched the TV for what brief reports about the typhoon the North American news displayed.

"It's amazing how little of the rest of the world we know," Bree said.

"I didn't realize just how insular my world was until I went," Mike confessed.

"I don't think any of us would. That's why this is so good for you to promote."

He nodded, waiting for John to respond to his email. He knew it was probably too early—or too late—and communications meant a conclusive answer regarding permissions might be weeks down the track, if at all. "Maybe we'd do well to have a backup plan for the photos. If we have one that includes faces and one that's more general market scenes or landscapes, that might prove less of a problem."

"Oh, that's a good idea."

Her approving smile sent strength to his heart.

"You know what else I think we could do? A website."

"A what?"

"Well, I was helping Moira with some preschool administration, and they have a simple website that's free to create and use. We could do a website that promotes the organization, and people could find the calendars, maybe see some of the sponsorships available or where their funds go. Don't you think that'd be cool?"

"You are so creative." Who was this woman, thinking so outside the box? "I think it's a great idea. I'll send John another email and see what he thinks."

She exhaled. "Hey, I'm hungry now. Do you think your mom has any of that fruit salad left?"

"If she doesn't, I'll make more."

"You're so good to me."

"The feeling's mutual, Bree."

She studied him, a small smile on her face that made him long to know what she thought. In some ways he hated this dancing around commitment. In other ways he loved it. It was like flirting, but with intention. Come January first, he'd know exactly how she felt.

His day passed in a world of images, memories, hopes, emails, and trying not to notice just how much he loved having Bree near. A day of mixed emotions as they worked beside each other productively, even as Mike still felt the gnawing ache of grief and concern.

But his most enduring image was at the close of day, when she hugged him goodbye. He'd head back to Boston tomorrow, and she'd return to work. Her hug was long, and as he wrapped his arms around her and buried his face into her hair, he was so tempted to turn it into something more. To admit the deepest revelation of his heart. A brush of lips on hers wouldn't really hurt, would it?

But he restricted himself to telling her thank you, kissing her cheek, and releasing her with the promise that he'd soon be in touch.

And watched as she climbed into her car, blew him a kiss, and drove away.

For once Mike's focus during preseason training was impacted, distracted as he was by the situation in the Philippines and that which was closer to home. He was exchanging texts and emails with Bree on a near daily basis—work-related, he told himself, and suspected she told herself too—as they discussed the calendar and website, as they worked together to do what they could to support John and Rose and MPFG.

His video had been received well, the guys using their own networks to raise awareness and talk about the extra need for funds in the devastated region. He'd felt their prayers as they supported him. Sometimes he'd feel a rising panic just dissipate, as if someone somewhere had prayed for him. Other times he'd pray, only to see an immediate answer, like God already had things sorted. God was so good. John had reported that the missing children had been found, and Rodel and his family were safe, and the church Mike had helped build in the mountains was still standing. He was so thankful.

Training camp saw some new faces, new lines, and he was partnered with Ledinberger for their first away game against Dallas. The next day they played against Phoenix, which at least provided a chance to find their groove and refine their plays a little more as they won. It also provided the opportunity to catch up with Beau before Mike—like a few other Canadian teammates—caught a flight home for Thanksgiving.

Time with his family, a brief catch up with Bree, then he was back to California for three games in four days. Two wins later and they finally flew back to Boston. All the travel made him weary, but Bree's messages, her work on the calendar and website—both now approved by John and Rose—lifted his heart.

"Mike!"

"Beatrice." He stepped back in the elevator and shifted his duffle bag so she had room.

Mrs. Gruber smiled. "It's been a while since we last saw you."

"Road trips. Back home for Thanksgiving. Then back to the west coast."

"You must be exhausted."

"Yeah, it's been a big few weeks, that's for sure."

"And how is that nice young lady of yours? I was ever so disappointed I couldn't have tea with her and her grandmother, but these things happen."

"Bree is doing well." He hoped. As soon as he got upstairs, he'd be giving her a call.

"Tell her hello from me and that I hope we'll see her again soon."

The doors opened, and he waited for Beatrice to exit before gathering his things and finally entering his apartment. The space smelled stale, so he inched open windows, threw his laundry in the wash, realized he'd need to go to the store for milk and essentials, but ignored that as he switched on his laptop and checked his latest email from Bree.

Hi Mike,
I thought you might enjoy seeing the latest progress on the website. I've included a section where people can purchase calendars and the framed prints we talked about last time. Let me know what you think. There's also the sponsorship page, which John and Rose can update with their latest children to be sponsored, and all the money is safely secured through the software used. Looking forward to hearing your thoughts.
Hope your flight home went well. Was so good to see you at Thanksgiving.
Miss you,
Bree

He wondered how long it would be before he could say the words from the depths of his soul. Would he need to wait until January? The way they were connected, it seemed much too far away.

He checked the time. Called her on the off-chance she might pick up. Knew his heart skipped a beat when she answered.

"Hi!"

"Hey, you. You're not at work?"

"I have Mondays off."

So she did. "Has work slowed up any?"

"We have a big Fall harvest thing for Halloween, then it's nothing until Christmas. How about you?"

"I'm in Toronto in a week's time, then we're back for a few games, then it's another road trip, this time to Florida."

"Oh, you poor thing," she mock sympathized.

"Yeah." He sighed. "It's sure gonna be hard to leave the snow and storms for the beach and sun."

"I'm feeling for you."

His lips curved. "Hey, I love your website ideas. I had a quick look at it while we were on a layover in Buffalo. It looks amazing."

"And John is happy?"

"Ecstatic. It's been yet one more of those things they've wanted to do but haven't had the time for. And now here you are, being amazing, making it happen."

"I'm just glad I can help."

So humble, too. "You know, I think the next time we get a chance, I'll need to take you out for dinner."

A beat. "But not as a date?"

"Definitely not as a date," he agreed, remembering. "Just as a thank you. Like a business perk. We can talk only about the website if you want."

"Yeah, not sure my brother will see it that way."

"Then I won't tell if you don't."

"My lips are sealed." She laughed. "Looking forward to seeing you again. Toronto in a week, you said?"

"I'll send you and your folks tickets to watch the game, if you like."

"I know Dad won't say no." She chuckled. "Maybe even Gran will want to come."

"She's pretty cool, your grandmother."

"Takes after her granddaughter," she said cheekily.

"Maybe she does. Although I kinda suspect she's had that sass for quite a few years."

"I think you're right. Regardless, I'll enjoy seeing you."

He smiled. "Me too. I can't wait."

CHAPTER 25

*A*h, the serenity.

The rose scented bubbles discreetly popped as the warm water soothed Bree's aching muscles. She leaned back against the bath headrest and closed her eyes. Quiet. Calm. Peace.

No fundraisers to organize—the calendar was at the printer's and the website was now live. No noisy children. As much as she loved her work, sometimes it was nice to escape. And with Mom and Dad visiting Dean in Vancouver, she had the house to herself for once.

She smiled, sinking lower until the water met her chin, the faint fizz of bath salts and gentle plop of bubbles the only sounds. She breathed in and out slowly. The past few weeks had been a little hectic, and now was her chance to relax and have an early night. After finishing work early, she'd grabbed takeout and eaten that while she ran a bath and thought about tonight's game. Mike was in Florida playing the Panthers. After her bath she'd watch the game in her PJs, text him congrats afterwards, and go to sleep. *Thanks, Lord.*

Bree cracked open an eye, lazily popping an enormous

bubble that had formed near her chin, smiling as the tiny droplets dispersed. Nothing to do tonight, no cleaning, no washing, no planning. Nope, tonight was all about finding some peace.

She took another deep breath, drinking in the sweet scent of relaxation as she sank deeper into the bath. Now all she needed was to have a nice cup of tea, watch Mike play, and then sleep, glorious sleep.

The game started, and Bree watched it with half closed eyes, brain only really pricking to attention when she recognized Mike's jersey. She liked to watch him skate—Mr. Cool on the ice, never throwing down the gloves or getting into the argy-bargy that others sought as entertainment. He didn't need to do that. He let his game speak for itself.

Pride swelled her chest. He was such a good guy—so relaxed, so considerate. Guilt whispered at times that she was being unfair, that to make him wait until New Year's to officially be a couple was simply an exercise in frustration. But the fact he seemed to understand her reasons, the fact he was willing to wait, made him even more wonderful.

The game continued. She sipped her tea. Prayed for his safety as he took to the ice again.

He and his new partner moved up on the ice, protecting their goal as the Panthers amped up their attack. Her thoughts ran slow, her blinks getting longer, when—

BOOM.

Man down on the ice. A man wearing Boston's 78.

No! She straightened, eyes widening, pulse pattering with fear. No, no. Mike wasn't moving. "God, let him be all right." She pumped up the volume on the TV, which had moved to the vision of a fight between a Bruin and a Panther.

"...and it appears Mike Vaughan has taken a nasty hit from

Woletsky, known as one of the bruisers in the game. Play has stopped, Boston's long-time trainer has taken to the ice, where Vaughan is finally moving. He seems to be clutching his chest after taking that hard hit from Woletsky straight into the boards. Let's watch the replay now."

Bree watched, chest tight, heart in mouth, as the hit was repeated on poor Mike. The vision slowed down, and she could see Mike move awkwardly as Woletsky angled him into the side. She caught a glimpse of Mike's face, his mouth guard hanging free as his jaw sagged before he hit the ice, his body lying ominously still for a second or two before his legs twitched and he slowly moved to his knees, wincing as he grasped his upper body.

The replay and commentary continued. "...appears he should have protected himself while Woletsky completed his check. Woletsky and Ledinberger have now been sent to the penalty box while Vaughan leaves the ice. I suspect we won't see him again this game."

"Dear God, let him be okay!" She grabbed her phone and called him. No answer. She texted, but knew it a futile exercise. How could she find out more? The game had moved on. There might be an update later about his condition, but she needed to know now.

Bree turned on the lounge's lamp, wishing the brightness would provide clarity to her whirling thoughts. Her brain was still too fuzzy. What to do, what to do?

Brent. Brent might know. And even if he didn't know, he might know ways Bree could know. She dialed his number, listening as it rang, hoping he'd watched the game tonight, seeing he wasn't playing. Five seconds later, he picked up.

"Oh, Brent! Did you see that?"

"Woletsky is a thug."

"Do...do you think he'll be okay?"

"I'm sure he will." Brent's voice softened. "He might have

bruised some ribs and need to spend the night in the hospital, but he'll be okay."

Moisture heated the backs of her eyes. She blinked. "I...I don't know what to do."

"You don't have to do anything, Bree. He'll be fine. Stuff like this happens all the time."

But it didn't happen all the time to the man she loved. She gulped. *Loved.* What if he'd died? "Hockey is so dangerous." Her voice was squeaky. "Should I call his mom?"

"Why would you? He'll be fine. Send him a text if you need to do anything. But hey, you saw him skate off. If he couldn't do that, then you'd know something was really wrong."

Brent's words eased a measure of the panic from her heart. Still, she chewed her lip. She didn't want to be a worrier, but she couldn't help this sense that she was supposed to do something but couldn't find her script.

"Bree, go and talk to Mom and Dad."

"They're in Vancouver, remember?"

"Oh, right. Look, how about I call him?"

"Would you? You're his best friend. Someone might answer if it's you, even if he can't."

"If it makes you feel better, then okay. Talk soon."

She waited, eyes fixed on the TV screen, but nothing more was being said about Mike's condition. Indignation rose. How could they ignore this? A man's life could be changed forever, but still the game must go on. What a joke. Sometimes she hated this sport.

She glanced at her phone. Still no answer from her text before. Should she try to call him?

Her phone rang, startling her into dropping it, and she scrabbled on the floor and picked it up, pressing answer. "Mike?"

"It's me." Brent. "He didn't answer."

"Oh."

"Look, it's really okay. You don't need to worry. I mean, it's nice that you're concerned, but when things like this happen the wife or family gets informed, but the team does what it can to help the player feel comfortable, and—"

"How can anyone feel comfortable with a broken rib?"

"You don't know that for certain."

"Why else would he be clutching his chest there? No, Brent, something is very wrong."

"Bree, it's not like he's your twin. This special empathy thing doesn't work for him."

Except it felt like it did.

Still, Brent's words had given her direction. "I should let you go. You're right, he's probably fine and will call us soon. Your next game is tomorrow night, isn't it?"

"Yeah."

"Well, take care of yourself, okay?"

"Yes, Bree. And you, don't worry. Pray, and trust God, okay?"

"Yes, brother dear."

"G'night, Breanna."

She made a face at that name and ended the call. Glanced at her phone again. Still no word from Mike. Maybe she should give his mom a call.

Two rings. "Mrs. Vaughan?"

"Why, Breanna, I...I wasn't expecting to hear from you."

"Please, how is he?"

"Mike? Well, the manager just called, and they're taking him to hospital. He's talking—"

Oh, thank goodness.

"—but they suspect broken ribs. He had a mild concussion, too, which means they want to keep him for a few days for observation."

Her eyes filled. Poor Mike.

"Breanna? Are you still there?"

"I...yes."

"Please excuse me. I'm racing to organize things so I can catch the next plane."

"Does one leave tonight?"

"I'm afraid it's too late. But there is one that leaves early tomorrow morning."

"Will…will Mr. Vaughan go with you?"

"I'm afraid he's in Nova Scotia on business, so I'm arranging this myself. And it's all rather new, and—" Her voice broke.

Bree swallowed. "Would you like me to arrange your ticket for you? You'd want the quickest flight there, wouldn't you?"

"Oh, Breanna. I—"

"You have a passport?"

"Yes, Callie insisted we get them to visit her in Germany. But I really couldn't impose."

"Mrs. Vaughan, if you don't think *I'd* be imposing, I'd really like to come to your house now and arrange this for you."

"You'd do that?"

"Of course. Is…is that all right?"

"That would be so helpful. I don't want to worry, but it's hard when you're on your own."

"I know exactly what you mean," Bree admitted.

"Oh, I forgot your parents are away. Well, if you don't think it'd be too much trouble—"

"I'm on my way. Sit tight, find your passport, and I'll be there in two shakes."

"Thank you."

Bree glanced at her PJs. Maybe she could get away with wearing them and remaining cozy if she wore a jacket. Some might consider this ensemble more lounge wear than the flannelette PJs she wore during the depths of winter, so provided she didn't have an accident driving there, it might work out okay.

Ten minutes later she was knocking at the Vaughan's heavy oak door, the stained glass either side permitting a dim view of inside. "Hello?" She knocked again. Tried the handle just as Regina opened it, a phone stuck against her ear.

"Hi." Bree pushed her messy hair behind her ears. Hadn't had time to brush it—or do much really, apart from get her bag and boots and keys.

Regina gestured her inside, whispering, "It's him." She spoke into the phone. "Yes, Bree has just arrived." She listened a moment more, then handed the phone to Bree. "He wants to talk to you."

Oh. She pressed the phone to her ear. "Mike?"

"Hey, what are you doing at Mom's when I'm not there?"

"Just trying to help her find a flight for tomorrow."

"I thought someone from the team would help do that." He coughed, and she heard him give a wheeze.

"Are you okay?"

"I'll be fine. Hey, thanks for helping out my mom. Be good to see her."

"Happy to," she said, wondering if he'd say anything about wanting to see her too.

But he didn't. Only said, "Can you please put Mom back on?"

He didn't want to talk to her? Her heart hurt so bad it was hard to breathe. She blinked back disappointment and handed the phone back to his mother, waiting as his mom listened a while longer then concluded the conversation.

"Mike had to go. His nurse is there. He thinks they'll organize a flight for me, but I'd still rather book this and sort it now."

"Sure. I'll do what I can." He didn't want to talk to her? She sighed. It didn't mean that. Not really. He was busy, there'd be doctors, team personnel. She shouldn't take it personally.

Regina led the way into a study, where the computer was on and her passport lay waiting. Bree glanced through the open tabs and quickly found the shortest flight. Two seats remaining. It left at 6:20 the following morning.

"Are you happy with this one?" Bree pointed to the tab. "You'd need to get to the airport pretty early."

"I don't mind. The sooner it gets there the better."

"Do you want one way or return?"

"What do you think?"

"One way we can book right now, but return can be cheaper."

"Oh, I don't care about the cost right now. If the team wants to pay, then they can sort that out later. I just want to see my son."

Bree swallowed. So did she. She completed the booking, printed off the e-ticket. "Here you go."

"You're a lifesaver."

"No problem. Have you booked a taxi to get to the airport?"

"Oh. I should do that, too."

Another phone call and that was organized as well.

"Thank you, Bree."

"I'm glad you'll see him. Tell him I said hello."

Regina studied her, glanced at the printed ticket. "You said there were two tickets available?"

"Now there's only one."

"You…you could come too, you know. I'm sure he'd like to see you."

Something within tugged to go. She tamped it down, shook her head. "I don't think so."

"Give it some thought? To be honest, I'm not used to arranging these sorts of things myself. Usually my husband is the one who arranges things like this, so I feel quite out of my depth. It would be good to have some company."

"Thanks, but I didn't get the impression he'd want me there."

"Why not? You know he"—a beat—"cares about you."

"I'm sure he's really busy."

"Think about it and let me know?"

Bree nodded, hugged her, then escaped back to her car and drove home.

Yet as she skidded on icy roads, her thoughts continued their desperate dance. Could she get away? She had no commitments this weekend. She didn't have to be at work until Tuesday. She had enough savings. And she *really* wanted to be there. Should she go, though? Brent seemed to think Mike would be okay, and Mike hadn't said he wanted her there. It certainly would make a statement if she went. Was this just fear-induced worry? But really, did those objections matter? Mike was in hospital. Of course she should be there! *Oh God, what do I do?*

Bree pulled into the garage, went upstairs, and exchanged her jacket for her dressing gown. Her phone still showed no word from him. Maybe a cup of tea might help. She moved downstairs to the kitchen. Watched the kettle boil. Sank into a chair and took a deep breath.

God, thank You that You are with Mike. Thank You for giving the doctors wisdom. Thank You for working this out for good. Show me what to do.

She stared blankly at the timber kitchen table until the jug signaled its readiness. She poured the hissing water over her tea bag and splashed in some milk. Took a sip of tea, wincing as the heat seared her mouth. Who cared about a minor burn? Mike had broken ribs! *Lord, what do I do?*

She went to the study to look at her dwindling bank account online. She bit her lip. If she went, almost all her savings would be gone. She shrugged and checked for available flights to Miami in the morning.

The last seat had gone.

Disappointment crashed against her chest. Well, she'd prayed for God to show her what to do. Apparently He had.

Tears welled. She blinked them back. She was just tired. Getting emotional. It had been a big few weeks, and tonight's early night had turned into a far, far later night than she'd expected. Sleep would help.

But back upstairs in bed, sleep eluded her as she wondered how Mike was feeling, wondered just how cute the nurses were, wondered if he was sleeping. Her mind raced, her emotions sliding all over the place, the panic kept at bay only by deep breathing. *God, help him. And help me...*

PALM TREES. Blue skies. How incongruous such things seemed. Bree blinked to see if this was still a dream. The trees blurred past as the taxi swerved away from the airport. True. But still unreal. How could God allow the sun to still shine? How could people still smile and laugh? Didn't they know what had happened?

But the fact she was here at all seemed a miracle of the most-loving-God kind. The lack of sleep that forced her to check for flights and cancellations. The sudden availability of a seat, one she'd instantly booked before sending a text to Regina, even though it was way past midnight. They'd met at the airport, exchanged hugs and yawns, and gotten a bite to eat. Their plane had changed at Charlotte, and they were now expecting to arrive at the hospital in the next five minutes or so.

Bree grasped Regina's hand, felt the return of pressure. She was still amazed Regina hadn't questioned her, had encouraged her to come. "Has anyone from the team called you today?"

"Oh, I should switch on my phone." Regina peered at her phone and sighed. "I'm sorry. In all that rush, I think I left my reading glasses at home. Can you read what this says?"

Bree peered at the tiny screen. "You have three missed calls."

"I should find out who they're from." She listened, glanced at Bree, and nodded.

The cab driver called, "We're nearly there."

Bree got her credit card to pay, and within minutes they

were in the hospital, being led along a corridor by a Boston representative.

"He's in with the doctor now, Mrs. Vaughan, if you'd like to see him." The representative glanced at Bree. She said nothing, just gestured Regina to follow him inside. She'd wait. She didn't want to intrude.

She stayed near the door in the corridor filled with noises and smells she didn't find restful, and she wondered how Mike had slept—*if* he'd slept any more than she had. She pushed a weary hand through her hair. She must look a mess. Was coming here just foolishness? What if he didn't want to see her? She blinked away tears.

"Miss?" A nurse paused. "Are you okay?"

Bree couldn't speak, the emotions she'd suppressed all morning rushing to clog her throat and eyes.

"Are you here to see Mr. Vaughan?"

"Mike," she finally managed. "Family friend. His mom is in there now."

"You came with her?"

Bree nodded. "Is he okay?"

"He will be."

Relief cascaded through her chest. "Good."

"Do you want to go inside?"

Bree nodded again.

"Come on." The nurse smiled. "But you might want to clean your mascara off from under your eyes."

Bree grabbed her mirror from her bag. "Oh, I look like such a fright." A minute's fussing and she looked more presentable, then finally, bracing herself, she went in.

The room was large, the window even holding the slightest glimpse of water. But she didn't care about the view. Her eyes were all for the man lying in the bed, whose own eyes widened as she drew near.

"Bree," he rasped.

She glanced at the team person standing in the corner, talking on his phone. The nurse, who'd accompanied her inside, moved to usher him outside.

"I, um, hope you don't mind that I came."

"How could I?" He stretched out a hand, and she moved beside the bed to hold it.

This. This was what she needed. To hold him—even if it was just his palm and fingers—and feel the warmth of his skin, his pulse, and know he'd be okay.

"Breanna has been such a godsend," Regina said from her chair on the other side of the bed. "Helping me last night and today. I would have been lost without her."

"I'm glad I could help." Bree offered a smile.

"You're a sweet thing." Regina's gaze shifted to Mike, then back to Bree. Then she blinked. Pushed to her feet. "Oh, you must excuse me. I have another call to make."

The knowing smile she offered was enough to make Bree wonder if she'd been getting lessons from Granny V on how to not be in the way. Bree waited until she'd left, then dragged a chair to the bed so she could sit close and still hold Mike's hand. "How are you? I was so worried. How are you feeling? Did you get any sleep last night?"

He chuckled, then gave a slight gasp. "I'm okay. But I have to take it easy for a couple of days. No skating. No laughing either."

"How is your head feeling?" Oh, how she'd love to smooth down that little curl over his forehead.

"I got banged up pretty good. I've got sore ribs and a killer headache, but I'll be okay."

"Are you sure?"

"I'll be a lot better now I'm seeing you."

Her eyes filled with fresh tears. "I…I—"

"Hey, don't cry. It's okay."

"No, it isn't," she said, wiping at her tears. She bet there'd be a new mascara tidemark soon. "I felt so helpless watching you last night. And even through all this, helping your mom and so on, I realized that I want to be the first person the team calls. Does that make me selfish?"

"It makes you wonderful."

His sweetness propelled further truth to spill from her heart and lips. "I realized that if you died, if you weren't in my world anymore, I'd always regret making you wait, for being so stupidly stubborn as to cling to a dumb vow I made, when really, Michael Vaughan, there is nobody else in this world I would rather be with, nobody else I want to date or whose hand I want to hold." She sucked in an unsteady breath, lifted his hand, kissed his knuckle. "I'm sorry for being such hard work."

"Bree, you're not hard work."

"No?"

"You're amazing. You're everything. I tried to call you before, but you didn't answer—"

"Wait, you called me?" She pulled out her phone. Saw she had three missed calls of her own.

"—and now I can say to you what I said on the phone. I stayed up last night thinking, as I couldn't sleep, and anyway, I'm sorry if I made you feel I didn't want you to come. I didn't want to presume, but I'm so, so glad you're here now."

She squeezed his hand. "There's no place I'd rather be. Well, obviously I'd rather you weren't injured and lying in a hospital bed, but I'm glad to be here with you. I'm always glad to be with you."

He smiled. "See? You brighten my day."

"Really?"

"Really." His gaze sobered, and in the blue depths of his eyes she could see all the sincerity and hope she'd dreamed of seeing. "I love you, Breanna Karlsson."

Her chest grew tight, as if her heart were holding in a

million radiant sunbeams. She slid a hand down the stubble of his cheek. "I love you."

"Really?"

"Really." She smiled and drew nearer, drew nearer still. Perhaps she could risk a brief hug—

"Ahem."

She jumped, straightened, and spun around. A doctor, followed by Regina and the team guy from before, looked at them with widened eyes. Bree took a step back, another, her cheeks aflame. Oh, what must Mike's mom think?

"Mom, Doc, Paul, excuse us."

"But—"

"You heard my son. We need to leave."

Bree bit back a grin as little Regina Vaughan propelled the two larger men from the room, exiting after them with a wink that told Bree everything she needed to know.

"Bree, come here."

She inched closer to the bed, found Mike's hand once again, gave his fingers a gentle squeeze.

"Come here."

She let his hand tug her nearer still, her eyes lingering on his face—his serious face.

"Come here," he said hoarsely.

Breath suspended, she lowered until she could feel his breath whisper against her skin.

"Bree."

And suddenly she knew what he meant and, in a moment that felt ordained by heaven, finally pressed her lips to his in a moment of utter rightness.

Oh. It was like his lips had been made for her and hers for him, so perfectly did they match and meld and move together. She slid a hand into his hair, felt his arm reach to her neck and ever so gently press her more deeply into his soul-tingling kiss.

Oh, this was perfection. This was romance. This was Mr.

Darcy kissing Elizabeth, this was Gilbert kissing Anne, this was heart-whirling, toe-curling sensation, and she needed—

Air. She needed air. So she could dive back into wonder again.

She pulled back, breathing unsteadily. Her lips felt swollen. She didn't care. "Mike."

"Bree."

"Why didn't you ever tell me you could kiss like that?"

"Why didn't you tell me?" He smiled, and her heart knew another palpitation most unconnected to her iron levels.

"Mike"—the Boston guy again—"we really need to—"

"Go away, Paul," Mike said, gaze still fixed on Bree, his expression like that of an explorer who'd just found Atlantis to be true. Like he couldn't quite believe it, though the proof stood before him still.

At the sound of footsteps retreating, she murmured, "You might need to hear what they have to say."

"I might need another kiss as well. Do you know how long I've waited for that?"

Long enough, if that soft expression on his face was any sign.

"Will you help me feel better?" he pleaded, heat—smudged with what looked like tease—in his eyes.

"We shouldn't," she murmured, caressing his jaw. "The doctor is waiting to see you, and we really shouldn't kiss again."

"Why not? Oh, because of Brent and your 'no dating a hockey player' thing." He sighed. Winced. "Well, I guess I can wait another six weeks."

"No."

"No? So this is nothing to do with Brent?"

"Who?" She smiled, drew near again. "No, it's because when we kiss I don't want to stop, and I'm worried I might do you an injury."

"Is that so?"

She nodded. "That is so."

"What was it you said back in Boston? It's not a date unless there's kissing. So what do we call this then?"

She bent and kissed his lips one more time, felt the tingles through to the very tips of her toes. "I think we'd better call this a medical emergency."

"I think I can see more medical episodes in my future."

She chuckled. "I meant me. I was going to combust if I didn't kiss you."

He laughed, winced. "Well, you let me know if there's anything I can do to help you with that."

"And as for this?" She straightened. "Still doesn't count as a date, because who wants to have a date in a hospital? So I think we can still count this as promise kept, right?"

"Absolutely."

"Mr. Vaughan." The doctor intruded.

"I'll let you go," Bree said, releasing his hand.

He gripped it more firmly. "Stay for a little while?"

"I'll stay as long as you'll have me."

CHAPTER 26

November passed in a blur of pain and medication, email and phone calls, as Mike adjusted to life at home in Boston, watching his teammates win some, lose some, and gel as a team without him. It wasn't all loss, though. The knowledge Bree had chosen him, wanted him despite this ridiculous promise, brought a joy and lightness that he hadn't felt in years.

Every moment she wasn't at work was one they could spend together. Texting, emailing, calling, online. They weren't dating, he told himself—and her—but only because they weren't in the same place. For all intents and purposes they were. He glanced out the window at the storm-tossed sea. Anyone else might definitely think they were.

He'd had fun trying to explain to Brent when he finally called.

"My sister was so worried about you."

Mike had had a choice. Admit she'd come to see him, or evade? He'd settled for: "She was a great support for my mom, helping to organize her flights and stuff."

"She's a great little organizer," Brent admitted.

Redirect, redirect. "Have you seen the calendars she designed?"

"I'm looking at mine now. It's hanging on the fridge. Looks great. Your photos worked out pretty good too."

"Yeah." Admit his photos were selling like hotcakes on the website and Bree had to keep ordering new ones to be printed? "People seem to like them."

"I checked out the website. It looks awesome."

"Yep, that's your sister's work too."

"Really? I didn't know she was so tech savvy."

"There's probably a lot you don't know about Bree," Mike said, smiling to himself, glad it was a phone call and Brent couldn't see his expression.

"Yeah. Hey, when have they said you'll be better?"

"A few weeks." Mike's mood sobered. "It's kind of tough seeing the team do stuff without me."

"They'll soon see how much they need you."

"Hope so, and that it's not the excuse they need to do a trade."

"Any more talk of that?"

"Not officially. But they've brought in a guy from the Providence development team, and he's looking a good fit with Leddy, the guy they teamed me with. Who knows what'll happen."

"God does."

Mike laughed, still felt some rib strain.

"What?"

"It's good to hear you talking like that again."

"I've come to realize that a lot of things I once thought important just aren't," Brent admitted.

"Sounds like you're getting old."

"I like to think it's maturity."

"Or you're just getting old."

"Yeah. Whatever."

Mike could hear the smile in Brent's voice. It felt good to be back to this tease again. "So how about you? The Wings seem to be doing well this season."

"Yeah. It's nice to see. Good to be racking up some points."

"It'd be good to be racking up any points," Mike had said dryly.

"It'll happen. Good things come to those who wait."

And wasn't that the truth?

Now Mike studied the boats in the harbor, already plastic-wrapped for the season, ready for the long months of waiting ahead.

He'd waited and prayed and trusted, and now, in just a few more weeks, he and Bree could finally make their relationship official.

Official. He shivered. Judging from the heat in their hospital kiss, they might need to ramp up the official status to something more permanent pretty soon.

Bree had mentioned inviting him for Christmas, but then his mom had shared that Callie planned to come back from Germany for a week or so. "It's been a while since you've seen her," he'd said to Bree. "Maybe we'll have to have you guys all come over."

"The army, right?"

"Medical corps. I get the feeling sometimes she wants to quit, but the job security and money is there, so she keeps on."

His last call with Callie had been a few days ago. Between his schedule and hers and the time differences between Germany and the east coast, there wasn't often much opportunity to talk, so he'd been glad to have the chance to talk with his older sister. Even if it hadn't taken too long before the chit-chat got personal.

"So, Mom mentioned you have a girlfriend." She raised her eyebrows. "Bree Karlsson?"

"You probably don't remember her. She's Brent's twin sister."

"The hugger."

"Well, yeah. But she hasn't been hugging me much lately. We're not dating officially. Not yet, anyway."

"Not yet? Why's that?"

He explained about Bree's vow, which scored a withering response from his sister. "Lame."

Maybe, but he felt he should stand up for Bree's resolution. "Well, I guess you wouldn't know what it's like to want to prove anything to your sibling," he teased.

"You're wrong. Why do you think I'm still here? I had to venture out and come all the way over here on my own so I wasn't just known as Mike's sister."

"Then you know exactly how Bree feels."

"Which is why I know it's lame, because it means I'm as insecure as your girlfriend even though I've got to be five years older. How do you think that makes me feel?"

"Lame?"

She laughed. "Brat. Anyway, I don't know why you say you're not dating. From what Mom said the other day, seemed things were getting pretty steamy down in Florida."

"It's a lot warmer there than here," he offered.

"Yeah. Seemed there was an awful lot of kissing going on for people who aren't dating."

He shrugged.

She smiled. "About time."

"That's what I thought too."

"You've always had a thing for her, haven't you?"

This focus on his love life was not what he needed, so he turned the conversation to other things. She'd mentioned she wanted to come home for Christmas, "seeing as I'll be back into things here from January."

"Be great to see you."

"Be great to see you—and Bree." She laughed.

Yeah, he wasn't sure how that was going to work. And the way his mom was talking, he probably needed to have a quiet word in her ear to not spread gossip about him and Bree any more than had already been done. It'd be nice to get to Christmas without feeling the pressure of unmet expectations or feeling the need to fib or redirect when Brent noticed what was going on.

But then, Christmas would mean only another six days to New Year's, and then everything could change for the better.

"WELL, it feels funny to be packing up so early, but I can't say I'm not glad. I'm glad this year ends soon."

Bree's heart panged as Sylvie put away the Santa hats used in the dress-ups today. Her friend had been a little down ever since her breakup with her chef boyfriend a few weeks ago.

Bree joined her in removing strands of tinsel draped across the windows. The twinkle lights would stay and continue to provide welcome decorations for the next week and a half that the center remained closed, but everything else would be cleaned and put away so the new year could begin with everything fresh and in order.

The new year. Bree shivered. Fought to keep the grin off her face.

"What's got you looking so happy?"

"I love Christmas." And she suspected she'd *really* love New Year's. Just the thought of kissing Mike again... Toe-curls. Tingles.

"What's your family doing?"

"Church on Christmas Day, and we do a family dinner the night before. My family has an open house Christmas night if you want to drop in."

"Will your brother be there?"

"Maybe. I know my cousins always hope he is. They barely talk to me when he's there. But I know Brent has a road trip happening pretty soon after Christmas, and I can't remember what day he has to leave to get ready."

"Hmm. Maybe I will." Sylvie pulled down the paper chimney with its paper puffs of smoke with the children's Christmas wishes and thanks written on them. Benjie: a new bike. Hannah and Grace: thanks their mom was better. Park Lee: new paints. Felix: thanks his dad was now living with them.

Bree blinked back happy tears. God had proved so faithful through this year. "And hey, church is always there on Sunday. Let me know if you want a ride."

"Will Dan be there?"

"Who?"

"Dan Walton, remember? Plays for Toronto."

"Oh, him." Bree shrugged. "I couldn't say." It didn't matter anyway.

It *did* matter that Boston were playing in Pittsburgh and she wouldn't see Mike until Christmas Eve. But at least he didn't have another game scheduled again until the 28th in Carolina. She hoped they could spend some quality time together over Christmas. Not kissing, of course. But holding hands wouldn't be breaking any rules. And she was now so close to proving Brent wrong.

"I'll let you know."

"I hope you do. You're always welcome at church." She felt conviction tug, and she moved to fold up the fabric panel displaying all the words of Jingle Bells. "You know I'm your friend and that I want you to be happy. And I know that your chef guy hurt you and you feel let down, but I promise you, God won't ever stop loving you."

"Yeah? Prove it."

Bree swallowed. "I think *you* should prove it."

"Huh?"

"You. Ask God to prove Himself to you and see what He does."

"What, you just want me to pray and ask God for a miracle?"

"I believe God does do miracles."

"Name one."

Her and Mike. Mike's rebound from injury, symptom free, now back on the team scoring goals. The amazing response to the calendar and website sponsorships. Looking back, she could see so many miracles where God had intervened, turning situations around for good. "This year has been an incredible year of seeing God bless people. Felix's dad being released into the community. Diana's healing. Don't you think that a miracle?"

Sylvie shrugged. "Experimental drugs."

"But the doctors couldn't explain why the tumor disappeared so rapidly," Bree said gently. "I've seen God do amazing things."

"Yeah, well, you've always been a good girl. I'm not surprised God does good stuff for you."

"Oh, I'm not that good. This year I've realized just how selfish I can be, how judgmental and vain and impatient. I think God has shown me how broken I really am. God does good stuff because He is good, not because of anything I've ever done."

"Come on. Are you trying to tell me that God isn't impressed with all your fundraising stuff this year?"

"I don't think He really is."

"Next you'll be telling me He doesn't care if I sleep around."

Bree swallowed. "I think He's more concerned about how those actions impact us."

"Does this mean you and Mike have—"

"No!" Her cheeks heated. "That would wait until we're married."

"Seriously? You'd wait until then? How would you know you're compatible?"

"I think I know," she said, remembering his kiss and the way every part of her body had screamed for more of him. "And anyway, don't you think it'd be a special thing to share your body, your heart and soul, with only one person?"

Sylvie stared at her like she'd suddenly started spouting Japanese.

"God is interested in our hearts, Sylvie. He wants us to make choices that don't make us feel ashamed. But even when we do mess up, I think it's amazing that being friends with God is not about what we do or how good we are. God loves you. Full stop. No matter what you do."

"No matter what I do?" The cynical smile was back. "I can't believe that."

Please, God. "You know Christmas isn't really about tinsel and Santa. You know it's about remembering the birth of a little baby, who grew up to be a man who faced a lot of prejudice in His life, and ultimately, despite doing nothing wrong, ended up on a cross. God gave the life of His son so that everyone who believes in Him can have eternal life. God loves you, Sylvie. He always has, He always will, and He wants what's best for your life."

"Like what?"

Bree swallowed. "Like a life that's not filled with regret. A life of peace and hope. Joy to the world isn't just a song we sing at Christmas. It's about the hope we find in God."

"Yeah, well, I don't think that hope is for me."

"I think it is. In fact, I know it's for you. He loves us, Sylvie." Her heart was racing. "He loves you. Ask Him to show Himself to you, and I'll pray you see His answer."

Sylvie shrugged, and Bree exhaled and moved to finish undecorating the foyer. Had she made sense? Gone in too strong? *God, touch her heart. Use my clumsy words.* Her prayers continued as she packed away more tinsel.

"Breanna!" Moira called.

Bree moved to the small office. "Yes?"

Moira extracted a small gift from under the table. "This is

for you. I know this year has been a little challenging at times, but I want you to know how much I appreciate your contributions this year."

"It's been a joy, Moira. Thank you for the opportunity." She accepted the gift, peeked at the tag. "Should I open this now?"

"Why not?"

Bree had given her fellow workers each an MPFG calendar and special soaps she'd bought at the UNICEF shop. It was enough to make her wonder if they should source similar things from the wider MPFG community and see if they could be sold at the website too. She'd mention the idea to Mike and John at the upcoming online meeting, a regular meeting since the typhoon with updates on progress with the children and in the villages, how the funds raised since the typhoon were being distributed, and technological—and other—ideas.

"Bree?"

She carefully unwrapped it and found a beautiful crystal vase. "Oh, how sweet! It's perfect for little posies."

"Or for a rose a special someone might give you."

Bree grinned. "I might have to drop a hint."

"I'm sure he will be very happy to oblige."

"Thanks, Moira." Bree hugged her. "I've really appreciated your flexibility with me this year. I know shuffling shifts wasn't in my contract, but it's made such a difference for me."

"We would hate to lose you, so we'll do whatever we can to help you want to stay."

Bree smiled. "Thank you." How wonderful to be wanted. Anything more about the future she couldn't say. Not until Mike said something. And then, who knew where he might play?

That night, she settled in front of the TV, flicking between broadcasts as Detroit took on Minnesota and Boston played St. Louis. She joined her father in cheering on Brent as he scored and prayed for Mike's safety as they succumbed to the Blues.

She'd likely get a call or text from Mike tonight, and she wanted to pay attention to every detail she could. Showing she paid attention was showing she loved him, a thought that drew remembrance of something he'd said months ago.

She bit her lip. How could she not have known? How could she have been so blind? He was everything she'd ever wanted, and Granny V, Mom, Holly, had all been right. He'd never been the sort to be blinded by her brother's fame. Mike noticed her. He wanted her. She couldn't wait to see him again.

SHE HAD to wait until after dinner on Christmas Eve to finally steal a moment alone with Mike, popular man that he was with her family, especially with Granny V. When she finally had him to herself, everything within her wanted to kiss him, but she held back. This might not be a date in the truest sense of the word, but there definitely was intention in his coming tonight—and by the look in his eye.

"I got a little something for you," he said, holding out a little red velvet bag.

"Oh, I love presents!"

"I know."

She kissed his cheek (that was allowed) and lingered (that might be pushing it) and slowly undid the drawstring on the bag. "Oh, how perfect!"

"I know you and Holly have exchanged charms, and I hoped you wouldn't mind if I joined in."

It was a tiny silver heart. "Does this mean what I think it means?"

He angled closer, his gaze dropping to her lips, then back up again. "It depends on what you think it means."

"Well, if I was to see something like this on Holly's bracelet, I'd assume that she had a secret—or otherwise—admirer."

"Would you now?"

"I would."

"Well, then you would be right." He threaded his fingers through hers. "Though the question is, how secret do you want your admirer to be?"

"If he can remain secret a few more days, then he doesn't need to be a secret anymore."

"No?" He smiled.

"No." She leaned up, kissed his cheek again, heard his intake of breath. "Would you put it on?" She held out her wrist.

"Sure." He bent and fiddled at her wrist, every so often brushing her skin—deliberately, she thought—with the pads of his thumbs, an action that rippled shivers across her skin.

"Thank you so much."

"I know you like charms."

"You pay attention." Could anything be sweeter?

"Of course I do. I know you don't like the tiny seeds of tomatoes. I know your favorite ice-cream flavor is butterscotch. I know you sometimes think you need to lose fifteen pounds but don't realize just how beautiful you are." He shifted closer, his voice dropping lower, becoming slower. "I know your eyes are like amethysts. I know your hair smells like roses. I pay attention, Bree. I care about you. I always have."

There was every chance her heart might explode. How could she not have noticed this? Mike was so wonderful, so perfectly perfect.

"I love you," she whispered, drawing a hand down his bristled cheek.

"Shh. Don't tell anyone. They'll start to get ideas."

She laughed and entwined his fingers in hers.

"Here you two are." Brent moved into the kitchen, stuffed a corn chip into his mouth.

Mike moved to release his fingers from Bree's, but she grabbed tight, folding her arm behind his back, shifting slightly to hide how close they were.

"Here we are," she said.

"What are you doing?"

"Just talking."

She glanced at Mike, fought the smile.

"What are you talking about?"

"Stuff."

"Like?" Brent's eyebrows rose.

"Like tomatoes. Ice cream. Roses. That kind of stuff."

"Riveting." Brent eyed them, stuffed another corn chip in his mouth. "Hey, are you two coming to the New Year's Eve party again this year?"

"Who are you playing this time?"

"St. Louis."

She leaned back, sent Mike an enquiring look. "You're not playing then, are you?"

"Got that night off. Yeah, I might be able to come."

Bree swallowed a smile. "It might be fun."

"Yeah." Mike squeezed her hand.

New Year's Eve. The chance to really start the year off right.

FUNNY HOW TONIGHT Detroit's score didn't seem to matter. Mike glanced around the venue—the same as last year, many of the same faces in the crowd. He nodded to those he knew and listened as people discussed recent trades. His gut tightened uneasily. He half expected a phone call from his agent any day now, the likelihood of Phil calling ramping up each day that brought them closer to the February 24 trade deadline.

His last two games—away games against Columbus and the Hurricanes—had also been losses, and while he'd been disappointed with the results and known it wouldn't do his cause to stay any good, such feelings were tempered by the anticipation of what tonight would hold. He'd flown here to see Bree, had enjoyed her company during the game, had been wowed once again by her impeccable dress sense and style. He moved toward her now, where she was laughing with Brent, their sibling bond fully healed.

"Have I mentioned how beautiful you look tonight?" he murmured in her ear as he handed her a glass of wine.

"Several times, but don't let that stop you." She smiled up at him. "What's the countdown?"

He checked his watch. "Still five minutes to go."

She sighed. "Why does it feel like time is going so slowly right now?"

"I have no idea."

Their gazes met, held, and the world seemed to shrink to just them.

"What are you two looking so intense about?" Brent asked.

"I was just telling your sister how beautiful she looks," Mike said truthfully. For Brent to accept this relationship, a little prep work might be helpful.

"Isn't he the sweetest?" Bree said, placing a hand on Mike's chest, sending every particle of his body tingling.

"Yeah," Brent said dryly.

Bree laughed. "Come on. Just because you don't have a date tonight doesn't mean you can't recognize beauty when it's standing right in front of you."

"You look very nice, Breanna."

"Very nice?" She turned to Mike. "I much prefer your words, Mr. Vaughan. Yours at least had a ring of sincerity about them."

"You know I'll never lie to you."

"I do know that," she said, her eyes filled with trust as she offered him a special smile.

"How long until we can get out of here?" Brent asked, tugging at his collar as he glanced around.

"You don't want to leave just yet, do you?"

Brent shrugged. "It's not the same."

Mike's heart softened. Yeah, he bet this felt different for his friend. The last time Brent had been date-free for New Year's Eve must've been ten years ago.

"You'll meet Miss Right one day," Mike said. "Maybe even this coming year."

"Yeah. I'm not holding my breath."

"Probably wise," Bree said. "But you never know who's out there who'll be perfect for you." She smiled up at Mike, and his heart did a little leap.

"So." Brent turned to his sister. "You didn't date a hockey player, huh?"

"Nope."

Brent's glance slid to Mike, then back to Bree again. "Well, good for you."

"See, brother dear? I can exhibit self-control too."

"Has self-control been needed?" Another glance at Mike.

"You know me," Mike said, hands up in self-defense. "Master of patience here."

"What's the countdown now?" Bree asked.

Mike checked his watch. "Two minutes more." Anticipation thrummed. Should probably move away from here soon so he could get Bree alone and—

"Brent, I hope you know that I do keep my commitments. This year has been a challenge, but I hope you can find it in your heart to recognize when I've accomplished things and kept my word. And I hope you can trust me to find the right man for me when it's the right time."

"I do," he mumbled.

"Do you? Really?" She eyed him, then waved a hand around the room. "If I should happen to find someone here tonight, that would be okay with you?"

"Sure. If you like him. And he's a Christian. And I like him."

"And our parents like him. And Granny V." She chuckled. "I think Granny V really likes him."

"What do you mean?"

"Ten, nine, eight—"

Mike grabbed her hand.

"—five, four, three, two, one. Happy New Year!"

Amid a shower of confetti and balloons, Bree turned to Mike and, with the biggest smile on her face, said, "Kiss me, Mike."

"Happy New Year, Bree."

"It will be now." She wrapped her arms around him, and he pressed his lips to hers.

She slid her hands around his neck, and he closed his eyes and finally kissed her in the way he'd always dreamed. Not on her cheek or brow. Not from the confines of a hospital bed. But where his regard and affection were met equally by someone who had never been less than enthusiastic in displaying hers.

"I love you," she said, her heart in her eyes, her eyes on him.

"I love you," he murmured back, sealing his words with another kiss.

"Finally," Brent mumbled.

"What?" Bree turned to him. "What did you just say?"

Brent heaved out a breath. "If you have to choose someone, it might as well be him," he said, gesturing to Mike with his thumb.

"Might as well—? Didn't you once tell me Bree was off-limits?"

"You said that to him?" Bree said, swatting Brent's arm.

"Hey, I was just looking out for you."

"I don't need looking out for, thank you, brother dear," she said, wrapping her arm around Mike's waist. "I can do perfectly fine on my own."

"Apparently you can," Brent said, hooking an arm around her and mussing her hair.

"Not the hair, Brent, not the hair. I spent *ages* making it look this good."

He mussed it even more. Glanced at Mike. "Take care of her, okay?"

"Always."

"And you"—Brent kissed the top of Bree's head—"take care of him."

"Yes, sir."

And with Brent's blessing—and that of Bree's parents, which he'd sought and gained at Christmas—Mike stole Bree away to a quieter section near the window where they watched fireworks before their lips created heated magic of their own.

CHAPTER 27

Mike skated off the rink after the team's training session in New York, his breathing as unsteady as his hopes to remain a Bruin seemed to be. He tried to think positive as the coach advised on switching up the lines, but since returning to play, he'd been getting less ice time, and the way the coach seemed to ignore his requests for more made him wonder where they saw him in the future. He was trying to trust God, but the trade deadline was inching closer, and conversation in the locker room and hotels centered on the latest moves teams had made.

"You hear about Woletsky?" Todd said as they moved back off the ice. "Traded to Edmonton. Good thing we don't play them often, right, Vaughan?"

Mike shrugged. "I don't care where he goes." And he didn't bear the guy any ill-will. Accidents happened. The guy had apologized. By text, but it was something. Not everyone did.

"Imagine swapping palm trees for igloos," chuckled Ledinberger.

"Edmonton's not that cold," protested Franklin. "It's really nice."

"Yeah, but you're a cowboy at heart, aren't you?"

Franklin shrugged. "I wouldn't mind if I got sent there."

"Have you asked your agent about a possible trade?" Mike asked as they unlaced skates.

"Yeah, my contract means it can't be for a few more years."

"I hope you get where you want to one day."

"Thanks."

Mike finished stripping off practice gear and reached up to the stall's shelf to collect his phone. Saw he had a missed call—from his agent. His pulse skittered. *God, help me with whatever this may be.*

He pressed the numbers. Heard it ring. "Mike. Calgary wants you."

He closed his eyes. Exhaled through clenched teeth. Awesome. "When?"

"They've done it; you need to get on a plane to Calgary tonight."

"What? I'm in New York. We're supposed to go to Montreal next."

"And Calgary wants you to come to them tonight. Someone from the team is gonna call you, help you arrange for your things to be shipped from Boston."

"You're serious?"

A glance at his teammates suggested they recognized the gravity of this moment. Todd looked stunned, Franklin looked sad, Leddy's brow puckered. Yep, this was serious all right.

He listened a little more, then ended the call, and slumped back in his stall, his mind whirling. *Seriously, God?*

"You're being traded?" Todd asked.

He swallowed to force emotion back down his throat. "Calgary."

"Really?"

He exhaled, managed a nod. "Tonight."

"Wow. That's brutal."

Yep. Talk about God breaking him…

"Do you know what for?" Leddy asked.

That at least was some comfort. Boston must rate him higher than he thought to let him go for a first-round pick in this year's draft, a winger and an up-and-coming prospect. That was something, at least. He shared what he knew.

Leddy chewed his lip. "You know which winger you're being traded for?"

"Phil didn't say. But hey, the speed this trade is moving, you might meet him tonight." As for Mike, he had to pack, say farewells, tell his folks, tell Bree, and envisage life in a place he'd rarely visited outside hockey rinks.

"I can help with your stuff if you like," Franklin offered.

"Thanks. I—" He dragged his hands over his face. "I just need a moment."

Okay, think. Think. What was the first thing to do?

"You okay?"

"Yeah. There's just a lot to take in." Where he'd live. His old place. What this would mean for him and Bree. Would she want to move to Calgary? He didn't have a choice. His signature on his contract last year meant he'd agreed to moves like these, but she, she certainly could choose.

The extra money would be good. Phil had mentioned the likelihood of guaranteed first pairing. This would be great for his career. But what would it mean for other parts of his future?

He called Bree a few hours later. "Bree?"

"Hi! Oh, it's so good to hear your voice. I didn't think I'd be hearing from you with your game tonight."

"Yeah, about that." He swallowed. "I got traded to Calgary."

A beat. "What?"

"I'm at the airport, waiting for my connecting flight." He slouched into his chair in the airport lounge.

"Where are you?"

"Dallas."

"Did you just say Dallas?"

"It was the quickest flight there. They want me there tonight."

"So instead of playing New York, you're going to be playing who?"

"I checked the schedule. There's no game tonight, but they play the Wild on Monday."

"Oh my goodness, Mike." Another beat. "How do you feel?"

"Stunned. Disappointed. A little broken. A bit excited. I know this is business and not personal, and it's not like this wasn't on the cards, but when it happens, it still hits you hard." And felt plenty personal. He swallowed. "It was tough to leave the boys." Tough also to say goodbye to those who'd nurtured him from his rookie days to now. His skating coaches. Trainers. Even the equipment guys. He'd kept it together during his conversation with his coach and during the phone call from front office. But this tightness in his chest made him wish there was a place he could hide and maybe release a tear or two.

"I'll be praying for you. I wish there was something I could do."

"Come and visit me sometime?"

"You know I will."

"At least there won't be pesky border controls."

"You've got to look at the bright side, right?"

He exhaled heavily, slumped forward, propped an elbow on his knee and his head in one hand. "I know it's not like a typhoon, and I haven't lost my family or house..." He swallowed.

"You don't have to suffer a tragedy to feel shocked," she murmured.

"I'm trying to trust God, but I don't mind admitting to you

that this is hard." The airport lounge blurred. He pressed his lips together.

"I'm so sorry, Mike," she said softly.

Her words held such compassion he felt emotion swell again. "I should go," he rasped.

"Will you call me tonight? I don't care how late it is. Promise me you'll call tonight."

"It'll be late. I've got no idea where I'm staying or anything." Reluctant laughter pushed out. "I've got no clothes except for a suit, a spare shirt, and what I'm wearing."

"Oh no."

"Yeah. Think of me."

"You know I do."

He sighed. "And maybe I can see you again soon. The mid-season break is next week, and I might try to move stuff then, say more official goodbyes."

"We can help you. Brent will be off too."

"Thanks. I might take you up on it."

"And if you need help house hunting in Calgary, let me know. I love looking at houses. Maybe I'm just nosy or something, but it's really fun seeing open homes and imagining living there."

He swallowed. Dared. "Do you think you could imagine living in Calgary?"

A beat passed. Two beats. Three. "If the right reason presented itself. And the right house, of course."

A knot in his heart eased. "Of course."

So much of this still felt plenty crazy, but at least one thing might work out right.

Bree ended the call, placed her head in her hands, and breathed. Try as she might to be brave, it felt like her world had turned on its axis and everything she thought she knew was about to change.

"Bree?"

"Oh, Mom." She swiped at a tear. "He's been traded to Calgary."

"Mike has?"

She nodded, welcoming her mother's arms around her. She didn't know why this felt so momentous. Maybe it was the sense he'd been fighting tears and really needed her support in this moment. Maybe it was something about the way he'd asked that question, one she wasn't sure she was ready to answer yet. Suddenly all the praying for God's direction, for Mr. Right to appear and for her future to be determined, seemed awfully real.

Did he really mean what her ever-romantic heart thought when he asked how she'd feel about living there?

"Want to talk about it?"

She nodded, tried to talk and explain as her mom listened and held her hand.

"He'll be there for a good few years, won't he?"

Bree thought back to what he'd once said. "I think that's what his contract says."

"Calgary is Canadian, so that's a plus." Mom smoothed her hair. "It's not as if it's England, Bree. You'll still see each other."

"But I..." She swallowed, unsure how to proceed. This relationship still felt too new to admit the deepest part of her dream.

"But you're not sure what this means for your future?"

"He...he asked me how I'd feel about living there."

Mom inhaled swiftly. "Really? He's that serious?"

She nodded. And that feeling of his intense regard—this was more than just kisses and cuddles. The fact he had even asked her showed the depths of his thoughts about her and both thrilled and scared her in equal measure.

"What did you say to him?" Mom asked.

"I said it had to be for the right reason. And the right house."

Mom chuckled. "He loves you, Bree."

"And I love him."

And surely that should be enough, shouldn't it?

THE EVENING SEEMED to drag so slowly, her prayers chasing her fears, so Bree risked a Zoom call to Holly. Holly was nothing but enthusiastic. "Calgary? That's awesome."

"Why?"

"Calgary has one of the best short track programs in the world. If I ever got such a miracle as to go there and you were there on a visit, then imagine how fun that would be!"

She wasn't sure Holly was seeing the big picture here. She tried to explain, but Holly was only pragmatic. "Look, sooner or later you're wanting to get married, aren't you?"

"Yes."

"To Mike?"

She couldn't imagine loving anyone else the way she loved him. "Yes."

"So you're going to need to move to wherever he's working, right?"

"Yes."

"So the fact it's in Canada, not a ten-hour flight away—what is it, four?"

"About that, yes."

"Oh my gosh. Four hours. How nice would that be? When I think of the long flights I have to deal with, four hours in a plane sounds like a picnic."

Bree laughed. "Okay, okay. I get it. Your life is way harder than mine."

"You know it." Holly grinned. "Seriously, though, Bree. If you love him and want a future with him, then look for the positives. I know there'll be many. Imagine all the skiing you could do!"

"I don't really ski."

Holly rolled her eyes. "Come on. The fact this is even a potential question is so exciting!"

Bree felt her enthusiasm kindle. "I don't know that he'd love to know we're all talking about what this could mean when he hasn't even said anything definite."

"He will, Bree. He's romantic. And he's patient. He's such a good guy. You two are perfect for each other."

"You think so?"

"Bree, how long have you been praying for Mr. Right to come along?"

"Years."

"Mike isn't Mr. Darcy or Gilbert Blythe or one of your fictional characters. He's real. This is life. Sometimes there are bumps in the road and we can decide to either push through and over or draw back and stagnate because it's too hard. If you want Mike to be part of your future, then do all you can to be his biggest cheerleader and Calgary's cheerleader also and he'll love you forever."

"When did you get to be so wise?" Bree grumbled.

"Don't know. Maybe it's God. Which reminds me: if you really are trusting God to direct your paths and close and open doors at the right time, and if this door has opened, then maybe it's time to trust Him with it and walk on through."

Wow. Bree exhaled. Maybe God could work this brokenness into something good. "Will you pray with me?"

"Of course."

Bree closed her eyes as Holly prayed for peace, wisdom, and clear direction. Felt a measure of new calm in her soul. "Amen."

"Amen."

"Thanks, Holly."

"Anytime." Holly blew a kiss and said goodbye.

Soon after, Bree talked with Brent and agreed they would do what they could to help Mike with his move in the following week during the break. "I think he'll really appreciate some moral support."

"Tell him I'll do whatever and he's in my prayers."

She passed the message on a couple of hours later when Mike finally called. "Hey, I'm sorry it's so late, but I've only just got in."

"Where are you staying?"

"The team set me up in an apartment downtown, supplied it with groceries. I meet the team tomorrow during a skate." He yawned.

"You must be exhausted."

"I slept a bit on the plane."

"And how are you feeling now you're there?"

"They seem really excited to have me, which is nice. There was someone from management at the airport to meet me, and they drove me here. They're saying all the right things, so that's something at least."

"You're going to be amazing," she said. "They won't know what hit them when you show up tomorrow."

He laughed. "Yeah, they'll probably be wondering about this sleep-deprived bulldozer of a dude and why he can't see the puck."

"They wanted you for a reason, Mike. I think it's good you're going somewhere where you'll be celebrated, not tolerated."

"Yeah."

She hoped her words hadn't sounded bitter about Boston. "I don't mean that you weren't celebrated in Boston, just that you weren't appreciated as much as you could have been. And Calgary are doing okay, aren't they?"

"They're tracking to make the playoffs."

"That's awesome! And they're sure to make it with you on their side," she added loyally.

"You're sweet."

"You're right."

He laughed. Yawned again. "I'd better go. I think I started my day twenty hours ago."

"Sleep well. Sweet dreams, and remember, God is working things out for your good."

"He is. For all of us. Love you, Bree."

"Love you too," she whispered. "Goodnight."

CHAPTER 28

So this was what it felt like to be appreciated. Mike skated onto the ice for his next shift, the red, black, and white uniform still taking time to get used to, the number 78 a thoughtful, unexpected nod to his tradition when he was officially welcomed to the team that first day by the general manager. The applause that had met his entry to the ice against Minnesota had been nice. It'd been even better to follow it up with play he credited more to God's help than his own skill, especially given his state of fatigue. But it was nice to show them that choosing him had been a good move.

He skated, blocked a shot, and sent the puck down to the waiting winger. Who'd have thought he'd be playing with Tyler Woletsky, the enforcer whose trade from Florida had taken an even more twisted turn than Mike's own. Traded to Edmonton, he'd been on a plane and halfway there when he learned that Edmonton had traded him to Calgary for a backup goalie and a seventh round pick. He'd arrived at Edmonton only to catch another flight straight back to Calgary. Pity for a predicament worse than Mike's own had made him welcome Tyler to the team, thus burying the last of any animosity from his hit.

"Here!"

He skated low, protecting his section of the blue line as the Chicago player advanced. He didn't care that Jai was his friend; he blocked him with a move that sent him to the boards.

Jai scrambled to his feet with a grin that said he appreciated the hit. Mike would catch him quickly for dinner before the Hawks flew to Vancouver tomorrow. These times to connect were fun—on and off the ice.

The puck slid his way, and he propelled toward center ice. Narrowed his gaze, checked for teammates. Aimed and shot.

The siren blared. He smiled. Accepted a round of back and helmet pats and skated to the bench. Grabbed his drink. Wet his throat. Followed the game.

He might be a commodity, at a team's disposal to go where and when they liked, but this was what it was about. Playing hockey. Doing this thing he loved. How blessed was he?

Later, after a loss of three goals to his one, he took Jai to a steakhouse his teammates had introduced him to close to the Saddledome.

"So, how's the move going?" Jai said as their steaks arrived. "Bet you can't complain when you have awesome food like this."

"Not gonna lie. It's a plus."

"You settled in yet?"

He shrugged. "It's only been a few weeks, but it's feeling more like home. The team's been great, really welcoming, and my digs are okay too."

"Brent mentioned last Monday at Bible study that he helped you out with the move."

"Yeah. The team had someone pack up the house, but it's the goodbyes you have to do in person." The Grubers, Bob, church friends, the staff at TD Garden. "Was nice to catch up with a few of the boys again before I came back here."

They'd thrown him a little party of sorts in one of the old

Irish pubs downtown. He'd enjoyed it, even as he wondered if he'd find the same sense of camaraderie with a new team.

"And Bree?"

Mike glanced up. Met the amusement in the hazel eyes. Shrugged. "What did Brent say about that?"

"Only that things were getting serious. Which is cool, by the way. Not that I'm ready to settle down, but hey, if you are, that's great."

Mike nodded, swallowed his piece of tender steak. He wasn't sure he was ready to admit just how close he was to wanting to settle down. A lot would depend on his trip east tomorrow, squeezed in between games and training, his good form having seen permission granted from the coach to skip a training session.

His trip east to see if he could secure Bree as part of his future, once and for all.

"LOVER BOY IS HERE!" Sylvie called.

Bree glanced up from where she was wiping down a table. Delight rippled the corners of her heart at the sight of Mike, dressed in his suit, carrying a bunch of red roses. "He's here early." She wiped her hands on her jeans, moving to the entrance with a big smile. "Hello, you!"

He grinned and swept her up in a big hug. "Hello, you."

Oh, how good it was to hold him, to smell his scent, to bury her face in his neck. "I've missed you," she murmured against his scarf.

"I've missed you," he said, putting her back down to gently clasp her face with his hands and kiss her thoroughly.

Oh, the man could kiss! She drew back, dizzy, senses awhirl and screaming for more as whistles and applause behind her said they had witnesses. She turned and, like a D-grade celebrity, waved her hand and bowed.

"You better take her away," Sylvie said. Moira had said Bree could leave early. "We don't want any mix-ups like what happened last year."

"That we do not," Mike said with a smile for Bree that made her heart skip. "I really don't want to be taking any old ladies I've never met before out for dinner tonight."

Bree laughed and brushed aside a hanging display of red hearts. There were no grand fundraising efforts this year. She'd learned her lesson last year. And with all the changes recently, she was glad to have conserved her energy and focus for tonight.

A few minutes later she was in Mike's rental car, snuggling, kissing until the glass fogged. Mike exhaled. "I'd better take you home so you can get changed while I go say hi to my folks."

"You'll come in for a moment?"

"Sure."

They arrived at her house, and sure enough, Granny V's car was there. Bree smiled up at Mike. "You said you didn't want to take any old ladies out for dinner, but I hope you'll say hello to this one at least."

"Michael!" Gran said, holding out her hands. "My, don't you look dashing?"

"It's good to see you, Violet," he said, kissing her cheek. "Hi, Pam."

"Mike." Mom smiled as he kissed her cheek too. "What lovely flowers."

Bree retrieved a crystal vase and filled it with water. "Don't tell anyone, but I think Mike is a romantic."

"Aren't roses expected on Valentine's Day?" he protested as she arranged the flowers then wiped her hands.

"The fact you've been sending her flowers every week

suggests you go beyond what's expected," Mom said affectionately. "So, how is life in Calgary treating you?"

"Treating me better than I hoped." His fingers wound through Bree's.

"I'm glad," Bree said, giving his hand a squeeze.

He chatted with them for a few moments longer, but Bree could sense his desire to leave so he could return and they could be on their own.

"Doesn't he look dashing, Breanna?" her grandmother demanded.

"Very dashing." Bree caught his amusement and smiled.

"Speaking of dashing, I need to dash off to see my folks. I'll be back in half an hour. Okay?"

"Okay."

He pressed his lips to Bree's, made his farewells, and Bree escaped upstairs to have a shower.

He'd said to dress nicely, and she had the perfect dress. Red for Valentine's Day, fitted, and with enough length and warmth to ward off the chilliest day. Not that she need mind that. When she was with Mike, she always felt warm.

Hair and makeup done, jacket and bag collected, she made her way downstairs to where Mike waited. "I thought you said thirty minutes."

"It's been forty-five, Breanna," her grandmother said. "But never mind. I think from the expression on that boy's face, he thinks it's worth it."

"Do you think it's worth it?" Bree asked, swiveling like a model.

He nodded. "Very worth it. You look beautiful."

His words, his soft expression, ballooned warmth through her heart.

A few minutes later they were driving to the mystery destination. He'd refused to tell her where they were going, and she was just fine with that.

"Isn't it funny that we saw each other just two weeks ago but it feels so much longer?"

"It's not funny," he said, sliding a look at her. "It's kind of hard."

She placed her hand on his, and he kissed her knuckles. "How are things going—really?"

He smiled. "I wasn't faking it earlier. It really is going so much better than I thought. I like it there, Bree." He shot her another deep look. "I hope you'll like it too."

Her mouth dried. There it was again. That look that said more than she knew how to answer. But before she could formulate a response, he'd pulled into a lane that fed into a parking lot outside an English-style cottage complete with slate roof and stained glass windows.

"What is this place?"

"This," he said, pulling up and switching off the engine, "is where I wanted to take you last year."

Then she noticed the sign. "This is the Gaugin Tea House?"

"The one and only. Are you ready?"

She nodded, and they escaped the cold into a world of romance and olde-worlde treasures. "Tell me you didn't bring Francine here last year," she whispered when they were seated at their table in a semi-private corner, the walls lined with antiques.

"I cannot do that, for that would be a lie."

"Oh, poor Michael," she said, covering his hand with her own.

He threaded her fingers with his and sighed. "The things I do for you." He tapped the menu. "I'm even prepared to eat cucumber sandwiches."

"A true hero."

"I'm glad you can recognize the sacrifices I make."

Oh, she recognized them all right. Flying to Toronto to see her like this, making time amid his own busyness to show her, through words, actions, and flowers, just what she meant to him. "I know you're the most wonderful of men."

He exhaled, lips twitching. "Just as long as you do."

A waitress came and took their tea choices—he wanted coffee, she had English breakfast—then a decadent three-tiered platter soon arrived at their table, the array of sandwiches, tiny pies and pastries, cakes, fruit, and handmade chocolates looking like it might satisfy even a hockey player's substantial appetite.

"Usually we advise our guests to move from the lower savory selections to the sweeter options on top," their waitress advised before pouring sparkling wine.

"This is so much better than I ever expected!" Bree said, her heart bubbling as much as her glass.

"I hope you enjoy," Mike said, affection in his eyes.

"You know I enjoy any time with you."

"So I could've taken you to a greasy pub somewhere?" His grin grew tender again. "Not that I would. Not when you look as sensational as you do."

She sighed. "That's it. That comment means I will most nobly eat any cucumber sandwiches you decline."

"True love."

"True love, indeed."

He wrapped his hand around hers. "Speaking of true love..."

Her pulse scampered, breath suspended.

"I was wondering if you'd given any more thought to coming to visit me."

Oh! She silently exhaled. "Is there a special reason you're asking?"

"Well, I may have found a house that could be nice."

"Oh." Had she mistaken that look in his eye? "Have you got a picture?"

He drew out his phone. Showed her pictures of a house of grand proportions and stylish interiors that seemed three times the size of Brent's in Detroit. "It looks beautiful," she said honestly. "But maybe a little large."

"You're right," he said. "It's probably more suited to a family than a single man."

She placed the phone down, picked up a tiny chicken pie, and swallowed meat, pastry, and disappointment. She'd really thought that, on Valentine's Day no less, he'd be saying something else.

"Of course, a single man doesn't always have to stay single," he said softly.

Her gaze slowly lifted from her plate to meet his.

"And a family can happen when a single man is no longer single. Or so I've heard."

She moistened her suddenly dry throat with tea. "I've heard that, too."

"So maybe a house like that could work. If the single man found a single lady who would like to live there with him."

Bree wet her lips, her nerves pattering like a drum. "What are you saying? You know I need things spelled out to avoid confusion."

"I'm saying that this single man has found a single lady he would love to live with there. Which means, for both this single man and this single lady, that they would need to be married."

Her hands were shaky as she reached for her teacup. Nope. Couldn't do it. She placed it back down with a clatter. "So, um, how would they do that?"

"Well, this single man might need to tell this single lady just how much he ardently admires and loves her."

Her heart fluttered. Had Mike just referenced Mr. Darcy's proposal to Elizabeth Bennet?

"And then ask if she would ever consider doing him the honor of marrying him."

"Really?"

"Really." He shifted to kneel beside her seat, hold her hands in his. "Please, Bree. I've loved you forever. You're everything to me."

"Oh, Mike." She slipped her hands to either side of his face, his wonderful, loving, ever-patient face. This man—hockey-player, best friend to her brother, and now her best friend too—was so much more than she had ever dreamed or imagined. "You know I love you. I suspect I always have. But first I have to know one thing."

"What's that?"

"Mr. Darcy. Did you know you were quoting him?"

"I might've had a helpful pointer or two from someone who thinks I'm rather dashing."

She laughed. "Granny V."

He nodded. "But she's not the one whose answer I'm desperate to hear. Please, Bree. My knee is getting sore. Say you'll marry me."

"You darling, patient, wonderful man. Of course I will."

And—heart tingling, with toe-curls galore—she bent her lips to his and kissed him most fervently, conveying but a fraction of all the love she wanted to share. What had begun as a breakup project had proved to be so much more, breaking and restoring, bringing them together, and leading to a future filled with faith, hope, and promise.

∾

Check out Love on Ice, the next book in the Original Six
contemporary romance series

Thank you for reading *The Breakup Project*, the first book in the Original Six contemporary romance series, which combines my love of ice hockey with appreciation for the cities that comprised the NHL's original six teams. If you enjoyed, make sure you check out the other books in the Original Six hockey romance series, a sweet & swoony, slightly sporty Christian contemporary romance series.

Love on Ice
Checked Impressions
Hearts and Goals
Big Apple Atonement
Muskoka Blue

Reviews help other readers find new-to-them authors, so if you can spare a moment to write a quick review at Goodreads and/or your place of purchase, I'd be very grateful.

I'd love for you to check out my other books and to sign up for my newsletter at www.carolynmillerauthor.com where you can grab an extended epilogue of *The Breakup Project* and be the first to learn all my bookish and contest news.

A huge thank you to the following people for their encouragement and eagle eyes: Iola Goulton (who originally suggested *Love on Ice* could have a prequel), Jacqueline, Ros, Caitlin, Abby, Rebekah, Nancy, Bea, Kaye, Brittany & Becky - I appreciate you all so much! Big thanks to the ladies in my Facebook group, Carolyn's Books & Friends, for all your support in helping promote my books.

The things mentioned in the Philippines, from peso notes floating from the ceiling, to fireflies on lapels, floods, found rings and healed eyes, are all things that have happened to my husband or friends of ours whilst serving in this beautiful country - God does amazing things!

Mission Possible for Future Generations is a charitable organization that helps underprivileged children in the Philippines to access feeding programs and education. To find out more, and how you can sponsor a child, please visit the MPFG website here: https://bmi-mpfg.weebly.com

Please turn the page for a peek at *Love on Ice*, next in the Original Six hockey romance series.

Chapter 1

Toronto, Canada
June

Not bad for a sports-and-science-focused tomboy, Holly Travers thought, eyeing the intricate paper rose she'd just fashioned, her lips lifted in satisfaction.

"That's beautiful!" Bree Karlsson peered closer, her long dark hair gleaming as the sun poured through the lounge window. "I swear, Holly Travers, you're full of hidden talents. How did you learn to do origami?"

"I saw it at a banquet earlier this year in Japan. It was good to focus on something other than this." Holly pointed to the pale scar on her upper arm that her T-shirt couldn't hide. Her stomach tensed. Ten stitches in a Tokyo hospital hadn't been fun. But it could've been worse. Thank God the other skater had shifted in time, otherwise Holly's face would be wearing a permanent reminder of the debacle that was Japan.

Her best friend shuddered. "I'll never understand why you do short track. It's so dangerous."

"What can I say? I have a need for speed." And she *loved* the sport. Mostly. "Now, do you want me to teach you how to fold the roses into place cards? I thought they'd be great for the tables at the reception. But it gets a little tricky, so you must be patient…"

Bree's laughter was as joyous as her vivacious personality. "It's so funny to hear you, the speed queen, go on about patience."

Holly grinned. Bree's perpetual bubbly smile was even bigger now that the family was counting down to Bree's wedding in seven days. "I brought some beautiful paper with me. I'll go get it."

Holly raced up the stairs to the guestroom of the Karlsson's family home. The room was painted white with apricot accents now, but the old oak tree in the backyard still spread welcoming arms. She smoothed her boring light-brown hair into its usual high ponytail, then retrieved the expensive mauve-flecked handmade paper from her suitcase. A car door slammed outside.

As she made her way down the hall, she studied the pictures on the walls. Cute baby photos, vacations, high school and college graduations, hockey photos. The only constants were the glossy dark hair and blue-gray eyes the Karlsson family shared. She smiled. Her time here in Toronto as an exchange student seven years ago had been the best year of her life.

As Holly headed down the stairs, she caught the vague murmur of voices. She paused at the sound of Bree's voice coming from the kitchen. "But Holly—"

"Holly?" There was a snort. "Bree, I'm over you and Mom trying to fix me up with one of your good little girl friends. I get enough offers as it is. Drop it, okay?"

Holly stilled. Little? So she wasn't a giant like the rest of the

Karlsson clan. And anyway, what was so bad about being good? So she didn't have a past you'd ever read about in *People* magazine. Where were the guys who could appreciate that? Not that she was here to find a man.

She bit her lip, uncertainty keeping her rooted to the step. Arrogance always made her prickly and defensive. Should she go in guns blazing or smile and just pretend she hadn't heard? Eavesdroppers never heard good about themselves, did they? She closed her eyes for a few seconds and drew in a deep breath. One of Coach Chan's mottos floated into memory: *Put on brave face; don't let fear win.*

She lifted her chin and headed into the sunny modern kitchen, pasting on a smile as three faces swung her way. "Hi!" Aim for bright and perky. "Mike, how are you?" She stepped forward to give Bree's burly hockey-playing fiancé a quick hug.

"Holly. Good to see you again." He eyed her with good humor. "Bree was telling us you got off the plane this morning and went straight into bridesmaid mode. The wonder from Down Under, eh?"

"Ha. Not that wonderful. But it's nice to know I've got some long-distance fans."

Her smile faded as she turned to the other man. Brent. Breanna Karlsson's twin. Bree's emailed photos of her family hadn't done him justice. Muscled, probably a foot taller than Holly, dark hair and blue eyes holding hints of gray and green— he'd grown even better looking than the guy she recalled from her time here on exchange. Back then, he'd lived away, playing junior hockey in Sault Ste. Marie. But on his few visits home, he'd made an impression.

Holly's hand strayed to the tiny scar on her forehead. Brent had made an impression, all right. His skating lessons—reluctantly given—might've left her with this scar, but they'd ultimately set the direction for her life. And his popularity with girls had further strengthened her resolve to never, *ever* throw herself at a guy or settle for cheering from the sidelines. Nope. She'd much rather be the one who actually did something worth cheering about, and between her skating and her university studies, she was going to do it. According to Bree's emails over the years, many girls continued to be charmed by that physique and those unusual eyes. Not that looks mattered if his attitude stank. "Hello, Brent."

He swallowed. Hopefully it was some pride. "Hey, Holly. How's it going?"

She pasted on a big smile. "Great!" Okay, maybe tone down the perkiness a tad. "Congratulations on your Cup win."

"Thanks." He still eyed her warily.

"How are you?"

He shrugged. "Can't complain."

Holly snickered. No, with his recent NHL championship win and multimillion-dollar contract with Detroit, she bet he had little to complain about.

He stared at her blankly. "What?"

Holly gave her sweetest smile. "I imagine the only thing you have to complain about is all the girls throwing themselves at you."

He blinked. Bull's-eye. What was it with women and pro athletes? Her stomach twisted. Girls could be so stupid. She shook her head as she carefully placed the package of special Ogura lace paper down on the marble counter top. "But you don't need to worry about me. You're not my type."

The room filled with Mike's laughter. "So, what is your type, Holly?"

Not arrogant, for starters. Brent might share the same genetic pool as Bree, but he seemed the polar opposite of Holly's warm-hearted, generous friend. Brent leaned back against the marble counter, watching them, eyes narrowed, arms folded across his broad chest.

"I like guys who are short, blond, and plump, who aren't

obsessed by sport and can show their feelings." She smiled, thinking of the little boys at church, their chubby arms that wrapped tightly around her whenever she was in town and able to help lead their Sunday school class. Yep, they definitely knew how to help her feel the love.

Bree chuckled. They'd emailed about Holly's "guys" before. "Now, before we start on the place cards, are you hungry? Mom said to make yourself at home, eat whatever. She was so sorry not to be here for your arrival. She had to take Grandma Violet to a doctor's appointment."

"No worries." Holly watched Bree hunt through a cupboard. "I hope everything's okay?"

"Granny V wants her blood pressure checked. She's a little excited about next weekend." Bree produced a container. "Ta da! Muffins. Mom said she tried to make them healthy for you."

Holly sighed, even as her saliva glands kicked into overdrive. "Your mum's such a good cook. But I need to be careful while I'm here. I can't afford to put on any weight."

Brent snorted as she grabbed an apple. "You one of these girls who's always on a diet?"

Bree laughed again, tossing her hair over a shoulder. "Just look at her, Brent. She's the only one of us who didn't need to diet before the wedding."

Holly stifled the sigh. She sometimes wished she weren't so lightly framed and had Bree's more voluptuous curves. It might help her feel more feminine. She'd never been a girly girl, too busy trying to keep up with her sporty brother and his mates, trailing after them on the bike or running, getting pretty good at the disciplines even before training started demanding it of her.

Oh well. Wishing never changed anything.

She eyed Brent. "I've a week off on the proviso I eat well, train, and visit the gym as much as possible. Competition season starts again soon, and my coach wants me ready."

His eyebrows shot up. "Your coach?"

Mike wrapped an arm around Bree. "Come on, man. Even I know she's the best short track skater in Australia." His blue eyes twinkled. "And going to compete at the Games in a couple of years."

Holly forced a smile. Crashing out in Japan had raised serious doubts about whether she should even be part of the skating program, let alone dream of competing in Vancouver. And yet this passion to prove herself burned inside and wouldn't be denied.

Brent shrugged. "Oh. I forgot what you do."

His indifference felt like a slap. Obviously she didn't rate too highly on Brent's radar. She bit into her apple, wiped juice from her chin.

"Maybe Brent can take you to the gym. He's always training and watching what he eats." Bree's smile widened. "He's like you, even if he's not exactly your *type*."

Holly slid a look at Brent, who seemed unimpressed. No way was she going to force her company on him. She shrugged. "It's fine. I'm sure I can walk or bike there."

Mike's lips twitched. "He's gonna need a new training partner now that I'm too busy."

Bree turned to her twin, her purple-hued eyes wide. "You don't mind, do you, Brent?"

The siblings engaged in a stare-off before Brent sighed, shook his head, and finally turned to Holly. "I like to go pretty early in the morning. Six thirty okay?"

She smothered the smile. Six thirty was an hour later than her usual training started. "That'll be fine. Thank you." She threw the apple core in the bin and carefully wiped her fingers, then turned to her best friend. "So, Bree, are you ready to start on those place cards now?"

HOLLY GLANCED UP from her muesli at the kitchen's new arrival. "Good morning."

Brent nodded, grabbed a bowl, poured in cereal and milk, and started eating silently.

O-kay. Obviously not a morning person. She refocused on her breakfast. Last night Brent had looked at her askance more than once as she happily answered questions from Bree's parents about her recent travels. Perhaps God's gift to women thought she was here to find a man—namely him. Her lips curled up on one side. As if he'd ever meet her boyfriend criteria.

Top of the list was someone whose actions and attitudes demonstrated his love for God. Second was someone who could cope with the demands her sport placed on her, like no time for a social life and constant jetting off for competitions around the planet. Hello? What guy could cope with that? Those two qualifiers always filtered out any prospective candidates. Handsome had certainly never needed to be factored in. Not that she could afford to be interested, even if Mr. Right should miraculously appear. Coach Chan said it best: *Firsts need focus, not distraction.*

Brent grabbed two bananas and nodded to the door. "Ready?"

Holly quickly scooped up the last mouthful. "Yep." After rinsing her bowl, she grabbed her gym bag and followed him to the Jeep outside. A few fat raindrops splattered against the windshield as they drove through Toronto's busy suburban streets.

As they waited for the red light to change, she tried out a tentative smile. He was Bree's brother, after all. "So, Bree mentioned you bought a house in Detroit last year."

"Yeah." His face grew animated for the first time that morning. "After staying in hotels and rooming with others for so long, it's great to have my own space."

"It would be." She nodded. "People think the travel for

competitions is glamorous, but staying in crowded dorms and long bus rides with all that gear isn't always easy."

"I had some of that growing up." He flicked a look at her. "It's easier now, of course."

Oh. Right. Of course. Mr. Millionaire, who flew with his team on private planes, stayed in five-star hotels, and had bought his first house at the ripe old age of twenty-five. Holly glanced out the window and sighed inwardly. She'd always had to trust God with finances. There wasn't much money to be made in short track, or much financial support, especially in Australia. Most skaters had to have a full-time job to help supplement the basic scholarship from the Australian Institute of Sport. She'd always had to work hard, save harder, and budget well to make ends meet.

Enough of the pity party. "So, how will you cope with being on your own? Will you get lonely?" Her cheeks heated. For goodness' sake—she sounded like a desperate groupie! "I mean, when you live by yourself, that'll be different…" She glanced over, noticing a twitch in his jaw as he pulled sharply into the gym parking lot and quit the engine.

He reached into the back to collect his gym bag. "I haven't thought about it much, to be honest."

So much for chit chat. She grabbed her gear. "Uh, thanks for doing this."

"No problem." He led the way in, holding the gym's front door open for her.

Maybe he was nice, and she'd misread the ego. "Um, sorry about yesterday."

He turned to study her steadily for a beat before shrugging. "Sorry for liking short blond guys?" A grin flickered. "Don't be. No skin off my nose."

She took a deep breath and lifted her chin. Ignore him. Act like a grown up. Usually she was pretty good at the ice maiden persona. Not for nothing did she train on ice.

He signed them in, and she followed silently as he gave a quick tour of the bright, spacious facility with its gleaming equipment. She swallowed a chuckle at the blatant ogling he got from some women working out. If only they knew. She stowed her bag in the locker, grabbed her towel, phone, earbuds, and water bottle, and headed back to the cardio room.

Brent was there, already warming up on an exercise bike. He glanced over. "So, should we be on the lookout?"

She moved to the treadmill, pulling her ponytail tight. "What for?"

He mimed short and plump before smirking.

Holly nodded toward the big-haired, big-busted woman in the far corner. Seriously, who wore that much makeup to exercise? She kept her voice low. "Funny. I thought you'd prefer a Barbie clone."

He looked over. The woman smiled a *hi there*. Brent nodded before turning back to Holly with a scowl. "Yeah, you sure got me pegged."

She gave him a tight smile and jammed in her earbuds, flicking her phone to her favorite workout playlist. Honestly, what was wrong with her? She wasn't normally so snarky. Maybe working up a sweat would help her heart and brain function normally. This was ridiculous.

BRENT STOOD at the front of his family's church, watching as Mike rocked gently on his toes, his eyes on the big double doors at the other end of the aisle. "How're you doing?"

"I can't wait to see her." Mike grinned. "This'll be you too one day, my friend."

Brent rolled his eyes. Not for a very long time. Miss Right had to appear first.

He caught the smiles of his older brother Dean and his

sister-in-law Laura, balancing their six-month-old son on her lap, then nodded to Jai Mullins, Beau Nash, and Dan Walton, fellow hockey Bible study friends, here for Mike's wedding.

Mike leaned closer. "So, is it me or are there a lot of women here checking you out?"

Brent glanced across the congregation. He couldn't help but notice that more than one lady sat up straighter, smiling wider. He grimaced. "It's pretty uncool if women are here checking *you* out on your wedding day."

"Everyone knows I've always been a one-woman man." Mike eyed him. "But you…"

How long would it take for him to live down the ladies' man reputation? Sure, he'd partied hard a few years ago, but since he'd started attending Reverend Josiah Abrahams' online Bible study group, he'd straightened out. He hadn't dated anyone for months, despite his teammates' offers of setups—and the loneliness that made some of those offers so tempting.

Brent stared down at his shiny black shoes. Maybe his mom and sister were right and he should make more of an effort to find someone with similar goals, who liked him for himself and wasn't obsessed with celebrity or the other superficial trappings of his sport. His mouth twisted. Like that'd be easy. How could you ever know?

The music in the background shifted, and the congregation turned to watch the first bridesmaid walk down the aisle. Brent's gaze lifted just in time to see Holly begin her approach. His eyes widened. With her pretty hair down for once and that pale green strapless gown accentuating her slender figure, she was…beautiful.

Mike snickered quietly. "Pick up your jaw, dude. You're embarrassing yourself."

Brent closed his mouth with a snap. He noticed some of Mike's teammates kept on staring as Holly moved gracefully down the aisle. His gut tightened. He'd made too many dumb comments this week. Holly's work ethic, loyalty, and sassy tease had intrigued him. She was nothing like the short, skinny, shy girl he vaguely remembered from seven years ago. Especially in that dress.

Her sunny gaze shifted to him. Brent smiled at her, catching the surprise in her green eyes before her lips thinned and she glanced away.

His lips hitched. Yeah, he definitely had bridges to mend.

"I KNOW IT'S HOT, but we need just one more of the groomsmen with their lovely ladies!"

Brent groaned at the photographer. Photos with Bree and Mike, photos with the bridal party, photos with various family members—on and on it went. His cheeks ached from smiling.

"Holly, move closer to Brent, please."

Holly sighed. Brent grinned, wrapping an arm around her waist. The photographer beamed. "That's it, Brent. Holly, let's see that lovely smile again!"

"I'm not six years old," she muttered through upturned lips.

That dress was definitely unsuitable for a six-year-old. "Relax, Holly, you look beautiful."

She arched her eyebrows, staring warily at him. Brent held her gaze. Her eyes were such a pretty green, like the sea, with violet rims and tiny golden flecks around the pupils—

"Brent! Holly! Pay attention!"

Brent ignored Mike's chuckle as he turned back to the photographer, trying not to squint as the afternoon sun beat down. The reception venue's rose gardens were super pretty, but his neck was getting sticky from Toronto's muggy heat. The photographer pronounced himself satisfied, and they were finally freed to go.

As they waited to be introduced to the cheering guests inside the function room, Holly looked up at him again. "Is my hair still okay? Hot weather makes it go frizzy."

He stepped closer and smoothed a few recalcitrant strands. "Relax. You look great." He leaned down, taking a delicate sniff. "What's your perfume?"

"It's Beautiful."

"Yeah, I know that. But what's it called?"

"My perfume?" Her voice was squeaky. "It's called Beautiful. It's by Estée Lauder."

"Oh, right." He glanced at her before focusing again on the door. "Suits you."

He caught the disbelieving side-eye as she raised her bouquet higher to match the angle of her chin.

"Ladies and gentlemen, let's hear it for our best man, Brent Karlsson, and the lovely maid of honor, Holly Travers." They stepped into the limelight and stopped for yet another photo before he escorted her to the bridal table and they turned to applaud the newlyweds' entrance.

The next two hours passed in a whirl of food and laughter as Brent chatted with numerous relatives and friends. He was listening to his grandmother when he glanced across the room to see Holly sitting at the main table, shaking her head at one of Mike's Calgary teammates. He frowned.

"Brent?" His grandma's faded-blue eyes peered anxiously at him. "Is something wrong?"

He quickly kissed her cheek. "Sorry, Gran, I need to go check something."

Ignoring the nearby group of smiling women, he strode over to Holly. Tyler Woletsky was too bold, on the ice and off. Brent sat down next to Holly and stretched his arm along the back of her chair. "Woletsky! Didn't see you there." Brent turned to smile down at Holly. "How's it going?"

Her eyebrows lifted. "Fine." She looked back to TJ, who still leaned against the table. "Thanks, Tyler, but I want to finish my cake." She smiled. "Besides, I'm not used to high heels."

Woletsky glanced between them, his blue eyes suspicious. "If you change your mind…"

"Thank you." The smile she offered was sweet as Woletsky lumbered off, then drained away as she faced Brent. "What was that about?"

Brent shrugged. "Woletsky doesn't always play nicely, especially with pretty girls."

Her eyes narrowed. She stabbed at her piece of cake. "And you think I can't take care of myself?"

He held up his hands. "Hey, I've seen you in the gym. I know you're tough." And super fit. The weights she could lift? "But, Holly, you need to be careful when you smile."

"What?" She twisted in her seat to study him. "What's wrong with my smile?"

"Nothing. Just that guys could get the wrong idea."

She blinked. "Are you serious? You sound like a caveman, blaming a woman for how a man acts, as if he can't be held responsible."

Huh? "I didn't mean it like that. I only meant to compliment you," he mumbled.

She stared at him for a long moment before shaking her head and looking away.

He followed her gaze back to the dance floor. "Want to dance again?"

"Once was enough. I hate dancing." Her smile held an abundance of sugar. "But don't let me stop you."

Dancing with random women sure wouldn't help him live down the reputation. Talking with Holly was far safer. "You're not that bad, for someone with two left feet."

"Two left feet? Hey, if you hadn't insisted on doing all that fancy twirly stuff, I might've been okay."

"Yeah, well, maybe I'm just a fancy kind of guy."

Her lips finally tilted up, and he felt like doing a fist pump to celebrate but settled for undoing his bow tie and slouching back in his seat. "So, are you having fun?"

"Yes. But I can't get over how big your family is." Her amusement faded as she picked off some icing with her fork. "Mine's so small now." She looked down at her plate, the white chocolate mud cake now thoroughly ruined. "I don't see them often enough."

"When do you go home?"

"I fly back to Brisbane tomorrow, but I won't get home to Wollongong until Christmas." Her face fell, and she started fiddling with the pretty paper rose place card she'd made, her slender fingers tracing the ruffled edges back and forth, back and forth.

Brent gazed across the chandelier-lit room, crowded with family members. It was amazing he'd been allowed to talk this long uninterrupted. "Big families aren't necessarily all they're cracked up to be."

Like his Uncle Ken, who sat in the corner, watching the girls dance. Bree had always found him slightly creepy. And there were those cousins who only ever called him when they wanted tickets to games, then got upset when Brent wouldn't work his connections to get them freebies. And as soon as he finished this conversation, he knew his grandmothers and aunts would buttonhole him to ask about that nice girl and wonder aloud when he'd get married.

He grimaced. "Hey, want to go outside?"

Holly cast another look at the crowded dance floor, raising her voice over the thumping disco music the DJ had begun to play. "But what about Bree and Mike?"

"I don't think they're going to miss us too much, do you? You know Bree. She never misses an opportunity to talk. And look, she's making Mike talk to every relative. They'll be here for hours."

"Poor Mike."

"And hey, if you disappear, Woletsky can't hassle you to dance again."

"Good point." Holly pushed back her chair. "Let's get out of here."

Brent found a side door that led to the reception venue's terrace, holding it open for Holly, then closing it firmly against the DJ's throbbing music. Her heels clicked on the tiles until they stopped at the far end near a marble fountain, lit up in the night by several spotlights. The stillness was broken only by the gentle song of insects and splash of water. The scent of roses filled the cooling air. Brent sucked in a deep breath, releasing it slowly. He looked over to see Holly standing still, her eyes closed.

"Are you tired? Want to go home?" Something about her today made him feel…protective. He swallowed. Like he would for his sister. That was all.

"No." She opened her eyes. "I'm just enjoying the peace and quiet. It's been a big week."

"And a big day." He leaned over the handrail, watching the water swirl around the base of the fountain. "But they seem happy, so all the hard work has been worth it." He glanced up to see Holly biting her bottom lip even as she nodded.

"I'm so glad. Bree's been like a sister to me." Holly blinked. "I'm going to miss that."

"You heard Dad before in his speech. Apparently, it's not about losing someone but gaining another." Brent shrugged. "But yeah, it won't be the same."

He frowned. It wouldn't be the same. Why hadn't he realized? Who would he call in the middle of the night to download the stress for the day? Mike had been his closest friend for years. He totally understood the pressures that went with playing in the NHL. Brent knew his sister loved him, but he'd bet Bree wouldn't appreciate too many late night interruptions.

Was this why his mom had ramped up the *find a wife* mantra? He sighed.

"Don't get me wrong, I am really happy for them," Holly's quiet voice continued. "They're perfect for each other." She peered up at Brent again. "But it's nice to know someone else understands." She smiled.

Her smile... Whoa. He blinked. Dragged his gaze away. Weddings were notorious for making people act weird. "I think people should be best friends with the person they marry."

"I agree," she said.

So they agreed on a couple of things at least. He turned away to watch the water again. "So, do you want to get married?"

Man, he must be super tired. Had that seriously just come out of his mouth?

"Is that an offer?" She laughed. "You're lucky I never believe anything you say."

His stomach twisted. "Why not?"

Holly's gurgling chuckle came again. "Come on. You flatter and flirt all night and expect a girl to believe you?" She patted his arm. "It's okay. I know you can't help it."

Ouch. "When was I flirting?"

Her cheeks reddened as she looked away, pushing her hair behind her ear. "I've seen how you act with girls."

"Hey, I'm a friendly guy. Besides, I do think you're pretty."

She rolled her eyes and shifted away.

So much for building bridges. He gazed at a tree lit up in the garden, trying to ignore the knot in his stomach. Tonight's rich dessert had been a bad idea.

Awkwardness stretched between them. What to say, what to say...

"So, you want to compete at Vancouver, eh?"

She straightened, energy vibrating from her. "Have you ever had a dream you feel you're on the cusp of living?"

He nodded. "I could barely sleep the night before my first game in the NHL."

"Then you understand what it's like to devote your life to something, to wanting to be the best, feeling like it's in your DNA, like it's who you are, what you were born to do."

He nodded again, her passion oddly inspiring. He'd taken a lot for granted these past few years, but the recent Cup success had only cemented his drive to win. There'd be selections for Canada's hockey team next year. The thought drifted, stilled, anchored. Maybe he should focus a little more too.

"So, even if I met Mr. Right tonight, I can't think about a relationship right now. Not for another two years, anyway."

So, the romance of today definitely hadn't gone to her head. Still, her steely-eyed focus curled fascination within. She sure wasn't like any other girl he'd met.

"How about you, Brent? Is marriage on your to-do list?"

"One day. I want to focus more on my hockey right now. But down the track, it'd be good. It just needs to be the right time… and the right girl."

He glanced over at her again. She was rubbing her bare arms, the right sporting a silvery-pink scar.

"Are you cold? Here, have this." He removed his jacket and wrapped it round her.

"Thanks." She glanced up at him again before gazing across the moonlit gardens. He studied her profile: the classic nose, determined chin, her long-lashed, beautiful eyes that the evening shadows only seemed to enhance. He swallowed. Her skin looked so soft. He reached out a hand—

"Oh, there you two are!"

He swallowed a groan as Holly turned.

"Are you okay, Bree? Do you need anything?"

Bree shook her head. "Mom just wanted your help with something inside."

"No worries." Holly shrugged out of his jacket and handed it to him with distracted thanks, then quickly strode back to the reception room without a backward glance.

He watched Holly disappear before turning to his smirking twin. "Breanna?"

"Anything I need to know about, brother dear?" Bree raised her eyebrows. "Anything at all?"

"Nope." He shook his head, hoping to shake off the strange mix of emotions he felt.

"I can give you Holly's email if you like." Her expression held hope.

His stomach lurched. He ignored it. "Nope. I'm fine."

Holly might be nice and all, but she lived on the other side of the world and had made her opinion about him and relationships very clear. So what was the point? How on earth could that ever work?

<u>Regency Brides: Promise of Hope</u>

Winning Miss Winthrop

Miss Serena's Secret

The Making of Mrs Hale

<u>Regency Brides: Daughters of Aynsley</u>

A Hero for Miss Hatherleigh

Underestimating Miss Cecilia

Misleading Miss Verity

'Heaven and Nature Sing' from the Joy to the World Christmas novella collection

www.ingramcontent.com/pod-product-compliance
Lightning Source LLC
Chambersburg PA
CBHW031003190726
48285CB00004BB/1451